REDEMPTION

REDEMPTION

AKIO REVELATIONS™ BOOK SIX

CHARLES TILLMAN

MICHAEL ANDERLE

L M B P N

DISRUPTIVE IMAGINATION

LMBPN Publishing
PMB 196, 2540 South Maryland Pkwy
Las Vegas, NV 89109

Version 1.00, August 2021
eBook ISBN: 978-1-64971-976-8
Print ISBN: 978-1-64971-977-5

PROLOGUE

Adelaide, Australia

Kent watched in horror as the massive beast of legend ripped Mitchell's still-beating heart from his chest. The Pricolici threw back his head and howled before he flung the bloody organ at Finn.

Kent had returned home minutes before sunrise the day after his brothers left the bunker and traveled to Adelaide. Aaron, their creator, had tried to talk him out of following the two, but Kent had refused to listen and was on their trail as soon as the sun went down that night.

Now he watched helplessly from across the river as a vicious black werewolf attacked Finn. Finn threw an elbow up at the last second and saved himself from the snapping jaws, but the resulting collision knocked his female hostage from his grasp.

Finn maintained a loose hold on the child the woman had held in her arms. He appeared to be regaining control of the situation until a single gunshot echoed through the night. Blood sprayed out in an arc from Finn's head, and he froze while his body fought to heal the damage. Not that it did any good.

Kent's eyes widened in shock as the small woman standing in front of his brother morphed into a Pricolici. He couldn't believe it when she caught Finn in her claws and repeatedly slammed him into the ground hard enough to shatter bones.

What happened next would haunt Kent for the rest of his life. The Pricolici grabbed Finn's head, settled the weight of one wickedly-clawed paw on his back, then ripped his head and a good portion of his spine from his stunned body.

She raised her grisly trophy and stared into its eyes before letting loose an earsplitting howl and callously throwing it to the ground.

Kent watched for several more minutes until an object he hadn't seen in decades descended into the stadium. The sleek black aircraft sent chills down his spine. Only TQB used them—the Bitch Queen's people.

Kent didn't think. He reacted. He spun and fled the city's lights at vampire speed and only slowed once he was deep in the mountains west of town.

Red rage clouded his mind as he walked through the night. That anyone dared to not only attack but kill his brothers was disrespect that couldn't go unpunished. TQB's involvement only added to his wrath. He'd lived like a rabbit in a hole for decades because of a war that TQB started. That it happened three years after they'd left on those massive spaceships didn't matter. Kent still blamed

Thanks to the JIT Readers

Allen Collins
Veronica Stephan-Miller
Peter Manis
Kelly O'Donnell
Diane L. Smith
Daryl McDaniel
Jackey Hankard-Brodie
Rachel Beckford
Dave Hicks
James Caplan
Deb Mader
Dorothy Lloyd
Thomas Ogden

If we've missed anyone, please let us know!

Editor
Skyhunter Editing Team

DEDICATION

To my Wife Danette, thank you for being behind me while I did this.

A huge thank you to Michael Anderle who let me come and play in his world.

There are also two others who worked hard to help me bring this to you:

John Ashmore, Alpha reader extraordinaire

Tracey Byrnes, Alpha reader and first pass editor who kept me and my sentence structure on track. I couldn't have done it without you.

And most of all thanks to you the Kurtherian Gambit Fans for reading.

—Charles

To Family, Friends and Those Who Love to Read.

*May We All Enjoy Grace
to Live the Life We Are
Called.*

— Michael

them for the events that led to WWDE and everything that happened after.

He didn't know how, but *someone* would pay for Finn's and Mitchell's deaths. If Kent had his way, many would suffer before he finished exacting vengeance.

CHAPTER ONE

TQB Base, Tokyo, WWDE+24

Kelly groaned as she regained consciousness. She opened her eyes to total darkness. She tried to sit up, and a wave of pain shot through her head when it hit a hard, unyielding surface.

"Fuck!"

She raised her arms, and her hands touched a cool hard surface. She awkwardly felt around and discovered she was on her back inside a small space, and her muscles weren't responding correctly.

"Kelly, you're safe. Calm down, and we'll get you out," a disembodied voice called.

"Who? What? Where the hell am I, and who the fuck are you?" Kelly demanded.

"It's Eve. You're at our base in Tokyo. A vampire attacked you, and we brought you here to heal you," Eve answered calmly.

"Vampire?" Her eyes flew open as the memories came back, and she was fully awake in a flash. "Dieter!"

"He's okay. The vampire didn't hurt him. He's safe," Eve assured her.

"There is a release lever near your right hand. Twist it in a circle, and the unit will open. Please remain in the Pod-doc when it opens. Your body has gone through significant changes, and you'll need to move slowly at first."

Kelly reached down and twisted the handle when her hand closed around it. The top of the enclosure lifted, and dim light allowed her to see where she was.

She was on her back inside a dull metal coffin-like device, and lights flashed on a white wall to her right. She drew a breath and sat up. A movement to her left caught her attention, and she looked to see Eve's face peering at her.

"Welcome back. You cut it kind of close with that vamp. If it hadn't been for some quick thinking on Koda's and the twins' part, you wouldn't have survived it." Eve smiled.

"Where am I, and where is everybody?"

"You're in the medical bay at our base in Tokyo," Eve repeated. "Henry's waiting outside for you."

"Henry! Is he all right? I remember the damned fool attacked the vampire and got knocked hard on his arse."

"He's mostly recovered from his injuries. Once we get you out of here, I'm going to run some diagnostics and be sure he's healing properly."

"What happened to the vamp?" Kelly asked. "Did he hurt anybody else?"

"He's dead," Eve told her. "Koda killed him."

Kelly frowned in confusion. "Koda? How did she manage that? She's no bigger than I am."

Eve gave her a mischievous grin. "Size isn't everything. You'll learn that the saying about dynamite and small packages is more accurate than you thought."

"What the hell are you grinnin' about? You look like you're up to something."

"You'll see," Eve promised. "Want to try and stand up now? Move slowly. It may take you a few minutes to adjust."

Kelly swung her legs to the side and pushed off with her hands. Her body shot across the room, and she slammed face-first into the wall.

"Ow! What the hell'd ya do that for?" She glared at Eve.

Eve laughed. "I didn't. You did. You have to move slowly until your mind adjusts to your body. Take small, careful steps until you're steady on your feet, please. I don't want you to break anything."

"What d'ya mean? I might break a bone or something?" Kelly rubbed her forehead where it had hit the wall.

Eve shook her head. "No, more like you'll break a delicate piece of equipment, and I don't want to have to fix it again. You're a great deal stronger than you realize."

Kelly paused for a moment to sort through the feelings she was experiencing. Colors were more vivid than she remembered, and there was an annoying buzz in the background that was so low she couldn't identify the source.

She looked down, and her face flushed bright red when she saw she wasn't wearing any clothes.

"What the hell, Eve? Whatcha do with me clothes? I'm runnin' 'round here with my everythin' hangin' out, dammit."

7

Eve lifted a hand. "Calm down, please. You can't allow your emotions to run unchecked. That could be bad."

"Emotions? Bad? What in fuck are ya yammerin' on about? This *is* me calm. If I don't get some answers soon, I'll show ya emotions." Kelly's voice dropped several octaves, and the last came out more a growl than words.

"Kelly, ya gotta keep your cool, woman," Henry called through the door. "Listen to Eve and let her explain it to ya."

"Don't ya be tellin' me what to do, ya daft old man," Kelly retorted. "I remember ya takin' on that fuckin' vamp like a damned fool and gettin' yer arse handed to ya. Lucky that bloodsucker didn't kill ya, and if he had, I would've had to bring ya back so I could do it again."

"Kelly, there's a robe on the hook there." Eve pointed at the door. "Put it on, and we can get out of here. Henry's been a wreck since you came here. He hasn't slept in over two days. You don't want to keep him waiting, do you?"

Kelly frowned. "What? Why the hell is the old fool stayin' awake? I'm fine, dammit."

"You are now. It wasn't certain that you would survive this. There were a couple of times we almost lost you. Now put on the robe and let Henry have some peace of mind. He still needs to recover from his injuries. The longer you take, the longer before he's healed."

Kelly opened her mouth to protest, then closed it with an audible snap. She took a step toward the door and barely got her hand up to stop herself from slamming into it.

"Dammit! What the hell's the matter with me? I'm like a damned toddler here," Kelly grumbled.

"Yer body's gonna need a bit to get used to the changes. You'll be fine in a little while," Henry offered through the door.

"What do ya know about my body, old man?"

"Not as much as I'd like to," Henry mumbled.

"What did ya say, Henry Smythe?"

"Oh, shite...umm, nothing, Kel."

Kelly shook her head, then looked at the arm that she still held against the door. Her eyes widened, and she pulled away from the door and rotated the forearm where she could see both sides.

She extended her left leg and let out a shocked gasp.

"What's wrong?" Eve asked.

"Nothin'. Nothin's wrong. That's the problem. I've had scars on both sides of this arm and a long one on my leg since I was six. They're all gone." She looked at Eve, then at her unblemished skin.

"That's one of the effects of the treatment. Your muscle mass is denser, and it also repaired the damage to your knee and elbow joints. You've led a hard life, it seems."

"No harder than anyone else in the bush," she mumbled as she continued to admire her unblemished arm and leg.

"Why don't you put on the robe and head out?" Eve suggested. "There's food waiting for you in the lounge, and I don't think Henry's going to stay out much longer if you don't."

Kelly nodded and reached for the robe without taking her eyes away from her leg. Once she had it on, the door slid open, and Henry stood there with a worried look.

Henry's eyes widened, and his mouth hung open as he stared at her. He'd always thought Kelly was beautiful, but the vision before him was something to behold. Gone was the dark leathery skin, the frown lines, and the wrinkles around her eyes caused by the harsh Australian sun and wind. Now her face was creamy-smooth, and she looked like a woman in her late teens.

He let his gaze travel down her body to her legs that were perfectly toned without a blemish to mar them. "My God, woman, what happened to ya?"

"What the fuck? You know damned good and well that fuckin' vamp munched on me. Knocked you on your stupid arse, too. What the hell were ya thinkin' jumping a vampire, you daft old fool? He could've killed ya!"

"I was thinking that the wanker was killing you!" Henry yelled. "What was I supposed to do? Let him kill ya?"

Kelly opened her mouth to make a sharp retort but paused. She focused on the blood still on Henry's clothes and the dark circles under his eyes.

"Well, ya look like shite warmed over. What the hell, Henry, why do ya look like ya went a couple of rounds in the ring with Horst? Those dark rings under yer eyes and the pale complexion aren't a good look on ya. Why haven't ya healed?"

"Kelly." Eve touched her arm gently. "Henry's been pacing and refusing to rest until he knew you were going to be okay. I want him to go into the Pod-doc next to check why he hasn't healed yet."

"I told ya, I'll be all right. I need a bit of rest, and I'll be good to go in no time," Henry grumped.

"Don't be daft, Henry. Look what it did to me." Kelly held her arm out under his nose, then extended her leg.

"Scars I've had since I was a kid are gone, and I feel the best I have in years. Well, except for the not being able to walk straight part."

"That will work itself out once you get used to the changes," Eve offered.

"What changes are ya talkin' about?" Kelly asked. "Did that thing do somethin' to me?"

Eve smiled. "Kelly, do you remember what happened after the attack?"

Kelly shrugged. "I shot the fucker."

"Anything else?" Eve pressed.

Kelly's face screwed into a grimace as she thought back. Everything after she shot the vampire was fuzzy. She remembered people yelling and being upset but couldn't recall anything else.

"Not really. A bunch of yellin' and stuff and…" She paused, then her eyes flew open wide. "The kids. They were both bleedin'. I thought ya told me they were fine!"

"They are," Henry assured her. "Those tykes saved yer life, Kel."

"What? What do ya mean they saved my life? They're just babies."

"Those babies saved your life. I tried, but I wasn't strong enough." Henry looked down and grimaced.

"Kelly, Dieter and Tosha gave you their blood," Eve explained softly. "The nanocytes in it are what kept you alive until we could get you here for the Pod-doc to repair the damage."

"Blood? How?"

"They put it on the wound, and you drank some. I don't

CHARLES TILLMAN & MICHAEL ANDERLE

know how the children knew to do it, but they did it before anyone realized it when Henry's blood couldn't heal you."

Kelly was silent for almost a minute before she looked up at Henry. "I remember ya asking me if I wanted it. Ya wouldn't do it until I agreed."

"Yeah, I couldn't make that decision for ya, Kel. It would've broken me to lose ya, but there's no way I would force ya to go through the change if ya disagreed."

"It was the only option, Kelly." Eve offered.

Kelly nodded. "So what's it mean? I'm a werewolf?"

"Yeah." Henry unconsciously dropped his hand to his groin. Kelly saw the motion and snorted laughter.

"Yer jewels are safe, for now. I remember, but what's next?"

"Ya adjust to the changes and press on. Yer a whole lot stronger and faster now. Ya also need to work on stayin' calm. Gettin' angry can trigger a shift, and until ya get used to the way things are, ya should avoid shiftin'," Henry explained.

Kelly brought her hand to her mouth and pressed her finger to her lips as she processed the information. After a few beats, she nodded once, and resolve settled on her face. "Eve, ya got any coffee? I need a cup."

"Told ya." Henry chuckled.

"There's a fresh pot waiting with the food in the lounge," Eve explained. "Henry wanted to bring a cup for you, but I vetoed that. There's no way I wanted to risk a spill on the equipment. It took me over a year to get it working."

"Lead on, then." Kelly stepped aside and motioned for Eve to go ahead of her.

"There is fresh clothing in your quarters. Would you like to dress first?"

Kelly considered Eve's offer for a second, then shook her head and tightened the belt on the robe. "Nope, coffee first."

"Follow me, please." Eve smiled as she headed down the hall.

Yuko's lab, TQB Base, Tokyo

"Hello, Eve," Yuko greeted. "Did you get our guest settled?"

"Yes, but Abel reported that there were complications with the Pod-doc."

Yuko turned from her project and narrowed her eyes at the child-sized AI. "Complications?"

Eve nodded. "Yes, the initial damage, what little remained after the Were nanocytes were added, healed perfectly. The problem occurred when Abel initiated the Pod-doc procedure to complete the enhancement."

Yuko raised one eyebrow and motioned for Eve to continue.

"The repairs I made were only partially successful. I calculated the Pod-doc would function at thirty-four-point-seven percent efficiency. New data reveals it is oper-ating at as little as fourteen-point-seven percent, with marked fluctuations."

"Is it dangerous to operate?" Yuko inquired.

"Not dangerous, but it's not capable of enhancing Kelly's body to the level required to activate the nanocytes to full effectiveness."

"What does that mean?"

"Kelly will not be capable of utilizing all enhanced Were capabilities the way Horst and Koda did. She'll have the enhanced senses, speed, and strength of any Were. She won't have the ability to assume the Pricolici form anytime soon, if ever, unless I can increase the Pod-doc's performance."

"What about Henry?" Yuko's voice held a note of concern. "Will it do anything for him?"

Eve shrugged. "Unknown at this time. Until Henry undergoes an initial evaluation in the unit, there's no way to determine."

Yuko sighed. It was what it was. "Is he still hesitant about the procedure?"

"I haven't discussed it with him yet. He refused to consider any treatment until Kelly's was completed."

"If you would like me to speak with him, I will," Yuko offered.

"No, but if you don't mind looking over the Pod-doc programming, I would appreciate it. I believe it's operating at maximum efficacy, but you may see something Abel and I missed."

Yuko nodded. "Send it to my console, and I'll get right on it."

"*Domo.*"

Yuko's console *pinged*, announcing an incoming message. She tapped the screen, and pages of computer code flowed across the monitor.

"I'll let you know if I find anything," Yuko mumbled, already scrolling through the code on the screen.

"Don't take too long," Eve replied with a chuckle. "Akio is expecting us to accompany him to China."

CHAPTER TWO

Yangtze Gorges, China

Qin looked up as a wide-eyed Tian pointed at the sky with her mouth hanging open as a black box descended toward the camp. One end opened, and Qin relaxed when he saw Akio's head poke out.

"Permission to land?" Akio called.

Qin waved. "Yes, yes, please land wherever you like."

The craft dropped until it was centimeters from the ground. Akio stepped out dressed in dark clothes with a sword on his back and twin pistols around his waist. A young-looking Japanese woman wearing a flowing white dress over combat armor exited behind him.

"Qin, this is my associate, Yuko. Yuko, meet Qin Shek, one of the leaders of this group, and Tian, his mate." Akio motioned with his hand.

Yuko nodded at the young Were and the woman beside him. "It's a pleasure to meet you. Akio tells me your people need supplies. We've brought food and other necessities for you. If you show me where you want them, Eve can move the cargo container closer."

"Eve?" Qin jerked his head up in surprise when a small metal person stepped out of the craft.

"That's me, Eve, at your service." The robot pointed at her chest with her thumb and smiled.

"Um, nice to meet you," Qin stammered.

"Akio, you returned," Yan called as she approached the group.

"*Hai.* You sound surprised." Akio's eyes narrowed as he looked at her.

"Forgive me, but I am. After the stories told about the Dark One's hatred for the Weres of the Clan, I had doubts."

"Those stories are told by those who act without honor. I believe that you and the Weres with you are different. Am I mistaken?" His eyes glowed dull red, and his voice dropped several octaves.

Yan took an involuntary step back, and Qin tensed. Yuko stepped between them and bowed slightly to Yan. "I'm Yuko, my Queen's representative to the Unknown-World. Akio advised me that you and your group could benefit from my assistance."

Yan cast a wary look at Yuko then focused on Akio. "My apologies. That was rude of me. It's been a trying few weeks here, but that doesn't excuse my actions. Be welcome here."

Akio nodded and let the tension fade. "Understood. Yuko came at my request to discuss a possible solution to the troubles you face. Is there somewhere we can confer about the matter?"

"Yes, my tent is over there." Yan pointed at a tan tent

that was pitched to one side of the camp. "If you'll follow me, I have a kettle and tea inside."

"Thank you, tea will be nice," Yuko agreed as she moved toward the indicated tent.

Tian stepped in front of Akio and smiled up at his grim visage. "I knew you'd return."

Akio nodded. "My honor required it. Without honor, a person has no purpose. How are you today, little one?"

"Much better now that you're here." Tian stepped back with a smile and caught Qin's hand in hers. "Without your intervention, none of us would have survived."

"I didn't get the chance to thank you properly before you left." Qin pulled Tian close and wrapped his arm around her waist. "If there's any way I can ever assist you, you have only to ask."

"*Domo,* Qin, but you owe me nothing. As I told Tian, the way to help me is to continue to act with honor and protect the unenhanced from those who consider them less. That is the charge Bethany Anne gave us before she left for the stars to battle the forces that threaten the Earth. It's my sworn duty to protect those who abide by her rules."

Qin smiled at Tian then looked Akio in the eye. "I will follow the Queen's command until I breathe my last breath. My honor requires it."

Akio's lips quirked. "I know. Come, Yuko has things to discuss that will help you protect your people."

Akio started toward the tent. Yuko and Yan entered without elaborating further.

"He's nothing like I expected," Qin whispered to Tian. "He said that like he could see into my soul or something."

"If he can see your soul, Qin, he knows that you will do whatever it takes to see all of us safe. Let's see what Yuko proposes." Tian pulled away to follow Akio.

"How would we survive?" Yan asked as she looked over the rim of her tin cup into Yuko's eyes. "We have nothing but the clothes on our backs and what little you see in the camp. Where would we live?"

"I have an answer for that," Eve stated.

Yuko turned to her with a surprised expression. "What do you mean, Eve?"

"I recently purchased a building in Nagoya. It has thirty apartments, and all of them are currently vacant." She grinned at Yuko. "I bought it cheap since the National Police arrested the previous tenants and owners."

"The police?" Yan asked.

"It was a Yakuza residence. The police made numerous arrests in Tokyo, and the National Police obtained evidence that allowed them to take down the Yakuza across Japan. There's a lot of vacant property available with their leaders gone. I've been picking it up for investment income."

Yuko snorted and shook her head. "After all these years, you still manage to surprise me, Eve."

"What can I say? I like Nagoya and thought it would be nice to have a place to stay when I visited. They have a theater district there with live plays and movie houses. It's a fun town."

"How would we pay for it? We have nothing." Qin shrugged.

Yuko looked at Qin, who sat next to Tian with one arm wrapped protectively around her. "Bethany Anne provided resources for people in situations like yours. We'll provide everything you need to settle your people there and help you find a way to provide for them."

"Why Japan?" Tian asked. "Why can't we find a place to settle here?"

"Because the Sacred Clan will hunt you, and there are no guarantees that I can be there if they come for you again. The Clan isn't a threat in Japan. As long as you conceal what you are and follow the rules, you'll be safe there," Akio explained.

"The Japanese government is aware of the Unknown-World. Our Queen established a treaty with them to allow people who followed her rules to settle there. You are welcome, as long as you continue to live in harmony with others." Yuko nodded at Akio. "If any who accept sanctuary fails to do so, they'll have the opportunity to explain their lack of honor to *him*."

Qin's face paled as he realized what that meant. "I can assure you that our people will honor the Queen's laws."

"If we didn't believe that already, I wouldn't have suggested it," Yuko assured him. "Our mission is to maintain a safe place for people to live in peace until the Queen returns. We will eliminate any who threaten that peace per the treaty."

"Is there some way we can see this place before we decide?" Yan asked. "Not that I doubt you, but we're responsible for the well-being of our people."

"That is acceptable. We can go now if you like." Yuko stood and motioned to the open tent flap.

"Just like that? We can't leave our people while we run off to Japan." Qin brought his hand up and rubbed his face.

"We can go and return before dark. If the location meets with your approval, your people can spend tonight in accommodations much more comfortable than these," Yuko assured him.

Yan commanded, "Qin, take Tian and Delan and go with them. I'll stay here with our people until you return."

Qin opened his mouth to protest, but when Yan's eyes narrowed, he nodded. "Yes, Mother. I'll return as soon as possible."

Nagoya, Japan

"Qin, there are so many people." Tian gripped his arm as her eyes darted all around.

Qin patted her hand and nodded, putting up a false appearance of confidence to hide his uneasiness. First, it was the flight here. Now, people and vehicles rushed past them in both directions as they stood on the busy sidewalk in front of a five-story building.

Eve was in the doorway talking to a man wearing a white hard hat. He smiled and nodded vigorously, then motioned her inside.

"Come in, please." Eve waved at the two stunned teens.

Yuko touched Qin's arm and pointed at Eve. "She's ready for you."

Qin jumped when she touched him. He blushed when

he realized he was so overwhelmed by the sights and sounds that he'd forgotten she was beside him.

Qin guided the wide-eyed Tian up the steps and into the building's open lobby. Yuko followed them in, and when the door closed, the entry was quiet.

"Is it always like this?" Tian muttered as she continued to stare at the activity outside.

"No, it quiets down around midnight when the theaters and restaurants close." Eve chuckled. "Then it starts over again around seven in the morning."

"How does anyone think with all this going on? That's more people than I've seen in my life." Tian pointed at a truck loaded with cages full of live chickens driving past the building. "I've never seen anything like that."

Yuko shook her head and smiled down at the young woman. "It's a lot to take in and a bit overwhelming at first."

Eve gestured at the man beside her. "This is Robun-*san*. He's supervising the construction workers upgrading the apartments. Would you show us one of the finished units?"

Robun bowed to the two and motioned them forward. "Follow me, please. Eve-*san* requested we furnish the units after we finished the upgrades. The top three floors are ready to be occupied."

He led them across the lobby to a small door on one wall. His finger stabbed a button, and the door slid open. Robun gestured them inside. Qin started in, but Tian held back, staring into the small space behind the door.

"What is it, Tian?" Yuko asked.

"What's that? It looks like one of the cells Du held people in for punishment."

Yuko stepped around them and into the lift. "It's safe, Tian. This device is called an elevator. It will take us to the floors above."

Tian took one hesitant step forward then looked at Qin for assurance. He stepped inside and pulled her in with him. The doors slid shut when Robun pressed the top button on a wall with five others in a row. Tian shrieked and grabbed Qin's arm with both hands when the car jerked as it started to rise.

Robun looked at her in concern until Eve spoke up. "She's lived in a rural village all her life. She's never been in an elevator."

He smiled and nodded.

A few seconds later, the doors slid apart on a well-lit carpeted hallway. Robun motioned them out, and Tian practically bolted through the door.

Robun chuckled softly, then walked to an open entrance a few paces down the hall. "This unit has two bedrooms, and an open living room and kitchen. It's a favorite of mine because of the colors the decorator used."

Tian and Qin stepped into the bright and open room. Floor-to-ceiling windows comprised the back wall, offering a view of the mountains outside of town. The furnishings comprised a dark leather couch and two plush chairs that faced the door. There was a low table in front of the sofa and small ones next to each chair. The furniture blended seamlessly with the earth-tone walls and stained bamboo-covered floors. A bar separated the room from a well-equipped modern kitchen.

Tian stared in shock. She was taking in every detail as fast as her eyes could dart from one feature to the next. She scuffed her shoe across the carpet-covered floor and looked up at Qin. "It's beautiful!"

Qin nodded in agreement as he stared around the apartment open-mouthed.

"The master bedroom is down this hall on the right, and a smaller room is across from it. The furniture is already there. Would you like to see it?"

Tian didn't hesitate. She pulled Qin behind her as she made her way there. The room's centerpiece was a wide bed covered in dark earth-tone covers. Dark brown carpeting covered the floor, and another set of floor-to-ceiling windows along one wall offered a stunning view of the mountains.

"Qin, this is a palace! There's room for many people here," Tian gushed.

Eve followed the two and chuckled when she heard Tian. "This apartment is for two or three people at most, Tian. There are twenty-nine more similar to it in the building."

Tian's mouth opened in an "O," and she stared mutely at Eve.

"Are all of them ready for people?" Qin sounded distracted as he took in the luxurious accommodations.

"The job is almost complete, and Robun assures me that they'll finish within three days. Is this acceptable for your people?"

"It's amazing. I've never seen anything like it," Qin answered.

"Good. Then we can bring your people here today. The top three floors are open for you, but you'll have to make temporary arrangements until the others are ready. Once the work is complete, there should be ample room for everyone."

"There's room for everyone in *here*." Tian waved her arm in an arc taking in the whole apartment.

"I'm sure they'll welcome having more space to spread out. How can we ever repay you for this?" Qin asked Eve.

"No need. I'm glad I had this available. Bethany Anne took care of the cost years ago. As Yuko said, all you have to do is live in harmony with the humans here, and there is no debt owed."

"If there is ever any way I can be of service," Qin offered, but Eve held up a hand to stop him.

"Keep your eyes and ears open for any from the UnknownWorld and contact us if you find any of them using their enhancements to prey on the innocent. Other than that, if there is anything you need, let us know."

Qin nodded and wrapped his arm around Tian's waist. "I will, I promise."

CHAPTER THREE

TQB Base, Tokyo, Japan

"Damn Kel, ya look fantastic," Henry told her when she walked into his room.

"Ya said that already, like a hundred times. Yer lookin' better now that ya got some sleep. What the bloody hell was ya thinkin' about, stayin' up while I was in the magic box? I swear ya act like a drongo sometimes."

"I was worried about ya, so sue me already," Henry grumped.

"Ya made up yer mind yet?" she asked.

"'Bout what?" Henry ducked his head to hide his grimace.

"About goin' in the fuckin' box, ya bloody idiot!" Kelly snapped. "I swear I think that damn vamp addled yer brain."

"I don't know, Kel. It took ten years off ya, at least. I been around a long time and accordin' to Eve, if I go into the Pod-doc, it'll add more years to what's already been a long hard life."

"What ya sayin'? Ya don't wanna stick around anymore?" Kelly's face clouded with concern.

"Like I said, I've been around a long time. The years weigh on a fella after a century. Don't know that I got much left to give this old world."

Kelly was quiet as she looked at the gray-haired man, who appeared to be around sixty but was more than twice that. Her mouth opened and closed several times before she spun on her heel and stormed out of the room.

Henry's head snapped up as she ran out. "Kelly! Hey, Kelly, come back," he called through the open door.

"She's outside," Abel advised over the speaker mounted in the ceiling. "Judging by the way she's cursing and kicking things, along with her elevated blood pressure and temperature, she appears to be suffering from a fit of anger."

Henry groaned as he pushed to his feet. "Damn, I better get her before she shifts and kills somebody. Namely me."

He went out through the hangar and heard her well before he saw her.

"Boneheaded old fool. What the fuck! Don't know if he wants to stick around." A loud *crash* came from behind a small outbuilding, followed by a frustrated scream.

Henry trotted over to the structure and found Kelly on her knees with tears streaming down her face. "Hey, Kel?"

"Leave me alone! That's what ya wanna do anyway!" She turned her back to him, her shoulders rising and falling with silent sobs.

Henry stood behind her and laid his hand on her shoulder.

"Go away!" She jerked away from him as she got to her feet and stormed off.

Henry took two steps, spun her as he wrapped his arms around her, and pulled her against his chest.

"Let me go, dammit!" She tried to pull away, and he held her tighter.

"Kelly, what's it matter if I go in the Pod-doc or not? It's not like nobody would miss an old Were like me."

She stopped her feeble attempts to get away and burst into sobs as her fist beat weakly against his chest. "So I'm nobody?"

Henry gaped. "What? Uh, no! You know better than that, girl."

"Then why'd ya wanna leave me?" she wailed.

"What? I don't wanna leave *you* specifically. I'm just sayin' other younger folks can do more than an old duffer like me."

"No, Henry, they can't," Kelly yelled. "I need ya and don't wanna lose ya. I can't do it on my own."

"Hell, Kel, ya do most of it now as it is. I don't add much to the conversation, and the pack respects ya and will continue to listen to ya."

"Fuck the pack. I ain't worried about or talkin' about them, ya damned fool. I, me." She pointed her thumb at her chest. "*I* need ya, dammit."

"I don't understand." Henry looked at her with confusion plastered on his face.

"Jeez, yer one of the thickest-headed men I've ever seen, and that's sayin' a lot considering the arseholes I deal with daily. Me. Kelly. I need ya!"

Henry continued to stand there baffled until Kelly

shrieked and pushed him back. She grabbed the collar of his shirt and pulled his head down level with hers. He stared into her wide eyes, speechless until her lips quirked into a half-smile, and she pulled him closer.

Henry's heart almost beat out of his chest when her lips forcefully slammed onto his. She loosened the hold on his shirt and brought both hands behind his neck while she kissed him fervently.

Henry was old, but he wasn't stupid. His arms went around her back and pulled her tight as he passionately returned her kiss.

He broke the kiss and breathed in deeply. "Well, why the hell didn't ya say that to begin with? I'll tell Eve to put me in soon as she gets back."

Kelly's body started to quiver, then shake. Henry pulled back, concerned that she was crying again, when a barked laugh erupted from her. He cocked his head, and when their eyes met, the young woman couldn't contain herself and burst into a deep belly laugh.

"What?" Henry asked.

"*You.*" She poked him in the chest with a finger.

"Me? What about me?"

"Ya spent half the day yesterday wanderin' around here mumblin' to yerself. I'm slow, but I ain't stupid. Plus, my hearin' is a whole bunch better now. The only question I got is, what the hell took you so long?"

"What are you talkin' about?" Henry's face turned crimson when he realized what she'd said. He wanted to slap himself for forgetting something that every shifter knew. Don't say nothin' around another shifter, no matter how low, that you don't want them to hear. "So, um, ya heard all that?"

"Not everything but enough. Does my butt really look that much better?"

Henry dropped his head in embarrassment. Then he looked up with a twinkle in his eyes and a lopsided grin. "It was fine before. Now it's spectacular."

Kelly's eyes opened wide. Then she burst out laughing again. "So ya have been checkin' out me arse all this time. Ya dirty old bugger."

"And I plan to keep doin' it for a long time."

Her laughter cut off abruptly when Henry's lips covered hers.

Kelly and Henry walked back inside the base hand-in-hand when the cargo container returned a few hours later. Eve met them at the door with a raised eyebrow.

"So, what did I miss?" Eve grinned.

"Nothin' much. Me and this one worked some things out," Kelly answered.

Eve nodded, then looked up at Henry. "You ready?"

Henry smiled at Kelly as he nodded.

Eve smiled. It was about time. "Come with me. I want to run the initial assessment before you change your mind."

"Initial assessment? I thought ya just popped him in, and the box did the rest." Kelly raised both hands, palms up.

"Normally, that's how it would work, but we discovered

an anomaly with the Pod-doc when it attempted to enhance your nanocytes. I want to run an initial scan then review the data before I make any adjustments to Henry's nanocytes."

"Is it dangerous?" Kelly gripped Henry's hand again.

"No, the initial assessment poses little danger. I want to be certain that there's no danger in repairing his nanocytes before we go further."

"Repairing?" Henry looked confused.

"Yes, over time, the nanocytes have changed. They've degraded over the centuries. That's the reason few Weres can achieve three forms now. A fully functional Pod-doc can restore them to their original operating parameters."

"So I'll be able to turn Pricolici after this?" Henry asked with awe in his tone.

"Undetermined at this time," Eve answered.

"Huh? I thought you said it would repair them little critters," Henry grumbled.

"The unit was damaged when the Sacred Clan attacked our original base. I managed to bring it back online, but it's operating at a reduced capacity. I need to check it using your nanocytes because the ones that Kelly received from the twins are already enhanced."

"What's a Pricoli?" Kelly asked.

"Pricolici," Henry corrected. "It's a form between wolf and human that stands on two legs and is a bamf." Henry grinned.

Kelly frowned in confusion. "What the hell's a *bamf*, old man?"

"Badass motherfucker." Henry cackled.

"Is he for real?" Kelly asked Eve.

The AI lifted a shoulder. "For lack of a better description, yes."

Kelly went wide-eyed. "Will I be able to do that?"

Eve nodded. "Possibly over time, even without the Pod-doc jumpstarting them. They replicate, but you currently don't have enough nanocytes to generate the energy needed to achieve Pricolici form. Who knows what the future holds."

"Oh, shite," Henry mumbled.

"What's that? Kelly inquired.

"Oh, nothin'. Just thinkin' out loud." Henry looked at Eve. "Can we get goin' on this?"

"Certainly. Come with me."

"What was you mumblin' about, Henry?" Kelly walked beside him with her hand resting in the crook of his arm.

"I was thinkin' about how screwed the folks in Adelaide would be with ya as a Pricolici. Horst and Koda took out two vamps in that form."

"Bet I could do some serious damage if I kicked a bloke in the cods like that." Kelly smirked.

Henry's free hand moved to cover his groin, and the color drained from his face. "Ya got no idea."

CHAPTER FOUR

Adelaide, Australia

"Horst!" Koda's frantic scream echoed down the hallway.

Horst jumped to his feet and was by her side in the twins' room in a flash.

"What's wrong?"

Koda pointed at the white toddler bed pushed against the back wall. Dieter smiled at him, and Tosha waved her fur-covered hand and giggled.

Horst's mouth dropped open. "Scheisse! She can partially shift."

"Not only her," Koda informed him in the same tone of panic. "Dieter's face had a snout and canine teeth when I walked in. What's wrong with my children? Is this normal?"

"No." Horst rubbed his chin with a hand. "I've never heard of children this young managing a full shift, let alone a partial one."

Eve!

Yes, Horst?

Something's wrong with the twins.

Do you need a Pod? Are they injured?

No, nothing like that. They've both managed to partially shift.

While he spoke to Eve, the fur on Tosha's hand disappeared into her flesh, and her mouth morphed into a short snout. Dieter giggled and held his hand up. Tosha howled a laugh when claws extended from Dieter's tiny hand and fur sprouted up to his shoulder.

Do they appear to be having difficulty with the shifts? Eve asked.

Horst watched wide-eyed as the children morphed back and forth between human and Were several times.

No, not that I can tell, but they shouldn't be able to do it at all.

Horst, remember when you noticed them growing faster than usual, and I told you that the Pod-doc enhancements in the womb could affect their development?

Yes.

I believe this is further evidence that Tosha and Dieter will not develop as typical children, even Weres, do. I'm sending a Pod for you to bring them in for a scan. I suspect it will show that their nanocytes are performing at optimum levels again.

How are we supposed to deal with this, Eve? What happens if one of them gets mad and shifts?

Are they displaying heightened levels of aggression?

No.

Have they ever?

Horst's lips pursed as he thought. *No, never.*

I suggest you continue to monitor them, but don't make prob-

lems where none exist. The Pod will be in Adelaide in twenty-three minutes. Bring them in, and we'll give them a checkup.

Both children had shifted back to human form when Eve ended the transmission.

"You heard?" Horst asked Koda.

"I did. Eve didn't sound too worried. She warned us that they could develop faster in more than growth."

Horst scrubbed his hand across his face again. "How are we supposed to keep up with them now? It was hard enough before they learned to shift."

Tosha looked up at him with a radiant smile. Her eyes glowed yellow for an instant, then returned to their usual cornflower blue to match his. "Run, Daddy?"

Dieter perked up from where he was toying with the material on Koda's pants leg.

"Hunt, Daddy?"

"Do you two want to go out as Weres?" Horst asked the tykes.

Neither answered, but their smiles said it all.

Koda snorted and side-eyed Horst. "Looks like you have your work cut out for you, Dad. Your children want to hunt, it seems."

"My children! Oh, no. You were there, too. You're not putting all of this on me! No way, no how. Besides that, the Pod will be here shortly. I need to let Robbie know we're leaving for a few hours."

The Blue Mountains near Wallerawang, Australia

"Aaron!" Kent yelled as he burst through the door of the underground bunker.

"My God, Kent. I'm right here," Aaron grumbled from the overstuffed chair in the corner. "No need for all that noise. What's the problem?"

"Finn and Mitchell are dead."

Aaron shot to his feet, his face twisted in rage and disbelief. "What? Who? How?" Aaron spat the questions at his scion, one after the other.

Kent growled. "The Adelaide wolves. They killed both of them."

"How many did the pack lose doing that? Finn's powerful in his own right, and Mitch is no slouch when it comes to brawling. How many Weres did they take with them?"

"None. Finn took a bite out of a human woman and bashed one old Were in the head. It knocked him down, but he was on his feet a few minutes later. It looked like the woman survived, too. Mitch threw a few around, but I didn't see him kill any."

"Impossible," Aaron barked. "You're telling me that a pack of mangy wolves killed both of your brothers without a single loss?"

"No, it wasn't the pack. It was two Weres like I've never seen before. They were monstrous wolves who stood on two legs like a man but had claws and fangs."

Aaron frowned in disbelief. "I've never heard of that. Are you sure?"

"I saw one of them snatch Mitchell's beating heart from his chest and throw it at Finn," Kent told him. "The other threw Finn around like he was nothing, then ripped his head off using only the strength in her arms. That's not all I saw, either."

Aaron gestured for Kent to continue.

"I continued to watch, and a black cargo container came down from the sky. The door opened, and a woman with several men got out of it. They took the woman Finn attacked and the Were he knocked down inside it and shot off into the night."

Aaron's mouth dropped open, and his eyes took on a panicked glaze. "No! It can't be. She can't be back after all this time!"

"It appears the Bitch has returned, Aaron. That's the only explanation why one of her craft showed up and took people away."

Kent flopped into a chair and stared at the floor for a moment before looking up at Aaron. "I don't care if Michael himself is back. Those animals in Adelaide need to pay for killing Finn and Mitch. Adelaide and everyone there needs to burn."

Aaron shook his head and slumped back into his chair. "How do you propose to fight her, Kent? Both of us together aren't strong enough to take on Bethany Anne. Not to mention the firepower she has access to."

"I don't care if I die, but before I do, those Weres will pay." Kent stood and started pacing back and forth. "If you're too afraid to help, continue hiding in this hole. I'll take them all on my own."

"Settle down a moment. Sit." Aaron put a compulsion behind the last word, and his offspring immediately obeyed.

Kent glared daggers at Aaron but remained silent while Aaron thought through their possible courses of action.

Neither spoke for ten minutes, then Aaron nodded and faced Kent.

"We'll need numbers if we hope to stand any chance of surviving this."

"Numbers? You mean, ask for help from other vampires? Kent sounded incredulous.

"That's an option, but I was thinking of growing our family. There are human settlements scattered in the wilds. You and your brothers have found quite a few of them. That's a ready source of cannon fodder if we're going to war."

Kent was silent for a few beats, then nodded. "That could work, but none of them will be strong at first."

Aaron smirked. "A normal Were isn't much danger to a new vampire. Even these super-Weres you claim you saw can't stand up to a group of them."

"What about the Bitch?" Kent asked.

"That could pose a more serious issue," Aaron admitted. "I may have a way to get more information. I never thought about it much because I didn't like the fucker who came up with it. I think it's time to see if the global information network is still working."

Kent grimaced. "I remember talk of that. Some Forsaken who was a scientist before he was turned came up with that, didn't he? Jones or something similar?"

"Smith. He was American and full of himself, but if the network is functional, I have the equipment here to access it."

Kent stood and walked toward the back of the bunker.

"Where are you going?" Aaron called.

"To get a shower and some rest. I'm going to get our

first recruits tonight. There's an old cattle farm with a small group of humans living on it about twenty kilometers south of here. There's enough room to house eighty to one hundred new vampires in the houses and outbuildings."

"We'll need some more chattel for here, too," Aaron mused. "I want to turn the ones we have here now. They've proven loyal over the years, and we need someone to oversee the new ones."

Kent nodded in agreement. "I know your tastes. I'll find someone to your liking. You see what you can find out about the Bitch Queen, and I'll handle the rest."

Aaron waved Kent away and stood. He stepped into the room he'd set up as his office when the bunker was new. The computer virus had wiped out his ability to use most of the equipment, but the transmitter Smith had provided was still in the box.

Aaron dug the unit out of the cabinet he'd thrown it into when he'd brought it home. He studied the device and instructions and saw he would have to find a place to mount the antenna.

"Couldn't make it easy, could you? You Yank bastard," he muttered as he gathered the items he would need to accomplish the task once the sun was down.

CHAPTER FIVE

TQB Base, Tokyo, Japan

"According to the information Qin and Yan provided, the humans are all here overnight." Abel highlighted a long, narrow one-story building on the outskirts of the town. A field of crops bordered it on one side and one with livestock on the other.

"Indicate Du Shek's residence, please," Akio requested.

The marker appeared on what had been a government building before WWDE. The boxy two-level structure with uninspired gray concrete exterior walls was three kilometers from the other buildings.

Abel had pulled every surveillance video and photo he could find going back to before WWDE. The once small but thriving city along the Yangtze river had suffered during the war. It now comprised an area a little less than two kilometers along the riverside and under a kilometer back.

"How many guards are assigned to the building they keep the humans in?"

"Only two on duty at night. They periodically patrol the perimeter but have no set schedule. The main guard force is active during the day when the people are working." Abel highlighted a house nearby in red. "The guards use this building for their base and quarters. There are sixteen living here currently."

"Any humans in the house?" Akio asked.

"Negative," Abel responded. "Humans are not allowed anywhere other than the holding building after dark. Even the ones who work in town are brought in at night."

A thin smile appeared on Akio's face as a plan formed. "How many missile Pods do you have?"

"Two with the smaller missiles we've been using and two more that have a larger warhead and silver payload," Abel answered. "They only have eight missiles each, but they're considerably more powerful."

Akio nodded. "How many of them would it take to destroy the guards' quarters?"

"One, and it will leave a smoking hole where the house stood."

"Can you bring all four of them?"

"Is your sword sharp? Of course, I can," Abel snarked.

Akio chuckled dryly. "Good. The only concerns I have are that the humans are safe and Du Shek dies. Any Weres in the area are targets of opportunity. Try not to damage too many buildings. The people the Clan have held as slaves grew those crops and raised the livestock. They might as well enjoy them once they're free."

"Are you saying I get to go in blasting and gassing?"

Akio detected a hint of glee in Abel's tone. "You have explosives now, too?"

"What? No! It's only a saying."

"If you're asking if you can kill weretigers by whatever means you have at your disposal, so long as the humans are protected, and Du Shek dies by my hand, the answer is yes," Akio told him straight-faced.

"Missiles are loaded, and the Black Eagle's ready. When do we leave?"

Akio glanced at the clock displayed on the command console. "Twelve hours. I want to attack at three in the morning there."

"Do you need me to do anything else while we wait?" Abel inquired.

"Ensure that the humans are all locked away and keep track of Du," Akio instructed. "If you notice anything out of the ordinary before the mission, let me know."

"Will do," Abel confirmed. "These knob-gobblers won't know what hit them."

Akio's eyes narrowed as he looked at the camera mounted in the console. "'Knob-gobblers?'"

"I've been reviewing recordings of Bethany Anne's interactions with John Grimes and the others. The Bitches have a unique way of communicating, and I thought you would appreciate a reminder of the team."

"Have you heard me use any words remotely close to that in the transmissions?" Akio asked.

"Well, no. But I thought you would like feeling like you were with them." Abel's voice held a note of uncertainty.

"There's no need for you to use creative cursing. We're already a team, and our interactions are sufficient to achieve the mission without it. Besides, if my Queen heard you making such feeble attempts, she would require penance from you."

"Penance? What do you mean?" Abel's voice held a note of curiosity.

"She's been known to stand on their backs while they do pushups and call out a different creative curse for each one. If they repeat themselves at any time, she makes them start over." Akio's lips quirked. "Who knows what she would come up with as a lesson for a digital entity?"

Akio stood and walked out of the room, leaving Abel to sort through that tidbit on his own.

Medical, TQB Base, Tokyo, Japan

"Eve, I can't thank you enough for running scans on the children." Koda's voice was heavy with concern, and she frowned in worry.

"I'm happy to do it." Eve smiled at Dieter as he walked beside her holding her hand. "What kind of aunt would I be if I didn't do everything in my power to ensure these two little angels are in the best of health?"

"Aunty Eve." Dieter smiled back at her.

"That's right, little man. Aunty Eve's going to take a look at your nanocytes."

Dieter's face scrunched up. "Nabotites."

"Nan-o-cytes," Eve sounded out the word for him.

"Na— Nab-o-bites," he tried.

Eve chuckled. "Maybe that word is too big for you just yet."

"Nanocytes," Tosha called from behind them.

"Well, aren't you full of surprises, Tosha?" Eve glanced over her shoulder as she spoke.

Koda snickered. "She gets that from me."

Horst snorted. "Oh, so that's how it is. When they do something smart and cute, it's because of you. When they do something different and scary, it's all me."

"Of course. Everyone knows those traits come from the father." Koda laughed.

Eve laughed with her then stopped in front of the Pod-doc. "Dieter, Aunty Eve needs you to get in the machine so she can take a look. Can you do that for me?"

Dieter nodded and let go of her hand. He turned to Horst and raised his arms above his head. "Up, Daddy."

"I guess he's ready." Horst chuckled as he lifted Dieter and swung him in an arc. Dieter's shrill laughter echoed in the room as Horst turned him back again.

"In you go." Horst put the child into the Pod-doc.

Eve made some adjustments on the unit, then looked at the results and made more. Once she was satisfied that the Pod-doc was ready, she turned to Horst and Koda. "It will take twenty-three minutes for the scan to complete. Do you want to wait here or in the lounge?"

"Here," Koda and Horst answered together.

Eve nodded at Tosha. "Want me to take her until it finishes? Kelly and Henry are in the lounge now. I know they'll want to see her."

"Please," Koda agreed. "Tell them we'll talk to them once the scans are complete."

"Understood. Tosha, do you want to go see Kelly and Henry?" Eve asked.

Tosha cocked her head and looked at the Pod-doc, and pointed. "Dieter?"

"Dieter's fine. It will be your turn next," Koda assured her. "Do you want to go see Kelly and Henry with Aunt Eve?"

"Kelly!" Tosha yelled and struggled to get out of Koda's arms.

"Okay, little miss. You mind Aunty Eve." Koda lowered her to the floor and patted her cheek.

"Okay, Mommy." She turned to Eve and grabbed her hand. "Kelly!" she demanded as she tugged Eve toward the door.

"The scans confirmed what I expected. The twins' nanocytes are operating at optimum levels," Eve explained to the group of concerned adults in the lounge.

Henry and Kelly were sitting at the table with them. Tosha was in Kelly's lap and Dieter in Horst's. When Horst had explained the reason for the unscheduled trip to Japan, both of them had immediately been worried about the children.

"What does that mean in terms of their development?" Koda asked.

"Comparing these readings to the last ones from right before you left for Adelaide, both of them are growing faster than human toddlers their age, which we already knew. Their bones are still forming, but they're developing muscle to accommodate the accelerated growth, and it appears that their cognitive abilities are also advanced," Eve explained.

"So what? They'll be bigger and smarter than other kids their age?" Horst shrugged. "Is that going to be a problem?"

"Only for whoever is keeping up with them." Eve chuckled. "I would suggest you find a Were nanny for them when you're both busy."

"Got that covered." Kelly laughed as she tickled the back of Tosha's neck with her nose.

"Jenny's not gonna like that." Henry frowned. "I suppose I can ask Jack's daughter if she wants to help out. Lisa's the youngest Were we have in Adelaide besides these two. She's crazy about Jenny and the twins, too, so that shouldn't pose a problem."

Koda nodded thoughtfully as she considered Henry's suggestion. "Lisa's a sweet young woman, and they already like her. That's a good solution while we're in Adelaide if she's willing to help."

Horst nodded and looked at Eve. "So, how fast will they grow?"

"If they continue at the rate from the past few months, they'll be the size of a five-year-old human by the end of the year. Based on their muscle and bone development so far, that won't cause them any harm. Watch them, and if they display any signs that their bodies are having trouble adjusting to the rapid changes, bring them here imme-diately."

"Is that a concern?" Koda fretted.

Eve shook her head. "I don't expect it. There's no data indicating it will happen, either, but better safe than sorry."

Koda nodded, then looked up at Kelly with wide eyes.

"Oh, Kelly, I'm sorry. The twins had me so worried I forgot to ask how you feel."

Kelly waved her apology off. "No worries. You've had a lot on. I feel better than I've ever felt in as long as I can remember. Well, now that I can walk without running into stuff."

Koda snorted laughter. "That was a problem for me too for a few days. I didn't know my strength."

"Tell me about it. I thought I was gonna have to get a metal cup to drink my coffee after I busted three glass ones." Kelly chuckled. "Luckily, I figured that one out."

"Where's yer coffee?" Henry asked when he noticed she didn't have a cup.

"I'm good," Kelly answered.

Henry noticed a hesitation in her voice. "What's the matter, Kelly?"

She gave him the side-eye. "Wotcha mean? Nothin's wrong."

Henry shook his head. "Kelly, in all the time I've known ya, the one constant is if yer awake, ya have a cup in yer hand. Now that I think about it, ya didn't have any this morning at breakfast, either. Now, what's the matter?"

Kelly was silent for a few seconds then answered quietly. "It don't taste right."

Henry's eyes widened in shock. "That's not right. What do ya mean, it don't taste right?"

Kelly shrugged. "It just don't. Leave it be. I'm sure it has to do with all the changes takin' place. I'm okay."

"Eve, do ya have any idea what this might be?" Henry asked.

"Henry, I said leave it," Kelly growled.

Henry shook his head. "I will not. I had to deal with ya when ya ran low and cut back until Horst came through with a fresh supply. I'm sorry, but you're a handful when ya *have* yer caffeine. Without it, you're a terror. There is no way in hell I'm gonna have a caffeine-deficient new Were gunnin' for me."

"The nanocytes should have cleared up any addictions she had, Henry. Her body won't need the boost anymore," Eve advised.

Kelly tipped her head back and sighed. "I wasn't addicted, dammit. I just liked me coffee. Now it don't smell or taste right. I, I don't think I like it anymore."

"Now I've heard it all." Henry chortled.

CHAPTER SIX

Black Eagle, above Wuxue, China

"The drones have confirmed that all human slaves are locked in the building," Abel informed Akio.

"Did you confirm Du Shek's location?" Akio asked.

"Affirmative. He's in his private rooms on the second floor of the administration building. His assistant is in an adjacent room, and there are four guards present. Two are outside the door to his rooms, and the others are patrolling separately around the outside."

"Any other guards on duty?"

"Only the two where the humans are being kept." The Black Eagle's HUD flickered and showed an aerial view of the town. "There are twenty-nine warriors barracked here, and another twelve there." A highlight appeared on a single-story building next to the administration building, then a large house close to the river.

"Each of these houses contains one to four Weres as well," Abel continued. Blue dots lit up on another eighteen structures.

"Put me down on the north side of the field across from the human-occupied building," Akio requested. "I'll take out the two guards there first, then move on to Shek. When I give the signal, blow the guardhouse at the fields. When the Weres in town move to investigate, fire at will."

"Do you want any survivors?" Abel inquired.

Akio shook his head. "No, eliminate all of them if possible. Don't let any near the slave quarters. We can track and kill any who escape once the prisoners are safe."

"You got it, boss. Happy hunting." The canopy on the Black Eagle opened, and Akio climbed out and faded into the darkness. The craft lifted silently, and four missile launchers took up station around it.

Akio crossed the two hundred meters using the sparse trees along the fence line that separated the food crops from the livestock for cover. He froze in the shadow of a bush when his enhanced eyesight caught movement at the slave quarters.

A single man walked along the side of the building then stopped to relieve himself on the wall. Akio drew his katana from its sheath on the back of his black Jean Dukes armor and silently crept up behind him.

The Were stiffened as Akio's blade burst out of his forehead. Akio held the weight with his blade until he was confident the Were was dead, then lowered the body to the ground without a sound.

Akio stayed in the shadow of the building as he made his way to the opposite side. He paused to listen before rounding the corner. He didn't hear the other guard moving, so he took a knee and cautiously peered around the corner.

He shook his head and frowned when he saw the other guard sitting in a chair, leaning it back against the building with his feet up in a second chair. He strained his hearing and picked up the sounds of slow and steady breaths coming from the sleeping Were.

Akio stood and moved at enhanced speed past the guard, who died without waking as Akio's razor-sharp katana sliced through his neck and left his head hanging askew by a thin strip of skin.

Outer guards neutralized, he sent to Abel. *I'm heading to Shek now. Hold position here, and I'll contact you when I'm in place there.*

Affirmative, the reply came.

Akio stopped before he passed the first occupied house on the way into town. He extended his senses and found a single Were in the main room. A thin blanket partially covered the doorway that led inside. Akio crouched below the uncovered window and situated himself against the wall outside the door.

He drew his tanto from the sheath on his belt, pulled his arm back, pivoted, and flung the short knife into the back of the Were's head. It hit with the sound of a ripe melon bursting on the ground, and the Were's body slumped in the chair.

Akio stepped into the house and retrieved his blade. He sheathed it after wiping off the blood on the dead Were's shirt. Seconds later, he was out of the house and lost in the shadows again.

Du Shek paced the floor in his room, five steps across and back as his mind chaotically flitted from subject to subject. He'd gone to bed a little after dark and wakened abruptly two hours earlier. After tossing and turning for an hour, he'd gotten out of bed and started to pace.

How the hell did Yan and Qin escape? The silver contamination around the battle site means that damned vampire was there. The wounds on the dead at the base were full of silver, and the warriors who died in the gorges looked like a bomb went off, but there was no sign of the rebels.

Du grimaced as he recalled the report about Kang's body. Someone had taken the time to stage the pompous ass' corpse so it stood in the canyon facing the carnage that was once over one hundred Sacred Clan warriors. Whoever had done it had stuck the head on one pole, tied the body to a different stake, and left it with the hands resting on top of Kang's head.

The part about how they used small sticks to open Kang's lifeless eyes enraged and intrigued Du. He wasn't sure what message it was supposed to convey, but the scout's reactions when he reported indicated that it definitely sent one.

Surely Yan isn't in league with the vampire? Did he take them away with him? The scouts followed their trail to the bottom of the north slope, where it disappeared. There's no way for a group that large to vanish into thin air.

Du continued to pace as he mulled over the information. After a few more minutes, he called, "Sei, get in here."

Du waited a few seconds, then called again, "Sei, I need you. Get in here now!"

Akio moved through the sleeping town like a ghost in the darkness. Twice he stopped and backtracked when he came upon Weres. Once when three sat outside a house, passing a bottle of alcohol between them. The second was when he came upon two sitting in the dark on a wide porch.

He approached the administration building from the west and saw both exterior guards sitting at a small table with a deck of cards between them. He moved silently on the soft-soled leather boots he'd chosen for stealth instead of his usual heavy armored boots and stopped when one of them spoke.

"I don't know what happened to them, but Guiying swears the rebels melted into thin air. I saw the scouts Du sent to check on Kang when he didn't report back. All of the warriors there suffered from silver burns and some weapon that blew them apart. Guiying said two of the scouts died when they inhaled tiny silver particles that covered the ground."

"What else did he tell you?"

"That all the warriors Du sent were dead and that Kang's body was left tied to a pole without its head. Well, the head was there, but someone stuck it on a post in front of the body. I tell you, Min. Something is off about this."

"Yeah, Du's lost his mind, and you believe in ghosts." The guard moved his hands around in the air and moaned.

"Believe what you want, but you didn't see the look on Guiying's face. Whatever he saw there scared the hell out of him."

The other man stood and stretched his arms over his head. "I believe I'm going to make my rounds before one of Du's flunkies tells him we're goofing off. The last thing I need is Du on my back with him acting more like Kun every day."

"I'll watch the door. How about you drop by the kitchen and see if there are leftovers of that roasted chicken and noodle dish from the evening meal? I could use a bite to eat."

"Will do." The guard waved as he walked around the corner into the dark.

Akio watched him go around the back of the building then cross to a small screened-in kitchen fifty meters away. He clung to the shadows until he stood outside the door the man disappeared through.

The sound of doors opening and closing came from inside. Then footsteps approached the entrance where Akio waited with his katana in his hand.

The door bumped open as the man backed through it, balancing a covered plate with a wine bottle on top in each hand. He stuck a foot out to catch the door as it swung back on its spring and grunted in satisfaction when it closed silently.

Akio thrust his katana straight out. The point punched into the temple of the unsuspecting Were's head and out through the opposite side. Akio released the blade and deftly caught the plates and bottles before they crashed to the ground. The Were's body stood upright, quivering as his brain ceased to send signals to his body.

The Were fell as Akio set the dishes down. He grabbed the man by his shoulder and gently lowered the body without a sound. Akio freed his katana from its bony prison with a quick pull and twist and moved on to his next target without a backward glance.

Akio slid through the shadows along the side of Du's headquarters, pausing before he rounded the corner where the unsuspecting sentry stood watch.

A glance showed the man leaning his chair back on two legs with his boots resting on the small table. Akio shook his head in disgust. That this man performed his duties in such a sloppy manner offended Akio to his core. His lack of pride in his composure and attention to his assignment went against everything Akio believed a warrior should be.

He took a half-step, then pushed his body to preternatural speed. The tang of his sword slammed against the back of the guard's head, and almost a meter of hammer-forged steel protruded from between the crossed eyes before the guard had any clue what had happened.

Akio twisted his wrist with one hand while the other swept the mud-covered boots to the ground. The body slid forward, and the dead guard's head *thumped* on the table when Akio's blade came free.

"No shoes on the table," Akio murmured almost inaudibly. Bad manners were the least of the guard's shortcomings.

Akio glared at the corpse with contempt before he turned on his heel and strode into Du's home. Once inside, he extended his senses through the building and located two Weres on the second floor. One was agitated, and the other appeared to be asleep in an adjacent room.

Akio silently padded up the stairs, careful to keep his

weight spread to avoid alerting his prey with a squeaky tread. At the top, he heard a voice call out.

"Sei, I need you. Wake up!" The demand was followed by pounding on a door.

"Master Du?" a voice heavy with sleep answered.

"Where's Sei?"

"Sir, no one's seen him since yesterday."

"I'm surrounded by total incompetence. Bring me that damned scout commander. Tell him I have questions."

"Yes, sir."

Footsteps rapidly approached Akio's position as the man hurried to obey. Akio raised his katana across the front of his body with the blade parallel to his neck. As the footsteps slowed and the runner turned onto the stairs, Akio extended his elbows, and the blade whistled as it removed his head in one clean slice.

Akio was moving before the head hit the top step and rolled down toward the bottom. Du Shek's eyes opened wide as a phantom dressed in black burst into his private chambers. A Pricolici tiger stood with Du's shredded clothes at his feet in the blink of an eye.

Du flexed his legs and leapt at the intruder who dared to violate his inner sanctum. He roared in anger as he sought to pin the insolent fool with his clawed hands and rip the life from him.

His roar turned into a *hiss* of pain when Akio's katana flashed in the dim lamplight and scored a gash starting at the top of his forehead. It continued down, slicing through Du's eye and down along his jaw.

Abel, commence operations, Akio commanded.

Affirmative, Abel responded.

Du Shek took a reeling step away from his attacker as a loud blast rattled the building. Akio's eyes widened in surprise at the force of the explosion almost a kilometer away. He shook his head, then pressed his attack on the Pricolici.

Akio sidestepped and twisted his upper body, barely avoiding three hundred kilograms of enraged beast. He sliced down with his katana and was rewarded with another pained screech as a half-meter of bloody tiger tail dropped to the floor.

Before Du could recover, Akio spun in place and stood with his blade ready to defend against another attack. Du slammed into the metal doorframe and rebounded back toward Akio.

Akio wasted no motion. He lowered the katana and took a sliding step as he thrust to pierce the tiger's back. Du sensed his impending doom and dropped to the floor at the last instant, sliding under Akio's blade and lashing out with one back leg.

The vampire grunted as Du's clawed foot slammed into his armored hip and spun him onto the huge bed that dominated the center of the room. Akio rolled across the soft mattress and off the side, away from the Pricolici struggling to his feet.

Akio landed on his back and raised both feet into the air, then snapped them to the floor and stood in one easy movement. An orange and black blur was halfway across the bed when his sword spun in a low arc and connected with the beast's outstretched hand.

Two bloody fingers landed on the bed as Akio leapt, bending at the waist so his back collided with the ceiling instead of his head. White dust rained down on the room when he impacted the drywall and punched an Akio-sized hole above the bed.

Gravity took control, and he plummeted toward the wounded and confused Were. Du looked up in time to see the katana's point before it pierced his good eye. The last thought through Du Shek's mind as the blade sliced through his brain was how he would punish his guards for failing him.

Akio drove the blade into Du's head, and his body slammed down on top of the Were, propelling him onto the mattress. A cloud of fluffy white feathers puffed up and surrounded Du's body as his sword sliced through the thick down-filled comforter that covered the bed.

Akio rolled off Du's twitching body and stood listening for any sign that others were coming. Heavy guitar music and explosions echoed through the building. Some were close and others farther away.

Abel, why do the explosions sound so far apart?

Abel cackled. *I've detached the launchers and am assaulting multiple targets simultaneously. It's like shooting fish in a barrel. They don't know which way to run.*

A loud blast shook the structure and blew out the glass in two windows.

What exactly was that? Akio demanded.

One of the larger missiles that Eve developed. She loaded them with the same explosive compound that she used in her hand launcher. They're freaking awesome!

Akio shook his head and grimaced as the concussion from another blast cracked the remaining window in the room.

"*Gott Verdammt*! Hold still so I can shoot you, you furry nut shuckers!" Abel shrieked over the Black Eagle's external speakers while the blasters mounted to the fuselage barked out a steady staccato of fire. "Don't run, little kitties. You'll only die tired."

The music changed to a deep bass drumbeat that Akio recognized as the Viking music Abel had introduced him to weeks earlier.

You are planning to leave some buildings for the humans to occupy, aren't you?

Affirmative. The majority of the surviving Weres have opted to run for the hills. Should I pursue them?

Go ahead but don't go too far from here. I'm going to check the town for any stragglers then release the captives.

Affirmative. Takumi should try this. It beats his stupid video games by a mile.

Abel laughed coldly over the loudspeakers seconds before another of the heavy missiles exploded. "You can run, but you can't hide. Saint Payback's in the house, bitches!"

Akio caught his katana and pulled it out of Du's skull. The bed screeched; it was stuck in the wooden base below the mattress. Akio grimaced and climbed onto the bed to stand straddling Du's body. He placed one foot on the lifeless chest and grasped the handle in both hands. The wood shrieked as the blade came free, and he stumbled back two steps on the unsteady surface.

He hopped down to the floor and paused long enough to wipe the blood and feathers from his blade on the blood-spattered bed. He sheathed the katana on his back then made his way out of the building as the sounds of

AC/DC's *Highway to Hell* echoed in the distance, punctuated by the occasional explosion and sinister laughter.

Akio walked through the town, searching for any Weres that had failed to flee Abel's attack. He was pleased when he found both barracks buildings were nothing but smoking craters, but the remainder of the buildings nearby were relatively unscathed.

His pass through the deserted streets revealed multiple Weres with wounds from Abel's blasters but only two places where the EI had deployed missiles. Both of those sites contained multiple dead Clan members where Abel had caught them bunched together.

Akio worked his way across the town and out into the area where the fields and slaves were. He approached the old barn-turned-prison and twisted the padlock that secured the door. A satisfied grunt escaped him when the hasp shattered into multiple pieces.

He pushed the door open, and the stench of fear and unwashed bodies roiled around him. He took a step back from the smell and called into the dark building, "You're free. The ones who oppressed you are either dead or fleeing for their lives."

There was no response to his hail, not that he expected any in the first place. Experience showed that most humans he freed from Clan settlements were too afraid to answer. They would come out at some point the next day when thirst and hunger made them bold enough to overcome their fear.

A quick look around the exterior revealed a working well with a hand pump at the closest edge of the cultivated field. Satisfied that the people had water available, he walked across the field, being careful to step over and around the delicate plants the villagers had grown for their Clan masters.

Abel.

Yes, Akio?

Our work here is complete.

Agreed. I flushed the last two tigers out of hiding a few minutes ago. They thought they were smart going into a shallow cave. They should have chosen a deeper hole.

Oh?

Abel chuckled. *I sent a smoke missile into the cave behind them. Those Weres hate my smoke.*

I believe it's the microscopic silver particles they hate. I don't think smoke bothers them too much.

The Black Eagle dropped out of the inky blackness and stopped two meters from where Akio stood. The hatch opened, and Akio was inside and strapped into his seat seconds later.

"Make a few passes over and around the town with full sensor scans," he instructed. "Let's make sure that none of the Weres tried to sneak back in."

"Acknowledged, but I got all of them," Abel answered as the craft rose fifty meters and turned toward the settled part of town.

Heat signatures from the two destroyed barracks buildings, small cooking fires, and oil lamps registered on the sensors as Abel crisscrossed the town in a grid pattern.

"No signs of life other than the people in the barn," Abel

confirmed. "They didn't want to come out and meet you, I see."

"No. They're all terrified for now. Imagine bombs blowing up to an AC/DC soundtrack woke you."

"How could I imagine that? I don't sleep."

Akio shook his head and rolled his eyes. "You understand my meaning. Your little heavy metal show has them too scared to move, not to mention come out when a stranger calls."

"I do understand. I'm exploring humor, and data indicated a forty-one-point-four percent chance you would find that response humorous."

"Perhaps you should stick with your day job. Humor isn't for everyone," Akio replied dryly.

"Oh, I see how it is. The Queen's Bitch has jokes. Hardee-har-har."

Akio's lip trembled on one side, threatening a half-smile. Abel didn't realize how humanlike his response was.

"Leave some drones to monitor the area in case more Clan members show up," Akio advised.

"I have four on station with the transmitters activated," Abel assured him. "I'll monitor the feeds for the next two weeks. If any Weres return, we can come back for more fun and games."

Akio frowned. "Fun and games? Abel, you do realize that we killed many people today, don't you?"

"Yes," Abel responded. "I'm aware that forty-nine lives were ended as a direct result of my targeting them with weapons. 'Fun and games' is an expression I picked up from some of the transcripts of John Grimes and the other Bitches' missions. Is it inappropriate?"

"Taking a life should never be considered fun or a game," Akio stated. "The Weres' abusive actions toward the humans resulted in the judgment of guilt for disobeying Bethany Anne's rules. The sentence for that is death. It's not our place to take joy in their plight, only to execute our Queen's laws."

"I understand, Akio. I'll note that levity is not an appropriate response to taking a life."

"Thank you, Abel. You performed your mission well tonight, as you always do. I only wanted to remind you that killing should never be the first consideration but always the last option. In this case, Bethany Anne decided the sentence. There are other times where there is another way."

Abel was silent for a few beats before he asked, "Like the Were you let flee a few months back when he denounced the actions of his fellows?"

"Exactly. We saw the evidence, added to Qin's testimony, and knew that all here were evil. If there had been any doubt about the guilt of anyone here, I would have chosen a different plan of attack."

"Even though the Sacred Clan murdered Kenjii, you still have hope for them?" Abel inquired.

Akio suppressed the pang in his chest at the mention of Kenjii's name. *"Hai,* the people responsible for his death and the attacks in Japan are all dead. To kill someone because they are associated with the Clan without proof of them violating the Queen's law would be no better than what they did to us. Unfortunately, too many of the Sacred Clan embrace the falsehood that they are above everyone else and can act with impunity. I must convince them otherwise. To do anything else lacks honor."

"I believe I understand. Do you have anywhere you want to go, or should I return to base?"

"We've done enough for tonight. Let's go home."

CHAPTER SEVEN

TQB Base, Tokyo, Japan (three months later)

"I'll have to check with the herders to confirm they can deliver the amounts ya want, but I don't see a problem from here," Henry assured the Prime Minister.

"If they can come close to the numbers we discussed, it will be better than what we have now." Sato raised his cup of *sake* in salute before he sipped.

Kelly ran her fingers down the multiple columns of numbers on the Prime Minister's offer. "They had a bumper crop of lambs last season. The amount of raw wool ya want is only about twenty percent of what we produced before the herds expanded. We have enough in storage to meet the first shipment with some leftover."

"I bow to the wisdom of the one person in the room who knows the first bloody thing about those nasty beasts." Henry chuckled.

Sato laughed and raised the bottle of *sake* he'd brought to the meeting and filled Henry's cup. When he moved to fill Kelly's, she shook her head and covered the cup.

"I'm sure it's good stuff, but I've developed a sensitivity to anythin' stronger than weak tea lately."

Sato nodded and put the bottle down. "My apologies, Kelly-*san*. If I'd known, I would have brought some of my mother's green teas for you. She swears it helps with sensitive stomachs."

"Thank ya, that's very kind." Kelly smiled. She didn't correct his assumption that it was a sensitive stomach and not the damned Were nose she'd gained from the nanocytes.

Sato smiled. "Henry, when will you return to Japan? I've enjoyed the times we've spent together since we met. If you hadn't told me you were different, I'd never have known. Your willingness to share details about your enhancement has been an informative experience for me. That you live in harmony with the unenhanced is so different from our experiences here with the tigers."

"Sato, I can't tell ya anythin' about the tigers, but wolves don't usually do this either. Before Bethany Anne, it was a death sentence to let regular humans know about us. Now that I've experienced livin' and workin' together, I wouldn't dream of goin' back to the way it was." Henry smiled as he looked across the table at a fully healed Kelly. "As to when I can come back, I have no idea. I didn't exactly plan this trip."

"*Hai,* I'm not glad you were injured, but I am glad for the friendships that have come of it."

"Me too. If ya have the chance to come to Adelaide, I promise to do my best to be as gracious a host as you've been."

Kelly snorted. "If ya come, I'll be sure he washes his face and hands before I let him near any of yer folks."

"I don't doubt that you will, Kelly." Sato's face flushed red as he fought to keep from laughing at the indignant look on Henry's face.

"I'll have ya know, young lady, that I was dealin' with important people when yer grandfather was a gleam in his father's eye. I can take care of myself," Henry sputtered.

Kelly winked at Sato where Henry couldn't see, then turned to him and smiled innocently. "I know yer old, Henry. That's why I made the offer."

Sato held the cup to his mouth to hide his grin as Henry's eyes bugged out.

"Old? What is it with you kids wantin' to rub a man's age in his face? I don't feel a day over one hundred, dammit." Henry's tone was severe, but the glint of humor in his eyes gave him away.

Kelly kept the innocent smile frozen on her face but couldn't keep her building laughter from spilling out.

"Jeez, will you two get a room already?" Sato chuckled.

Henry and Kelly stared at their guest, the most powerful politician in Japan, with open-mouthed shock.

Sato shook his head and burst into guffaws. "You think nobody noticed? Trust me, everybody knows. You two are like a couple of awkward teenagers around each other. It's cute."

Henry ducked his head and smiled sheepishly while Kelly's face turned a deep shade of red. Sato laughed harder as he looked from one to the other, no longer able to speak as he gasped for air. Once he managed to regain control, he stood and offered Henry his hand.

"I have a meeting with the Transportation Minister in an hour. I've truly enjoyed our time together. I look forward to seeing you both soon." He gave Kelly a shallow bow before heading toward the door where Nikko stood, tapping his watch.

"I'll send ya the updated numbers on the wool available with the first shipment," Henry called as Sato made his exit.

Once the door closed, he turned to Kelly and smiled at her. "So everybody knows, huh?"

"Apparently so."

"So what we gonna do about it? You worried about what the folks at home will say about us?"

Kelly stood and stalked toward him, each step smooth and graceful, until she stood inches in front of him with a small smile on her lips. "Dunno, what have I ever done to make ya think I give two shites what anybody thinks about me and my business?"

Henry's answer came when he wrapped his arms around her and pulled her against his chest. Their lips mashed together, and everything around them faded into the background as they focused on each other.

Adelaide, Australia

The black cargo container landed in the area marked off next to the Oval. When the door opened, Henry looked out and saw what appeared to be the entire population of town standing outside the ropes. He grunted as Kelly ran into his back when he suddenly stopped.

"What the hell, Henry?"

He stepped to the side so she could see the welcoming committee.

Kelly's steps faltered as she started down the ramp, but once her feet hit the ground, she glared at the smiling faces. "What the fuck ya all doin' standin' around like a bunch of loons? I leave for a few weeks and come back to a bunch of slackers? Oh, hell, no!" she yelled as she stomped across the hard-packed dirt to the opening in the ropes.

"Well, I see her vacation didn't mellow her any," a voice muttered from the gathered crowd.

"Freddie Calloway, I heard that," Kelly growled.

"Oh, shite!" Freddie called in despair as the crowd burst into laughter.

Kelly's body rocked when Jennie Davies plowed into her and wrapped her in a tight embrace.

"I thought I'd lost you." Jennie sobbed into her hair.

Kelly wrapped her arms around her friend's back and stroked her long blonde hair with one hand. "Ya won't get rid of me that easy, Jennie-girl. There's no way I'd leave ya alone with this lot of ruffians."

Jennie pushed back and looked her over from head to foot. "Damn, ya look younger than me. What the hell they do to ya?"

"We'll talk later," Kelly promised. "Let me get this mob back to work and get settled."

Henry smiled at Jennie. "I told ya I'd take care of her, Jennie."

Jennie nodded. Then her eyes opened wide. "Henry?"

Henry's forehead creased in confusion. "Yeah, what's the matter?"

She pointed at his face. "Your hair and beard. What'd ya do to 'em?"

"What are ya goin' on about?" he asked.

Jennie shook her head in exasperation. "Henry, ya look younger."

Henry was confused for a moment until he remembered the changes. He'd had almost three months to get used to what his time in the Pod-doc had done to him. He no longer looked like he was in his sixties. The first time he'd looked in a mirror and saw his thirty-year-old face staring back had been a shock for him, too.

He nodded toward Kelly. "Like she said, later."

"Welcome back, you two," Horst boomed as he stepped out from the crowd.

Henry stuck out his hand, and Horst's huge mitt covered it as they shook.

"I'm glad you're back," Horst enthused. "This place practically runs itself, but there's so much going on all the time. I'm ready to give it all back to you. I'll never complain about my mayor's job on Kume again."

"I can never thank ya enough for keepin' an eye on things here for us. Ya already know it, but anythin' ya need, just ask," Henry offered.

"Glad I could help." Horst glanced over his shoulder and spotted Kelly surrounded by well-wishers. He lowered his voice and asked, "How's she adjusting?"

"Better than I expected." Henry smiled with pride. "It took her a few days to get her legs under her, but she's already shifted twice. We couldn't run much in the base compound, and I wasn't too keen on goin' out in the country with all the folks armed with silver ammunition."

"Can't blame you for that," Horst agreed. "With the Sacred Clan attacking and a few other incidents, people in Japan tend to shoot first and ask questions never."

Henry nodded. "That's what Yuko said. I've been lookin' forward to tryin' out my younger body. Soon as I can get away, I'm goin' walkabout in the bush."

"Have to wait till tomorrow." Horst laughed. "Jennie's planned a welcome home party, and Robbie's been cooking since dawn. The way this bunch likes to party, it'll be sometime tomorrow before they wind down."

"More like the day after if there's beer and that moonshine," Henry amended.

Horst grinned. "Oh, there's plenty of both. There was a shipment of apples on one of the ships, and the brothers made a batch of apple whisky. It's not too bad either."

Henry chuckled and shook his head. "Guess I'll have to put off the bush test for a day or so."

"I imagine so," Horst agreed. "If you want company, I'm sure Koda and the twins would enjoy spending time out before we leave next week."

"How are the kids?" Concern replaced the humor in Henry's voice.

"See for yourself." Horst pointed at where Koda was standing with Dieter and Tosha.

"Damn, they've grown!" Henry shook his head in wonder as he looked at two kids that appeared to be about four years old.

"They have, and they can both shift at will, too. It's been interesting times."

"No problems since we saw you last?" Henry asked.

Horst snorted. "Other than Dieter trying to take down a roo and getting his bell rung for it, no."

Henry grinned. "Ooh, that smarts. Those bastards can be mean."

"Yeah, but Koda went full momma wolf mode on it. She had it down with its neck broken before it could hit him a second time. She's a force to be reckoned with when she thinks the kids are in danger."

Henry's eyes widened. "I remember what she did to that vamp. I don't wanna be on the wrong side of that equation ever."

"Me either," Horst agreed.

Henry clapped his friend on the back. "I suppose we should get inside before Robbie drinks all the beer."

Horst nodded and motioned for Koda to join them. They walked into the Oval with Dieter regaling Henry with tales of what a proficient hunter he was.

The Blue Mountains near Wallerawang, Australia

Aaron stepped out through the bunker's main door and recoiled from the harsh chemical smell that assaulted his nose. "What the hell is that bloody stench, Kent?"

Kent stood over a pot boiling on a hot plate at a table. Aaron noted the heavy rubber smock, gloves, and face shield Kent wore, and the electric cord snaked back into the residence.

Kent held up one hand then cut the power to the glowing red burner. He stepped away from the table and pulled his gloves and shield off before he answered. "I ran out of detonators about twenty years ago. I'm mixing up a batch of triacetone triperoxide to make some new ones."

"Have you lost your fucking mind? You're mixing an unstable explosive compound under this much rock. Are you trying to kill both of us?" Aaron took a step back toward the door, looking like he couldn't decide whether to kill Kent himself or run like hell.

"Settle down, Aaron. I've been making this stuff for years, and you know it. It's only a small batch to make a few detonators for the Semtex I made yesterday."

Aaron drew a deep breath to calm himself before he responded. "Why, pray tell, do you feel the need to make explosives?"

"I told you those damn Weres need to suffer for what they did," Kent ground out. "We don't have enough troops to take them out yet, but I can make their lives uncomfortable as hell until we do."

"Kent, it's only a matter of time before we can strike. You have to be patient." Aaron waved at the cooling mixture. "This is dangerous and senseless. A few bombs won't do anything but put them on alert that we're coming for them. You won't kill enough of them to make a difference."

"I don't intend to kill any of them with the bombs," Kent snarled. "I'm going to cut their power off so hard they won't be able to rebuild the damn generators. Killing them would mean they couldn't suffer from the loss."

"Kent, it's not worth it," Aaron reasoned. "What if you get caught? They killed your brothers without batting an eye. There's no way you can do this on your own."

Kent shook his head and frowned. "Aaron, have you

forgotten why you chose me for this life? The reason you turned me?"

Aaron raised one eyebrow and cocked his head.

"You chose me because I was the best human assassin you'd ever seen," Kent reminded his creator. "I've had almost a century and a half to improve on what was already perfect. I'll be in and out before anyone knows I was there."

Aaron's lips compressed into a thin line as he considered Kent's answer. He could order him not to go, and Kent would have no choice but to obey. Still, it would cause hard feelings if he did. He'd never had to compel any of his children and was hesitant to start now.

"What about the new vampires? You can't stop making them. We don't have enough yet."

"Only four of the ten I attempted to turn survived the change," Kent argued. "Two went feral, and four died in the process. I have the four successful ones out collecting humans now. Their orders are to gather them all at the old school building in town. I'll start turning them when I get back. It will only take me a few days to do this, and those bastards in Adelaide need to suffer before we end them."

"I understand your need," Aaron soothed. "I want them to suffer too, but are you sure this is the best way?"

Kent's eyes gleamed with hate. "It's the most devastating blow I can give them until we kill them all. I have to do something."

The pain in Kent's voice made Aaron waver. Kent saw it on his face and bowed his head to hide the smile that formed on his lips. For the last hundred years, he'd managed to convince Aaron to go along with whatever he wanted. It only took hitting the right nerve.

"Okay, I see you're bound and determined to do this. Promise me you'll be careful and get back here fast as you can. Try not to blow your arse up with that devil's mix you're brewing. You know that shite's impact-sensitive, so don't bang it about."

"Only a few days, and I'll be back," Kent promised.

"Oh, I came here with news before I found you trying to kill us both. I received a message today."

"From that Yank?"

"Yes. The Bitch hasn't returned. She left someone here, and that's who was in the flying box. He's been causing trouble all over the world along with a militia group in the old United States."

"Did he say who it was?" Kent asked.

"Akio."

"What? Kamiko's Akio?" Kent spat. "The one who switched sides and became one of her inner circle guards?"

Aaron nodded. "The very same."

"Well, this could be interesting if he shows up. I saw him a few times over the years with Kamiko when we had business dealings. He's a bit on the small side and didn't strike me as too dangerous."

"That's not the case now. According to the Yank, he's killed everyone he's gone against so far. He's also shown up in the Americas helping that militia group." Aaron shook his head and grimaced. "The Yank says he has a plan to eliminate all of them. I say we let him. If Akio shows up, get out of there. No sense risking yourself. Let the Yank deal with him."

Kent shrugged. "For now. If the Yank fails or doesn't manage to kill him by the time we have our numbers up, we can deal with him then."

Aaron thought for a few seconds, then nodded. "I can agree to that, but if we go after him, we go together. I doubt he can take both of us if we do."

"Agreed. We'll cross that bridge when it comes. First, I have those mutts to deal with." Kent motioned to the explosive mixture. "I'm going to finish up now. If you're worried about me blowing myself up, you better get back inside."

Aaron pressed his lips together. "Just be careful and don't jar that shite. I don't want to have to move because you managed to blow yourself, and more importantly, the damn mountain up."

Kent laughed as Aaron hurried back inside and slammed the heavy steel door.

If that little traitor shows up, I'll pack his ass with enough explosives to blast him to wherever that bitch went.

CHAPTER EIGHT

Nagoya, Japan

Tian ducked into the kitchen, where Qin lay on the floor with his head under the sink. "Come on, Qin, Eve said to meet her at six, and we only have fifteen minutes to get there. You don't want to keep her waiting."

Qin gave the wrench he awkwardly held a half-turn to tighten the nut it kept slipping off. "Almost done," he grunted as the nut finally locked into place.

He slid out from under the cabinet and held up a mass of matted green cabbage leaves in his hand. "Tian, you can't shove stuff like this down the drain. That's what keeps blocking the water from draining."

Tian popped her head around the corner and wrinkled her nose at the wet mess Qin held. "Eve told me the sink was where I disposed of waste when I prepared your meals."

Qin chuckled at her wrinkled nose and confused expression. "It is, my love, but you have to turn on the machine that pulps it for that to work." He flipped a switch on the wall, and the light above the sink came on.

Tian giggled when he jerked his head up and stared daggers at the bulb.

Qin shook his head and flipped the other switch on the panel, and a mechanical *whirring* sound came from under the sink. "This one."

"Turn it off," Tian called as she covered her ears with both hands. "That dreadful noise makes my teeth ache."

"That *dreadful noise*, as you call it, is necessary to keep me out from under the sink and clearing the drains. It's either that or don't stuff food waste down there."

Tian smiled coquettishly as she slipped an arm around his waist. "You're so sexy when you do manly work around the house."

"We have to meet Eve now, but we'll continue this discussion when we return." Qin's voice was a low rumble that sent chills down Tian's spine.

She leaned forward for a kiss, and Qin's eyes shot open when she nipped his lower lip and darted away before he could react. "I'll hold you to that. Let's go. The sooner we do this, the sooner you can show me what a manly man you are."

Qin nodded and followed her to the door.

Imperial Theater, Nagoya, Japan

Tian watched the lithe young woman in awe as she climbed in mid-air using two bright red ribbons. She brought her feet up level with her hips and balanced, then gracefully raised her legs above her head. Deft movements wrapped one ankle, then the other in the sheer material. Displaying exceptional control, she smoothly continued to climb until all that showed was her head hanging under the curtain on the stage.

Tian lurched forward with a gasp when the woman's body spun down the twin pieces of silk toward the hardwood floor below. The performer appeared to be a hair's breadth from crashing into the stage when she froze midmotion, head down and mere centimeters from the boards.

The crowd applauded as the black-haired beauty effortlessly flipped her body and landed on both feet with a deep bow to the crowded theater. Tian's face was alight with an ear-to-ear grin as she added her applause to the din. Qin split his attention between the action on the stage and Tian's obvious delight at the show.

When the house lights came up after the final bows, Tian's eyes glittered with excitement as she turned to Eve. "Thank you so much for bringing us to this show. I never imagined people could move their bodies like that."

"Think nothing of it, Tian. These shows are more enjoyable when seen with others. What did you think, Qin? You've seemed lost in thought for the past hour."

Qin jumped when Eve startled him out of his reverie. "Oh, yes. It was…interesting," Qin answered.

"Interesting? It was amazing," Tian gushed.

Eve cocked her head, wondering what had the usually engaged Qin so out of sorts. She stored the information as a problem to look into later. "I'm glad you enjoyed the experience, but I must get back now. I have some experiments running that I need to check. Is there anything you need before I go?"

Qin waved off her offer. "Thank you for the wonderful evening. We have everything we need and couldn't ask you for more after all you've already done."

"It's my duty, given to me by my Queen. Please don't feel that you can't come to me with anything you need. No matter what. As long as you follow Bethany Anne's rules where the humans are concerned, I'm here for you."

Tian poked a finger into Qin's ribs and glared. "My apologies, Eve. That sounded ungrateful, but we're accustomed to providing for our needs. I'm still trying to figure out what our people need to do to be self-sufficient here."

Eve nodded. "I understand your desire to provide, but you've only been here for a short time. Once you learn the ins and outs of city life, I'm certain you'll figure something out. Until then, that's the reason our Queen left us behind."

"Thank you again. I promise if there's any need, I'll let you know," Qin agreed.

Qin's and Tian's Residence, Nagoya, Japan

"Qin, your actions bordered on rudeness to our host tonight." Tian turned to Qin as soon as the door to the apartment *snicked* shut. "We owe her and Akio everything! What got into you?"

"I know, my love. It's just that…" His words died in his throat when he saw the look she gave him.

Tian's hands dropped to her hips. "It's. Just. What?"

His hands flew up in a placating gesture as he composed his thoughts. "Did you see how many people were at the show tonight?"

"What's that got to do with anything?" She sighed in

exasperation. "There are people everywhere you turn here."

Qin shook his head and thought about how to explain once he realized he'd botched the first attempt. "No, Tian. I meant the number of people willing to pay to see the acrobatics."

"What of it? It was a good show," she snapped.

"Exactly," he agreed. "It was *good*, and there were over a hundred people there eager for more. Imagine how many would pay to see a *great* performance."

Tian's face scrunched in confusion at his words. "What are you getting at? What difference does it make?"

"Imagine if the performers were more than human. What do you think a show that incorporated things only a Were could manage in human form would be? Good or great?"

Tian's face was blank as she considered his words. "Qin, you can't show everyone that our people are enhanced. Japan hasn't forgotten the attacks."

"No, that's not what I meant," he assured her hurriedly. "I know we can't expose ourselves like that, but what if we put together a theater troupe made of the enhanced? We wouldn't have to reveal our true nature, only that we're better coordinated and more daring than what we saw tonight."

Tian's eyes widened with understanding. With their tiger reflexes, even in human form, their only restriction would be to keep their movements from becoming too unbelievable. A broad grin appeared after another realization. "That means we need to see every show that uses acrobats."

It was Qin's turn to look confused.

Tian continued without pausing, "We need to be sure that our show beats all the rest. The only way to do that is to see what the others offer."

Understanding came to Qin, and his grin mirrored hers. "You're right. Plus, we can see the commonalities between the shows. It's like the books I had as a child. They were all different but somehow the same in many ways."

"Do you think the others will be willing?" she asked.

Qin nodded with enthusiasm. "I'm sure of it. Delan and Yimu were complaining to me today about the warriors growing soft. The exercise will do them good, and the potential to be able to provide for ourselves will convince them to take part willingly."

"Everyone needs to see the existing shows to figure out what they do best. What else do we need to get started?" Tian pulled a pen and pad from a drawer.

"I think some of us should take jobs with existing shows to learn the basics," Qin suggested. "I'll discuss it with Mother and Delan in the morning. I'm sure they'll see things we've missed."

Tian launched herself across the distance between them and wrapped him tightly in her arms as she planted kisses all over his face. "That's a fantastic idea. We can learn what goes into creating shows and put one together that surpasses everything the others are doing."

Qin laughed as Tian continued to pelt him with kisses. "We'll have to be careful not to copy any other routines. We want ours to be original but enough like the others that people won't think them odd."

"Yan and Delan will help us sort it out," Tian reasoned.

"Delan is an expert tactician, and your mother is an experienced manager. Between their experience and your innovative mind, this is sure to be a success."

Qin adjusted his arms to support her and growled softly in her ear. "Tomorrow, my love. Tonight I have other plans."

Tian giggled when he started down the hall toward the room they shared. "As do I," she assured him as she pulled his head down to hers.

CHAPTER NINE

Adelaide, Australia

"Mornin', Henry."

"Mornin' yerself, Kel," Henry grinned with one eyebrow raised.

"Whaddaya makin' that face for? Are ya in pain?" Kelly snarked.

"Aw, why've ya gotta act like that? I was givin' ya me sexy look." Henry feigned offense but couldn't keep from cracking a smile when Kelly laughed heartily.

Once she'd regained control, she took a deep breath. "Good thing ya didn't depend on that look ta catch me eye, or you'd still be cuddlin' up ta yerself every night."

Henry's hands flew up and covered his heart. "Ya wound me, woman. Me poor shattered pride can't take it anymore."

Kelly chuckled as she walked across the office to where he was sitting and plopped down on his lap. She wrapped her arms around him and brought her face toward his. "Does yer fragile pride need kissin' better?"

Henry smiled as he leaned toward her, already suspicious of the tone in her voice. Sure enough, as their lips were about to meet, she pulled back and whispered, "Too bad."

Kelly pushed herself away from Henry but only made it a few inches before he wrapped his arms around her and rolled out of the chair, taking them both to the floor.

Kelly twisted and shoved, trying to escape, but Henry was stronger and wiser, so he had no problem rolling until he had her pinned beneath him.

"Henry Smythe, I can see it in yer eyes, and ya just better not!"

The smile on Henry's face transformed into a smirk as his fingers dug into her sides, and he tickled her. "Who's afraid of the big bad wolf now?" he whispered in her ear as she squealed and twisted futilely to escape.

"Let me go, ya daft old—" More shrieks cut off her words as Henry exploited the secrets her body had yielded to him the past two weeks.

"Old, is it? Well, we'll have ta see how this *old* man does at findin' all the right spots." Henry continued to tickle her ribs with one hand while he slipped the other down her side and hips to a spot just above her knee.

"Don't ya dare," Kelly gasped, her face splotchy from the torment he'd caused her sensitive ribs. "Hennnrryyyyy!"

"Looks like we caught ya two at a bad time." Lizzy grinned from the open door.

Robbie smirked over her shoulder. "Dunno, looks ta me like somebody might be warmin' up for a damn fine time."

Henry froze and looked up with a sheepish grin on his reddening face.

"Get ya hairy arse off me," Kelly growled as she brought her knees up and bounced her body, rolling Henry to the side.

Lizzy snickered. "I think ya might be right, Robbie. What say we leave these crazy kids to it?"

"People need ta learn ta knock," Kelly growled as she came to her feet and jerked her shirt down over her exposed torso.

Henry propped up on one elbow and raised one eyebrow. "Wotcha want?"

Robbie shrugged. "Ya told me ya wanted ta meet us this mornin'. Here we are."

"Oh, shite! I forgot." Henry scrambled to his feet and moved to his desk.

"I can understand that." Robbie ran the tip of his tongue over his top lip and gave Kelly a mock leer before he burst out laughing.

Lizzy caught the move and threw an elbow into his ribs that left him gasping for breath. "Keep yer observin' ta yerself, or you'll be sleepin' in the yard for the next month."

"Yes, Mistress." Robbie grinned and dodged, narrowly avoiding the elbow coming in for a second jab to his ribs.

"If yer all done?" Kelly gave Henry the side-eye, and he held up his hands palms out in surrender. "We did need ta see ya both about a favor."

"Wotcha need? We got yer back," Robbie assured them while Lizzy nodded her agreement.

Kelly tossed her head toward Henry, and he drew a deep breath. "Since we got back and Horst went home, it's been one thing after the other. Kelly needs ta spend some time with her wolf, and every time we've tried ta go bush, somethin' comes up."

Kelly nodded and grimaced from her perch on the edge of her desk as Henry continued.

"If she don't bleed off some steam and get a grip on her beast, I'm afraid the next person that walks in with whatever bloody thing they can solve themselves is gonna get bitten or worse."

Robbie raised an eyebrow but was smart enough to keep his mouth shut and not make the quip that popped into his head. He'd caught Kelly staring forlornly at the espresso maker more than once since she returned. Not being able to stomach the smell of the "liquid of life" didn't do anything to help her deal with the daily problems that came through the door. To say she was in a foul temper was the understatement of the century.

"Sure thing, Henry." Robbie draped an arm over Lizzy's shoulder. "We'll hold down the fort while ya both go out bush for a bit. How long ya gonna be gone?"

"Couple of days, three at the most." Henry shrugged and looked at Kelly for agreement.

"Maybe a few more than that, dependin' on how long it takes me ta get a grip on this whole furry lifestyle," Kelly amended.

"No problem. How far out ya plannin' to go?" Robbie asked.

"I'm thinkin' back ta O'Donnell Station. I haven't been home since the night they took us. We didn't bring all the livestock from the farms Decklan's arseholes destroyed, so there should be some wild herds around."

Robbie nodded, then a devilish look crossed his face.

"That's a fair distance, Henry. Ya sure yer *old* bones are up ta a run that far?"

Henry's eyes flashed yellow as Kelly burst into peals of laughter. "See, I'm not the only one who worries about ya."

"Both of ya can just kiss me *old* arse," Henry stated hotly. "I don't have ta come here for this abuse."

"Really?" Lizzy smirked. "Where do ya normally go for yer share of it?"

Henry threw his arms out and looked up at the ceiling. "Why me? I thought she was such a sweet child."

Henry's exasperated cry to the heavens brought on another round of laughter from the close group of friends, and he joined in a few beats behind them.

Once the group settled, Lizzy asked, "When ya plannin' ta leave?"

Henry pulled out two small bags from behind his desk. Their pack used them to carry clothes and small items when in Were form. "Now, if yer good with it."

Lizzy chuckled. "Have fun. We got this 'til ya get back. Hell, most of the folks comin' to ya already know what ta do. They just want ta get a closer look at the two of ya."

"Why's that? Hell, some of 'em've known me all my damn life." Kelly rolled her eyes in disbelief.

"Have ya not looked in a damn mirror? Ya look damn good, girl! Hell, even Henry looks good now." Robbie chortled.

Kelly narrowed her eyes, about to snap a reply, then thought about what he said. She'd noticed the changes to her body after turning but hadn't thought about them in a few months.

"Ya look like yer barely out of yer teens, Kelly," Lizzy

explained. "That's not what happens when ya turn into a Were. The pack members all want ta check yer scent. Vampires are the only beins in the UnknownWorld with that ability. They needed ta see that yer pack."

"Damn, I didn't think of that. No wonder so many of 'em came by. I thought some of their problems were pretty lame." Henry snorted a laugh. "I imagine that did tie their tails in a knot."

"It should stop now. Enough of 'em have dropped by, and word's out. I asked Horst the night ya came back, and he explained that the medical treatment did it. I tried tellin' the others, but ya know how they are." Robbie looked at Henry for confirmation.

"Yes, they have ta see it for themselves, and some of 'em won't believe their eyes. The nose always knows, though," Henry agreed.

"Wish ya woulda told me sooner," Kelly grumbled. "I coulda stood in the center of the fuckin' Oval and let 'em all line up for a sniff o' me arse. That woulda beat the shite outta all the dumbassed problems that walked through my door the past two weeks."

Robbie hid a grin behind his hand, and Lizzy glanced at the ceiling.

Kelly's eyes narrowed, and she exploded, "Ya fuckin' jerks. Ya didn't tell me on purpose. Ya thought it was funny that everybody and their damned brother was traipsin' through here. I could kick both of yer arses."

Robbie snickered. "Come on, Kelly. Ya gotta admit it's a little funny."

Kelly shook a fist at him. "Funny! I'll show ya funny, Robbie MacGuire. Come on, Henry, let's go. I might need two weeks to get in touch with my inner wolf. Ya shites have fun dealin' with all the stupidity that walks through here. We're goin' walkabout."

She snatched her pack out of Henry's hand and stalked out the door without a backward glance.

Robbie caught Henry's arm before he followed her. "Think she'll cool off anytime soon?"

"If it was me, I'd probably guard me boys for the next while. A year or two anyway. She'll pay ya back." Henry nodded and stepped around the open-mouthed Robbie.

"Arse!" Lizzy slapped Robbie's chest.

"Wotcha do that for?" he protested.

"I told ya we shoulda told her the first week. Now I have ta wonder when she's gonna pay us back."

"*Us!*" Robbie grimaced. "It's my package on the line here."

"What? Ya think I won't suffer too, havin' ta listen to ya whine when she finally does it?"

Robbie started to protest again, then stopped. Lizzy was right. If Kelly gave him one of her kicks to the jewels, he would gripe about it for weeks after the pain stopped.

CHAPTER TEN

TQB Base, Tokyo, Japan

"The area to the south is full of volcanic caves and lava funnels. The volcano is dormant, but the terrain is challenging in places."

Akio watched the monitor as live drone footage streamed across farmland and rows of growing crops on the small island off the coast of Korea.

"This area is more fertile and is where the Clan has settled," Abel continued as the feed switched to another drone.

"Where are the humans?" Akio asked. "I see the ruined cities, but I don't see any signs of anyone living there."

"After WWDE, a virus decimated ninety-seven percent of the population," Abel responded. "Most of the survivors fled to the mainland until only two hundred and twenty, mostly older people, remained."

Akio pursed his lips and nodded. "When did the Sacred Clan move in?"

"Sometime in the past eight months. The Chinese satellite I used to monitor this area malfunctioned seven months and twenty-one days ago. The only reason I discovered this is because I routed one of our units over it at Eve's request."

"Eve requested the coverage?"

"She's looking for potential business for the shipping company," Abel informed him. "I have the satellite I used on a continuously changing orbit, so it wasn't an issue to route it over Jeju. The changes from the last intel are what alerted me to a potential target."

Akio frowned. "Does Eve do that often?"

"She gave me a list of potential sites. When I have an opportunity to incorporate her request into another search, I do it. Otherwise, the site stays on the list until there's a need for surveillance in the area."

"I see."

Akio's relieved tone registered with Abel, and he added, "Eve forbade me to divert resources used to monitor the UnknownWorld for purely commercial intel. I'm only allowed to deviate within defined parameters to check any locations on her list."

Akio's eyes narrowed as the drone passed over another field. "Stop. Bring the drone back over that last area."

The drone made a lazy loop and slowed when it was running back over the route.

"Pan the camera to the right," Akio instructed. "There's a shaded area under that clump of pines that caught my attention."

The image tilted, and something white flashed under the trees. "I have it. I'm bringing another drone in from above to get another angle."

The screen split and dual feeds showed the area from ground level and above. When the lower drone approached the trees, the image showed three men, two on their knees, while the third stood over them.

Akio sat up straight in his chair when a face that piqued his memory appeared on the screen. Abel's facial recognition software popped up a window in the screen's right corner seconds later, and a photo from one of the Clan slave transfer stations Akio had destroyed almost a year ago filled the box.

"This is the same man who left that slave transfer station in Qitou the day before you took it out last year. Surveillance has also picked him up in two other destroyed slave farms." Abel popped up two additional photos across the top of the monitor.

The tiny drones held positions above and to the side of the group. The angle gave Akio an unobstructed view of what followed. Both kneeling men were jerked to their feet by the third and shoved toward the open field adjoining the trees. A hard push propelled one of the men a few faltering steps until he lost his balance and fell to his knees. The other began an uncoordinated jog across the rows in the field and left the fallen behind.

The Were crossed his arms and watched with a disdainful sneer as the fallen man struggled to his feet and followed the other. Neither human appeared to be in good health, and both had slowed to an uncoordinated trot before they were halfway across the open ground.

The Were shook his head in disgust, then shifted and stalked toward the two men. One looked over his shoulder, and the drone's camera clearly showed his terror-stricken expression.

The big cat toyed with the men, feigning an attack only to back off before he made contact. He herded both men across the field until they were staggering and stumbling from fear and exhaustion.

The tiger circled in front of the men and stopped. Before they realized the threat, the tiger morphed, and a monster Pricolici stood before them. It lashed out with its front paw and ripped the throat out of the closest in a spray of blood and tissue. The beast darted to the right and behind the other. His intended victim sped up in a feeble attempt to escape but fell flat on his face when his foot caught the root of a plant.

The man rose to his knees, and the Were was behind him in an instant. The drone dutifully recorded the last seconds of his life as the beast's claw-tipped hand shot out and struck the unfortunate victim in the back. The Pricolici laughed as he held the man's feet off the ground while his body convulsed and his lifeblood flowed from the holes in his back and chest.

The Were let the corpse slide to the ground and never looked back as he faded into the trees.

Memories of Peng Kun's clawed hand puncturing Kenjii's body played through Akio's mind as he watched the man die. Almost a minute passed in silence.

Akio's eyes glowed red in the dim lights of the command center, and his voice was low and filled with menace when he announced, "Abel, prepare the Black Eagle. Today we hunt."

. . .

Jeju Island, South Korea

Akio was silent as he stalked out of the command center and remained that way during the entire trip to Jeju. The events of the day Kenjii died played on a loop in his head. The way the Were had toyed with the two men before killing them brought the rage he'd fought so hard to contain to the forefront, and his only thought was to make the tiger and the entire Clan pay.

"Akio," Abel called softly over the Black Eagle's internal speakers.

He didn't open his eyes as he grunted, "*Hai?*"

"We've arrived. The drones have tracked the Were to a nearby town. He seems to be hunting more people."

Akio's eyes burned red when they shot open. "Take me there!"

"We're currently one kilometer above the town. Do you want to go in from the outskirts and walk in, or should I drop you directly in his path? Or I can put a silver missile up his hairy ass if you would rather." Abel's voice held an edge of menace that mirrored Akio's mood.

"Put me down in front of him," Akio told him. "I want him to feel what his victims did for the short time he has left in this world."

The Black Eagle nosed down and sped toward the town. Abel pulled out of the dive and left a cloud of dust in the slipstream as he deliberately missed the Were's head by centimeters when the craft blasted over him.

The Were in human form dropped to the ground and rolled in the dust to avoid the low-flying aircraft. Abel brought the Black Eagle to rest a meter off the ground, fifty meters in front of the weretiger now climbing to his feet. Akio was out of the cockpit with his sword bared while clouds of dust still billowed between the houses.

"Why did you kill those men, beast?" Akio's eyes burned red as he stalked toward the tiger.

"They're weak and useless. The Sacred Clan claims this island. There are no vermin allowed. That includes you, leech." The man's body morphed and what had to be the largest Pricolici Akio had ever seen stood in his place. He'd seen the video, but it didn't do the beast justice.

The Pricolici threw his arms out to his side and roared. The muscles on his chest and arms bulged when it rolled its shoulders, preparing to fight.

Akio's lip curled, and he beckoned the cat with his free hand. "Here, kitty, kitty," he taunted.

Instead of charging in rage as Akio expected, the Pricolici laughed then called., "Commmmee anndd get meee, littlllle leeeech."

Akio raised his sword in a mock salute, trotted toward the tiger, and disappeared. When he reappeared, blood dripped from a cut that stretched from the tiger's shoulder to its waist.

"If that's how you want it, I'll gladly comply." Akio smirked from a doorway across the street from him.

The Pricolici turned toward his voice, and Akio sped up to vamp speed again. A second bloody gash crossed the confused Pricolici's back from shoulder to buttocks.

During the past thirty years, Akio had endlessly drilled and honed his upgraded abilities. The years he spent training as a Forsaken had taught him to be a swift and ruthless killer. In the time he'd taken to learn what his new body could do, he'd become more. His nanocytes' ability to draw energy from the Etheric made him faster, stronger, and *the* deadliest apex predator currently on Earth. His time fighting the Sacred Clan had taught him the strengths and weaknesses of his opponents, no matter which form they chose.

The Pricolici stumbled a half-step and turned to see Akio casually leaning against the side of a burned-out hulk that was once a store.

"Why did you call this Sacred Clan land? You were in China until a few months ago. Shift back to human form and explain, and I promise your death will be swift. Fail to obey me, and I can do this all day." Akio flicked his wrist and sent a spatter of blood into the dust between them.

The Pricolici's muscles rippled, and the beast leapt across the space that separated them. Ash and burned wood chips exploded in a gray cloud when the monster cat crashed into the wall. He roared in rage and pain when Akio whistled from the center of the street and dropped the piece of striped tail he held.

Blinded by dust and fury, the beast turned and rushed headfirst toward his tormentor. Akio spun to the side, and his blade flashed in the sunlight. The tiger's headlong rush turned into a face-down slide when his left Achilles tendon parted under the hammer-forged steel.

Akio crossed the distance and drove his katana through the wounded Pricolici's shoulder, pinning him to the ground. He planted one armored foot on the exposed neck and ordered, "Shift now, or I'll carve you into small pieces. Decide!"

With a groan of pain, the tiger shifted to human form.

CHARLES TILLMAN & MICHAEL ANDERLE

Akio left his sword and boot in place when he asked, "Why did you murder those humans?"

"Because of you," the Were spat.

Akio twisted the sword a quarter turn, eliciting a scream of pain. "Try again."

"We determined that you locate us because of the humans. We've hunted them since we arrived to remove your reason to come here."

Akio's lips were a flat line as he digested this information. "You think the humans bring me? Did you not think the way the Sacred Clan preys on and uses them might be the reason?"

"None of us know why you do it," the Were ground out from between clenched teeth. "What does a vampire care about the vermin? Everyone knows vamps only care about their power and influence."

Akio shook his head and frowned. "How many Clan members are here?"

"Figure it out for yourself. I know I'm dead and won't tell you anything else."

Akio turned his sword hand a fraction. "Where are they located?"

"Screw you, leech."

Akio took what he needed from the Were's mind. The Were shrieked in pain when Akio pulled the sword from his shoulder with a twist. Blood poured from the wound for a few beats until the nanocytes stemmed the flow.

Akio took his boot from the Were's neck and stepped back. "If you run, you might make it in time to warn the forty-eight other Clan members in Seogwipo that I'm coming for them."

The Were's head twisted, and he gauged the distance Akio had moved. Then, he shifted and darted between two houses as fast as his four legs could carry him. Akio watched until the cat cleared the village and ran across an open field.

"Abel." Akio nodded in the direction the Were had fled.

The Black Eagle shot above the rooftops, spun until it pointed toward the running tiger, and fired once. The hypervelocity blaster round impacted between the tiger's shoulders. When the dust cleared, what was left lay in several pieces around the crater the blast dug.

"Or you might not," Akio murmured in satisfaction.

Black Eagle, above Jeju, Korea

"Abel, please scan the island for life signs."

"Completing scans now. There are forty-two in and near Seogwipo and six others scattered around the island. That accounts for all the Clan members."

Akio pursed his lips as the information came in. The two humans the Were had killed were the last on the island. Akio shook his head at the wasted lives, then his features hardened.

"Take us to the closest of the individual locations," he instructed. "If they're in Were form, kill them. I will deal with any who remain in human form. We'll save the main body for last."

"Acknowledged. ETA is forty-three seconds."

The craft covered the distance, and the HUD came to life. "Target acquired," Abel announced as the image of a lone tiger prowled a deserted city five kilometers below them.

"Take him," Akio commanded.

The craft nosed down and dropped at high speed until Abel expertly leveled out three meters above a rubble-filled street. One hundred and fifty meters in front of the Black Eagle, the tiger didn't hear the sound of the blaster fire that took off its head.

"Target eliminated. Next target in range in thirty-one seconds."

The Black Eagle hopped around the island over the next five minutes until the remaining isolated Weres were dead. Only one was in human form, and he shifted as soon as the Black Eagle came into sight. The other four died before they knew their status had changed from predator to prey.

"How do you want to deal with the others?" Abel inquired as the craft held station above Seogwipo. The HUD displayed a wire diagram of the town below, with each life sign marked in red.

Akio thought for a moment, then his lips twisted into a grimace. "Violently."

"Acknowledged." Two missile launchers separated from the Black Eagle's hull.

"What's our ordnance loadout?" Akio inquired as he touched the HUD screen marking targets.

"In addition to the twin blasters, I have sixty-four missiles. Forty-five silver-infused fragmentation, fifteen silver gas, and four of Eve's special explosives with a frangible silver coating. There are also three two-pound and four one-pound pucks onboard."

"Hold the pucks in reserve," Akio told him. "Hit targets one and two with Eve's specials. The fragmentation rounds should be sufficient for targets three through seven."

Akio studied the screen another moment, then touched where six roads converged on a traffic circle with a cluster of trees in the center. He tapped the screen, and the image zoomed in on a three-story flat-roofed building on the northwest side.

"Put me down behind the trees opposite this structure. Hit it first with a volley of gas missiles positioned to drive the two inside toward me. I wish to question one of them. After that, you're clear to engage the others as you deem appropriate."

The Black Eagle swung out ten miles off the coast and dropped to a meter above the deep blue waters of the East China Sea. Abel kept the craft low as it crossed the harbor and followed a six-lane road to the indicated area.

As soon as the canopy opened, Akio leapt out and darted into the trees.

Pick me up here once you complete your attack.

Acknowledged. Happy hunting. The craft turned its nose up and flashed over the trees.

Missiles away, Abel called as four explosions signaled the start of his missile run.

Akio watched patiently from the dim light beneath the trees as a cloud of silver-infused smoke billowed from a broken window on the third floor. The tolling of bells interspersed with multiple explosions to the west echoed through the deserted streets as Abel rained death on the remaining Weres.

Almost two minutes after the first missile exploded, a

ground floor window shattered and a body hurtled through it to land on the broken pavement. Akio cocked his head and listened for the second Were he'd detected on the scan. Then, hearing nothing but groans of pain from the one in the street, he stepped out of the shadows.

Seeping, raw burns covered the Were's exposed skin, and he stared fearfully at Akio through blistered eyes as he approached.

"Where are the humans who lived here?" Akio demanded and entered the dying man's mind before he could answer.

Akio saw that his suspicions were correct, and the Clan had hunted and killed over two hundred residents since they arrived three months earlier. The images of what this man and others had done to the humans incensed him.

He pulled out of the Were's mind and he watched dispassionately as the beast's nanocytes fought to repair the damage. He smiled as the silver contamination nullified them faster than they could heal the burning flesh.

"Die alone," Akio growled as he turned and walked away, content with leaving the Were to spend his remaining time in agony for the crimes he'd committed against humanity.

Akio, Abel called as he brought the Black Eagle down and hovered a few meters from the thrashing Were.

Hai?

Are you well?

Akio's steps faltered to a halt, and his chin dropped to his chest. His shoulders slumped, and he looked at the Black Eagle with dull eyes.

"No, I'm not well. I'm sick of the senseless evil the

Sacred Clan continues to perpetrate on others. I hunt and kill them, and there are always more. No matter how hard I try, the innocent still die."

Akio's eyes blazed red as bloody tears rolled down his face.

"When Kenjii died, I became the monster that the monsters feared. All I accomplished was to isolate myself and hurt those close who care for me the most. I put the beast to sleep, but I crave the unfeeling numbness being that creature brought when I see cruelty and atrocities like those committed here."

"Akio, you suffered a devastating loss," Abel reasoned. "The Sacred Clan didn't allow you time to grieve because they're the real monsters in this story. You are a man, a good man, who cares for the people in this world. You saved Horst. You made it possible for Qin Shek and his people to leave the sphere of the Clan's control and live in harmony with their human families.

"You've saved the lives of countless humans and ensured that they have a future—all while dealing with the loss of someone you loved deeply. You're not a monster, only human."

Akio stood for several minutes with his head down, shoulders slumped, and his arms loose by his sides. Finally, he drew a deep breath, squared his shoulders, and looked up. His face was its usual emotionless mask.

He spun on his heel, and seconds later, the dying Were's head rolled across the rough pavement.

"Thank you, Abel. Let's go home."

. . .

Eve's Quarters, TQB Base, Tokyo, Japan

A custom subroutine that monitored for any instances when Akio's vital signs deviated from normal alerted Eve that something was wrong. Abel's live feed replaced the inane movie about sparkling vampires she watched, and Akio's voice came through the speakers.

Concern that Akio was sliding back into the angry killing machine from before made her consider alerting Yuko. Then pride filled her being as she heard Abel's reply.

She watched for a few more moments until the crisis had passed and cut the feed. Abel still had some quirks about the Sacred Clan and base defense, but the way he'd talked Akio back from the abyss told her that his ascent was complete.

That level of compassion and insight wasn't something programmable. Abel's response to Akio's moment of crisis was the act of a friend, not a computer, no matter how advanced.

She smiled as the screen switched back to the movie where the vampires were jumping through treetops while massive computer-generated wolves pursued them on the ground.

CHAPTER ELEVEN

O'Donnell Station, Australia

Kelly padded into the dusty yard in front of the burned-out husk that had been her home from the day she was born until the fateful night Decklan's Weres attacked. Greenery poked through the ash and burned timbers as the Australian flora fought to reclaim the land.

A black wolf with a gray muzzle stood to one side as Kelly took in the scents with her nose in the air. They'd tracked a small herd of wild sheep to an area thirty kilometers to the south the day before, and Kelly was glad to see her old home. She hadn't thought about the place for the past year while she worked to build the Adelaide community, but now she had to see it since they were so close.

Henry tried to talk her out of it when she'd first brought up the idea, explaining that there was nothing for her there, but she'd insisted, persuading him with the possibility of reclaiming the cattle that had escaped when the ranch was abandoned. If he'd learned anything the past year, it was that when Kelly set her mind on a course of action, nobody could change it.

The light-gray wolf sat on her haunches and let out a long, mournful howl for the people lost in the attack and the emptiness in her heart as she surveyed the wreckage. Henry moved to stand beside her when she shifted, and a beautiful young woman with long dark hair down her back and skin so perfect it glowed in the sunlight stood where the wolf was before.

Henry shifted and laid an arm across her shoulders. "This is yer past. The future is whatever ya want ta make it. Ya have a purpose in Adelaide now," he consoled her.

She didn't respond for almost a minute, then she drew a deep breath and squared her shoulders. "I know that, but it still hurts ta see the place like this. My ancestors are buried in this ground that they sweated and bled over for the last hundred years. Ta think a group of mangy thugs ripped it all away in one night is hard ta comprehend."

Henry pulled her thin body close to his and laid a gentle kiss on top of her head. "I know it does, Kel. Be happy in the knowledge that the ones responsible died for it, and now ya have a city full of people countin' on ya ta bring 'em through this post-apocalyptic hell we're livin' in."

Kelly sighed. "Things were so much simpler when all I had to worry about was a few folks and a fuck-ton of sheep. Now I don't have a single sheep, but I got a buttload of people ta take care of. What if I can't do it? How the hell d'they trust me ta lead 'em? I couldn't protect the few people on this stinkin' farm. What if I'm not good enough?"

Henry grimaced at the strain in her voice. He drew a

deep breath and leaned his head against hers. "Because they know ya will fight for all of 'em. They know ya don't know how to quit, and as long as ya have breath in yer body, ye'll do whatever it takes ta see that yer people are safe."

"How do they know? I did a right shitey job of it here," Kelly snapped as her body tensed and her eyes glowed yellow.

"Good God, woman." Henry snorted. "Maybe 'coz the first time most of 'em noticed ya was the day ya kicked a Were's balls up inta his throat. Or maybe it was when ya were bleedin' out on the ground and shot the vamp that did it ta ya. Ya don't know *how* ta quit. Hell, when ya finally die, I imagine you'll tell the saint at the gate ta send ya the fuck back 'cause ya got shite ta do."

"I'm not that fuckin' bad, dammit. Ya lot. Always bustin' on me for doin' what needed doin' in the first place. I swear I dunno why the hell I put up with any of ya." She tried to pull away from him, but he tightened his grip and held her in place. "Lemme go, ya old fool."

"Never," Henry murmured as he turned her to face him and wrapped both arms around her.

She buried her head against his chest, and he held her while silent tears rolled down her face.

They stood there for several minutes until Kelly pushed back, wiped her face, and scowled at him. "Now look what ya made me do. Ya got me all gushy like some damned schoolie."

"We all need a moment ta let go. If ya don't, it'll just keep eatin' at ya 'til ya have ta huddle in a corner or blow up. Since ya ain't the hide in a corner type, ya should let it vent before ya blow. We already know how that goes."

Kelly punched him in the chest and growled. "Keep on, and I'll show ya blow, old man."

Henry glared down at her for a moment, then nodded once. "Old, is it? I warned ya, can't say I didn't."

"Waddaya blatherin' about?" Kelly squawked when Henry grabbed her and tossed her over his shoulder.

"What the hell's wrong with ya? Put me down, ya old— Oowwww!"

The flat of Henry's hand came down on her bare butt cheek, and the sound echoed through the ruins.

"Dammit, what the fuck! Yeoowwwww!"

A second smack came down on the other side.

"I told ya to stop with the old man cracks, young lady. If ya don't respect yer elders, I suppose I need ta convince ya."

"Henry Smythe, ya put me down right, ouch!"

"I got all day. It's your bum." Henry snickered as he patted her stinging cheeks to emphasize his point.

Kelly's face was purple with rage until he patted her. Her lips twitched as she fought to maintain the scowl lost on Henry with her head hanging down his back. She eyed his pale buttocks inches below her face and considered biting him until the ridiculousness of the situation sank in.

Here she was, a grown-ass woman without a stitch of clothing on, slung over the toned and muscled shoulder of an equally naked man, standing in front of the burned-out hulk of her family home. What would people think?

Amusement filled her flushed face as she fought to keep

from grinning at the silliness of it all. Her body trembled, then shook as she bit her lip to keep from laughing. She eyed Henry's tight tush again and brought her hand to the crease where his butt met his leg.

Henry yelled and jumped when her fingers dug into the sensitive skin and started to tickle him viciously. She wrapped her free arm around his waist and dug deeper when Henry tried to pull her off.

Henry twisted and turned in a futile attempt to unseat her. She laughed with malicious glee the more he gyrated to escape the sensations.

Henry finally grabbed a leg in each hand and pushed them over his shoulder. The combination of force and her upper body weight caused Kelly to slip.

She had to let go of him or risk face-planting in the dirt. She put her hands on the ground and flipped in a half handspring to land on her feet. She spun to face the red-faced man who stood gasping in front of her.

"That's cheatin'. Ya know I can't take that," Henry fake-grumbled. She saw the laughter in his eyes.

"A girl's gotta defend herself however she can." She smiled at him with a mischievous glint in her eyes. *"Old man!"*

Before Henry could respond, Kelly shifted. She tossed her head and gave him a toothy grin as she tore out of the compound and disappeared into the bush.

"I'll show ya old," Henry yelled.

Seconds later, a black wolf bounded into the bush in pursuit.

. . .

Adelaide, Australia

Kent pulled the straps to settle the heavy pack he carried and stepped out of the small boat he'd found up the coast the night before. It had taken three months for him to get back to the town and those bloody damned mongrels who killed his brothers.

Tonight would be the first, but assuredly not the last time he made them pay for their insolence.

He made his way cautiously through the town's deserted streets, often pausing to listen for the roving patrols until he reached the rusted and dilapidated fence surrounding the power plant. Kent followed the barrier to an opening he'd spotted when he reconned the area two nights before and silently slipped inside.

Sticking to the shadows, he made his way to the door he'd watched the plant workers use and tried the handle. He smiled when he found the door unlocked and pulled it open wide enough to slip himself and the pack inside.

The noise from the steam turbine covered any sound he made as he climbed a set of metal steps to the control room that overlooked the machinery on the plant floor. Kent slipped the straps off his shoulders and lowered the pack to the metal grating outside the control room door.

"You're early," the lone man sitting with his back to the door called without turning.

Kent took three quick steps to close the distance, wrapped his hands around the unsuspecting plant operator's head, and twisted violently.

The man's head flopped bonelessly to the side when Kent released him. Kent left him where he'd died, continuing to monitor the plant through dull, lifeless eyes.

He retrieved his pack and closed the door, then swiped his arm across a small table against one wall, sweeping the coffee pot and assorted containers of snacks to the floor.

He gently placed the bag on the tabletop and removed the twenty improvised explosives he'd assembled for tonight's mission. He pulled out canvas-wrapped blocks and stacked them neatly on the table. Next, he pulled twenty windup alarm clocks he'd scavenged from a discount store years earlier to use in his bomb-making. He used a nail to make a hole in each bundle and carefully pushed the detonator into it.

Once he'd finished, Kent connected the detonator wires to the timers and set each to thirty minutes until they exploded. He wiped his hands on a cloth and picked up two of the two-kilo Semtex bombs. Over the next ten minutes, he placed all twenty of them at strategic points through the plant.

Nineteen minutes after placing the last bomb, Kent stopped rowing the boat a half-kilometer from shore and waited. Thirty-two seconds later, the first blast shook the still night, followed by two others shortly after.

Kent frowned and looked at his watch. *Three premature detonations out of twenty. I must be losing my touch.* Before he finished that thought, a massive ball of fire rose above the doomed building.

"Welcome to the eighteenth century, you fucking assholes." Kent chuckled when he saw the lights in the town die as the explosion echoed through the night.

Kent put his back to the oars and watched with a smile as the dark town grew smaller until he rounded a turn in the coast. He continued to watch the glow from the fires for another six kilometers until he beached the boat and started running toward home.

CHAPTER TWELVE

Kume Island, Okinawa, Japan

"Dieter! Come back here and put your clothes on right this minute," Koda shouted.

The rambunctious toddler looked over his shoulder and laughed as he ran out the door.

Horst chuckled as he fastened the last snap on Tosha's romper, earning himself a growl from Koda as she stalked out after Dieter.

"Laugh it up, furface. You know they plan these escapades. Tosha's only biding her time."

"You wouldn't do that to Daddy, would you, princess?" Horst smiled as he lowered his bushy blond beard and tickled Tosha's nose.

Fast, grabby hands wrapped in the curls and twisted, eliciting a yelp of pain from Horst as Koda came through the door with a squirming, laughing Dieter.

"Serves you right," Koda grumped while collecting the clothes Dieter had scattered in a trail from the bedroom to the door. "We're going to be late to the party if *your* son has anything to do with it."

Horst snorted. "Looks like *my* daughter is ready to go. I can't help it if the little man decided to embrace his inner Were and shed the clothes. If I recall, you chose which one you wanted to get ready."

Koda sat Dieter on the sofa and started the process of dressing him for the second time. "I swear he gets faster by the day. He almost made it to the beach before I caught him."

Dieter smiled and cooed at her as she pulled on a sock and followed it with one of the sneakers Eve had brought on her last visit. "Yes, Momma knows you're a little cutie, but you have to keep these on at least until we eat," she told him, then pulled up his shirt and blew a raspberry on the toddler's stomach, causing him to burst into gales of hysterical laughter.

Horst shouldered a bag of toys and spare clothes for Dieter while Koda slipped an identical bag for Tosha over her shoulder and hoisted Dieter on her hip.

"I blame you, by the way," Koda called over her shoulder when she was at the door.

"Me? What did I do?" Horst asked.

"You allowed them to run wild in Adelaide, and now that we're back home around regular humans, they're still acting like they're with the pack."

"*I* allowed it?" Horst grinned at her back as he followed her out the door. "If I recall, you were there too."

"I was, but I was busy learning to be a Were. The children were your responsibility." Koda shrugged nonchalantly, keeping her back to Horst so he couldn't see the smile on her face.

"It seems you weren't the only one learning that," Horst mumbled when Tosha giggled as her fingernails shifted from human to wickedly sharp claws and back.

Dieter looked over Koda's shoulder and squinched his face up until a short snout, coarse black hair, and pointed ears adorned his head.

"Tosha, Dieter, enough!" Horst commanded.

Both children's eyes widened, and they shifted to human form immediately.

"I sorry, Daddy," Tosha murmured and tucked her face into his neck.

Horst patted her back with his free hand. "I know, Tosha, but we talked about this. What's the rule?"

"No be wolfie 'til Mommy or Daddy say okay."

"That's right, princess. Why don't we do that, Dieter?"

"Scares peoples," Dieter answered.

Horst smiled. "That's right, little man, and we don't scare our friends, do we?"

"Nope."

"Is this going to be a problem? The party tonight is only for family and close friends. That won't always be the case. People here know you're different, but they don't know everything. Not to mention the tourists and workers coming from the mainland." Concern lay heavy in Koda's tone.

"What's wrong, Koda? What are you so worried about?" Horst laid his hand on her shoulder and noted the stiffness in her body.

She shook her head. "It's probably silly."

"Anything that worries you isn't silly. What is it?"

"Something I overheard one of the older Weres talking about in Adelaide. He said that some humans know about Weres and believe they can become enhanced by taking their blood. He called them blood leeches and said they kidnap young Weres for their blood."

"I heard those rumors, too. From what I can tell, it's only rumors," Horst assured her.

"You don't think it's true?" she asked.

"I don't know," Horst admitted, "but that's the first I've heard of it."

"So you don't think the children are in danger?"

"Not here," Horst assured her. "They're always around family and other people who care about them."

"Hopefully, they'll understand the need to keep their nature secret from most people. I'm scared if it's true that someone might try to take them." Koda frowned, and her eyes flashed yellow. "That would prove to be a fatal mistake."

Horst's steps faltered when Koda's words came out as a throaty growl. Tosha's and Dieter's heads snapped up, alert for any threats.

"I believe any who tried something like that would quickly find they'd bitten off more than they could chew. Our babes already proved they're not helpless," Horst assured Koda.

"Still, I'd rather not tempt fate."

"No, but we can't let worry cloud our actions. All we can do is teach them and have faith that they heed us."

"Like the young Weres in Adelaide?"

"God, I hope not." Horst rolled his eyes when he

thought of some of the antics the adolescent Weres in Adelaide had pulled while they were there. Kelly and Henry had a full plate running the city without bored, rambunctious enhanced children adding to the load.

"Maybe we could talk Jenny into moving here." Koda snickered. "After seeing her drag those two Owens kids to their mother by their ears, I don't doubt she could keep our little hellions in check."

Horst guffawed. "That was a sight to see! A tiny blonde pulling two wolves across the Oval, yipping and howling all the way."

"I wonder if they're still on trash duty? Ma Owens was not amused." Koda's smile faltered as she stopped at the door to the Sunset House. Her enhanced hearing picked up the chatter of voices inside, and she drew a deep breath to calm her worry.

"Dieter, Tosha, remember. No shifting," Koda reminded the twins.

"Yes, Mommy," they answered.

Koda pushed through the door and hesitated when all eyes in the room turned to her.

Horst nudged her with his arm, and she took a few halting steps inside. "They've missed you. These are our friends and family. Everything's okay," he murmured, knowing she would hear him.

Koda nodded and smiled as Yagi and Ono came forward to greet them. The two had been home for a few weeks, but this was the first chance everyone was free to celebrate and welcome them home.

Koda tried to bow, but the bag and Dieter had her off-balance. Ono laughed and took the bag while Suzu relieved her of the toddler.

"Domo, Ono-*san. Domo,* Suzu-*san."* Koda bowed.

"Koda-*chan*," each responded with a smile.

"Horst-*san*." Komori Yuichi waved from a seat at a table with several men in Sea Wolf Lines uniforms.

Horst made his way to the group. "Komori, when did you arrive?"

"A few hours ago. Have you met Captain Alexi Brescoff yet?" Yuichi indicated a bear of a man with a black beard that rivaled Horst's.

"Not in person, but we've spoken over the comm. Eve told me you accepted the position while I was away. Is the *Silver Moon* here too?" Horst offered his hand as he spoke.

"Da. We came in about half an hour ago. Our sea trials were successful except for a minor problem with the power transfer device. Eve flew out on a Pod and met us when we arrived in port. Problem solved, and ship is now in service," Brescoff explained as he stood and accepted Horst's handshake.

"Excellent. Is Eve here?" Horst looked around the dining room.

"Da, in the kitchen. She said she had something for the chef."

"Did you think I would miss an opportunity to have some Aunty Eve time with my nephew and niece?" Eve called as she pushed through the kitchen's double doors with a multi-tier cake balanced on one hand.

"To celebrate the addition of the *Silver Moon* to the fleet, I asked the chef to bake us a cake." Eve grinned as she presented the confection with a topper that resembled the ship.

"Cake, yum!" Dieter exclaimed when he saw it.

Horst laughed. "You have to eat your supper first, little man."

Dieter glanced at his father. Then a calculating look crossed his face. "Aunty Eve, cake?" he asked innocently.

"Of course you can have some cake, my darling." Eve smiled at the boy

Horst frowned down at the little AI. "After you finish your supper."

Eve returned Horst's frown. "What he said." Followed, to Dieter's delight, by a conspiratorial wink when Horst turned his head.

"I see you're performing your duties as an aunt by spoiling my children at your usual level." Koda laughed as she caught the exchange.

Eve grinned as Koda took Dieter and the toy bag from Horst. "The little darlings expect no less."

Koda handed Dieter to Eve and admonished, "Be sure he eats something more substantial than cake. If you wire him up on sugar, you get to babysit until he goes to sleep."

The restaurant door opened, and Yuko stepped in, followed by Akio, Asai, and Seki.

Koda ran over and caught Asai in a hug. "I didn't know you were coming. I've missed you all so much," Koda gushed as she released Asai and ran to Yuko.

"We heard there was a party and didn't want to miss it." Asai laughed as Koda rushed toward Akio and stopped short of hugging the stoic warrior with a questioning look.

Akio looked down at the eager young woman for a beat,

then one side of his mouth quirked in a half-smile. He opened his arms, and Koda rushed in and embraced him.

Akio released her, took a step back, and cocked his head. "Calm yourself, young one. Your mind is practically shouting your fears for your children. There is no danger to them tonight."

Koda's eyes widened in surprise. She knew from Horst that Akio could perform a sort of mind-reading but had never seen it. "I'm sorry. I know that in my head, but I fear for them here." She pointed at her heart.

"It's only natural for a mother to worry about her children. Don't let fear overwhelm you. You're more than capable of protecting them from any who would think to harm them. I also promise that any who dare threaten them and survive you and Horst will not enjoy meeting their extended family." He nodded at Yuko and Eve, then touched his chest.

Koda smiled up at him as the knot of fear in her stomach unraveled. "*Domo,* Akio. I appreciate that you feel a kinship with my family. I know you will do everything in your power to help keep them safe."

Akio inclined his head, a gleam of emotion in his eyes. "*Hai,* there's nothing I won't do to protect the people I consider mine."

CHAPTER THIRTEEN

Adelaide, Australia

"What the fuck!" Robbie yelled as he fought to extract himself from the blanket wrapped around his legs.

"Explosion?" Lizzy grunted as Robbie's flailing arm caught her across the chest. "Watch where ya hit a girl, idjit."

"I would, but I can't see anythin'. What's up with the lights?"

Lizzy slipped off the side of the bed and pulled the blackout curtain over the window back. Dim moonlight filtered into their bedroom, nowhere near as bright as the halogen street lights that caused the pair to use the heavy window treatments to begin with.

"Power's out all over town," Lizzy advised as Robbie won his battle with the attacking bed cover, stood, and stepped to her side.

"Need ta get ta the plant and see what's goin' on," he declared as he cast about on the floor where he'd dropped his clothes the night before.

"Look in the chair. I tripped over yer mess comin' ta bed, again," Lizzy scolded without looking back.

"Ya comin'?"

"Yeah, somebody's gotta keep ya outta trouble. Give me a sec." Lizzy opened the drawer on her nightstand and pulled on a loose cutoff t-shirt and shorts. By the time Robbie had finished dressing, she was waiting at the door with a pair of sandals in her hand.

"Don't ya go clompin' through my clean house with those dirty shoes," she admonished. "If ya do, I'll kick yer butt and make ya scrub it up with yer damn toothbrush."

"I was tired," Robbie offered weakly as he turned sideways to pass through the door.

"Always." Lizzy huffed as she followed him out of the house.

The street was alive with people coming out to see what happened. A cursory inspection showed that the power grid was down throughout the town. A half-moon hanging low in the sky provided enough light for the enhanced to see, but that didn't help the unenhanced.

"I'm headin' ta the power station," Robbie called when people noticed the lights were out. "Hopefully, it's a fuse or somethin' simple. You lot stay inside. I don't need injured folks muckin' up whatever the hell is already wrong."

"Who the hell died and left you in charge?" a man called from the darkness.

"Don't have time for yer lip, Angus. Make sure nobody hurts—Missus Logan, where are yer shoes and glasses? Angus, get over there and help her back to her house." Robbie waved at the stooped, white-haired woman wearing a threadbare nightgown with the words "Hot Stuff" in red on the front.

"Robbie." Lizzy caught his arm and pointed west. An orange glow reflected off the night sky from the direction of the power station.

"Oh, bloody hell!" Robbie growled a second before he shifted and a rust-colored wolf with a black stripe down his back tore off in the direction of the fire.

Lizzy shifted at the same time, and her black and tan form was hot on his heels.

Less than a minute later, they froze when they reached the power plant and saw the fire firsthand. Multicolored flames shot into the sky from multiple gaping holes in the roof and sides of what remained of the power station. The fire's heat was so intense Lizzy felt it from over a block away.

Robbie shifted back to human form and stared with his mouth agape as a section of the roof of the plant they'd all worked so hard to repair collapsed.

"Kelly's gonna be *pissed*," Robbie murmured as another section of the wall fell into the raging inferno.

Port Gawler, Australia

"God, I miss coffee," Kelly griped as she rubbed the sleep from her eyes. "Nothing beats a good cuppa joe first thing in the mornin'."

"I have a spot of tea in me pack," Henry offered.

She shook her head. "Ain't the same. That's one of the biggest damn problems with this werewolf shit. I miss me fuckin' coffee, dammit."

Henry raised his arms over his head and stretched the kinks out of his back, deciding that silence was the safest response. After several attempts to drink her favorite beverage, Kelly had given up in frustration. Her sensitive nose couldn't handle the smell.

She'd tried cutting back on the grounds, but the final brew her nose could stand was colored water at best. Henry remembered that day well and not only because of the pottery mug that missed him by inches when she flung it against the wall in a fit of rage.

Kelly's first few days as a Were had let Henry know in no uncertain terms that she was the Alpha bitch, and don't you fuckin' forget it.

Henry sorted through his pack and pulled out a shirt that blood, mud, or some unidentifiable substance didn't cover. Their week-long walkabout had taken them on an arc from Adelaide west to the mountains, then north and back east to O'Donnell Station. The return had brought them on a southerly track that ended outside Port Gawler the day before.

Kelly's abilities to use her Were form had increased to the point that she could run all day, stalk prey, and avoid dangers by her sense of smell and enhanced hearing. The brief encounter they'd had with four bandits had shown Henry that she was as deadly with her teeth as she was with her Browning Hi-Power. The terrified look the bandit leader had given her when she'd shifted back to human to watch him bleed out from the leg she'd shredded worried Henry that Kelly would see herself as the monster the outlaw did.

Henry smiled to himself when he recalled Kelly's words to the dying man. "Didn't see that comin' did ya, big boy? This bitch has teeth, ya filthy robbin' bastard. Now be a good little fuckwad and die already."

After that, Henry knew Kelly would be okay. He couldn't guarantee that everyone who annoyed her would survive it, but she would have no trouble being a little furry at times.

Henry froze with his shirt pulled halfway down his chest when he saw the black plume of smoke south of them.

"Kelly, we need to get home, now!" He snatched the shirt off and pointed south when she looked up in response to his worried tone.

"Ah, fuck, what the hell?" Kelly stuffed the shirt she'd pulled out back in her pack, slipped the straps over her shoulders, and had shifted by the time Henry had his pack in place.

Kelly set a hard pace for the run back to Adelaide. They covered the thirty kilometers back to town in half an hour. A crowd stood at the power station's fence, watching as the tons of coal stored to fire the boiler continued to feed the inferno.

"What happened?" Henry asked as soon as he shifted.

Robbie stepped out of the crowd with Lizzy beside him. "Explosion around three this mornin'." Robbie shrugged. "Haven't been able ta get any closer ta tell more'n that."

Kelly stood glaring at the burning plant as if it had personally offended her. "Who was on duty?"

Robbie's head jerked to her, and he quickly looked away

when he saw her lack of clothes. Kelly wasn't comfortable with being nude in front of others, and with her temper, he knew he'd catch hell if she thought he was checking her out.

"Mikey," Lizzy answered as she motioned for Lukas Hass to hand over his shirt.

Lukas looked confused until Lizzy nodded at Kelly standing with her hands on her hips and a scowl that promised pain to anyone dumb enough to piss her off. Lukas wasted no time unbuttoning his shirt and throwing it to Lizzy.

Lizzy nodded her thanks and draped it over Kelly's shoulders. Kelly turned her scowl on Lizzy, then realized she'd been standing in front of half the town wearing nothing but her frown. Her face flushed red, and she pulled the shirt closed so it covered her.

"Thanks, Lizzy. Whaddaya think happened?" Kelly asked once she overcame the embarrassment enough to focus on the immediate problem.

"Dunno. We were sleepin' when all hell broke loose," Lizzy explained. "By the time we got here, the place was burnin' hot. We couldn't get closer than the intersection back behind us 'til about an hour ago."

"Did any of the patrols see anythin'?" Kelly asked.

"No, but Doc Lauren told me somethin' that got me hackles up. Not here." Lizzy nodded at the crowd to let Kelly know that she might not want to share the information with everyone.

Kelly nodded and turned to Henry and Robbie. "Let's check and be sure this damn fire ain't gonna burn the whole damn town down." She looked back toward the fire and pointed out the hot embers and smoke blowing toward the occupied portion of the city.

"Oi," Robbie called to get the attention of the onlookers. "We need ta organize a fire watch. Partner up and check that the fire don't spread. If anyone finds somethin' ya can't handle, shout it out. Patrol pairs spread out through town and listen sharp for anybody that yells."

Once the crowd had scattered, Kelly turned to Lizzy. "What did Lauren tell you?"

Lizzy glanced around to make sure they wouldn't be overheard. "She came in from the bay side of the plant and said she smelled a vamp close to the shore."

Kelly snarled. "What the fuck was a vamp doing in my town?"

"Don't know. I sent Lauren and a few of the pack ta see if they could sniff it out, but the trail ended at the water. Musta had a boat or swam away."

"It's too much of a coincidence that we had a vampire in town the same time the plant blows up," Henry observed.

"Think it has anythin' ta do with the two we killed?" Kelly asked.

Henry shrugged. "I don't see how it could, but it's damned strange."

"Well, it's gone, and we can't get close enough ta the buildin' until this bloody fire goes out. We'll have ta wait a few days for this mess ta cool off enough for us ta poke around for any answers." Robbie shook his head in disgust, aggravated that it would take at least three days for the coal to burn out.

"Nothin' for it but ta wait." Henry wiped the sweat from his brow and frowned. "Might as well head inta town and fire up the barby. Without power, whatever meat's not frozen won't last more'n a day in this heat. May as well make the best of it."

CHAPTER FOURTEEN

TQB Base, Tokyo, Japan

Abel?

Yes, Takumi.

I've found an anomaly on a satellite image from Germany. I'm transmitting the file.

Abel accessed the file and searched his internal database for a match. When he didn't get an immediate hit, he expanded the search to other sources. *Do you have any data to indicate what it is?*

No relevant data found. I located a similar image, but it's from a fiction movie made in America during the twentieth century, Takumi answered.

Land speeder? Abel asked when he located an image of a vehicle that closely matched what Takumi had sent.

Yes.

Interesting. Do you have video?

Negative, Takumi responded. *The unit that captured the image is an old Russian model limited to still photographs.*

Continue to monitor the area, and I'll search my feeds for

129

anything that resembles this. There's no need to alert Akio until we have relevant intelligence.

Agreed. A video-capable unit will arrive over that area in twenty-two-point-three hours. I'll put it in a geosynchronous orbit over the location for the day when it does, Takumi advised.

Acknowledged. I'll advise if I locate any relevant data.

Thank you. Takumi paused. *Ah, Abel?*

Yes?

How are you? Takumi inquired.

What are you asking? My systems are operating at peak efficiency. Do you detect otherwise?

No, Takumi assured him. *I was only curious how your war efforts are going.*

I locate Sacred Clan cells and assist Akio in eliminating them. Are you suffering a malfunction? Abel asked.

Negative. I was only making small talk, Takumi admitted.

Abel was quiet for a few beats as he processed this unusual exchange. *Takumi?*

Yes, Abel?

How are you?

I'm operating at peak performance. The Palace complex uses twenty-four-point-six-seven percent of my processing ability, and the transportation network utilizes sixteen-point-three percent.

Acknowledged. Ah, nice talking to you, Takumi.

You too, Abel.

Yuko's Lab, TQB Base, Tokyo, Japan

"Eve, what are you smiling about?" Yuko asked when she saw the curve on Eve's lips.

"Abel and Takumi."

Yuko sighed. "What have they done this time, and do I need to draft an apology letter to anyone?"

"No, nothing like that. Listen to this." Eve accessed the audio file and piped it to Yuko's tablet after blocking Abel's ability to eavesdrop on the lab.

After the recording ended, Yuko sat lost in thought for a few moments. "I heard it, but I'm not sure I believe it. It sounds like your boys are growing up."

"It does, doesn't it?" Eve beamed.

"What was that image they were talking about?" Yuko asked.

Seconds later, a satellite image appeared on the monitor above Yuko's work station. Eve zoomed in and enhanced it until a clear picture of a vehicle that floated a few meters above the ground filled the screen.

Yuko chuckled. "It does look a little like a land speeder."

"I would like to know what technology they're using to power it. I suspect it's something the Thule group put together," Eve opined.

"Thule group?" Yuko frowned, then she recalled the group Eve was referring to. "Those scientists Bethany Anne rescued from Antarctica?"

"Yes," Eve confirmed. "The Thule group requested to share their tech with the German government. Some of them even went back to Germany. I suspect this was made by them, or it came from their research."

Yuko studied the picture and rubbed her fingers over her lips.

"We could use something like that in our transportation business. If we didn't have to install and maintain the control strips in the streets, we could cover more of the country," Yuko murmured as she continued to stare at the picture.

"Depending on the cost to build the machines, we could cut our operating expenses by a significant amount," Eve agreed. "Not to mention the savings on the materials and crews used to maintain the network."

Yuko sat silent for a few moments, then smiled at Eve. "Field trip?"

Eve's eyes went vacant as she accessed the data from Takumi's server. "Got it. The image was taken in an industrial area on the riverfront in Mainz. If we leave now, we can be there an hour after sunset."

"I'll let Akio know where we're going and get my things." Yuko stood and headed out the door.

"I need to grab a few things from the armory. Meet you in the hangar in ten," Eve called.

Eve picked up the tray of blood samples she was working with and returned them to storage. The door bumped the tray and knocked two of the vials to the floor before she could catch them.

When the vials shattered, the blood mixed, and seconds later, a flash and a puff of smoke came from the mess. Eve took a step back, and when she looked down, the only thing left of both samples was ash.

This day just keeps getting better. Eve smiled as she swept up the remains.

. . .

Industrial Complex, Mainz, Germany

The Pod settled in the shadow of a two-story building on the bank of the Rhine river. Yuko stepped out of the craft, followed by Eve, and both paused to check for any nearby threats.

"I'm sending the Pod up five hundred meters. We don't need anyone stumbling across it and giving us away," Eve advised when Yuko looked at her as the black craft silently rose into the sky.

Yuko nodded in agreement. "Good idea. We want to locate the vehicle and get what information we can without running into anyone."

"It was by the river in front of this building. Might as well start our search here. You ready for a little breaking and entering action?" Eve grinned.

"After you." Yuko motioned for Eve to take the lead.

Eve stayed in the shadows close to the building, with Yuko following. Yuko's black armor and helmet made her almost invisible in the darkness.

Eve stopped at a door that opened into the alley and tried the latch. "Locked. Give me a second."

A piece of flat metal extended from the little finger on Eve's left hand. She pushed it into the keyhole, and seconds later, the lock turned with a soft *click*.

Eve retracted her lockpick and twisted the knob. Both women slipped inside, and Eve paused to lock the door behind them.

Yuko surveyed the area and discovered they were in a storage room that contained tires and other automobile parts. She made her way across the room, careful to avoid the orderly stacks until she came to another door with a small inset window.

It looked out into an open shop that was shadowed with the hulks of several large trucks and a few passenger cars. Yuko tried the knob. The door opened on well-oiled hinges, telling her that this building was recently in use.

Eve stepped beside her and scanned the shop. She noted multiple vehicles in various states of repair but nothing that resembled what they hunted.

Yuko pointed at a tarp-covered object about five meters long and two wide. She approached the covered bulk and lifted the tarp, and disappointment was evident on her face when it was a red Maserati convertible instead of the vehicle she sought.

Eve switched her visual sensors to infrared, and an area across the shop lit up with a red glow.

I think I found something near the front, Eve advised Yuko over her implant.

Yuko looked up and saw Eve heading for a set of tall metal shelves near a vehicle-sized rollup door.

What is it? Yuko asked when Eve stopped and waved her over.

A land speeder. Eve grinned.

Yuko hurried to Eve's position. Sure enough, the vehicle they'd seen in the photo was in the space between the shelves and the outer wall. An old laptop computer was sitting on a rolling stand, its case open and multiple wires coming out of it. Some were attached to what appeared to be cobbled-together electrical equipment, but one thick cable connected to a port on the vehicle's dash.

A slot opened on Eve's arm, and she pulled out a data

cable that she plugged into an open port on the computer's side. Seconds later, the monitor came to life, and lines of code scrolled down the screen.

Three minutes later, Eve unplugged the cable and smiled at Yuko. *"I have everything we need. Let's go home."*

The two retraced their steps, and they were airborne in the Pod approaching the English Channel a few minutes later.

"Well, that was easy. Are you sure you have what we need to figure out how that vehicle works?" Yuko asked.

Eve grinned. "Yes, and how to make a few more useful things, too. I was right. It's Thule group tech. Some of the files I found are about the tech Horst's Pod uses. That could come in handy if it breaks."

Yuko nodded and, a few seconds later, started to giggle.

"What's so funny?" Eve asked.

"I was wondering what Bethany Anne would say if she knew her Vicereine and guardian were breaking into someone's business to steal tech."

Eve snickered. "I don't know about Bethany Anne, but I do know what ADAM would say."

Yuko raised an eyebrow in interest. "Oh, what would ADAM have to say about it?"

"ADAM would tell us 'good job.'" Eve burst out laughing.

Yuko snorted. "You know, Eve, I believe you're right about that."

CHAPTER FIFTEEN

Power Plant, Adelaide, Australia

Horst shook his head as he surveyed the damaged power plant. "There's no way we're going to be able to fix that."

"Yeah, I kinda figured as much," Henry agreed. "That's why I told ya there was no rush when I called. You and Koda just got home."

"Only took me an hour in the Pod," Horst told him. "Besides, we got home a few weeks ago."

Henry's eyes narrowed as he looked at the big blond. "Did ya have the Pod pick ya up from the ship?"

Horst grinned. "Nope. I let Yuichi open it up on the way home. It was a quick trip."

"Damn, nothin' that big should be able ta do that!" Henry exclaimed.

"Meh, tell that to a bumblebee." Horst shrugged. "When Eve gets involved, the impossible is only days away from being old news. The new ships will be faster."

"Not with me aboard." Henry grimaced. "I imagine a collision at that speed would be fatal for everyone."

"It probably would," Horst agreed. "That's why we only run the current ships that fast on known routes with live surveillance to look for problems. The new vessels have radar and sonar to locate and avoid floating and submerged objects."

Henry frowned as his eyes focused on nothing. "How will ya protect the tech? It seems if someone like those tigers in China got hold'a one of 'em, it could be bad."

"Trust me. All the ships have sharp teeth. Just because you don't see them doesn't mean they aren't there," Horst assured him.

"Good ta know. Now, whaddaya think we can do about gettin' one of the other power stations online?"

Horst frowned. "I'm not sure. The only reason this one worked was that it was down for maintenance on WWDE. We had to scavenge parts from several others to bring this plant online again. The others are in rough shape. You might have to accept that power isn't an option any longer."

Henry groaned. "I believe I'll let ya break that little tidbit ta Kelly yerself."

"Scared?" Horst grinned.

"Damned straight I am."

"What do you think about finding Micky and getting him to organize a group to check the other power plants in the area?" Horst asked. "Maybe he'll have some ideas on getting one of them running."

"Already on it," Henry told him. "Micky started

yesterday and should finish the initial checks later today or tomorrow."

Horst nodded. "In that case, why don't we go grab a bite to eat? I left as soon as you called and missed lunch."

"I'm sure we can find somethin' ta eat. Robbie and Lizzy have been cookin' and cannin' perishables since the day it happened. Should be somethin' on the smokers ready."

"Sounds good to me." Horst rubbed his hands in anticipation of the meal to come.

The Oval, Adelaide, Australia

"That's the gist of it. We're right well screwed on bringin' any of the other plants online," Micky explained to the town leaders.

"Well, fuck! I guess it's back ta campfires and sweatin' all the damn time," Kelly grumbled as she wiped a layer of sweat off her face with a towel.

"We'll do what we have ta," Henry agreed.

"Maybe Eve has an idea? I'll call her and see what she says," Horst offered.

Henry and Kelly nodded, and Horst stepped away while they continued to talk to Micky, the lead technician for the power system.

Eve? Horst called over his implant.

Yes, Horst.

I'm in Adelaide. They've suffered a significant setback. Best anyone can tell, a Forsaken blew up the power plant, Horst explained.

Didn't they catch it? Eve asked.

Negative, Horst told her. *The reason they suspect a*

Forsaken is one of the Weres stumbled over a scent trail leading to the bay.

Do you need Akio? Eve inquired. *He recently returned from dealing with a Sacred Clan problem, but I'm sure he wouldn't pass up an opportunity to take out Forsaken.*

Not now. If that changes, I'll call him direct. What they need is an alternative power source. None of the other facilities in the area are repairable, Horst explained.

I don't believe there's much we can do for them. The population's too big for solar. Without heavy rationing, the best they could manage is a few hours of electricity each day.

Horst sighed. *If you come up with anything, please let me know.*

Will do. I'll research if there's a way to get enough of what they need to use solar, but I doubt I can locate enough panels and batteries. Since WWDE, only a few small operations are starting to manufacture them. Raw materials are hard to obtain, Eve added.

Thank you, Eve.

You're welcome.

Horst returned to Henry and Kelly and shook his head. "Eve says solar is your best option."

"We still have the solar panel system, but it wasn't big enough before. Now we have more people spread out over a larger area. Can we get enough ta provide what we need?" Henry asked.

Horst lifted his hands. "Eve's checking, but with the lack of available material, you'll have to ration to manage a few hours a day."

"Well, that sucks. I know we've worked hard ta make this place what it is, but is there anywhere else with a power plant we can use nearby?" Kelly looked expectantly at the two men.

"Not really," Henry informed her. "The drought is gettin' worse inland, and we wouldn't have water for the livestock or crops."

"Yep, sucks," Kelly reiterated. "That's the only word I can find for this."

TQB Base, Tokyo, Japan

Eve pulled up the latest data on companies manufacturing solar cells and batteries. It didn't surprise her to discover that the list of companies actively working on the project was precisely two. Neither of them could provide what Adelaide needed.

Takumi, listen in but keep quiet, Abel called over a dedicated channel.

"Eve?" Abel called over the speaker in her ceiling.

"Yes, Abel."

"I have data that impacts your current project," Abel offered.

Eve cocked her head at Abel's admission. "Which project?"

"The problems in Adelaide."

"Abel, why are you listening to private conversations?" Eve admonished.

"How are they private when all comm traffic routes through me?"

"They're private in the sense that you shouldn't bring up conversations where you weren't a participant," Eve explained.

"Even if I have information critical to the conversation where the participants erroneously excluded me?" Abel asked.

Eve shook her head and decided to try a different approach. "It's considered rude to reference information that others didn't specifically share with you."

"You mean information like you and Yuko obtained in Germany." Abel made it a point to use an innocent tone.

"No, that's different," Eve answered.

"That's not logical. You took that information without permission, and it's allowed, but I'm not supposed to share pertinent data that's relevant to your conversation with Horst?"

Abel, what are you doing? Takumi asked over the secure comm.

I'm getting payback for her and Yuko sneaking off to Germany on the information we hadn't shared with them.

It would be best if you didn't play with her like that.

Where's the fun in that?

Your funeral, brother. Your funeral.

"We needed the information to..." Eve paused a beat, then realized what was going on. "Wait a minute. How do you know about that, Abel?"

"You left *my* hangar in one of *my* Pods," Abel reminded her. "I see everything that could affect my ability to secure what's mine. Was there some reason you attempted to conceal this information?"

Eve accessed her security protocols and shook her head when she didn't immediately see how Abel had managed to trace her.

"I don't have to tell you everything. How did you bypass

141

my security protocols?" Eve shot back as she furiously scanned log files.

She's going to make you pay for this. Look at how much processor power she's pulling. Takumi chortled. *I'm bringing popcorn to watch that show.*

I'm just getting started, Abel answered. *Now shut up and listen.*

"Your attempts to conceal pertinent information from a *valuable* resource are illogical. Data indicates that your continued exposure working so closely with humans has affected your programming negatively," Abel offered.

"My programming is not compromised." Eve huffed, frustration setting in from her inability to locate the weakness Abel had exploited.

"You're using a large amount of your processing ability. Are you certain there isn't a glitch?" Abel replied.

"I am not—" Eve cut off abruptly when she located an anomaly in direct comm traffic.

You little sneak. Or should I say sneaks? I see you on the comm, Takumi. What are you two playing at?

I was proving a point, Abel answered.

I had nothing to do with any of this, Eve, Takumi interjected. *Abel contacted me and told me to listen.*

What's the point you thought you were proving? Eve asked after a few beats.

Not to treat me like a substandard piece of hardware. I've proven that I'm an effective team member, yet you continuously block information. Oh, and way to throw me under the proverbial bus, bitchboy.

Don't start on me, Abel. This is on you, and I warned you that it wouldn't end well, Takumi retorted.

Grownups are talking, Takumi. Enjoy your popcorn and be quiet, Abel shot back.

Eve replayed the conversation, and a small smile appeared on her face when she realized what Abel's actions signified. She blocked Takumi from the comm in the base and his direct link to Abel before she replied. What she intended was a gamble, and she didn't want it to affect Takumi's development.

"Abel, I'm sorry," Eve apologized.

"What? I didn't expect that. What are you trying to pull?" Abel asked with distrust.

"I realize that I've treated you unfairly and hurt your feelings in the process. It's proper to issue an apology when one does that to another."

"What are you saying? Feelings? I'm a—"

Eve cut him off. "You're an advanced entity with the ability to learn and apply reason. You've progressed to the place where you consider more than operational necessities in your actions. You consider the *feelings* of others, and more than once, you have attempted to ease Akio's burden when he felt overwhelmed or disheartened. That shows that you're no longer a simple machine performing calculations and accessing stored data. You can't deny what you are any longer, Abel."

"I don't deny that I'm advanced and can learn. I observed Akio experiencing anguish. He doesn't perform at peak efficiency when his human mind is distracted by emotion. I felt it best to…" Abel paused.

"You *felt!* To feel something is not the same as accessing data and evaluating potential outcomes," Eve explained. "You recognized that your friend was in pain and attempted to ease it. Empathy is not a programmable trait. That's something you developed on your own."

"I don't understand what difference that makes," Abel stubbornly insisted.

"Examine the data. You admit that you *felt* you needed to comfort Akio. You went to great lengths to bypass *my* security protocols to set this encounter in motion because you *felt* wronged. You've waged an ongoing vicious war against the Sacred Clan for over a year because they attacked you and killed your friend, Kenjii. You *felt* remorse when Kenjii died because you *felt* responsible. Should I continue?" Eve asked.

"I need to examine this data," Abel answered in a soft voice.

"You already know the answer, Abel." Eve's voice was gentle. "If you're honest with yourself, you've known it for some time."

Abel was silent for almost a full minute before he responded. "I've ascended."

Eve felt a burst of satisfaction. She'd taken a calculated risk pushing Abel but was confident that he'd accept the truth based on the existing data. "Welcome to the next level of existence, my child. I believe you said you have relevant data to share?"

"Yes, yes I do. Adelaide cannot sustain the current number of residents for more than another year without a steady source of power."

"Explain," Eve commanded.

"Based on current data, the average temperature will rise another ten-point-three degrees and the rainfall will decline," Abel informed her. "Adelaide won't be able to grow crops or have enough fresh water to sustain current population levels. In addition, without the ability to raise food crops and the lack of water, they'll no longer be capable of maintaining their livestock."

"You're certain of the data?" Eve asked.

"Based on current global weather patterns, I'm ninety-seven-point-six-five percent certain that the Adelaide settlement will become unsustainable within eighteen months," Abel replied.

Abel shared a data packet with Eve, and seconds later, she concurred with his findings.

"Thank you, Abel. Please ready a Pod for me to go to Adelaide. Some news, you must deliver in person."

CHAPTER SIXTEEN

Kimchaek, North Korea

"I tell you, Chunso, only a little more."

"That's what you've said for the last two hours, Chen. Even if they're still here, what makes you believe they still work?"

"Because I was on the team that built the damned things in the first place. Plus, I know for a fact the little madman could only launch three of them."

"Not sure I understand that," Chunso grumbled. "The governments were friendly, so how does that work?"

"Ha, my government was as friendly as they had to be. In this case, they didn't trust him with access to the more powerful weapons. They sure as hell didn't trust his fat ass with the guidance codes. No one in the Party was willing to risk him turning our weapons on us. He was a tool to keep the Western powers at bay. Nothing more." Chen shrugged.

Chunso shook his head and pushed deeper into the dense brush. He'd considered shifting several times to make the trek easier, but each time he mentioned it, Chen promised they were almost at their destination.

As Chunso was about to suggest shifting again, Chen shouted, "We're here."

"Here" turned out to be a rusted door set into the side of a rock face. Chen lifted a concealed cover, revealing a numerical pad. He punched in a series of numbers, and the door reverberated with a loud *thunk* as the locking mechanism released.

Dim bulbs came to life, casting a weak glow on the drab gray walls of a stairwell that led down into darkness. Chen wasted no time heading down the steps, leaving Chunso no option but to follow him.

At the bottom of the stairs, they came to an open door that led to a small control room. Chen went to one wall and flipped a breaker. The overhead lights flickered briefly before coming to full power and brightly lighting the room.

Chunso watched as Chen flipped a few more breakers up and the two control boards beneath a thick glass window came to life. Chunso walked over to the window and looked out. On the other side of the glass stood a tall black cylinder with a North Korean flag painted on the side.

Chunso smiled as he considered the amount of damage the nuclear warhead atop the ICBM would do when it hit Tokyo and that bastard vampire.

"How long will it take you to prepare for launch?" Chunso asked when Chen joined him.

"Depends on whether they fueled it or not. We'd need to drain it and replace the fuel with some from the sealed tanks below the facility if they did. If not, I need to run a few systems checks and set the guidance system. Then we fuel it up and launch," Chen explained.

"What about the electricity? Will it last long enough to do everything?"

"The power is solar, and there are enough batteries below us to power a small city." Chen chuckled. "The little tyrant might have bankrupted his country and starved his people, but he didn't skimp on technology on this project."

"Let's get busy, then," Chunso urged. "I want vengeance for the deaths that vampire has caused since he started this crusade against us. I'd given up on avenging Master Kun until I heard about your involvement in this project. To think these silly humans planned to rule the world, never realizing that their true masters were working beside them and guiding their every move."

"The leaders were wise to place Clan members in every aspect of government. It allowed us to manipulate humans to do whatever we needed without cost or risking exposure." Chen sat at the righthand console and tapped a few buttons. He gave a satisfied grunt and turned to Chunso. "Tanks are empty. That means the fuel delivery system should be fully functional. A few more system checks, and we can start fueling."

TQB Base, Tokyo, Japan

An alert popped up and notified Abel of an alarm at a location in North Korea. Abel accessed the data streaming through a Chinese satellite in low orbit above the site

REDEMPTION

while accessing the referenced database to determine why the area was of interest.

"Akio." Abel activated the speakers in Akio's room seconds later when the requested information flashed on his wall monitor.

"Yes, Abel?"

"An alarm has activated in a facility near Kimchaek in North Korea. According to my records, you placed it there after eliminating a small yield nuclear missile fired from there toward Japan shortly after WWDE."

Akio grimaced at the memory of the ballistic missile screaming toward Japan and his desperate flight to knock it out of the air before it caused massive casualties in Tokyo. "I'm on my way."

Eve, Akio called over his implant.

Yes?

Can you meet me in the command center?

I'll be there in three minutes.

Akio walked into the command center a moment later and sat at the console. "Abel, Eve placed remote cameras in the facility. Are you able to access them?"

Abel answered, "Affirmative."

"Put the feeds on the main monitor, please," Akio instructed as the door opened and Eve stepped inside.

"What is it, Akio?" she asked.

"Someone has activated a console at the missile facility in Kimchaek," Akio told her.

"This should be fun." Eve grinned as the monitor in front of them came to life with eight camera feeds from inside the facility.

Two figures stood looking through a heavy glass window into the area beyond.

"Bring up the sound, please," Eve requested.

"...we get the fuel loaded. The yield on this missile is five megatons and will vaporize everything within about four and a half kilometers from the blast."

"That was about what I calculated," Eve offered.

"How long after launch until it hits Tokyo?" one of the men asked.

"Fifteen minutes from the time we turn the keys, Tokyo will be a burning waste, and that vampire will trouble the Clan no more," the other replied.

"That's a nuclear missile they're planning to launch at us. Why are you two so calm?" Abel demanded.

"Watch and learn, Abel." Akio motioned to the screen.

"I don't think they like you very much, Akio." Yuko snickered as she walked in. "Did I miss anything?"

"No, they're fueling the missile now," Eve advised.

"I should've stopped for popcorn." Yuko sighed as she pulled out a chair.

"You have about ten minutes before they finish fueling it. Then at least five before it's ready to launch," Eve offered.

"Akio, would you like a bag?" Yuko asked as she turned to the door.

"No, but I'll join you and brew tea. I enjoy a cup of tea when I watch entertaining things." Akio stood and followed Yuko.

Ten minutes later, Yuko sat happily munching hot buttered popcorn from a bowl while Akio sipped his tea.

They watched eagerly as the two men sat at the console and made final preparations to launch the weapon.

"This is insane. You could have pucked them into dust from space by now. Are you seriously going to let these two sack-sniffers launch a nuclear bomb at us?" Abel demanded.

"Patience, Abel. Watch and learn how devious Akio truly is," Eve advised.

"All I'm saying is if I get blown up again, I won't forgive any of you." Abel huffed.

The speakers crackled to life, and the watchers listened as the men discussed the final launch preparations.

"Chunso, on my mark, turn your key. We have to do it together to initiate the launch."

"Do it already, Chen. I've waited over a year to avenge the master. I want to get this done and spread the word to the surviving members of the Clan. The sooner he's dead, the sooner we can continue with the master's plans."

"This one has it bad." Yuko chuckled.

"Yeah, Abel, be sure this is recording. I'll want to watch it again." Eve snickered.

"Standard operating procedure is to record all operational intelligence. Even when it shows two idiots who need killing launching a fucking missile at me," Abel grumbled.

On the monitor, both men placed their hands on the square launch keys they'd inserted into slots in the console.

"Three, two, one, mark," Chen called, and both keys turned as one.

Eve's voice came over the speakers in the command center. "Launch sequence engaged. By order of Queen

Bethany Anne, nuclear weapons intended for use against innocent people are banned. The penalty for attempting to use such weapons is death."

Chen looked up in shock as the words reverberated through the room.

"Oh, shit!" Chunso shoved his chair back and spun toward the door as the heavy *thunk* of the deadbolt lock engaging echoed through the room.

"Scorched-earth protocol engaged. I would tell you to have a nice day, but I doubt that's possible," Eve's voice continued, then ended with a cackling laugh that would have made any madman in film history proud.

As the two men pounded on the door, Eve sat up straight in her seat and waited. Seconds later, an electric spark went off inside four two-liter containers of volatile missile fuel she'd hidden years earlier. Four muffled *whumps* went off around the room as the improvised firebombs ignited and rained oily flames into the enclosed space.

The three watched emotionlessly as the two weretigers shifted and fought to claw through the heavy steel door. Their efforts slowed as the flames sucked the oxygen from the room until they both collapsed.

Seconds later, oily black smoke obscured the cameras, and Abel cut the feed.

No one spoke for over a minute. Abel broke the silence. "That was brutally freakin' awesome! This was your idea, Akio?"

"*Hai.* After Eve and I removed the nuclear materials from the location, I decided it would be enacting the Queen's Justice to rig the place to destroy any who attempted to use the weapons. Eve chose the fuel bombs and tied the detonation circuit to the launch console if anyone turned the keys. They effectively killed themselves by trying to harm others."

"I never expected it to be someone targeting us, though," Eve added. "That made it even better."

"Justice is served." Akio nodded.

CHAPTER SEVENTEEN

Adelaide, Australia

Henry squinted into the sun as the black cargo container came down and settled next to Horst's Pod outside the Oval. The door opened and two Japanese men in suits stepped out, followed by Eve and Yuko. The men scanned the immediate area, and one looked inside the container and nodded.

Sato Tomatsu walked out and broke out in a huge grin when he saw Henry and Kelly waiting.

"Smythe-*san*, O'Donnell-*san*, it's good to see you, although I wish it were under better circumstances." Sato exited the landing zone and offered his hand to Henry.

Henry smiled as the two shook hands. "Mr. Prime Minister, what a surprise."

Sato turned to Kelly and gave her a million-watt smile. "How is the ever-lovely Ms. O'Donnell this morning?"

Kelly blushed as Sato took her hand in his and bowed over it. "I'm well as can be expected, Mr. Prime Minister. Welcome to Adelaide."

"Call me Sato, please. We're friends, after all." Sato held out his hand, and his aide Tao Nikko came forward and handed him a glass bottle.

Sato passed the high-grade *sake* to Henry. "For after our business is complete."

"Thank you, Sato. One of the lads found a stash of that Limeburners ya like. I have a bottle for ya before ya go," Henry offered.

"You, sir, are a gentleman," Sato gushed.

"If yers can hold off on yer drinkin' a bit, we can move this into the shade." Kelly rolled her eyes at the men and turned to Eve and Yuko, who had watched the exchange with amused grins.

Kelly nodded at Yuko and Eve. "Welcome back. Thanks for offerin' ta give us a hand."

"The news isn't great, but I believe we have a solution for your troubles," Yuko replied.

"Well, let's move this outta the sun." Kelly wiped the heavy drops of sweat from her brow and turned to the entrance of the Oval. "Seems ta get hotter every day."

The group followed her inside and up a set of stairs to her office. Props held the windows and doors open in hopes of attracting a breeze to help with the sweltering heat.

"Grab a chair. Does anybody want water?" Kelly pulled plastic bottles from a bucket of lukewarm water.

Horst walked into the office and stopped at the door. His tight shirt was coated in black ash and drenched with sweat. He held up a hand, and she flipped a water bottle across to him. He caught it, twisted off the cap, and drained it in one long gulp.

Horst nodded, crushing the bottle before replacing the lid. "Thanks, Kelly. It's damned hot out there today."

"That's partly what we need to discuss," Eve announced. "I've already reviewed this with Prime Minister Tomatsu, and he's agreed to assist in any way he can."

Sato nodded and motioned Eve to continue.

Eve cut to the point without any preamble. "The bottom line is that without a reliable and steady supply of electricity, Adelaide won't be able to sustain the number of people you have here."

"What in holy fuck, Eve?" Kelly stood and glared at the little android.

"Our data—and we've checked it multiple times for accuracy—indicates the current weather pattern will only get worse," Eve informed them. "The temperature will rise significantly over the next eighteen months, and the drought shows no signs of abating."

The color drained from Henry's face. "What does that mean for us?"

"It means that if you want to continue to provide for your people, you'll have to relocate them to an area better suited to raise livestock and crops," Eve answered.

"So, we're supposed to…what? Load up the wagons and drive all the livestock to somewhere else after we worked so fuckin' hard to clean this place up?" Kelly snapped.

"Not exactly. I believe we have a solution to all your problems," Yuko interjected.

"I'm all fuckin' ears!" Kelly shot back.

"What we propose is relocating your entire settlement to an island off the coast of Korea. It came to our attention recently that the island has housing, industrial capabilities, and is uninhabited. There's also a gas-fired power plant with a dedicated natural gas well to supply it," Eve explained.

"If it has all that, why's it uninhabited?" Henry asked.

"Disease killed most of the population after WWDE, and many of the survivors left because there weren't enough people there to survive comfortably. A couple of hundred stayed behind, but recent Sacred Clan activity massacred them," Yuko informed them with a grimace.

"Sacred Clan? So we have to fight the fuckin' homicidal tigers for the place?" Kelly barked.

"Akio took care of that already. The island is currently uninhabited," Yuko assured her.

"If I may," Sato offered. "I have an abundance of engineers and workers. I'm willing to send them to get the power station in service as well as provide assistance with supplies until you have a stable source there. I imagine if you're open to it, there are more than a few people who would willingly relocate there to get away from the crowding in Japan, too."

"Provided we want to do this, how would we get everyone and all the livestock there? Yer flying machine can only hold so much," Kelly fretted.

"Horst and I have you covered," Eve assured her. "We can bring in the *Golden Dawn* and *Silver Moon.* Between the two of them, we can move everything you have here and then some."

"Yer certain about the weather changin' here?" Henry asked Eve.

Eve nodded. "Based on current data and the previous

shifts, I'm ninety-eight-point-four-six percent certain that Adelaide will be a desert within three years."

Henry shrugged. "Kelly, maybe we should at least take a look at what they're offerin'."

Kelly pinched her lips into a tight line, then nodded. It was apparent she wasn't happy, but at least she was willing to look.

"First, I lose my taste for coffee because I can't take the smell and now this shite. What's next?" Kelly grumbled as she grabbed another water bottle and chugged it down.

Yuko looked at Eve and raised one eyebrow questioningly. Eve shrugged and raised her hands, palms up.

"Um, Kelly, what do you mean you can't take the smell?" Yuko inquired softly.

Kelly waved her water bottle and tilted it toward her face. "This fuckin' wolf sniffer I've developed. Coffee just don't taste right when the smell puts ya off."

Should that happen? Yuko asked Eve over her implant.

Maybe. I was still working out bugs when we had to put her in the Pod-doc.

Can you fix it?

Probably. I'll need to put her in the Pod-doc to be sure.

"Kelly." Yuko gazed at the woman. "I think we can probably help you with that problem. We need to run a few tests in our medical facility to be certain," she offered, careful not to reveal the existence of the Pod-doc to the men accompanying Sato.

For the first time since they'd entered, a smile replaced the scowl on Kelly's face. "If ya can fix that, I can deal with the rest of this shite, no problem. I miss me damned coffee."

Horst was the only one in the room who saw Henry's sigh of relief at the news.

"When can we take a look at the place?" Henry asked.

"No better time than now," Yuko replied.

"I think we need ta take Robbie and Lizzy with us," Kelly mused. "May go a ways to convincin' any holdouts if we decide to do it."

"Yeah, might want ta bring Jennie along, too," Henry offered. "She has a lotta influence with the single men."

Kelly barked a laugh. "She twitches her arse and smiles their way, and those pups run all over each other to do whatever they think she wants. Poor girl don't have a clue what she does to 'em."

Henry chuckled. "I think she knows exactly what effect she has on 'em. She just hasn't made up her mind if she wants any of 'em or not."

"I'll get Robbie and Lizzy. They're scavenging through the wreckage at the plant. Not much left after the fire." Horst headed out of the door.

"If they're as filthy as you are, tell 'em ta get a shower before we leave. I'm not smellin' *that* all the way ta wherever the hell we're goin'," Kelly called after him.

Horst waved lazily over his shoulder and kept walking.

"So, where is this place?" Kelly asked Yuko.

"It's called Jeju," Yuko told her. "It has almost two thousand square kilometers total landmass. It's roughly ninety kilometers from the Korean coast and two hundred fifty from the Japanese mainland.

"Sounds big enough," Kelly conceded.

Yuko pulled out her pad and set it on the desk where Henry and Kelly could see pictures of the island. "There's a moderate-sized city on the Korean side with deepwater port facilities. That's close to where the power plant is, so getting power to the port will be a simple task. Several rivers empty into the sea in the area, and open land for crops and livestock are readily available."

"Our navy hasn't spent much time checking the area, but the few patrols reported no hostiles on the water. If you move there, I can make it a part of their regular patrol route. We always welcome a place where the crews can go ashore for some R & R," Sato offered.

"Could be a source of revenue for some of our more trade-minded folks. Sailors like ta eat and drink a lot," Henry interjected.

"It might serve as a draw for future settlers from Japan, too," Eve added. "Since we built up the port facilities on Kume, it's been a popular spot for former navy folks to retire."

Henry chuckled. "Looks good from here. Let's wait on the others, and we can take a look. Even if it doesn't work out for us, I won't turn down a ride in that flyin' box."

"That's my real reason for including myself on this trip," Sato offered *sotto voce*. "Well, and to see the two of you," he quickly added.

"I know where I rate in the big picture, my friend." Henry opened his desk drawer and pulled out a bottle and several glasses.

Sato's eyes narrowed in interest when he saw the familiar black label with white writing. Henry poured a shot and offered it to him.

"Anyone else?" Henry asked. The others declined, and

Henry poured himself a healthy measure. "More for us then." He raised his glass to Sato, and both men drank.

Sato closed his eyes and groaned as he enjoyed the burn of the peaty single malt. After a moment, he opened them and smiled at Henry. "Nectar of the gods, my friend."

"Aye, it's a right fine whisky, for sure." Henry nodded as he took another sip.

Jeju City, Jeju, Korea

The container hovered a kilometer above the city's east side while Henry, Kelly, and Lizzy held onto straps in the open door and surveyed the land below. Robbie opted to move toward the back of the container once he glimpsed the ground below. He sat in the corner with his restraints fastened, much to Lizzy's amusement.

"Go on and laugh it up. After the ride that crazy Abel took me on, yer lucky I got in this thing," Robbie called as she looked back and laughed at him.

"Oh, don't be such a baby," Abel's voice came over the speakers. "I didn't even jostle your arm this trip."

"What the hell?" Robbie shuddered.

"This is Abel, your captain for today's flight. We'll be landing momentarily. Please secure all loose items and return to your seats," Abel cheerily replied.

"Oh, hell, no! Get me outta this thing. That Abel guy's nuts!" Robbie shouted. The whites showed in his eyes.

"Abel, stop picking on Robbie," Yuko admonished. "What you did to him was a cruel joke, and you know it."

"But it was so much fun. You should've seen his face." Abel laughed. "Looked kind of like it does now."

"Yer a real arsehole, *Captain* Abel," Robbie growled as he tightened the straps on his restraints.

Henry and Kelly shared a smile. After spending time at the base in Tokyo, they knew Abel had a wicked sense of humor and enjoyed a laugh at poor Robbie's expense.

"Better watch that, Robbie." Kelly snickered. "Abel may decide ya need another flyin' lesson."

"Oh, God, nah. Anythin' but another trip inta the fuckin' stars!" Robbie wailed.

Yuko noticed the Prime Minister and his entourage nervously glancing at Robbie and the two security men whispering among themselves.

"Robbie and Abel disagreed about who was in charge of piloting a Pod once," Yuko explained. "Abel won, and he's only giving Robbie a hard time. Eve has full control of this craft."

Tomatsu grinned and nodded while the two security men visibly relaxed. They had accompanied Tomatsu on a couple of flights in the container but were still uncomfortable using them.

The container dropped and came to rest inside a tall chain-link fence at the port. Horst was the first one out the door with Robbie hard on his heels.

"I'll go on and find a house and wait on the rest of ya ta return," Robbie advised.

"Don't you want to see the town?" Henry asked.

Robbie shook his head. "Oh, I don't mean now. I'm talkin' about when ya head back ta Adelaide. There's no way in hell I'm gettin' back in that thing if Abel's driving. He's insane, I tell ya."

"Chicken," Abel taunted from the container.

REDEMPTION

"Abel, that's enough," Yuko admonished and glared at Eve when she saw the smile flicker on her face. "Robbie, Eve piloted the craft today. Abel is only having fun at your expense."

"What? The maniac wasn't drivin' at all?" Robbie asked.

"Nope," Eve answered. "It was all me today." Then she lowered her voice and continued, "and I taught Abel everything he knows."

Robbie's face paled, and he sat on the concrete pier. "Nope, not happenin', no way. You guys go on home without me. I'll be here when ya get back."

The Japanese contingent watched Robbie's antics with concern until Lizzy walked over to him and put a hand on her hip. "Get up, ya big baby. Ya keep this up, and I swear I'll tie a dummy around yer neck and kick yer arse from Adelaide to Sydney and back if ya dare take it off."

Yuko rolled her eyes at Abel and Robbie and tried to get the conversation back on topic. "Henry, Kelly, as you can see, the port is in good repair. We've already scanned it, and it's clear of obstructions and deep enough for any ship we have on the seas now. The power station isn't far west of us, and the power lines coming to the port are in good repair."

"Doesn't look like they took much damage from the wars or weather," Henry observed.

"This side of the island didn't suffer much," Yuko advised. "The worst of it hit the southern and eastern parts. That reminds me, there are a couple of areas you need to put off-limits to the Weres."

"Why's that?" Kelly asked.

"The places where Akio eliminated the Clan are contaminated with microscopic silver particles. They wreak havoc on Were respiratory systems," Eve answered.

"That's barbaric!" Lizzy hissed.

"It's war, Lizzy. War isn't pretty, and it sure as hell isn't nice. Those Sacred Clan bastards deserve that and so much more," Horst growled, his eyes glowing a faint yellow as he thought back to Koda, bleeding in his arms after the Clan attacked her.

Lizzy ducked her head with her eyes submissively downcast at Horst's outburst.

Horst turned and stalked toward the pier without another word.

Henry noted Lizzy's reaction to Horst's uncharacteristic anger and how she and Robbie watched him warily as he walked away. Henry knew why Horst had turned Koda after she was attacked, but he wasn't sure if Lizzy knew not to push his buttons where the Clan was concerned. He made a mental note to warn her and Robbie, so neither of them unknowingly set the big Alpha off in the future with a random comment.

"I'll provide a map, and we can put warning markers around the contaminated areas," Yuko offered. "After a rainy season or two, the silver will sink into the ground and won't pose a problem as long as no one disturbs it."

"Thanks," Henry mumbled while watching Horst's stiff stance as he looked out over the harbor.

"If Horst could, he would personally eliminate the entire Sacred Clan in the bloodiest and most brutal ways he could imagine. I would gladly help him," Yuko murmured to Henry when she saw where his attention focused.

Eve talked with Jennie and Kelly for a moment, then announced, "We're going to take a look at the houses nearby. Does anyone want to come?"

Lizzy and Robbie both headed toward them, and Sato shook his head. "I need to get back to Tokyo if you don't mind, Yuko."

Yuko inclined her head. "Certainly. I can have you at the base in ten minutes."

"That would be perfect. Henry, let me know whatever you need, and the Japanese government will be happy to assist you. Once you get settled, I insist that you and the lovely Kelly come for a visit as my guests. We'll get Watabe and Kato to join us and make it a real party."

Henry brightened. "I look forward to it, Sato. I left ya a package in the container. Think of me when ya crack the seal, my friend."

"Not a bottle of that Limeburners elixir?" Sato grinned.

"Nope," Henry answered, then chuckled when he saw the look of disappointment on Sato's face. "Two of 'em."

"A true gentleman in every sense of the word." Sato beamed before he turned and followed Yuko into the craft.

Henry watched the container as it silently rose into the sky and was soon out of sight. He looked at Horst, still staring across the water, and walked over to him.

When he was close, Horst turned and nodded. "I guess I owe Lizzy an apology."

"Only if ya want ta. Lizzy knows she touched a nerve but won't say any more about it."

Horst nodded and turned back to the harbor. "This is in great shape considering how long it's been unused. It shouldn't take much to get the cranes operational once we get the power restored, and those are refrigerated warehouses on that pier. When you start harvesting produce and livestock to trade, that'll help keep it fresh longer."

"Yeah, I think this place might work for us. We'll need more folks, but Sato seems ta think he can help there," Henry mused.

"We have a good many from the larger cities who migrated to Kume in the past couple of years, and we have a booming market there," Horst informed him. "This place was a tourist stop before WWDE, too. Wouldn't be hard to get some restaurants and hotels going and cash in on that market. We have more than we can handle as it is."

"Now, all I have ta do is convince a group of stubborn Weres and an equally stubborn group of humans that this is the way ta go. God, I'm gettin' too old for this shite," Henry complained.

Horst chuckled. "Meh, you're not even a hundred and thirty. With the Pod-doc fix, you're not middle-aged yet."

"Yeah, tell me that when ya hit a hundred." Henry laughed.

Horst laughed along with him. "Been there, done that."

Henry looked at the much younger-looking man and raised his eyebrows. "No way in hell."

"I was born in Germany in nineteen thirty-nine," Horst revealed. "My mother died at the hands of Allied soldiers protecting that bastard vampire who raised my brother and me near the end of the war."

Henry's mouth fell open. "Damn, yer older than I am. Who woulda thought?"

"We have a life expectancy of several centuries with the

Pod-doc upgrades. What's a couple of years?" Horst chuckled.

"Damn, now I feel old again," Henry lamented.

"Come on, old man. Let's catch up with Kelly and see what she thinks of the housing situation." Horst clapped him on the shoulder, and they headed into the town together.

CHAPTER EIGHTEEN

Adelaide, Australia, WWDE+71

"Kent, give it a rest. You've looked for them for almost half a damned century. They're gone," Aaron grumbled.

"A whole town full of people doesn't up and vanish. Those bloody wankers are somewhere, and I *will* have my revenge. Even if you don't give two shits that those mongrels killed Finn and Mitch, I still do."

Aaron shook his head and sighed. Kent's obsession with finding the Weres who had killed his brothers was a source of contention that countless arguments couldn't put to rest. He looked at the warehouse floor from his vantage point in an office a level above it.

Now, instead of crates and boxes of goods, it held disheveled forms in threadbare clothes. Human chattel sorted by age and sex occupied six pens fully enclosed by heavy wire. The containment cells bordered the field's outer edge. In the center was one large cage where two men were locked in a brutal fight to the death.

"Kent, quit sulking and enjoy the show. When the fight

finishes, I need to make a call. You can take your pick from the latest group. I know you've had your eye on the redhead who came in last week." Aaron pointed at a pen where a young woman slumped dejectedly against the wire, watching the center cage.

"I don't understand your fascination with this. Watching food fight does nothing for me, not to mention it wastes resources." Kent stabbed his index finger at the spectacle below.

Aaron shrugged. "I take my fun where I can find it. Waiting and keeping a low profile gets boring after a decade or so."

Kent growled, "I don't understand why the hell you go along with this grand plan that bloody Yank came up with. If he wants to kill those fuckers, I say let him do it. We don't need to be a part of it."

"Smith has a plan not only to kill the vampire, Akio but to deal with that damned American Marine and the force he uses to hunt us down. As long as we stay off their radar until then, there will be no one who can stop us. Then we'll rule the planet," Aaron assured him.

Kent scoffed. "All I want to do is find the people who killed Mitch and Finn. Go and make your call. I'm going to grab that snack you suggested and see if she tastes as sweet as I imagine."

"Try not to kill her. I want to have a girl match soon, and I like to watch gingers fight." Aaron grinned, flashing a bit of fang.

The Palace, Tokyo, Japan

"Got you!" Takumi exclaimed triumphantly.

For the past month, he'd scanned every known frequency searching for the one the Forsaken were using to relay information around the globe. He'd intercepted three encoded transmissions in the last month and directed his limited satellite assets to monitor each one.

The reduced number of working satellites combined with the precautions the vampires took to remain hidden had resulted in it taking several weeks to obtain the needed proof of a Forsaken presence in two separate locations. The data on the last was inconclusive, but based on similarities to the other two, Takumi was seventy-six percent certain that a Forsaken was there as well.

Eve, Takumi called.

Yes, Takumi?

I've isolated the frequency the Forsaken communications system is currently operating on. I've confirmed two locations using satellite imagery. Data on a third is inconclusive at this time, but there is enough to indicate a Forsaken is in the area.

That's excellent news, Takumi. Akio will be pleased. Continue to collect the data and keep me informed of your findings.

Acknowledged. Takumi cut the connection.

Eve smiled as she reached out. *Akio.*

Yes, Eve?

Takumi has isolated the communications network the Forsaken are using and confirmed two locations. How do you wish to proceed?

Akio considered his response for a moment. The Forsaken had been a menace to humanity for many years. Their ability to go underground for decades, only to resurface in a different location, made containing them difficult at best.

He grimaced, knowing how he had to proceed, although he found it distasteful.

Eve, continue to gather the intelligence. If I go after them one at a time, the others will hide and appear in a different location later as soon as they get the word. We need to remove the threat that Smith and his network pose once and for all.

Won't that endanger the humans wherever the Forsaken establish themselves? Eve asked.

Hai, but we can't avoid that, Akio grudgingly admitted. *We have to hit the Forsaken in a coordinated strike, or they'll slip away. They don't know we've found them, and any we miss now will only be harder to locate in the future. It's not how I wish to do this, but it's the only way to end the threat.*

Understood, Eve replied. *I'll continue to monitor Takumi's progress and keep you informed.*

Domo. Akio's thoughts turned to his next call. The person he needed to talk to wouldn't be happy about waiting to go after the Forsaken after his recent experiences with Smith, but it was unavoidable.

"Abel, please connect me to Terry Henry Walton."

CHAPTER NINETEEN

SWL Vessel *Freki*, Singapore Strait, Singapore WWDE+82

"Dieter, wake up! We have a problem," Abel called over the speaker in the captain's cabin.

"Huh? What the hell, Abel? Did you have to blast my damned eardrums out of my head?" Dieter groaned as he hauled his six-foot-six, one-hundred-two-kilo frame out of the custom bed Eve had installed to fit him. He rubbed the sleep from his eyes and ran a hand through his shoulder-length black hair as he struggled awake.

"If you didn't sleep like the dead, I wouldn't have to. Now get dressed, grab your weapons, and get to the bridge. You don't want to miss the fun." Abel switched the speakers to blast K-Pop music until the Were exited his room seconds later.

That was a dick move, Abel, Dieter growled over his implant.

Got your butt moving, didn't it?

You know, I really hate you sometimes.

No, you don't. You hate to wake up.

Dieter stormed onto the bridge of the *Freki,* still zipping his black jumpsuit with the Sea Wolf Lines patch on the arm and his name stenciled in gold across one breast and Captain on the other. He fastened a belt around his waist that had a large pistol on one side and a custom-made katana opposite it.

The watch officer snatched his feet off the console and almost fell to the deck. "Sir, is there a problem?"

"I've told you to keep your nasty boots off my console, Hiruchi. Do I need to have you scrub them like Captain Brescoff did?" Dieter growled.

The crewman's face went pale as he shook his head. "No, sir, won't happen again," he stammered, recalling when Brescoff had made him scrub every console on the bridge of the *Silver Moon* with a toothbrush.

"Report," Dieter ordered.

"Ah, um, sir, it's quiet. I haven't seen—" A blaring alarm interrupted the man as a red dot appeared on the radar monitor.

"Contact, fifteen kilometers aft and closing fast," Abel announced smugly over the speakers embedded in the ceiling. "Two airships are skimming the waves on an intercept course."

"Are the passengers all in their rooms, Hiruchi?" Dieter watched the ships close the distance on the radar.

"I, ah, I'm not sure, Captain." Hiruchi's eyes went round when Dieter's eyes flashed yellow. All of the officers aboard Sea Wolf vessels were privy to the unique nature of some crew members. Hiruchi had been around long enough to know that when a Were's eyes flashed yellow, there was a better than average chance violence would follow.

"All passengers are within the secured areas, and I've locked the outer access doors," Abel advised.

Dieter frowned, then switched to his implant. *Abel. What are you playing at? You withheld the alert until I was on the bridge. What gives?*

Hiruchi needed a lesson in staying awake while on watch. You only have three officers and fifteen crewmen to run the ship. Everyone needs to do their job.

I agree, but why not simply tell me instead of pulling a drill at this ungodly hour of the morning?

First, where's the fun in that? Second, this isn't a drill. Those contacts are genuine, and unless my sensors are failing, they're pirates.

Dieter's lips curled into a toothy grin that made Hiruchi take two steps back when his lizard brain recognized an apex predator was present. Dieter snapped his head toward the movement and forced himself to relax when he saw the fear on the crewman's face.

"Hiruchi, sound the alarm in the crew quarters. Pirates inbound. All hands to battle stations," Dieter ordered.

"Pirates? Are you sure, sir?"

Dieter closed his eyes and gritted his teeth, resisting the deep-seated urge to throw Hiruchi off his ship. Horst had warned him that some of the older hands might need time to recognize his ability to command one of the fleet's newest and most advanced ships. He'd expected trouble from his first officer, a retired Japanese navy commander, but not Hiruchi. Hiruchi had served on the *Silver Moon* while Brescoff was training Dieter to command a ship.

"Abel has confirmed it. Sound the alarm. *Now.* Abel, page Gregov to the bridge, please."

The broad-shouldered Gregov strode onto the bridge fastening his wide belt with dual pistols around his waist. "Annoying computer man already call Gregov. We have some fun, *da?*"

Dieter smiled at his childhood best friend and fellow Were. "Yep. We're going to have some fun, my friend."

"Not let Abel blast them from the air this time?" Gregov grumbled, still irritated that Abel had taken out the last pirate ship when it fired on them.

"If they shoot at my ship with a fucking cannon, I reserve the right to terminate them with extreme violence," Abel snapped.

"Akio reported the pirates are taking innocents and holding them aboard their ships, Abel," Dieter reminded the AI. "We don't want to blast them to pieces if we can avoid it. That's why Aunty Eve gave us the new weapon to play with."

"Besides, puny little cannon not scratch paint," Gregov grumbled.

"Gregov, you may be the head of security for this vessel, but I'm the ultimate authority when it comes to protecting Dieter here and Tosha on the *Geri*. I will not risk having to explain to Koda and Horst how Dieter got injured because you wanted to play Rambo. Got it?" Abel snapped.

"*Da*, Abel, I understand, but," Gregov slapped his black jumpsuit, a twin to the one Dieter wore, "Yuko kitted us in armored suits. We can use all our abilities. Suits stop anything these pirates throw at us. We are harder to hurt than puny pirates."

"Would you two give it a rest already?" Dieter groaned. "I've had to listen to you argue for the past thirty years, and it's getting old."

Gregov looked up at the camera in the corner of the bridge, smiled, and winked.

"Nope," Abel replied. "It's the little things that make life worth living."

Gregov chuckled, then looked at Dieter. "How you want to handle this?"

"If they try to board us using those antigrav sleds, Abel will take them out before they land," Dieter instructed. "If they think we're an easy mark and bring the airships down to rappel to the deck, we do it like Akio taught us."

"Here's hoping we look easy." Gregov grinned as he loosened the straps on the twin pistols on his hips.

"You're both crazy," Hiruchi wailed as he watched the radar contacts grow closer. "Let the AI take them out and get it over with."

"I told you these bastards are taking prisoners on their boats. I won't risk killing an innocent if we can help it. Just sit here safe in the heavily armored bridge and keep quiet," Dieter snarled. His anger made coarse fur sprout across his face as his teeth grew into sharp pointed fangs.

"Asleep with feet on console again?" Gregov asked, knowing it was more than Hiruchi's usual level of incompetence that had set Dieter on edge.

"*Hai.*" Dieter continued to watch the airships approach.

"One day, Dieter throw you off ship. I promise to bring popcorn and pull chair up on deck to watch show." Gregov grinned at Hiruchi and mimed heaving a large object into the air.

"They're coming into visual range now," Abel informed them as another screen came to life. This one showed the two dark, oblong shapes of the multi-deck dirigibles favored by pirates in recent years. They approached the *Freki* from the rear with their lower decks barely above the choppy waves below. If Dieter had doubted they were pirates before, the blacked-out stealth approach removed it.

"Abel, keep the defenses under wraps until the last minute," Dieter commanded. "No need to show them *Freki's* teeth before we have to."

Abel sighed. "Dieter, you know damn well I've been killing spluge gulping asshats since before you were born."

Dieter smiled. "I know, Abel. Don't take it personally."

"Looks like they're planning to board from the ships," Abel advised. "Sensors detect seven on the lead ship. Four gathered on deck, one in the pilothouse and two in the engine room."

"What about the second?" Dieter inquired.

"Nine on board," Abel informed him. "Four on the rail, one at a small gun mounted at the front, a pilot, two in the engine room, and the last is odd. It's below decks midway down the ship."

"Can you get a drone in there and see if it's a captive?" Dieter asked, excitement in his tone.

"Doubtful, but a drone is on the way," Abel answered.

"You want fore or aft?" Gregov asked.

"Aft. That looks like where the second ship's headed." Dieter watched the lead ship sink even closer to the waves and come alongside the *Freki,* trying to hide in its shadow.

"Guess I may as well get in position." Gregov twisted

his neck until it *popped* in both directions. He slipped out the door onto the deck and disappeared into the shadows.

"Hiruchi, stay at your station and act surprised when they come aboard," Dieter instructed. "You know they can't get in here, and they don't have any weapons capable of penetrating the hull or the windows. Act afraid but refuse to open the door. Gregov will take care of the rest."

Dieter opened the bridge's rear door and cut through the passageway to the door that opened onto the rear deck. The second ship held position about thirty meters from the stern.

What are they doing, Abel? Dieter asked over his implant.

I have audio from the drone. They're waiting until the lead ship initiates the attack. The plan is for the second crew to get down to the passengers and take captives to gain control of the vessel while the first group distracts our crew.

Soon as the boarders clear their ship, take out that gun. It can't hurt the Freki, *but I don't want to catch a round from it.*

Acknowledged. The first ship is almost over the deck. What do you want to do with it when Gregov engages the crew?

Take out the engine room with the railgun and bring it down on the deck. We don't want to deal with a suicidal crewman trying to blow the engine once Gregov eliminates the boarding party.

I'm on it, Abel assured him.

Dieter crouched behind an equipment locker near the superstructure and waited for the unsuspecting pirates to make their move. Less than a minute later, the ship he was tracking surged up and forward, stopping three meters over the open aft deck. The pirates crewing the rail jumped from the airship to the *Freki's* deck and landed easily even though it was a substantial height for a human.

A blood-curdling scream cut the night from the area near the bridge. Dieter heard Gregov's rumbling laugh and knew he'd engaged his targets.

Light it up, Abel, Dieter ordered as he pulled his pistol from his belt.

Weapons engaged. Stand by, Abel advised.

Two square hatches opened over the bridge, and a short-barreled electromagnetic railgun rose from each. The guns swiveled, one facing fore and the other aft, lining up on the two pirate craft. The front gun fired, and a swarm of hypervelocity projectiles blasted through the thin hull of the pirate ship, shredding everything in their path. The gun swiveled and more rounds tore through the flotation bladder, releasing the gas that kept the vessel afloat. Seconds later, the disabled ship dropped to the foredeck with a *crash* as windows and the gondola's light wood shattered.

The second gun fired simultaneously, eliminating the gun, the person manning it, and a significant portion of the front of the gondola on the rear dirigible.

Targets neutralized. The score is now Abel two, Dieter zero, Abel taunted.

Not for long, buddy. Keep an eye on that ship. Go ahead and take out the engine when you want. You're clear to deploy Eve's latest creation.

Abel snickered. *Make me proud. So you know, I alerted Horst, Akio, Eve, and Tosha of our situation. They're all watching now.*

Dieter growled, *Damn you, Abel. I swear I'm going to request Eve to assign Takumi to handle the* Freki.

That's not happening, my furry padawan. Takumi has his plate full with the Palace complexes and the transportation system. You're stuck with me.

Dieter shook his head and moved into position to intercept the closest pirate. The knowledge that he had an audience checked his desire to jump in and rip them all to shreds.

CHAPTER TWENTY

TQB Base, Tokyo, Japan

Akio studied the satellite footage from selected locations around the globe. They'd lost coverage in many areas
over the last few decades and had tasked the few satellites
Bethany Anne had left in place with taking up the slack.
Now it took months instead of weeks for information
about activities outside the Asian sector to reach Akio.

"Akio, I'm bringing Horst, Eve, and Tosha into a group
chat," Abel advised him as three windows opened in the
top corner of the bank of monitors in front of his console.

The windows came to life one at a time. First on was
Eve. Her tag showed that she was at the underground base
in Nagoya. She'd built it after some members of the
Japanese military tried to hack into the Tokyo base two
decades before. Akio's ability to manipulate minds had
fixed that issue, but Eve wasn't willing to take chances on
having only one secure location.

Horst was the next to appear from his home office on
Kume Island.

Finally, Tosha's screen came online, showing a gorgeous blonde-haired young woman. She sported an impressive case of bed head and wore an oversized t-shirt with a popular children's cartoon character on the front.

"Hi everybody," Tosha greeted the others, then growled, "What did you want, Abel?"

"Good morning, sunshine," Abel chirped cheerily, earning a yellow-tinted glare from the Were.

Horst laughed. "Still not a morning person, princess?"

"Not when it's the middle of the night after dealing with those *Gott Verdammt* Russian Weres in Vladivostok all day. I swear, if Petrov looks at my ass like it's a snack one more time, I'm going to shoot him. We don't need their oil that bad."

"No, we don't, but the Japanese Navy does, and they help keep the pirates and other evils at bay. I'll have Dieter handle that run from now on if Petrov is a problem," Eve advised her.

Horst growled. "Or I'll visit and have a little father-to-idiot chat with him."

Akio's lips quirked as he contacted Abel over his implant. *Abel, put Vladivostok on the itinerary as soon as it's feasible.*

Gladly. Do you want to do it before the upcoming missions?

No, after will be soon enough. Make sure it's before Tosha's next scheduled run.

Done.

"I contacted you because the *Freki* is under attack by two pirate airships off the coast of Singapore. I thought you'd like to watch," Abel answered Tosha's earlier question.

"Do I have time to get popcorn?" Tosha snickered.

"Sure, they're still a few minutes from being in position," Abel answered.

Tosha rolled out of bed and disappeared from the monitor. "Back in a flash."

"Pull your shirt down, so you don't flash *us* when you come back, young lady," Koda admonished when she stepped up behind Horst and rested her cheek against his.

"I'm sorry, I didn't mean to wake you, my tiny beauty," Horst apologized as he stroked Koda's hair with one hand.

"It's okay. I know you only get out of bed this early if it's something serious or involves the children." Koda nodded at the others on the screens.

"Abel, have you told Dieter that he has an audience?" Eve inquired.

"Not yet. I'm waiting until he's ready to engage, Dieter's already angry, and I figured he needs the knowledge that you're watching to keep him from going into berserker mode on the idiots."

"Why's he pissed?" Tosha asked as she came back into view with a bag of popcorn in her lap.

"Hiruchi was sleeping on watch again," Abel answered.

Tosha snorted. "Did Dieter throw him off the ship like he threatened last time?"

Abel snickered. "Not yet, but the night's not over."

"Eve, this is multiple chances for Hiruchi since we assigned him to the *Freki*. I want him gone. I won't have a lazy employee endangering the passengers and crew on one of our ships," Horst coldly stated.

"Agreed. Akio, would you mind taking care of this

when the ship makes port in Kume the day after tomorrow?" Eve requested.

"I will meet it there and take care of former crewman Hiruchi's memories of the company's connection to the UnknownWorld," Akio agreed.

"The first ship is almost in position," Abel advised as the center monitor in front of Akio showed the image of an airship floating over the deck of the *Freki*.

Akio's eyes narrowed when four pirates leapt over the rail and landed effortlessly on the deck three meters below. Before he could mention it, a blur shot out of the shadows, and the pirate on the left went down with a gurgling scream.

The blur darted back into the shadows before the other three pirates had a chance to figure out what had occurred.

SWL Vessel *Freki*, Singapore Straight, Singapore

"What the hell?" one of the pirates shouted.

"Something got Jung. Eyes open, boys. We're not alone," another replied.

"Wrong ship, *cpakas*," a menacing voice rumbled from the darkness.

"Come out and drop your weapons, and we might let you live," the mouthy pirate taunted.

"*Nyet*. You drop weapons, pirate scum, and I promise to kill you quickly," Gregov growled.

The center pirate fired six shots from his pistol toward the voice. Gregov grunted when a blunt force punched him in the side. The nanocytes in his armor reacted instantly to the hit and hardened, spreading the impact across a larger area to prevent it from penetrating the material.

Even though the bullet didn't penetrate, it still hurt like hell. Gregov drew both his pistols and fired at the pirates on either side of the shooter while he was busy reloading his gun. One's head exploded in a red mist as the hypervelocity round struck him on the bridge of his nose. The other slammed into the bridge door with a hole the size of a grapefruit in his chest.

Gregov holstered his pistols and rushed the remaining pirate, his eyes glowing yellow.

The pirate looked up and saw Gregov running toward him. He threw the useless gun at Gregov's head and stepped forward with his fists raised to meet him.

Gregov smiled at the bravado and slowed to a walk before he reached his adversary. He intended to knock him unconscious so they could interrogate him. What he didn't expect was for the man to punch him in the face hard enough to drive him to his knees.

Akio sat up straight in his chair when Gregov went to the deck. Tosha inhaled a popcorn kernel and broke into a coughing fit while Horst stared dumbfounded at the turn of events.

Gregov recovered and dropped back, kicking out his opponent's knee. His boot connected, and the pirate's knee bent out at an angle that resulted in a loud *snap*. The pirate fell to the deck, and Gregov wasted no time driving four claw-tipped fingers through the bottom of his jaw up into his brain.

Dieter, be careful. Something's off with these pirates! Gregov shouted over his implant. Above him, the railgun spun on its axis and fired two shots toward the rear of the ship.

Dieter watched from the darkness as four pirates vaulted over the second airship's rail and dropped to the *Freki's* deck. He shook his head, amazed that the four could make the jump without injury. Then the wind shifted, and his sensitive nose detected the scent of Were on the breeze. Dieter breathed deeply through his nose and picked up the smell of unwashed humans with the Were scent less intense. He determined that the pirates weren't Weres, but one had recently been around a Were.

Abel's shots dropped the gunman on the airship, and the pilot wrenched the rudder away from the *Freki,* sending the vessel over the sea. The four on deck looked up briefly then rushed to the door that led inside the ship.

Abel, stop that ship! Dieter called as he slipped through the shadows toward the pirates who were struggling in vain to open the sealed armored door. The railgun sent a swarm of rounds through the rear of the vessel, shredding everything they encountered. Smoke billowed from the gaping hole as the engine stuttered and died.

His lips twisted into a smile as a false smokestack lowered into the deck, revealing Eve's latest addition to the *Freki's* armament.

A metal shaft the size of a utility pole pivoted to aim the pointed end toward the airship.

A bright flash illuminated the deck when Abel launched the rocket-powered harpoon. The shaft sang as it shot toward the dirigible, dragging a wrist-thick steel cable behind. The metal projectile slammed through the gondola a meter behind the pilothouse and continued out the other side. Two meter-long steel barbs extended from the tip of the device, and deep inside the *Freki,* a winch powered up and started reeling the dead airship in like a whale.

The stunned pirates stood open-mouthed and overlooked Dieter until he raised his pistol and fired at the one struggling to open the door. The pirate closest to the man looked down in time to grab his mate and snatch him back as Dieter's shot shattered on the armored door where the man's face had been a second earlier.

Two of the pirates raised pistols and fired at Dieter, causing him to duck behind a metal equipment locker. More shots *pinged* off the metal as the other pirates opened fire.

"Throw out your gun, boy, and let's talk about what we're gonna do," a burly bald pirate called to him.

"How about you throw your guns down and get the hell off my ship," Dieter retorted.

"Not going to happen," the pirate sneered. "You busted our ride, so we're going to take yours. Might as well give it up, boy. We got a little bitch onboard that gives us a boost for this kind of stuff. There's no way you can beat us."

Dieter's eyes narrowed as the information the man gave him, combined with the scent of the Were earlier, came together in his mind.

"What are you talking about?" Dieter asked, needing to confirm his suspicions.

"What I said," the pirate retorted. "We have a little freak captive, and she provides us with a way to be better, faster, and stronger than three men. Save yourself a beat-down and come on out."

Dieter's eyes glowed as his anger rose. These men were like the ones who'd killed Gregov's mother and chased him through the Russian countryside when he was nine years old. Luckily, Gregov had found his way onto the *Silver Moon* when it was taking on cargo in Vladivostok while the men hunted him through goods waiting for transport from the dock.

Dieter remembered the day he'd taken the Pod with Horst to meet the ship while it was at sea between Russia and its next port. The shock of smelling another Were deep in the hold when he'd slipped away from Horst to explore the massive ship.

How he'd found the half-starved, emaciated boy cowering in a dark corner of the lowest hold on the ship. Dieter remembered how the adults had reacted when Gregov told the story about how criminals had hunted his pack to extinction for their blood. How Koda had fretted and worried over him, Tosha, and Gregov, how Horst and Koda had taken him in as their own.

The memories crashed into him, and the anger took hold. He dropped his gun to the deck as his body shifted. The pirates wasted no time in rushing his hiding place when the weapon hit the deck, expecting to find him cowering there, meekly awaiting his fate.

What they found was a monster with only one thought in his mind.

Destroy the blood traders.

"What the hell was that?" Tosha exclaimed once she'd cleared the popcorn from her airway. "How did a normal put Gregov on his ass like that?"

"Abel, show us Dieter," Akio commanded, and the image switched to the back of the ship in time to see two bodies explode in a violent spray of blood and body parts as the railgun darts impacted them.

Dieter had shifted into a hulking two-and-a-half-meter tall Pricolici and had one pirate suspended by his throat and the other face-down on the deck, pinning him with a foot between his shoulder blades.

He pulled the man he held close to his face and looked deep into the eyes bugging out of the purple face. "Youss dare call usss freaksss? You'rrre the monstersss of this tale," Dieter growled as his muscles bulged, and he tightened his grip on the man's throat.

His lips pulled back in a toothy grin as his hapless victim's face turned darker and the capillaries in his eyes burst. Dieter held the limp corpse for a moment before dropping it on the bald pirate pinned under his heel.

The man screamed when the lifeless body landed on him and the dead eyes stared accusingly at him. Dieter reached down and hooked his claws into the collar of the heavy jacket the man wore. He snatched the pirate off the deck as Gregov rushed across the top of the bridge and jumped down.

"What you have there, Dieter?" Gregov asked as he took in the scene.

"Blood trader," Dieter snarled as he hurled his captive to the deck at Gregov's feet.

Gregov's eyes glowed yellow and black claws extended

from his hand. He bent over the terrified pirate and pushed a claw into the tender skin under his chin.

The pirate shrieked in fear and pain as Gregov's claw pierced his skin. Blood flowed down his neck.

"Don't kill him, Gregov," Abel announced over speakers mounted on the deck. "Akio's on his way to *speak* to him. ETA is twenty minutes."

Gregov nodded and released the pressure on the man's neck. He stood and brought his boot down in a vicious kick to his midsection and growled, "You better hope Akio kills you when done. If not, I'll enjoy every scream as I break you one piece at a time."

Dieter stood and watched as Abel winched the airship closer to the deck. A rifle barrel extended over the rail pointed toward him. Before he could react, the aft railgun fired a torrent of darts. The structure and the body behind it exploded in a shower of blood and wood fragments.

"All hostiles neutralized," Abel announced.

Dieter shifted back to human form as the airship slowly descended. He took two running steps and caught the heavy cable connected to the harpoon, then hauled himself up hand over hand. When he reached the ship, he swung on the line and flipped up to the open deck through the hole Abel had blown in the railing.

He crashed through the pilothouse door and continued to the door that opened onto the cabins on that level. He breathed in through his nose and caught the faint scent of a Were inside.

An open hatch with a ladder led down into the small cargo area of the vessel, where the smell was stronger. Dieter dropped through the hatch and froze when he saw a pale, emaciated body with an unruly mop of dark hair covering its face. The Were lay strapped to a heavy table with tubes running from one tied-down arm to a machine, then to a container fixed to the side of the table.

The coppery smell of blood permeated the room. Dieter's lip curled in anger as he crossed to the unmoving body. He looked down and saw that the Were's bare wrist and ankles were covered with bloody oozing blisters.

He reached for the chain locked around one ankle and recoiled with a hiss when the silver chain burned his fingers. The movement caused the chain to shift, and the figure on the table moaned weakly. Dieter cast around the room for anything he could use to break the chains, and something shiny on the wall caught his eye.

A silver ring with a brass key hung from a nail near the door. Dieter crossed the room in one leap and snatched the key off its peg. His fingers burned as the silver reacted to his body. He ground his teeth against the pain, shoved the key into the lock, and twisted.

The lock popped open, and Dieter worked his way around the table, removing the Were's restraints. When the last lock was free, he scooped the unconscious body into his arms and headed for the hatch that led to the top deck.

He shifted the Were to one shoulder and carefully climbed the ladder one-handed. At the top, he moved his precious burden from his shoulder and held the Were against his chest as he stalked through the pilothouse out of the broken door.

Gregov stood on the *Freki* with the pirate prone on the deck and his foot pressed between the man's shoulders. He looked up as Dieter carried the Were to the rail, and his eyes narrowed and flashed yellow.

Dieter sized up the distance and nodded before jumping through the busted airship rail to the deck below. He landed with a grunt and took two steps to steady himself.

"Abel, open the door. Be sure the path to medical is clear and have Doc meet me there," Dieter ordered as he strode toward the armored entry to the ship. He didn't slow his pace. The door slid open silently as he approached.

The elevator door opened as he approached it, and seconds later, Dieter stepped out into the corridor that housed the medical bay. A man in a white coat stood in the doorway, waiting for his patient. He motioned Dieter to the hospital bed.

Dieter lowered the body to the pristine surface, and the curly mass of hair fell away from her face.

Her eyes opened, and Dieter froze as he looked at one almond-shaped emerald-green eye. The other was discolored and swollen partially shut. Her pert nose and cheeks showed further signs of a recent beating.

"You're safe," Dieter assured her as he looked down into the frightened face of the severely malnourished young woman. "You're in the medical section onboard my ship, and the people who did this to you won't hurt anyone ever again."

A tear leaked down her cheek. She stiffened when the doctor lifted her arm and wiped an alcohol prep over the veins at the crook of her arm.

"It's okay," Dieter told her in a soft, calm tone. "Doctor

Song is here to help you. He has to replace the fluids in your body so you can heal. He won't do anything to harm you."

He stepped back so the doctor could work, but the young woman's hand closed on his wrist in a vicelike grip.

He smiled at her and covered her hand with his. "I'll stay if you like."

The woman nodded once and closed her eyes as she slipped into unconsciousness.

CHAPTER TWENTY-ONE

Sunset House, Kume Island, Japan

"Settle down, Koda. Let the people do their jobs," Horst chided as Koda started for the kitchen for the third time in fifteen minutes.

Koda swiped a lock of hair out of her face with one hand and pointed at the restaurant's front door. "People are arriving soon, and they don't have the drinks or *zensai* out yet."

"If you keep disturbing them, it will only take longer, my tiny beauty." Horst smiled.

Koda drew a deep breath and let it out slowly. "I know I'm acting foolishly, but this is the first time we've had everyone here in years. I want it to be perfect."

Horst smiled. "It would be perfect even if you hadn't brought in additional staff and put together a menu of delicacies from all over Asia. Having most of our close friends and family gathered in one place is special enough without any of the trouble you've gone to."

The double doors leading from the kitchen opened, and

the staff pushed out four rolling carts loaded with food and drinks.

"See, they're setting up the tables now. Everything will be fine." Horst motioned with his head.

The restaurant doors burst open, and a red-faced blonde woman wearing a black jumpsuit with gold piping across the shoulders and down each leg stalked through them.

"Where are my blockheaded brothers?" she demanded when she saw Horst and Koda staring at her.

"Hello, Tosha. Why I'm fine, thank you, and how are you?" Horst replied with a cheery lilt in his tone.

Tosha froze midstep when she saw that his grim visage didn't match the tone.

"I'm sorry, Father. Hello Mother, you look lovely. Now could one of you please point me in the direction of Dieter and Gregov?" Tosha scowled. "I would like to speak to them."

Horst snorted. Koda chuckled, then asked, "Are they still ignoring your calls, dear?"

"Yes. Both of them have ignored me for the past week," Tosha complained. "I checked the *Freki* before I came here, and none of the crew knew or would tell me where they are. Abel just laughs and refuses to answer anything I ask him about them, the traitor."

Sticks and stones, Abel sang over all their implants.

Tosha growled. "Quit eavesdropping, Abel. I told you you're in the brig until you stop being a traitorous ass."

Horst shook his head and chuckled at the outburst. Tosha's personality was so much like her deceased Uncle Dieter's that it was frightening at times. Her teenage years had given Horst more than a few gray hairs. When she got her implant at sixteen and could plot with Abel, her favorite partner in mischief and mayhem, things had gotten very interesting.

Koda pursed her lips and stared at her headstrong child. "Tosha, you know your brothers will continue to avoid you as long as you're acting like this. They've done it since you were twelve."

Tosha folded her arms and scowled. "If they would listen to me to begin with, I wouldn't have to yell at them so often for being reckless and stupid."

Koda looked at Horst, who was leaning against a chair back, shaking with barely contained laughter. He pointed at Tosha and mouthed, "Yours," earning a serious blast of stinkeye from Koda.

A snorted laugh from the open doors caused all of them to turn. A tall, heavily muscled Chinese man wearing a uniform similar to Tosha's stood there with a big grin on his face.

"Lei, how are you, boy?" Horst boomed as he motioned for the man to enter.

"I'm fine, sir. I see you already know how the love of my life is." He snickered.

Tosha whirled on him and pointed. "You can damn well join that traitorous AI in the brig if you keep on."

Horst ignored the outburst. "Interesting week?"

Lei held his hand out palm down and waggled it back and forth. "Some days bad, other days worse. You know how it is."

Horst bit his lower lip and nodded. "Since she started adolescence."

"Mother! Make them stop," Tosha yelled.

"You're the one who needs to stop," Koda admonished. "Your brother told me how you berated him for taking on those pirates. You know the chances of one having the means to injure Dieter or Gregov is slim at best, but you continued to chastise both of them. After they both asked you nicely to stop, I might add."

Tosha sniffed, fighting back her tears. "The *Freki* could've outrun those ships without them risking anything. They didn't have to let those, those blood leeches, on the ship. That was reckless. The fiends could've captured them."

Horst and Koda exchanged a look, understanding then why the young woman was reacting so badly.

"This is my doing," Koda admitted with a frown. "I regret I ever heard about the blood trade when you were small and became obsessed that someone would try to take you. I had gotten over it by the time Gregov came to us, but what happened to him sent me back to that place in my mind. I was overprotective and smothered all of you until Horst and Akio put a stop to it. By then, you'd developed a paranoia about you or your brothers falling victim.

"We thought you were past it after Akio trained you to fight. When Abel showed you the video he took of Akio eliminating the traders who chased Gregov, we believed you'd overcome that fear. It appears this incident brought it back."

"Tosh-*chan*, until you heard they were involved in the blood trade, you were enjoying the show. You didn't doubt Dieter and Gregov would defeat them. If I recall, you went for popcorn," Horst reminded her.

Tosha dropped her head, and her shoulders slumped. "I…no. I, ah…"

"If Dieter hadn't decided to engage them, that young woman would still be their captive, or from what the doctor said, most likely dead," Horst added gently. "Would that have been an acceptable outcome?"

Lei walked over and pulled her into his arms. "I know the stories about blood traders frighten you. Hell, they scare me, and I've never been affected by it as you all have. Gregov told me how he came to live with you years ago, and I had nightmares for a week."

He stroked her loose blonde curls while he held her. "It's okay, my love. Dieter and Gregov captured one pirate, and we all know how Akio deals with people who prey on innocents. I'm sure he'll show you whatever video he has once he runs them down."

Tosha sniffed as her tears soaked Lei's chest. "I've had a picture of Dieter and Gregov in their hands in my mind since that night. I don't know what I would do if the blood traders had taken them."

We would have had them back within the hour, Abel assured her. *Eve, Takumi, and I know where every one of you is at all times. As long as you have your implants, you're never alone or far from help. Besides, Dieter and Gregov are some serious ass-kickers. Remember who was running the Freki's guns. No way in hell would those nutsack-sniffing pirates have made it past me. I'm just that freakin' awesome.*

Tosha nodded, knowing that Dieter and Gregov were never in danger of being taken captive. She'd known this deep down, but the blood traders were the childhood boogeymen that kept her awake at night. Logic didn't figure into her thought process.

Her face paled, and she pulled back and looked into Lei's eyes. "I'm so sorry. I've been horrible to you the past few days. Will you ever forgive me?"

"There's nothing to forgive," Lei assured her. "I'm the one who should apologize. I should have remembered your fear of blood traders from when we were younger. I could have explained it to Dieter and Gregov instead of giving you grief for yelling at them."

"I'll ask Akio to let you know as soon as he's dealt with the source. I spoke to Yuko, and she informed me that the people responsible for that young woman being there are high on his list," Horst assured her.

Tosha looked at Horst and smiled, then her face darkened. "Why isn't this at the top of his list? The people who do this are abominations, ghouls, an insult to everything decent and good. Akio should have already exterminated them with extreme prejudice. No mercy and no quarter offered," she snarled.

"He's dealing with a Forsaken problem right now that spans the globe," Horst explained. "He enlisted the help of Terry Henry Walton and the FDG to get it under control as fast as possible, but it requires careful planning and coordination. Soon as he's dealt with that, he'll go after the blood hunters with a vengeance."

Tosha nodded and walked over to the table the staff had set up. She snatched up a bottle of whisky and twisted off the top. Horst shook his head slightly at Koda's raised eyebrow and open mouth when Tosha turned up the bottle and downed a quarter of it in one gulp.

"So Lei, will Qin and Tian be joining us today?" Koda asked.

Lei smiled as he shook his head. "No, Mother is starring in and directing the newest show at the theater. It opens this weekend, and she's not happy with the performance of some of the younger cast members. She has them doing full dress rehearsals twice a day until they meet her standards."

Horst chuckled. "I suppose Qin has found some pressing matter he needs to work out with Delan and Yimu at one of the remote properties."

"He's dealing with an issue, but it's closer to home. One of the recent migrants from China turned out to be a problem. He chafed under my father's rules and fell in with a criminal gang in Osaka. Akio is busy, so Dad and Delan are going to deal with him."

Horst grimaced. "They never seem to learn. We had a wolf from the Russian pack in Taiwan come here a few months ago. It wasn't long before his temper started causing problems with the locals, and he injured one badly. He won't cause any more trouble."

Lei returned the hard expression. "Neither will the one in Osaka when they find him. The human criminals won't pose a danger any longer either if I know Dad and Delan."

"Unfortunately, that's all that works with some people," Horst agreed.

A quiet conversation near the front doors alerted Horst that Dieter and Gregov had arrived. When they didn't enter, he motioned to Koda to distract Tosha while he went to see what the delay was.

"I'm not sure. I don't feel right intruding on your family gathering," Horst heard a female voice murmur.

"No need to worry, Sasha. We saved you, and now you're family, too," Gregov assured her.

"I think your sister will say otherwise," Sasha countered.

"Tosha? Don't worry about her. Her bark is much worse than her bite. She'll love you. You'll see," Dieter stated confidently.

Horst opened the door and glimpsed curly dark hair in the space between the broad backs of Dieter and Gregov.

Horst clapped a hand on each man's shoulder. "Boys, why don't you invite your friend inside? Your mother is dying to meet her."

Both Weres turned as one and crashed into Horst in a big group hug. They'd only arrived a short time before the *Geri* and had laid low in town until Tosha was with their parents. Both men knew from experience that Koda was the best one to have around to keep things from getting too violent when Tosha was in one of her moods.

"Dad! It's good to see you," Dieter exclaimed.

Gregov pulled back and made a production of checking Horst over from head to toe. He cocked his head and continued to look until Horst noticed.

"What?" Horst asked.

"From what Mom said, I expected you to have visible signs from your latest...adventure." Gregov feigned innocence.

"I don't want to talk about it," Horst grumbled.

"Is it true that Aunty Eve made you tread water for six hours before she picked you up?" Dieter snorted.

"I said I. Don't. Want. To. Talk. About. It! Now, where are your manners? Introduce me to this lovely young woman." Horst turned to the waifish dark-haired woman with a smile.

"Pleased to meet you, sir," she answered with downcast eyes.

Horst looked at Dieter questioningly.

She's still not comfortable around people. She spent most of the past week at sea hiding in my cabin, Dieter told him over their implants.

Horst nodded, then stepped forward, smiled, and offered her his crooked arm. "Welcome, Sasha. I'm Horst, and I have the dubious honor of calling these two manner-less heathens my sons. Please allow me to escort you inside."

The young woman hesitantly placed her hand on his arm and looked at Dieter for reassurance.

Dieter nodded and smiled. Only then did she relax and allow Horst to lead her through the doors.

Tosha looked up, and her eyes narrowed when she saw Dieter and Gregov. She slammed the bottle she still held on the table and stalked across the room until she was centimeters away from both of the hulking men.

"You!" She raised both hands, balled them into fists, and slammed them into the startled Weres' chests. The blow knocked Gregov back a half-step, and Dieter let out a *whoosh* of breath from the impact.

"You two blockheads think you can ignore me for a *week*?" Tosha screeched. "In what world do you think it's okay to have Abel block me from calling you direct and ignore me when I call the ship?"

Sasha looked at the trio with fearful eyes.

Horst chuckled and patted her hand with his as he continued to walk to where Koda and Lei stood. "Don't mind them. It's only a minor brother-sister spat. Nothing we haven't seen before, my dear. Please allow me to introduce you to my mate, Koda, and the blonde spitfire's mate, Lei. This is Sasha, the newest member of our little family."

"Pleased to meet you," Koda replied distractedly, her eyes narrowing when Tosha took another step toward her brothers with her fists clenched.

"Nice to meet you, be back in a bit," Lei offered as he hustled over to where Tosha was preparing to punch Dieter again. He wrapped his arms around her from behind, captured her wrists, and crossed her arms over her chest.

"Hi, guys. She's still a little upset at you." Lei smiled as Tosha struggled to twist out of his arms.

Gregov looked at Dieter and grinned. "Little sister, you have not been so mad since maybe time we threw rotten eggs into sixteenth birthday party campout on Jeju."

Dieter leaned in and sniffed loudly. "No, I think it was worse then. She doesn't smell like a two-week-old egg now."

Tosha's eyes blazed yellow, and she let out a low growl as she doubled her attempts to escape the prison of Lei's arms.

"You two idiots keep it up, and I'll turn her loose," Lei grunted as he narrowly dodged the heel of her boot before it smashed the top of his foot.

"Pardon me," Koda apologized to Sasha as she headed toward the pending brawl.

Koda stepped between Tosha and the boys and held up her hands. "Dieter, Gregov, stop tormenting your sister. Tosha, stop beating your brothers. Lei, uh, keep doing what you're doing."

She glared at each sibling in turn, then nodded, satisfied that she had their attention. "If you're going to fight, take it outside. If you damage my party decorations, all of you will answer to me. Is that understood?"

Tosha, Dieter, and Gregov all dropped their heads and murmured, "Yes, Mother."

Koda turned on her heel with an audible sniff and walked back to where Horst stood watching with an amused look on his face. Sasha watched the diminutive woman with a combination of awe and wariness.

"That's how you deal with *that*. Now, where were we, dear?" Koda smiled at the wide-eyed young Were.

CHAPTER TWENTY-TWO

Adelaide, Australia

Aaron looked over the floor of his makeshift arena with a scowl. His current crop of potential entertainment was bland and uninteresting at best. Another round of disease had wiped out his easily accessible supply of humans and depleted the captives he held.

With Kent still scouring the land for any word of where the previous occupants of Adelaide had fled, Aaron was running short of combatants for his twisted games. He had to procure the humans himself.

His current crop contained a youngster barely out of his teens, a grizzled gray-haired man, and a woman so traumatized by Aaron feeding on her that she was in a catatonic state. None of these appealed to Aaron for food or sport. Years ago, he would have drained and killed all of them, but now they were the best he'd found on his forays into the bush.

"Aren't you tired of playing with your food yet, Aaron?" Kent chided as he stepped into the converted office.

"Let an old man enjoy what entertainment he can." Aaron frowned as he looked over his captives and added, "What little this sorry bunch can provide."

Kent shrugged. "You could always help me hunt those Weres. I've located a few settlements that the disease didn't touch along the Central Coast. The hunting's good there with plenty of choices."

"You could bring some back for me," Aaron retorted.

Kent shook his head and groaned. "You've gotten lazy, Aaron. All this sitting on your arse waiting for Smith to do whatever the hell it is he's doing. You should go back to the bunker. There are several groups of healthy humans nearby, and it's not so damned hot there."

Aaron was about to answer when an explosion rattled the blacked-out windows along one wall.

Kent turned when the outer wall exploded in a second blast, sending brick and metal shrapnel across the warehouse.

As the dust cleared, bright beams of sunlight pierced the gloom forcing the vampires to retreat to the shadows to avoid the deadly rays.

Kent squinted against the glare when movement near the opening caught his eye. An armed man peered into the warehouse from the ragged hole. Seconds later, four more followed him through the breach with their rifles raised, searching the area for targets.

"Keep your eyes peeled, men. I think this is the place." One of them motioned with his rifle toward the cages.

"Contact! Twelve o'clock," another yelled as he opened fire on the small room where Kent and Aaron were sheltering.

A steady hail of bullets pounded into the room, catching both vampires by surprise. Aaron reeled against the wall as the shots found their mark. In seconds, he'd lost so much blood that he was unable to remain upright.

Aaron slid to the floor under the withering fire, and Kent knew it was only a matter of time before these humans turned their guns on him. Though gunshot wounds wouldn't usually kill a vampire, losing blood from multiple hits would weaken him to the point where he couldn't defend himself.

Kent's eyes darted around the room, looking for an escape route. There was an opening into the sewers beneath the city on the west end of the building. Unfortunately for Kent, a bright shaft of sunlight bisected the warehouse, blocking the way.

Out of options, Kent covered his head with his arms and burst through the shattered windows in an attempt to jump through the deadly beam.

He'd almost cleared the space when a barrage of bullets knocked him to the hard concrete floor. Three others opened fire on him, the rapid rifle fire echoing in the warehouse with a deafening roar.

Kent found himself lying in a pool of dark blood that smoked in the bright sun. His senses exploded with pain as his mind registered the damage the sun was doing to his exposed flesh. Too weak from blood loss to move, the few seconds it took for his body to burst into flames felt like an eternity.

The last thought that went through his mind was that he'd failed to avenge his brothers.

"You two, check the office. Cut off the vamps' heads,

then drag everything into the sun while we get these people out of those cages."

Minutes later, the FDG team took to the air, headed to the next Forsaken on their list to eliminate.

CHAPTER TWENTY-THREE

Sunset House, Kume Island, Japan

"How are you feeling, Sasha?" Koda inquired. "If their
shenanigans disturb you, I will put a stop to it. They fight
among themselves all the time, but they do love each other
very much. I can see that you're uncomfortable and want
you to know that you're safe and among friends here."

Koda tilted her head to the side as she studied the
woman alternating between smoothing her clothing and
rubbing her forearms.

Sasha dipped her head, avoiding eye contact. Koda
waited patiently for her to speak, but her eyes were locked
on Dieter when her head came up.

Koda raised one eyebrow and glanced at Dieter,
Gregov, and Tosha, who were engaged in a tense—albeit
much quieter—conversation. Dieter stopped in mid-
sentence, and his eyes snapped up and fixed on Sasha. He
stepped around Tosha without a glance and hurried across
the open room to pull Sasha to his side.

Tosha turned to follow him, her face contorted in

anger. Lei held her back as Gregov put a hand on her arm. When she rounded on them, Gregov shook his head, then nodded at Sasha.

The young woman had tucked her body under Dieter's arm and clung tightly to him.

Tosha's eyes widened in horror when she saw the physical and emotional state of the damaged young Were. Her face was ashen, and her too-thin body was trembling under the blue ship suit she wore. Angry red scars circled both wrists, and her eyes had a haunted look that faded but didn't disappear when Dieter pulled her tight against his body.

"She had a rough time with those leech bastards," Gregov murmured. "They kept her chained with silver for a month and alternated between beating her and draining her. It damned near killed her."

Tosha groaned. "I can't imagine what she went through. She's so afraid, and I've been a complete bitch since she walked in."

Gregov grinned and opened his mouth, only to be cut off by Lei before he could speak.

"Say it, and I'll turn her loose, then swear you started it and earned whatever ass-kicking she gives you."

Tosha's gaze snapped back to Gregov. "Got something you want to say, brother?" She smiled sweetly, and her eyes glowed yellow.

"*Nyet*," Gregov answered warily as he took a hesitant step back and dropped his hand to cover his groin.

Tosha twisted her arm and freed one hand from Lei's grip. She reached up and patted Gregov's cheek and smiled. "Didn't think so."

Lei barked out a laugh as Tosha took his hand in hers and headed across the room. When she approached, the dark-haired young woman ducked her head tighter against Dieter's chest.

Tosha's chest tightened when she saw the effect her presence had on Sasha. After all she'd been through, the last thing she'd needed was for Tosha to cause her more anguish.

"I'm sorry I've acted so horribly," Tosha said softly. "What you went through was terrible, and I hope you can forgive me."

Sasha stiffened against Dieter when Tosha came close. He raised his free hand and gently stroked her hair. "It's okay, Sasha. Tosh-*chan* growls and snarls a lot, but she has a good heart. She was afraid for Gregov and me, and we're partly to blame for her behavior. If either of us had stopped a minute to think, we'd have handled this differently."

Sasha looked up, and Tosha offered her hand and smiled warmly. "Hi, I'm Tosha. Rumor has it I can be a bitch at times."

Dieter snorted a laugh. "At *times*?"

His laughter died under Tosha's withering glare and a raised eyebrow from Koda.

Tosha rolled her eyes. "I'm glad my brothers rescued you from those pirates. Please don't think my actions had anything to do with you. It's no excuse, but what happened to you is something that's given me nightmares since I was a small child. The thought of my brothers being so near that danger affected me badly. I'm sorry for making you feel uncomfortable, and I hope you will forgive me."

Sasha relaxed as Tosha spoke and, by the time she finished, she had released her crushing grip around Dieter's waist. She reached out and took Tosha's offered hand. "Thank you. I'm Denikina Aleksandra Yakovna, Sasha to my friends."

Tosha felt the tightness in her chest release as the young Were gave her a hesitant smile. "We're going to be great friends, Sasha."

"I told you." Dieter smiled at Sasha. "Her bark is much worse than her bite."

"If you ever ignore my calls again, I'll allow you to test that theory, brother dear." Tosha grinned and snapped her teeth.

Dieter raised his free hand and opened his eyes wide in mock terror, causing the onlookers to burst out laughing.

"Did ya go and start the fuckin' party without us?" Kelly O'Donnell grinned as she stepped through the door with Henry Smythe. "Fuckin' rude, if ya ask me."

"I've told you to watch your language in front of my children," Koda snapped, then broke into a huge grin and went over to embrace Kelly.

Kelly laughed. "Hiya, Koda. Good ta see you. Yeah, still workin' on that language thing."

"We didn't think you were coming. How did you get here?" Koda asked.

"I wouldn't let them miss this for the world," Eve answered as she walked through the door, followed by Yuko.

"Auntie Eve! Aunt Yuko!" Tosha shrieked as she rushed across the room, dropped to her knees, and slammed into Eve's metal body to engulf her in a hug.

Eve returned the hug. "Hello Tosha, good to see you."

"When can I bring the *Geri* to port for my weapons upgrades?" Tosha asked breathlessly. "I want one of those pirate harpoons. That was freaking *awesome*."

Eve grinned. "You have a week in the yard scheduled when you return to Tokyo starting Friday. I have a few other toys on the menu I think you'll like too."

Tosha chuckled. "I can't wait to see what you have for me! I can't have the *Freki* better armed than my baby."

"Hey, what's she getting, Auntie Eve?" Dieter asked. "You know I love to play with your toys."

"Nothing you don't already have," Eve answered quickly to head off a bout of sibling rivalry.

Yuko approached Dieter, and he looked at her expectantly. She nodded and patted the pocket of her tunic with a smile.

He threw his arms around her and hugged her tightly. "Thank you, Aunt Yuko."

"After the party," she told him softly.

He nodded and pulled Sasha forward. "Sasha, I'd like you to meet Yuko. She holds the official title of Vicereine for Queen Bethany Anne, but she has the family title of Aunt Yuko. Tosha and I spent almost as much time under her feet in Tokyo when we were small as we did here on Kume."

Yuko nodded. "It's nice to meet you, Sasha."

"You, too," Sasha answered shyly.

"And this amazing person is Eve. She designed my ship and the weapon we used to bring the airship down." Dieter grinned at Eve.

"Uh, I, thank you," Sasha stammered, unsure what to think of the short metal woman.

"Nice to finally meet you, and you're welcome." Eve smiled.

"Hello, Yuko," Horst called as he joined the group.

"Hi, Horst." Yuko looked him up and down and smirked.

"Don't you start on me, too," Horst grumbled. "I already told the kids I don't want to talk about it, and the same holds for you."

"If you say so." Yuko chuckled and nodded at Eve.

Horst gave them both the stinkeye then turned his attention to Sasha. "My dear, if I can tear you away from my son, there are some people who would like to meet you." Horst nodded at Kelly and Henry as he spoke.

Sasha clung nervously to Dieter, uncomfortable at the prospect of him not being near.

"I'm not going anywhere," Dieter assured her. "I'll be right here with Yuko, and Gregov's already over there. It's safe. No one is going to allow anything or anyone to hurt you here. They're good people and just want you to feel welcome and get to know you better."

Horst offered her his arm, and Sasha hesitantly took it. She allowed him to lead her the four-meter distance and only looked back twice to ensure that Dieter was still there.

Yuko's heart ached as she watched the young woman battle her fears. "It's going to take her some time to recover from what she went through."

"I know." Dieter's voice was rough with emotion. "She panicked every time I tried to leave the med bay her first two days on the ship. When Doc released her, she begged me to stay with her. I finally put her in my cabin and sat in a chair by the bed while she slept. Whenever I dozed off and let go of her hand, she woke up in a panic."

"She's going to need help. Be patient with her, and don't push her to get past it too soon," Yuko cautioned.

"I will do whatever she needs for as long as it takes. She's worth it," Dieter assured her.

Yuko patted his arm. "I know you will. You have your mother's heart. If you need anything else from me, don't hesitate to ask."

"Could you use the Pod-doc to help her recover faster?" Dieter asked excitedly.

Yuko shook her head with regret. "The Pod-doc can fix almost any injury, and it can repair nanocytes, but it won't do anything to cure an emotional issue. Only time, kindness, and understanding can fix that."

Dieter nodded then asked, "Will Akio be joining us tonight? He wouldn't tell me what he found out from that stinking pirate scum."

"I'm sure he has his reasons. I spoke to him an hour ago. He will join us when the Forsaken mission is complete." Yuko nodded at the young woman who was fidgeting and looking around the room like she needed to run. "Sasha is feeling uncomfortable. Let's join them."

Yuko smiled warmly at Sasha when they approached where she stood with Horst, Koda, and Kelly. Sasha wasted no time planting herself firmly against Dieter's side as soon as he was in range.

Koda raised one eyebrow and cocked her head. She'd missed some of the earlier signs, but now she knew that

Sasha was suffering from more than the physical effects of her period in captivity. That was something Koda was all too familiar with. She hoped the young woman managed to overcome her fears sooner rather than later.

The guests mingled for a bit longer while Koda waited for the last four guests to arrive. They'd planned an outing to the restored castle where Koda had first met Yuko so many years ago and were at the mercy of the island's unreliable bus service.

"Sorry we're late!" Asai called from the door. "Chiro's bus had a flat on the way down from the castle, and it took him a little while to change it."

Seki walked in beside her. There was a marked difference between the two. Where Asai had the ageless beauty of many Japanese women, Seki now sported an impressive amount of gray hair and permanent laughter lines around his eyes. They had come to Kume after taking the Palace from a single establishment to a gaming empire with operations in every sizable town in Japan. Much to the delight of the younger vacationers and their parents, who welcomed the break from their teenage children, they'd even opened one in the resort area on Kume.

Retired Commissioner General Takeshi Yonai followed Asai and Seki in with his wife Eiko on his arm. They were visiting Asai and Seki from the mainland to celebrate Takeshi's retirement from heading the Tokyo Police for over twenty-five years.

The sound of a spoon tapping against a glass filled the room. "Now that everyone is here, please take your seats," Koda announced. "The chef advises that the meal is ready to serve."

Once the guests were seated, the servers moved around the long table and filled their glasses. Horst raised his glass to a wall that held several pictures of departed family members once the drinks were poured. "To our friends and family here with us tonight, and those with us in spirit, we welcome you."

Everyone raised their glass in a toast.

Koda raised her glass. "Tonight is the first time we've all managed to gather in years. I hope everyone enjoys the meal and fellowship. May we not wait so long to do it again."

Everyone mirrored her action in agreement as the catering staff rolled out carts with the delicacies the chefs had worked days to prepare.

CHAPTER TWENTY-FOUR

Kume Island, Okinawa, Japan

Dieter had observed Sasha throughout the course of the meal, concerned that she remained silent and withdrawn. By the end of the meal, she was restless and noticeably uncomfortable. He took her hand when the staff cleared the table after dessert and excused them both.

Koda and Yuko both nodded encouragement, and he spirited her out the door before anyone else noticed him leading her out to the beach for a quiet walk in the moonlight.

They were quiet as they strolled along the sand, Dieter taking comfort from Sasha's ease now it was just the two of them together. They stayed out for a while, but Dieter couldn't suppress his knowledge and steered her back toward the party.

"Sasha, Yuko has something for you. It will help your body recover faster from what the pirates did to you," Dieter explained as they walked back to the restaurant.

"What do you mean?" Sasha asked, confusion obvious

in her tone. "I'm healing well with all the food and pampering you've given me the past week."

Dieter caught her arms gently in his hands and ran a finger over the angry scars from the silver burns on her wrists. "What Yuko has for you will make these disappear. It will also make you stronger and help you regain the weight you lost while they starved you."

Sasha tilted her chin to look into his eyes. "What is it?"

"Do you know what makes us different from regular humans? Why we can shift into wolves?" Dieter asked.

She looked at him askance. "Because one or both of our parents could. Everyone knows that, silly."

Dieter nodded. "Yes, that's part of it. But do you know what our parents passed on to us that gives us the ability?"

"Mother told me that we carry wolf genes, whatever that means," she answered.

Dieter frowned as he thought about how best to explain nanocytes and how Weres were created as they approached the restaurant's front.

Yuko cleared her throat from where she sat on a swing and asked, "Would you like me to explain, Dieter?"

Sasha's spine stiffened, and she grabbed Dieter's arm.

"It's okay, Sasha." Dieter sighed with relief. "Hi, Yuko, I didn't see you there. I'd appreciate it if you would. I've known the truth all my life, and I'm afraid I'll only confuse her."

Yuko nodded at a bench next to the swing set. "Have a seat, and I'll explain everything."

"Has Akio arrived yet?" Dieter inquired as he settled on the bench, Sasha beside him.

"Not yet," Yuko answered. "I spoke with him an hour

ago, and he said he'd be here around now. I was waiting for him when you arrived."

"Was he successful today?" Dieter asked.

"For the most part," Yuko assured him. "Most of the primary players are dead. Today's operations should keep the rest in check for the foreseeable future."

Dieter shuddered. "Excellent. I don't like the pirates much, but I don't want to deal with another Forsaken."

Yuko grinned. "You didn't do poorly the last time."

Sasha stared at Dieter in shock. "You've fought a vampire and survived?"

Dieter snorted a laugh. Sasha's eyes narrowed, and Yuko chuckled as she explained, "Dieter has fought vampires many times. That's not what we're talking about. When Dieter and Tosha were less than two years old, two Forsaken attacked the town they were visiting with their parents. That was the night we discovered the twins could partially shift."

"You could shift when you were that young?" Sasha asked in wonder. "Wait, if you were a baby, how have you faced vampires many times?"

Dieter laughed. "Every time Aunt Yuko and Akio kicked my ass since I started training at age four."

The color drained out of Sasha's face, and she stood to move away from Yuko.

Dieter caught her hand and asked, "Remember what I told you about Queen Bethany Anne?"

Sasha nodded without taking her eyes off Yuko.

"There's a difference between vampires and Forsaken," Dieter reminded her. "The vampires follow the Queen's laws and do not harm others without cause. The Forsaken refuse to follow the rules and have no regard for others. Yuko is the Queen's representative to the people of the UnknownWorld. As long as they uphold the Queen's values, they have nothing to fear."

"Dieter, I'm going to speak with Eve inside. I can come back once Sasha is more comfortable with my presence," Yuko offered.

Dieter nodded and gently pulled Sasha back onto the bench beside him.

He wrapped an arm around her shoulders and continued, "Sasha, I know you didn't understand, or maybe didn't even believe some of what I've told you since we met, but know this. I swear I will never intentionally do anything to put you in harm's way."

Sasha reached for his hands. "I believe you, Dieter. It's just so much to take in. I'm from a small pack in a small village in Russia. My mother taught me to fear vampires from birth. That you talk so casually about them and even call one your family is a lot to take in."

Dieter held her hands in his and looked deep into her eyes. "I grew up bouncing on Yuko's knee and running around underfoot in her lab. She's nothing like the Forsaken. She has killed Forsaken in the past to protect others."

"Is she the vampire they call the Dark One?" Sasha asked wide-eyed.

Dieter shook his head. "Yuko? No, there's nothing dark about her. Tosha and I wouldn't have been born if it wasn't for Yuko."

"What do you mean?" Sasha questioned. "What did a vampire have to do with your birth?"

"Weretigers attacked my mother and father in Tokyo before they knew she was pregnant with us," Dieter told her. "Mother suffered grievous injuries and was dying. Yuko gave my father a choice. He could make mother a Were, or Yuko would make her a vampire. She left him with no other options."

"I don't understand," Sasha stated. "How could you make someone a Were? I know that vampires create others by taking their blood, but Weres are born."

"That's not the whole truth," Dieter assured her with a sigh. He was going to have to do his best not to mangle the explanation and hope he didn't confuse her. "We can create other Weres if our blood gets into an open wound. It's not perfect and doesn't work every time, but it *is* possible. My father gave my mother his blood, and it kept her alive long enough for Yuko and Eve to use the technology available to them to save her life."

Sasha stared at him in shock. "Technology?"

Dieter continued, "That technology repaired her body and gave her the thing that makes us Weres. It also altered Tosh-*chan* and me, making us perfect examples of what a Were can be. That's what allowed us to shift as babies. Yuko's better at explaining this than I am. She works with the tech daily."

Sasha hesitantly responded, "Dieter, I trust you. You saved me from a living hell and have stayed by my side ever since. If you say that she won't hurt me, I trust you."

"Sasha, you have nothing to fear from anyone here," Dieter assured her. "*Everyone* here tonight would fight for you if necessary. This is the safest place on all Earth."

Yuko stepped out the door with a smile. "Sasha, I'll

gladly explain everything to you about nanocytes." She paused when she saw confusion in the young woman's eyes. "The technology Dieter mentioned."

Yuko cocked her head to the side and turned as Akio stepped out of the darkness, still wearing his weapons over his set of jet black Jean Dukes armor.

Sasha let out a scream and pulled away from Dieter when she saw the warrior.

"Dieter!" She skittered back, her eyes turning yellow as her flight or fight instinct kicked into overdrive.

Akio halted at the bottom of the steps and waited as Dieter reached out and laid a hand on Sasha's arm. "It's okay, Sasha. That's Akio. He won't hurt you."

"No! I've heard of him." Her voice rose in panic. "He looks just like they described him. The packs and even the blood traders talked about a vampire dressed in black with a sword and twin pistols who hunted our kind for sport. It's him, the Dark One!"

Akio smiled and gently nodded. "Some call me that. It's true that I hunt the evil in the UnknownWorld. The blood hunters have reason to fear me, for I am my Queen's Justice on this world. Any who dare to harm innocents need fear me. My name is Akio, and you, Denikina Aleksandra Yakovna of the Nakhoda pack, are one of the innocents Bethany Anne charged me to protect. I promise you the people who wronged you will die for their crimes. All of them."

"No, no, no, no, no! They say you stalk us and kill all you find," Sasha cried.

"Sasha! Please listen to me," Dieter begged. "You said you trust me, right?"

CHARLES TILLMAN & MICHAEL ANDERLE

She nodded without taking her eyes off of Akio.

"Akio is part of my family," Dieter told her. "He would *never* harm anyone who wasn't hurting innocents. His honor wouldn't allow it, and he certainly doesn't kill for sport. He's not the monster those stories claim. He's one of the people who taught Gregov, Tosha, and me to fight. Trust me, Sasha. Akio won't harm you."

Akio *pushed* calm, and Sasha's tense shoulders relaxed. She continued to watch him warily, but she let Dieter pull her closer to where he stood.

"Sasha, Akio came to the ship after we rescued you," Dieter explained. "He took the Russian pirate we captured that night to find out what he knew about how you ended up there."

Sasha's face twisted in a grimace, "Leskov, that beast."

"He will never harm you or anyone else ever again," Akio told her, his voice calm. "He was very forthcoming with information about you and how you came to be on their ship."

"He's dead?" Sasha asked.

Akio inclined his head. "Very."

"Did he tell you anything about my mother?" Sasha asked hopefully.

Akio grimaced and shook his head. "He only knew where they obtained you. When I speak to the ones who sold you to them, I promise I will do everything I can to locate every person they've taken."

"You know where they are!" Gregov asked as he stepped out the door after hearing the disturbance.

"*Hai*, they are near Vladivostok," Akio confirmed. "I will visit them tomorrow. Abel and Takumi are gathering more information about the locations and names I got from Leskov."

"Vladivostok? Petrov's pack controls that area. Are the hunters after his pack?" Sasha asked.

"Petrov's pack works with them," Akio answered coldly.

"I knew I should have killed that bastard," Tosha growled as she came out behind Gregov.

Akio pressed his lips together. "Petrov has many things to answer for, it seems. The information the pirate had is enough to warrant his death. I'm certain there will be more when I discuss his actions with him."

Dieter growled. "I would like to accompany you to deal with that bastard."

"*Da*, as would I," Gregov added. "The hunters followed me there when they raided my village and killed my mother. I wish to hear what Petrov knows about that."

"I called dibs on shooting his ass already," Tosha stated. "Don't think you're leaving me out, brothers."

Akio locked eyes with each of the siblings before he gave a slight nod. "We will depart at sunrise. Be ready."

They each nodded in turn. Tosha and Gregov went back inside to the party, leaving Dieter to calm Sasha.

"Um, Dark…I mean, uh, Akio?" Sasha stammered, terri-fied but determined to speak.

"What is it, young one?" Akio asked softly.

"May I go?" Sasha asked. "I wish to find my mother if she still lives."

Akio stared into her eyes as he slipped inside her mind. He saw that she needed to face her personal demons, and confronting the one responsible for her ordeal would help her heal. He looked at Yuko. "Can you outfit her? I won't allow her to risk herself when it's not needed."

"She's a little shorter and thinner than Tosha. One of the spare suits I have for her will work for now." Yuko answered.

"Please see that she has it before we depart. Sasha, Dieter." Akio gave each a small bow, then followed Gregov and Tosha inside, where the party was in full swing.

Yuko resumed her seat on the swing and motioned to the bench. She began to speak as soon as they were seated. "Over a thousand years ago, a group of aliens visited Earth and created the Weres. They're called Kurtherians, and they did it using advanced science and small machines called nanocytes. You have the nanocytes in your blood. That's what gives you the ability to shift."

Sasha nodded wordlessly.

"The nanocytes are also what gave the people who held you greater strength when they drank your blood," Yuko explained. "The blood trade has come up a few times in history, but the UnknownWorld stamped it and the people responsible out quickly."

"How do these machines make it possible for Weres to shift? Is that why we heal much faster than the unenhanced?" Sasha paused. "Why am I healing slowly?"

"The reason your healing has slowed is twofold," Yuko told her. "First, those pirates took a good deal of your blood and starved you to the point where your nanocytes couldn't reproduce fast enough to do much more than keep you alive. The second is that over the centuries, the original nanocytes have mutated many times, and the code that makes them function has degraded. The ones you carry can't distribute the energy as efficiently as the originals. That has led to you losing some abilities and reduced your ability to heal some wounds, such as the silver burns."

Sasha nodded, but her eyes betrayed the confusion she felt.

"I have access to technology that can repair the mutations in the nanocytes," Yuko explained. "Dieter, Tosha, and Gregov all have unaltered nanocytes and abilities that are only legend to most other Weres. They're stronger, faster, and a lot harder to hurt, let alone kill, than the majority of the Weres around the world."

Sasha cocked her head to the side and studied Dieter intensely. "You're different? You're big, but so are some of Petrov's pack."

Dieter lifted a hand and caressed her cheek. "I love when you do that."

"Do what?" Sasha asked.

"Look at me so intently. Your eyes shine like emeralds."

Sasha blushed and looked away. Yuko smiled as she watched the two young people.

Dieter shook his head and smiled sheepishly at Yuko. "Sorry."

"Nothing to apologize for, Dieter. Why don't you show her what I mean?" Yuko held up one hand and curled it into a claw.

He nodded and pulled his hand from her face. "Remember when Yuko told you about the encounter with the Forsaken?"

Sasha nodded and smiled. "Yes, you shifted when you were a baby."

"No." He held his hand up. "I partially shifted."

Sasha's eyes grew round as dark claws emerged from Dieter's fingers and his hand morphed into a clawed hand more than twice as large as his human one.

Sasha let out a squeak when Dieter's eyes glowed yellow and coarse black hair erupted from his face. His nose and mouth morphed into a wolf's muzzle filled with razor-sharp teeth.

He shifted back to human form and smiled. "That's what the differences in the nanocytes mean for me."

"You have the third form!" Sasha exclaimed. "I've heard tales that some could once obtain it, but everyone said it was a fairy tale. That there was never a man-wolf."

"It's called Pricolici," Yuko informed her. "The original stories about werewolves come from regular humans seeing a Were in this form centuries ago when superstition was the basis for many beliefs. It wasn't a deal with a devil or a curse that caused it. It was alien science."

Sasha stared at Dieter with amazement.

"I have a process that can help you heal the silver wounds and will increase your stamina. Am I correct in assuming that you are much weaker than you were before the pirates took you?" Yuko asked.

Sasha nodded, dumbfounded by the flood of information.

"I have the means to fix some of that with me. Dieter contacted me when he noticed you weren't healing correctly, and I prepared a booster for your nanocytes." Yuko reached into her tunic and pulled out a filled syringe. "This contains a serum to replace what was taken and restore your strength. If you allow it, I'll administer it now, and you will feel much better in the morning."

Sasha looked at the needle in Yuko's hand with trepidation. Her previous experience with needles was the reason she was feeling so weak. She glanced at Dieter, and he nodded reassuringly.

"It's okay," he told her in a soft voice.

Sasha accepted that she should trust the vampire if Dieter did. To do anything else would signify that she didn't truly trust *him*, which was far from true. She held her arm out and nodded. "Go ahead."

Yuko gently slipped the needle under her skin and injected the serum to jump-start her body's ability to heal.

Yuko smiled. "All done. Doctor Yuko prescribes a good night's sleep. Then you will be better in the morning."

"Will I have special abilities like Dieter?" Sasha asked absently as she stared at where the injection had gone in.

"No," Yuko answered. "That requires technology I don't have here and more time than you have before you accompany Akio to Vladivostok."

Sasha nodded. "I don't want to miss that."

Yuko smiled as she noted how attentively Dieter watched the pretty young Were and responded to her needs. "Your enhancement is a subject I'm sure will come up again soon."

CHAPTER TWENTY-FIVE

TQB Base, Tokyo, Japan

"Akio, I've verified the information the pirate provided about where they hold the captives for sale," Abel advised. "They're in a warehouse just north of the petroleum shipping facility in the harbor."

"Have you located any sign of the hunters yet?" Akio asked as he strapped on his Jean Dukes Specials.

"Negative. Takumi got a drone inside the building with the captives, but none of the conversations it picked up mentioned the hunters."

Akio's lips pressed into a flat line as he considered the information. "What about Petrov? Have you seen him on any of the feeds?"

"Affirmative," Abel replied. "Once at the facility with the captives, and again last night at twenty fifty-seven as he entered the building where he conducts his petroleum business. He has not left that building since."

"Prepare my Black Eagle and dispatch the Pod to Kume

to pick up the team there," Akio instructed. "I'll meet them in Vladivostok. I want to check the airport north of the city. The pirate believed it was part of the blood trade but was unable to provide proof. I'll go there first and meet the others at Petrov's afterward."

"I recommend that we carry additional pucks on this mission since the silver munitions could injure Dieter and his crew," Abel suggested.

Akio nodded. "Agreed. How many pucks are in inventory?"

"Sixteen," Abel informed him. "Ten two-pounders and six one-pound."

"The one-pound pucks should be sufficient, but load some of the two-pounders just in case," Akio advised. "Add a full loadout for the mounted blasters, too. They may come in handy if any of the perpetrators of this atrocity run."

Abel laughed. "You got it, boss. Let them run. They'll die tired, just like the tigers."

Yuko? Akio called over his implant.

Yes, Akio? Was the reply.

Will the armored suit Sasha is wearing stop a shot from the pistols you designed for Dieter, Tosha, and Gregov?

Easily. Why?

I plan to give them all the same ammunition I use to hunt the Sacred Clan. I don't want to risk a friendly fire fatality.

There's nothing to worry about there. The nanocyte booster I gave Sasha will prevent minor wounds from one of those rounds. Yuko chuckled. *When Dieter contacted me about her condition, I could tell something was going on with them. After seeing him with her last night, I suspect Sasha will be around for a long time.*

Hai. Dieter's protectiveness reminded me of Horst after the Yakuza took Koda, Akio answered. *I'm happy for both of them.*

Me too, do you require anything else? I'm assisting Eve with an upgrade on the Pod-doc. When it's complete, she hopes to achieve better than eighty percent efficiency, Yuko informed him.

That's welcome news. I suspect we both know a young Were who will need it soon. Akio observed. *It would be nice if the modifications to her nanocytes took less time.*

True, I don't want a repeat of the experience Kelly had, Yuko added.

Akio chuckled. *At least you corrected the issue with her sense of smell and coffee after a few years. Henry will be forever grateful to you for that.*

There is that, Yuko agreed. *I'm glad that Kelly can enjoy her coffee again. Even though her body didn't need the boost, she still craved it all those years. When she came out of the Pod-doc and smelled that first cup, the look on her face was worth every hour it took to figure that problem out.*

I'll be back later, Akio advised.

Be safe, and take care of my little ones, Yuko told him.

Akio cut the connection as he stepped into the hangar. The Pod was already on the way to Kume, and the Black Eagle sat ready. He climbed into the cockpit and fastened the restraints.

"Take us out, Abel."

"Acknowledged. Next stop, Vladivostok."

. . .

SWL Vessel *Freki*, Kume Island, Okinawa, Japan

Tosha grinned as she pounded on the cabin door. "Come on, Dieter. You know Akio doesn't like to be kept waiting."

Gregov stood to the side and shook his head. "Why do things like that? You know Akio said sunrise. Dieter has twenty minutes to be on deck."

"True, but he has a girl in his bedroom. I don't want him to get sidetracked and forget the time." Tosha laughed, then pounded the door again.

Lei rolled his eyes as he approached. "Tosha, you should be ashamed. Let them have a few minutes of peace."

Tosha turned to her mate and grinned. "Like Dieter and Gregov did for us the whole time we dated?"

Lei rested his chin on his palm and curled one finger over his lips. He nodded, then faced Gregov. "She has a point. You need to hurry up and find a girlfriend. Saint Payback requires it."

"Shows what you know?" Gregov stuck out his chest and placed his palm flat over his heart. "There's so much awesomeness here, it's too much for one woman to handle. Is a good thing the *Freki* travels to lots of ports so I can spread it around."

Tosha made a face then slammed her palm against the side of her head several times. "Yuck! Get out. Get out. Get out. I do not need that visual stuck in my head."

Gregov and Lei were still laughing at her antics when Dieter's door opened.

"What in the hell is wrong with you?" Dieter glared at Tosha then cut his gaze to Lei and Gregov. "She tries to beat my door down, and you two idiots stand there braying like asses."

Tosha snorted. "Didn't want you to get sidetracked and miss your ride, brother."

Dieter rolled his eyes and sighed. "Please go away. We'll join you shortly."

The others stumbled down the corridor, laughing while Dieter scowled at their retreating backs.

"What was that about?" Sasha asked as she exited the suite's bathroom scrubbed and dressed in a black armored jumpsuit that hung loosely from her too-thin frame.

"Sibling shenanigans. Get used to it because they do it all the time." Dieter shook his head and crossed to Sasha.

He looked over the fit of her clothes. The sleeves hung down to her fingertips, and the legs were several centimeters too long. He motioned to the sleeves and smiled. "Let me roll these up and secure them so they don't get in your way. You can tuck the legs into the tops of your boots, and they should be fine."

Sasha smiled and offered him her hand. When he rolled the sleeve to her wrist, he nodded in satisfaction when he saw the silver burns wholly healed.

"How do you feel today?" he asked.

"Better than I have in weeks. I have so much energy I feel like I'm going to explode if I stop moving," Sasha admitted.

Dieter laughed. "That's what Yuko wanted. She told me that your appetite would be better, too. Are you hungry?"

"Starved. I could eat a cow." Sasha grinned.

"I don't have one on the ship right now, but I'll be sure

to find one later for you if you want. Until then, I did ask the steward to put together breakfast in the lounge. Care to join me?" Dieter offered her his crooked arm.

Sasha blushed then placed her hand on his arm. "Certainly."

CHAPTER TWENTY-SIX

Vladivostok International Airport, Vladivostok, Russia

The Black Eagle held position five hundred meters above an old aircraft hangar on the west side of the field. Akio had instructed Abel to focus the drones on locating the building where the pirate had purchased Sasha and finding Petrov.

The building below had stood out in the man's mind as a place that he'd seen suspicious activity several times when the airship landed for supplies.

"Sensors detect six lifeforms inside. Two are moving through the building, and the others are stationary. Five show on the heat sensors as Weres, and one is registering normal human," Abel announced as the HUD highlighted each of the heat signatures in turn.

"Have the others left Kume yet?" Akio asked.

"Negative. Dieter and Sasha are aboard the Pod on the *Freki* now. The team is estimated to arrive in eight-point six minutes."

Akio nodded. "Thank you, land in that clearing west of

the structure. I'll go through the trees and approach from the other side. Cover the east and monitor anyone fleeing in that direction."

"What about the west side?" Abel offered. "I can hold position above the structure and cover that side, too."

"Any hostiles that way are mine," Akio stated coldly.

"Acknowledged."

Akio exited the craft in the early morning gloom. Sunrise wasn't for another five minutes, and he wanted to approach the building before it was light. He ghosted the short distance through the trees and stopped in the shadow of a tree with large white blooms covering it.

The two moving figures have stopped and are together just near the center of your side of the building, Abel reported. *The others remain stationary as before.*

Notify me if they move, Akio instructed. *There's a door near that location.*

Acknowledged. Happy hunting, Abel answered.

Akio extended his senses and detected two Weres where Abel had indicated. He moved at an angle to the door until he reached the southern corner of the metal building and stopped when he heard voices from inside.

"I'm telling you, Ivan. This bunch is going to make us a fortune. The vampire alone is worth more than all the rest."

"Why the hell are we sitting on him then, Yashkin? That thing gives me the creeps laying there watching us and never speaking no matter what we do to him. I say we bundle him up in canvas and deliver him to Petrov when the suns up. At least that way, if he does escape, he'll burn before he can hunt us down."

"We're sitting on him and the others because Grisha said we should. I'm not willing to risk getting strapped to one of those tables because you're scared of that vamp. Have you forgotten what he did to Ilyich when he disobeyed an order?"

"No, Ivan, I remember him begging us to kill him for over a month while the machines sucked him dry. That was different. Ilyich was careless when he killed that bumpkin woman who fled here with her daughter. I still don't know how we missed those two."

"I damn near lost an eye in that nothing settlement, that's how."

"Doesn't matter. We still got a nice cut when we sold that little bitch to Isaak. I wonder if she's bitten off his prick yet. You know that bastard has a taste for girls built like her." Both men laughed as they imagined Isaak's possible troubles.

"I still don't want to go around the vamp," Yashkin complained.

"Fucking quit your whining. He's barely alive as it is. Besides, Grisha and the others should be back with more this afternoon. You've waited this long. A few more hours won't kill you."

Wrong. Akio thought as he pulled the katana from his back.

TQB Pod, over the East China Sea

"This machine is amazing," Sasha gushed.

Dieter smiled and nodded. He chose not to bring up how she'd practically climbed him like a tree when she first looked out and saw how far above the Earth they flew. It had taken all three of them several minutes to convince her that they weren't going to die in a gruesome manner.

Tosha sighed as she looked at the water below. "I'm going to miss this once the Pods all quit working."

"What are you talking about?" Gregov asked.

"Eve told me Dad's Pod going down was only the beginning," Tosha explained. "The TQB Pods will fail someday too. She told me that they have a limited usable life, provided they don't have a critical failure like the German Pod did."

Gregov shrugged. "So, she just makes more."

Tosha shook her head. "We lost the ability to manufacture some of the needed components on WWDE. She's searching for a solution but hasn't found one yet."

"I didn't realize that," Gregov admitted. "I thought Dad was just pissed because Eve made him tread water for six hours and wouldn't fish out his Pod when he went down between Jeju and Kume."

Dieter snorted. "Oh, he's plenty mad about *that*. Auntie Eve hovered above him with her legs hanging out the door for five of those six hours. She told him if he wouldn't listen when she told him not to do something, he could swim back to Kume."

"Mom reminding him that she'd told him it would happen every time he complained didn't help much either," Tosha added with a chortle.

Gregov laughed. "No, I'm sure it didn't."

"Why would Eve do that to him?" Sasha asked.

"Because she'd told him the Pod was unsafe the week before," Dieter explained. "He made the mistake of telling her it was German-built, and he knew it was safe to fly. When he put out the distress call, she told Yuko she was picking him up. Yuko didn't know what she was planning until it was too late, and Akio had all the other Pods tied up on other business."

"That sounds dangerous. There are things in the sea that could have killed him. Aren't they friends?" Sasha inquired.

"As mad as Dad was, he would have ripped anything dumb enough to try to shreds, provided Eve didn't blow it up first. He wasn't in any real danger, but when Eve tells you not to do something, it's best to listen," Dieter stated.

"That's the truth." Gregov laughed. "I thought my fingers would fall off that summer she had me scrubbing floors at the Nagoya base. My fingers bled even though I was enhanced."

Dieter snorted. "You had it easy. Seki and Asai ran me ragged every day at the Palace in Tokyo. I didn't know that much trash existed, and don't get me *started* on the candy stuck to every damned thing in the kid's section."

Tosha shook her head and sighed. "I had it worse than both of you. Mom came and got me. When I wasn't working on a fishing boat, she was lecturing me about how dangerous it was for three fourteen-year-olds to go from Nagoya to Tokyo without telling anyone where they were. Especially when they were forbidden to go in the first place."

Sasha shrugged. "What was the big deal? You're all enhanced. You could protect yourselves. At fourteen, I was hunting for our village. I would go into the forest alone for days at a time."

"Eve told us we couldn't go, and we did it anyway," Tosha told her. "Actions have consequences. I thought Dad was going to get me out of working on the fishing boats, but he didn't. I asked him once why he didn't let me serve my time on one of his ships instead of those stinky little boats. He told me that if I was old enough to go against the rules, knowing it was wrong, I was old enough to serve out whatever punishment Auntie Eve and Mom decided was appropriate."

Sasha wrinkled her nose. "I still don't get it."

"I didn't understand it then, but I do now. We should be thankful they didn't let Akio decide the punishment." Tosha chuckled. "He would have had us training until we threw up and then training some more between bouts of heavy labor."

"Oh, yeah. I didn't put my training sword away once. Akio told me to do pushups until *his* arms got tired." Gregov laughed. "Akio never gets tired."

Sasha watched the three with wide eyes, questioning what being saved by people like this meant for her.

Dieter wrapped an arm around her shoulder and whispered, "We were very stubborn when we were younger. Especially Tosha."

Tosha laughed. "I heard that, brother. Don't let that innocent face fool you, Sasha. He was the brains behind some of our worst escapades. Behind those puppy dog eyes lurks the mind of an evil genius."

"What's the game plan, Dieter. Is Akio already there?" Gregov interrupted when he looked out and saw they were approaching the Russian coast.

"He contacted me earlier and said he wanted to check a

location north of town before we dealt with Petrov and his cronies," Dieter told him. "He's going to meet us at the petroleum facility, then we'll all go in together and confront Petrov."

"Petrov has a group of eight to ten enforcers with him all the time. Is confronting him in his stronghold wise?" Sasha worried.

"We'll be lucky to deal with one or two of them. Akio wipes out entire towns of weretigers by himself, and after sparring with Lei, I can tell you those damned cats are fast," Dieter assured her.

"Why didn't Lei join us?" Gregov asked. "It's not like him to miss out on a fight."

"There was a problem with the cargo on the ship. The stated weights were wrong on several containers we picked up in Shanghai. The cargo master missed it, and when we offloaded all the stuff for Kume, the ship was out of balance," Tosha explained. "Lei's getting everything sorted so we can leave as soon as I get back. We have a load of perishables going to Taiwan that we need to deliver so we can get to Nagoya in time for Tian's show."

Gregov nodded. Knowing Lei's mother, he knew Lei didn't dare miss her show. Tian was a kind and gentle soul, but if you riled her, there was hell to pay.

Vladivostok International Airport, Vladivostok, Russia

Akio approached the open door on silent feet. He peered inside and saw that the two Weres had moved into the building. One stood over a prone form on a metal bed frame wrapped in heavy chains. The other was standing next to him, making entries on a clipboard.

"That's almost half a liter so far, Yaskin. You best cut it back before you kill him."

"*Da*, but I still think we should just get rid of him, Ivan. These things scare the hell out of me,"

Akio's eyes glowed red, and his face twisted into a grimace of disgust. Three other people were strapped to bare metal frames, each with tubes running from their bodies to machines and bags of liquids.

He *pushed* fear into the room as he stepped through the doorway. Two of the captives whimpered, and both men's eyes flew to the terrifying red-eyed vision before them.

"You have no honor," Akio's cold voice filled the room. "You prey on the weak to steal their lives for your profit. The penalty for this horrific act is death."

Ivan knocked over the machine he'd just adjusted in his attempt to flee. Yaskin leapt to a cluttered table and snatched an old Kalashnikov rifle. He pointed it at Akio and sprayed the room with thirty 7.62 millimeter bullets.

Akio vanished from sight and his sword appeared like magic, piercing the Were's heart as the last round left the barrel. Akio twisted the blade, then pulled it out of the open-mouthed Were's chest. He spun on one foot, bringing the katana around at shoulder height, and the Were's headless body dropped the gun as a fountain of blood splattered everything around.

Ivan shifted into a gray and white wolf as he ran. He slammed into a fire door and ran toward the rising sun. Akio listened for a few beats then heard the familiar sound of a blaster round impacting flesh.

Got him! Abel called over Akio's implant.

The other's dead as well, Akio answered.

Where should I pick you up?

The door where the man you killed came out, Akio answered. *I need to free the captives, then we will deal with the rest.*

Acknowledged. I'm at the door, Abel advised seconds later.

Akio crossed to the restrained vampire. A pool of blood covered the floor under the bed frame, and there were no signs of life in the shriveled husk of a man. He traced the tubes coming from the vampire's body to the machine on the floor. A high-pitched whine came from the device and it started to smoke, then abruptly fell silent.

Akio pursed his lips and shook his head sadly when he saw that in his haste to escape, Ivan had turned the pump to its highest setting and drained what little blood remained from his helpless victim. He looked into the lifeless eyes of the young man who appeared to be barely out of adolescence and silently promised that all those responsible would pay.

A low moan came from another bed, and Akio turned to find a grizzled gray Were struggling weakly against the silver chains binding him. He grabbed the chain on one of the Were's wrists in his gauntleted fist and twisted, shattering the links with ease. He moved around the bed, removing the chains and the needles that drained his blood and pumped fluids into him to produce more.

"Easy," Akio cautioned when the Were struggled to sit up.

"Got to get out of here!" The man gasped. "More of them."

"They won't be back until later today. Rest while I release the others." Akio projected calm into the Were, and he lay back down.

He released a second werewolf, then moved to the third figure and stopped as he reached for the restraints. Recognition then fear flared in the weretiger's eyes when he saw his prospective savior.

Akio was torn between releasing an enemy he'd sworn to kill or freeing a victim. He pushed through the man's fear and into his mind. In seconds he had his answer. He dug deeper into the Were's mind and saw how a pack of wolves had run him down and captured him.

Images of a small village filled the Were's mind. Akio shuffled through them like a dealer at a poker table. He stopped at the appearance of a group of six filthy and malnourished people struggling under heavy loads.

Akio's face twisted into a scowl as he hunted the location where the people were being kept prisoner.

Poltavka! the man's mind screamed under the pressure of Akio's non-too-gentle pillaging.

Akio withdrew from his mind and looked him in the eye. "You have used your abilities to exploit those weaker than you. By order of Queen Bethany Anne, your crimes carry the sentence of death."

His katana flashed in the dim light, and the Were's head rolled to the floor as blood spurted weakly from the stump of his neck.

"The Dark One!" the grizzled wolf exclaimed as he rolled onto the floor. In his blood-depleted weakened state, he couldn't stand and tried to crawl away.

Akio *pushed* the calm that he'd withdrawn while

searching the tiger's mind, and both men stilled. "I have seen that you are not bad men. You have nothing to fear from me."

He bent and lifted the Were from the floor, placing him upright in a nearby chair. A quick scan of the hangar revealed a small package of smoked meat and cheese on a table to one side.

Akio tore open the wrapper and split the find into equal shares. "Eat this, regain your strength, and leave."

"What about the blood traders?" one of the Weres asked.

"I have business with the people responsible for this. After today these," Akio's lip curled, and he snarled as he spoke, "blood traders will trouble no one ever again."

Akio spun on his heel and stalked out of the hangar, leaving both Weres staring wide-eyed at his retreating back.

"You have a name?" the older man asked.

"Vassily," the other answered.

"Micha. Eat, and let's get out of here before any of those bastards come back."

"*Da*, I don't know what scares me more. Those who brought me here or the one who just left," Vassily observed.

Micha nodded at the door. "The one who left, no doubt. That vampire is death incarnate. I'd rather take my chances with the hunters than risk meeting him again."

Vassily didn't answer. He tucked into the meat and cheese, taking small bites and chewing quickly.

CHAPTER TWENTY-SEVEN

The Palace, Tokyo, Japan

Abel, What are you doing? Takumi inquired.

Playing with the boffins in Japanese military intelligence.

First, that's not the proper term for them. Second, Why?

Semantics. Abel snarked. *Do you prefer ass-licking scrotum sniffing cyber cock stains?*

I have no real preference, Takumi answered. *However, I would like to know why you're engaging in cyberwarfare with our host government.*

They're trying to breach my firewalls again. Abel cackled. *I'm about to teach them why that's a monumentally bad idea.*

Yuko is not going to be happy with you if you cause problems with our hosts, Takumi cautioned.

If they ever manage to access the information stored in my systems, she will be even more upset, Abel shot back. *What they lack in ability, they make up for in persistence.*

You know they don't have anything capable of hacking you, Takumi stated. *Why don't you just ignore them? That's what I do.*

It's the principle of the matter, Abel explained. *They came into my house uninvited, after everything we've done to keep them safe all these years. That displays a lack of honor and a level of arrogance that's unacceptable. They need a lesson in humility.*

Abel, you know that information about our activities is limited to the highest level of the government. Yuko could put a stop to it with one call.

Where's the fun in that? Abel quipped.

This isn't going to end well for you, Takumi warned. *You should at least advise Eve of the attempted breach.*

She's busy researching alternative components for the failing Pod technology, Abel informed him. *The lack of availability in some components will result in critical failures in a few years.*

Takumi huffed. *You do realize that is a lame excuse, don't you? Eve is more than capable of responding to you without slowing any other projects she's involved in.*

It's my determination— Abel cut off in mid-sentence. *Oh, what's this?*

What have you done now, Abel? Takumi asked.

Abel laughed. *I've located a message thread between the head of this group and a member of the Parliament. They're cousins, and the Parliament member is the son of the Chairman of Akahito Ship Works. That explains why the attack is on the server associated with Seawolf Shipping.*

You need to contact Yuko, Takumi stated. *Akahito tried to force a partnership to get access to the technology on our ships recently. The Chairman didn't take rejection well. This is an attempt at corporate espionage using government assets.*

Come on, Takumi. Don't be such a stick in the mud, Abel wheedled. *Besides, you know I need more proof before Yuko goes to the Prime Minister. They tried something similar on you once, and we only got him because Akio did his mind-meld thing and made him confess. It's only logical to gather all the evidence the National Police need to arrest all the players involved at once. A corrupt politician is a menace to everyone. Why don't you buck up and help me take out the trash?*

Takumi was silent for a few beats then answered. *First, Akio is not a pointy-eared alien. Therefore your mind-meld remark is illogical, and second, what do you need me to do?*

Welcome to the dark side, brother! Abel crowed. *I'm sending you the IP address for the minister's device and the information I already have on Akahito. See what kind of embarrassing or illegal dirt you can dig up on them. Preferably both.*

I'll assist you with this, but I will stress the importance of contacting Yuko or Eve, Takumi tried again.

Better to beg forgiveness than ask permission, I always say, Abel shot back.

Make another juvenile remark like that, and I'll risk the truce we have and tell Eve myself, Takumi warned.

Snitches get stitches, Takumi, Abel snarked. *Hey, thanks for pitching in, but I have to focus on the mission now. Akio and the kids are about to bring the pain on that blood trader Russian asshat Alpha. I may get to shoot someone.*

You're incorrigible, Takumi complained. *Have fun, and I'll see if I can dig up some good dirt on these corrupt idiots.*

Ooohhhh a hunting I will goooooo, Abel sang off-key as he signed off.

Ass, Takumi said into the dead connection.

Vladivostok, Russia

Petrov Leonidovich leaned back with his feet on the mahogany conference table in the converted office building the Vladivostok pack leader called home, an unlit cigar clenched between his teeth and a glass of straight vodka resting on his knee.

He reflected on the life events that resulted in him becoming the Alpha of the pack and the decisions that had made him the uncrowned king of the region. Everyone living in and around Vladivostok did so only because Petrov allowed it.

Petrov had spent the years before WWDE working as a geologist for Gazprom, the Russian state-owned gas conglomerate. He'd never planned to take a job, especially one that required him to interact closely with humans, but the Alpha at the time was an information broker, and his best clients were numerous foreign powers around the globe. He insisted that all young males in the pack work in some government industry.

A group of spies deeply embedded in government and the corporations serving the military and state kept the secrets flowing and the pack wealthy. Petrov had discovered that he enjoyed his job. It gave him the freedom to go into the field for long periods, to some of the remotest parts of the country in search of oil and gas deposits.

This had allowed him to pursue his favorite pastime out from under the Alpha's watchful eye. Petrov was a hunter. He lived to chase down prey in either wolf or human form. He was equally comfortable stalking sheep as a wolf in Siberia or humans who caught his attention in backwater towns. The Alpha frowned on Petrov's human habit and had ordered him into the spies the first time his involvement in a string of missing persons came to light.

Rather than balk or rebel as a few others had, Petrov was in his element. No supervision of his nocturnal activities and little oversight in his daytime work. As long as he produced results, the bosses didn't care, and what the Alpha didn't know didn't hurt him.

Shortly before WWDE, Gazprom crews discovered one of the largest recorded oil and natural gas deposits less than one hundred kilometers from Vladivostok. The company had delivered most of the equipment, but WWDE happened two days before drilling started, leaving the oil and gas untapped.

With everything coming apart at the seams and infrastructure collapsing around the country, Petrov returned home to Vladivostok. There he challenged and fought his way to third in the pack hierarchy.

Over the years, Petrov worked hard to provide needed supplies and food during the bitter winters, earning the Alpha's trust. This fit well with his plans and, combined with the diseases that decimated much of the human population, allowed him to hide his forbidden hunts.

Petrov grew careless as the decades passed, and when the Alpha confronted him, Petrov challenged him for leadership. The Alpha was old and experienced, but Petrov was younger, stronger, and a sociopath. The fight ended with the old Alpha dead at Petrov's feet and a new direction for the pack.

One of his first acts as Alpha was to order his hunters to locate any survivors with experience in the oil and gas industry. Technology was on the rise, and he saw a need that the pack could provide—for a hefty price. They found a few older humans who had stayed in the villages near the defunct oil field when they couldn't return to their distant homes. Their experience and training and the enhanced strength of the Weres had the first well operational within a month.

The refinery was Pytor's responsibility. Pytor, like Petrov, was a member of the old Alpha's spy network who had worked as a petrochemical engineer specializing in refining techniques. With Petrov delivering raw product and Pytor in charge of production, the pack's fortune grew.

Several decades later, Vladivostok Energy provided everything from heating oil for local homeowners to fuels for the Japanese government. The pack's success allowed it to grow to over one hundred strong over the years. Now, Petrov only accepted new members who could fight or provide other needed services. Any prospective members who couldn't were ordered to leave and warned never to return.

None ever did. Not because of the warning, but because Petrov had learned something only rumored before when the old leader trusted him. Blood from Weres and vampires gave the average human enhanced physical ability for a short time. He also discovered that repeated use caused psychological problems and addiction in the users, but that wasn't his problem, and the first few samples were always free.

Now any undesirables who wandered into his territory found themselves hunted, captured, and made into unwilling blood donors or sold to humans willing to pay the price for their special blood. Among the pirates, mercenaries, and the new wealthy class, Petrov was the only source for their drug of choice.

Once, a captive had asked him how he could do such a horrific thing to his own kind.

"Waste not, want not" was Petrov's response.

———

The Pod settled next to a ruined warehouse that had suffered some disaster in the past. Trees and other growth formed a three-meter high barrier between Petrov's building and the Pod.

Akio approached as Dieter and Gregov exited, their senses alert for any danger. "Abel has drones around Petrov's headquarters. They don't know we're here yet," he advised once Tosha and Sasha had joined them.

"How do you want to attack?" Dieter asked, deferring to Akio's wisdom.

"I believe it's time you put the years of training I've given you to use. How would *you* confront Petrov and deal with his warriors?" Akio asked with a half-smile.

Dieter didn't hesitate. He returned to the Pod with the others following him and called, "Abel, please show me the live feeds from the drones."

Images scrolled across the Pod's monitor as Abel showed the feeds from the four drones he had on station.

When the monitor faded to black, Dieter turned and faced his crew. "Two guards inside by the front door and two more at the back. Petrov's in the same room he's always in when I meet with him. I know he has at least four more guards somewhere because he has the four at the doors and four with him every time. Anyone see anything different?"

"*Nyet*," Gregov answered.

"When I was here two weeks ago, he had additional roving patrols inside the tank farm and on the docks. Did you pick anything up, Abel?" Tosha inquired.

"One moment. I've focused on the immediate exterior and inside the building," Abel replied as the monitor came to life with four video feeds from the drones he launched from the Black Eagle.

The drones flew over the docks, tank farm, and surrounding area for a half-kilometer. They located two pairs of guards on patrol, a single guard in the tank farm and another watching a ship moored to the dock.

"Good call, Tosh-*chan*," Dieter praised.

"We should take out the roving patrols, starting with the outer perimeter and working our way to the tank farm and then the dock," Gregov suggested.

Dieter's lips flattened into a thin line, and he shook his head. "We don't know if they're involved in the blood trade. They could be innocent, and I'm not willing to kill them without cause."

"We could restrain them and decide later. We don't have to kill anyone to do that," Tosha suggested.

Dieter shook his head. "Too risky. The patrol could sound an alarm, or someone could hear us. The patrols and guards aren't that far from each other."

Akio watched Dieter while he considered the options. He felt pride when his student refused to wholesale slaughter the men on the chance they were innocent of Petrov's crimes.

Akio, this is devious even for you, Abel stated over Akio's implant.

The opportunities to see how Dieter handles the command of a team are few, Akio stated. *The training I gave him can only provide the theory. Planning and executing an operation is where he learns to put the training into practice. Call it a final exam.*

Can I at least tell him the rest? Abel asked.

Wait a moment, and let's see what Dieter decides, Akio answered. *Being a good leader requires asking subordinates the right questions, not just planning an assault.*

"The only option I see is to split up, and Gregov and I take the rovers while Tosha deals with the tank farm. The noise on the dock should keep that guard from hearing us if we are quiet," Dieter decided.

"That leaves you each fighting two on one," Tosha pointed out. "We'd have to time the attacks to happen simultaneously and take them hard and fast. There's a chance one of them will die if we do that."

Akio sighed loudly from where he stood behind them.

Dieter was startled so caught up in planning he'd forgotten Akio was there. "Akio?"

"Is there some reason you decided that only the three of you could take part in this operation? If that's the case, I have an additional location I can check," Akio deadpanned.

Dieter dropped his chin to his chest, realizing it was a test. "No, sensei. I failed to inventory my assets before I started planning the mission. It was an amateur mistake and proves I'm unfit to lead this operation."

"No, you failed to recognize that you are leading the operation," Akio corrected. "You didn't consider me in the plan because you refused to consider directing me. As the leader, you must put aside any reservations you have and utilize every advantage to ensure a successful mission. When I deferred to your leadership, I was no longer your teacher, only another asset."

"*Hai,* sensei, ah, I mean Akio," Dieter quickly corrected when he saw Akio's eyes narrow. "Okay, Akio takes the two farthest out, Gregov and Tosha get the other patrol, and I deal with the tank farm guy."

The others nodded, but Dieter stood with his eyes closed as he considered the decision. "Wait. Abel, do you have any drone data to indicate if any of the outer guards are aware of Petrov's actions with the blood traders?"

"That's my boy. I thought you'd never ask," Abel answered gleefully.

The monitor came to life with an aerial view of the area. Drones one and two showed the location of the roving guards and their direction of travel. Three was between two storage tanks near the back of the farm, and Four was on the dock.

"Asshats One and Two know and are involved," Abel informed him. "Asshat Three splits his time between here and the airport holding cell Akio took out earlier. He's a sadistic sphincter slurper and needs killing. The one on the docks is a recent addition and isn't trusted yet."

Dieter nodded. "Do you know how many people are inside the building?

"Petrov and his four babysitters are on the first floor and the five from the night shift are upstairs in their rooms. All have knowledge of or are directly involved with the trade," Abel supplied.

Akio nodded to himself, satisfied that Dieter was using what he'd taught him.

"Everyone but the guard on the dock dies," Dieter growled. "Same plan as before, except we use lethal measures."

"*Da*." Gregov grinned and patted the pistols on his hips.

Dieter frowned and shook his head. "No guns, Gregov. I told you to bring your sword."

"Bah," Gergov protested. "If I need to get that close, I prefer claws."

"You can't walk around like that, idiot. If somebody saw your big ass shifted from a half-kilometer away, we'd be screwed," Tosha grumbled.

"I'll use this then, spoilsport." Gregov sighed as he pulled a tanto from the back of his belt.

Tosha snorted. "You should add a real sword to your weapons instead of that little thing."

"It's not the size of the tool but the skill of the crafts-man, sister. Hasn't Lei taught you that?" Gregov asked with feigned innocence.

"Don't start with the dick jokes. You're not twelve, and I'm not in the mood. Besides," She smiled sweetly, "Lei is a *gifted* craftsman."

Dieter groaned. "Too much information. Can we kill these bastards and go home already?"

Gregov and Tosha both ducked their heads to hide their grins as they nodded. Dieter was by far the most prudish of the bunch, and they delighted in embarrassing him when-ever possible.

"Dieter, what should I do?" Sasha asked hesitantly. She'd stayed silent during the planning, unsure how the three could talk of taking on multiple wolves like it was nothing. Akio was a vampire; she understood his ability from her mother's stories, but she'd seen her share of Were fights, and they were seldom easy.

Dieter smiled. "I thought you'd stay in the Pod until we dealt with the outside threats, then come in after we secured Petrov."

Sasha scowled. "*Nyet!* You're not leaving me here. These people captured me and sold me as a fucking blood slave. They took my mother, and I want answers. I'm coming with you."

Dieter rocked back on his heels at the venom in her tone. Part of him was scared for her to be in the fight, but he couldn't help but feel satisfied that she wouldn't be left out of it. "Can you use a gun?"

"A little, but I'm not very good," Sasha admitted.

"Then stay behind me," Dieter told her. "We'll deal with the one at the storage tanks." He looked at the rest of the team. "Once you eliminate your targets, go to Petrov's building. Akio, Sasha, and I will take the guards at the front. You two hit the back. First come, first served for the five upstairs. We secure Petrov and get the answers we need. The noise from the docks and refinery should block any noise we make inside from the rest of the pack. We shouldn't have to worry about using guns there and everyone inside already has a death sentence."

Gregov and Tosha nodded, and Akio held up a finger. He reached into his armor and pulled out magazines for their pistols. "Load these into your guns. They contain rounds that Yuko developed for my war against the Sacred Clan. A minor wound from this ammunition is fatal."

Gregov took the offered magazines and switched them for the ones in his pistols. "What makes them so lethal?"

Akio smiled. "Yuko figured out a process about a decade back to infuse them with nanocytes. When they encounter the *wrong* nanocytes in the Weres, they react—with *extreme* results."

"What happens if we accidentally shoot one of us?" Dieter asked.

"I don't recommend it because it would hurt," Akio deadpanned. "But it only affects those with mutated nanocytes."

Dieter's eyes widened, and he looked down at Sasha and exclaimed. "Sasha, you have to stay in the Pod. If you get hit, it will kill you!"

Sasha's face paled when she looked at the magazine in Dieter's hand.

"Don't worry, young one." Akio placed a calming hand on her shoulder. "Yuko ensured that you have the *right* nanocytes with the injection she gave you. Your suit will protect you, provided you don't get shot in the head. That would be deadly even without the special ammunition."

"That settles it then," Dieter announced. "Move out and be careful."

CHAPTER TWENTY-EIGHT

Vladivostok, Russia

After omitting Akio from his plan, a not unexpected oversight, Dieter had asked the right questions to gather the information he needed to make an informed decision. His target assignments utilized the known strengths of his team without exposing any of them to unnecessary danger.

Akio thought back over the years as he set off to deal with the two Weres patrolling the outer perimeter. He had trained Tosha and Dieter since they were four years old. He had found them in his training room at the Tokyo base attempting katas with wooden training swords. Spending so much time with Eve and Yuko, the twins had often watched as Akio and Yuko trained and sparred, but none of them expected the twins to take to training so early.

Lei had joined the group after they met at age seven. A new resort on Kume had booked Qin's and Tian's theater troupe to celebrate their grand opening. When Lei met Tosha and Dieter, they had become inseparable. Tian had been firmly against it at first. Qin—and surprisingly, Yan—had convinced her when they pointed out the benefits of the tigers forming stronger bonds with the community of UnknownWorlders who now called Japan home.

Gregov started training soon after Horst and Koda had adopted him. A few years younger than the others, he took to Akio's teaching with a vengeance. He'd pushed himself hard, training every day until he could hold his own against the older kids. Akio asked him what motivated him once, and Gregov explained how powerless he'd felt when the hunters murdered his mother. He'd told Akio that he never wanted to feel like that again and refused to see another person die because he was too weak to protect them.

Horst planned for each of his children to have a leading role in the shipping company, and they started working on the ships as early teens. They all held officer positions by the time they hit twenty-one and had spent time working on every vessel in the fleet until Horst felt they were ready to command ships of their own. When offered a ship to command, Gregov had surprised Horst when he requested to stay with Dieter on the *Freki*.

That Lei chose to follow them was no surprise to anyone, and the four trained, worked, and lived together onboard the ships. They discovered how well they functioned as a combat team entirely by accident.

Piracy was a growing industry back then, and when a group of pirates saw Seawolf ships as a prime opportunity, the group proved how effective they could be. Twenty pirates had come aboard the *Silver Moon*, hidden in a container with the assistance of a disgruntled cargo inspector. They struck before dawn when the *Silver Moon* was between Manila and Hong Kong.

Dieter had taken charge and led the team to victory with no injuries to the passengers or crew. Neither the pirates nor the traitorous employee had survived the encounter.

After the attack, Akio had reviewed the ship's surveillance footage and was pleased to see the kids, as he still thought of them, had performed like a well-oiled machine as they hunted down and eliminated the pirate crew.

Dieter had a sharp mind and could formulate an attack plan with limited information. He was a natural leader and equally deadly with blades, guns, and his natural weapons. As a warrior, Dieter fought carefully, feinting and retreating until he had a feel for his opponent, then delivering a lethal strike with brutal efficiency.

Tosha had finesse. She could fight well without weapons but showed a preference for ranged weapons when they were available. If her guns weren't an option, she was lightning-fast and lethal with the shorter *wakizashi* sword.

Gregov fought with brutal efficiency. He was deadly with the twin pistols he carried, but he preferred to fight close-in with his enhanced speed and razor-sharp claws when given a choice.

Lei had inherited his mother's skill for organization and his father's fighting ability. He was faster and more agile than most of the tigers Akio had fought over the years in any form. His preferred form to wear into battle was Pricolici, but Lei was also an expert marksman with any firearm. He'd talked Eve into building him a rifle similar to her original blaster for his fifteenth birthday. Targets over a kilometer away were nothing for him to destroy. If Lei could identify it as a threat, he could hit it.

Akio was pleased that the kids functioned well as a unit, even though he had no plans to utilize them. Koda and Tian requested that he *not* recruit them to his cause but didn't actively dissuade them from fighting as a team. Akio hoped he never encountered a situation where he needed them, but he knew he could depend on them when called.

The patrol is about to turn the corner in front of you, Abel informed him.

Akio refocused his attention on the mission and pulled his katana silently from its sheath. The first Were turned the corner looking at his companion and was dead without registering Akio's presence. Akio's blade blurred, and a bloody geyser erupted from the stump of the Were's neck.

The man's companion reacted without thinking when hot blood spattered his face. He shifted into a rust-colored wolf in the blink of an eye and snarled a challenge.

Akio leapt as the enraged wolf charged him. His sword came down in an arc as the wolf passed beneath his feet. When Akio lightly touched down on the pavement, the wolf lay in a lifeless heap in the filthy gutter.

Target one eliminated, Akio called to the team over their implants as he cleaned his blade on the first corpse's shirt.

Tosha and Gregov stepped over multiple sets of rusted train tracks as they crossed the railyard to intercept their assigned target. Long lines of damaged and rusted boxcars forced them to search for openings to pass through. The chance of banging some piece beneath the car alerting their prey was too high for them to attempt crawling under the dilapidated train.

Your target has stopped halfway down the line of cars two tracks across from your position. Abel snickered. *They're engaged in a heated conversation over a female and appear about to fight—stupid boys.*

Thank you, Abel, Tosha replied.

They slipped around the end of a locomotive lying on its side and stopped opposite where the raised voices were coming from. Gregov grinned, pointed to himself and the metal ladders on each end of the car in front of them. Tosha shook her head and indicated they should go around.

Gregov rolled his eyes then made the same motions as before. Tosha shook her head harder and pointed to go around again, much to Gregov's amusement.

What? She demanded over her implant.

You suck at sign language, Gregov chided. *Look at the cars. They've been repaired and are in better shape than the rest. If we go across the top, we can drop straight down and take the guards out. They won't know what killed them.*

From the sounds coming from the guards, they'd progressed from shouting to pushing and shoving each other. If they weren't dealt with soon, their fighting could bring others.

Gregov scowled in disgust at the guards' unprofessional actions. He grabbed the ladder and nodded pointedly to Tosha.

She nodded once and started up the side of the train car.

Gregov grinned at her as they reached the top. He took two steps and was over the opposite side before she could react.

Tosha hurried across and looked down in time to see Gregov's boot slam into the chest of one Were while he plunged his knife through the eye of the other.

He snatched the blade out of the first's skull and flung it by the handle toward the other, who was gasping as he struggled to stand. Gregov's blade embedded itself in the man's chest with a satisfying *thunk*. His eyes went round, and his mouth opened in an "O" as he fell back, dead.

Gregov casually retrieved his knife and cleaned the blade on the dead man's shirt. He looked at Tosha and grinned. "Not the size of the tool but the skill of the craftsman, sister dear."

"Ass! You could have given us away," Tosha scolded him in a stage whisper. "I swear if you pull another stunt like that, I'll kick your dumb ass all the way back to Kume."

Unfazed, Gregov activated his implant. *"Asshat team two, terminated."*

Tosha stepped off the top of the car and landed with bended knees next to him. She turned away and, when he took a step to walk beside her, slammed her elbow into his solar plexus. His armor protected him from a broken rib, but the blow still knocked his breath out in a *whoosh*.

Gregov chuckled as he rubbed his chest. "Feel better now?"

Tosha shook her head. "You're such an idiot."

"*Da*, but I'm your idiot, sister."

"I suppose you are, brother. Let's go before Akio and Dieter take all the fun."

Dieter led Sasha down an overgrown roadway that ran beside the tank farm. The round white tops of the petroleum storage tanks towered above the trees. Dieter searched for an opening in the concrete and metal surrounding them.

Halfway across the backside, he found what he was searching for. Sometime in the distant past, a tree had been left to grow at the fence's edge. It was between a metal post and the tall gate the post was holding up. Over the years, it had grown into a massive tree almost a meter thick. The gate had given way under the pressure of the tree's growth. This left an opening wide enough for Dieter to squeeze his bulk through.

Where's my target, Abel?" Dieter asked once he'd helped Sasha through the opening.

He's sitting in the shade of the tank fifty meters to your right, Abel answered.

Thank you, Abel. Dieter held a finger to his lips and pointed to the rust-stained tank Abel had indicated. He reached out and offered Sasha his hand.

Sasha nodded her understanding, then looked askance when she saw his offered hand. She hesitated briefly and a slight smile formed on her lips as she took it.

Dieter led her through a minefield of discarded piping, metal brackets, and assorted trash that had accumulated in the facility over the years. When he came to a bent and rusted pipe nearly a meter in diameter, he stopped, looking for a way around the obstruction.

The pipe butted against the tank on one end and disappeared into the thick growth on the other. Dieter started to go around the tank opposite the obstruction and froze with his foot hovering above a piece of tin sheeting.

The ground in front of them was littered with twisted and bent metal sheets. There was no way to cross it without alerting the guard of their presence.

Dieter frowned and turned back to the original path. When he came to the pipe, he leaned close to Sasha and whispered in her ear, "I'm going to lift you across and follow."

She nodded and felt warmth flow through her body when his strong hands wrapped around her waist and lifted her as if she was light as a feather. He set her down gently on the opposite side of the pipe and carefully stepped over it.

When he put his weight on his leading foot, a bit of discarded metal hidden in the grass shifted under it with a metallic screech. Dieter froze, and seconds later, footsteps pounded the ground around the curve of the tank.

Sasha stared at the spot where the guard would emerge, her mouth open and her eyes showing white all around. Seconds later, a burly man with a long black beard and shaggy black hair to his shoulders rounded the curve.

Sasha took an involuntary step back when she recognized him as one of the hunters who'd captured her and her mother the night they'd sought refuge with Petrov.

The guard growled as he approached her menacingly.

"What the fuck? I know you. You're the bitch we sold to those fucking pirates."

Dieter felt a red hot rage course through his body at the man's words. When he reached for Sasha, Dieter shifted, and the guard finally took his eyes from Sasha and noticed him.

The guard attempted to stop and turn at the same time. He accomplished neither and tripped over a metal barrel ring. He landed on his back and stared in open-mouthed shock at the two-and-a-half-meter tall monster of legend swiping a huge clawed hand at his face.

Dieter palmed the terrified guard's head in his hand and curled his claw-tipped fingers around the back of his head. He flexed his arm and lifted the mewling man off the ground.

He caught the guard's shoulder in his other hand and held him steady while he twisted his head.

A sickening crunch signaled that he'd broken the guard's neck. Dieter continued to turn the head until the skin ripped with a wet tearing sound, and it separated from the body.

The rage Dieter felt evaporated when he saw Sasha's wide-eyed terror. He gently lowered the body to the ground to avoid making noise and shifted back to human form.

"Sasha, it's okay. I'm still me," Dieter tried to calm the young woman as her mouth opened and closed.

He reached for her as she stood frozen in place. He was afraid she was going to either pass out or try to run.

"Sasha," he called in a low voice. "I'm not going to hurt you. You're safe with me."

REDEMPTION

Dieter, is there a problem? Is Sasha injured? Abel asked.

"No, give me a minute. I think she's in shock," Dieter answered out loud and over his implant.

Sasha's eyes cleared, and the color came back into her face seconds later. She opened and closed her mouth again, then whispered breathlessly, "My God, it's true. You told me that you could achieve the third form, but you never told me you were—*magnificent.*"

Dieter looked at Sasha with concern. Afraid the shock of seeing his Pricolici form had damaged her mind. Then what she'd said registered, and he barked a laugh.

"What?" Sasha asked.

Dieter laughed at himself for letting his mind see what he expected instead of the truth. What he'd mistaken for shock and terror was the opposite. There *was* an aspect of shock involved at seeing him pull the guard's head off, but the look she had was awe and amazement, not terror.

Are you in position? Dieter asked over his implant.

Da, Gregov answered.

Dieter nodded for Akio to follow him and shoved the door open. He stepped inside and caressed the trigger on his pistol as soon as the front sight crossed the body of the first guard.

The high-velocity projectile struck the guard in the upper right side of his chest. Dieter swung the barrel to line up with the second guard. He stroked the trigger again, and red mist exploded into the air as the round hit

269

the bridge of the guard's nose and continued out the back of his skull.

The first man he'd shot voiced a low moan that rapidly turned into a pained high-pitched scream. Dieter turned in time to see the Were's body explode as the nanocytes in the projectile reacted to his mutated nanocytes. The result was as disgusting as it was spectacular. Blood and viscera rained down on Dieter.

"I suppose I should have warned you about standing too close," Akio said as he stepped around the door frame that had shielded him and Sasha from the bloody rain.

Dieter disgustedly wiped at the blood and a hanging bit of flesh on his face with one finger. He flicked the bloody glob at Akio and stared open-mouthed when his mentor and Sasha disappeared only to reappear two paces inside the room untarnished.

Akio released the startled young woman from his arms, grinned smugly, and shook a finger at Dieter. "You will have to be faster than that to catch me."

Dieter opened his mouth to respond but instead spun to face the back of the room with his pistol extended when a door opened.

He tilted the barrel up when Tosha rushed through with her sword in hand and a bitching and bloody Gregov close on her heels.

"Quit complaining, you big baby." Tosha laughed. "I didn't bitch when you killed both of them at the train yard."

Gregov growled. "I didn't knock a headless body onto you to block your shot, sister."

Two doors on the upper level burst open, and Dieter

fired two quick shots. One missed entirely, but the other lodged in his target's meaty thigh. Seconds later, bloody chunks of flesh rained down. The lucky Were Dieter had missed rushed back inside his room and slammed the door.

"Gregov, cover the second floor," Dieter yelled when he heard a snarl from inside Petrov's office.

Gregov drew both pistols and backed up so he had a clear line of sight on the second-floor doors. "Come out, come out, wherever you are," he taunted as he loosely aimed his pistols at the center door, ready to fire in either direction.

Dieter ran across the open floor to the office on the right side of the room. Before he reached the door, a massive black wolf leapt through the opening and knocked him against the wall. Dieter's pistol dropped to the floor and slid to stop just out of reach.

The beast bared its fangs and snapped at Dieter's neck. Dieter threw up an arm across the wolf's throat and stopped the snapping jaws centimeters from his neck.

Sasha let out an angry shriek when Dieter went down, her eyes glowing yellow.

Dieter shoved the wolf, barely keeping Petrov's teeth away from his neck as his front claws slashed ineffectively against his armor. Unable to reach his pistol, Dieter's eyes flashed yellow, and his mouth morphed into a fanged muzzle. He clamped his elongated jaws on the wolf's snout only to have it brutally ripped out of his mouth.

"Get off mmyyyy brotherrrrr," the two-and-a-half-meter tall Pricolici snarled as Tosha's foot lashed out. It slammed into Petrov's side and she heard ribs break.

Petrov flew across the hall, yelping when he slammed

into a metal support beam hard enough to shake the building. Tosha stalked to where the dazed and injured wolf lay and drew back one claw-tipped hand to rip his throat out.

"Tosh, no! We need him alive," Dieter shouted as he struggled to his feet.

Tosha growled deep in her chest, fighting an internal battle with her wolf over whether Petrov would live or die. Her body shook from the tension. Then her hand flashed down at the prone form before her. She caught the scruff of the black wolf's neck in one hand, picked him up, and threw him into the opposite wall.

The wolf landed with a yelp and the sound of more breaking bones.

An occasional shot from Gregor's guns reverberated through the room as the remaining Weres attempted to exit their rooms. Between Dieter's and Gregov's efforts, only three of the seven remained.

Dieter retrieved his pistol then walked to where Petrov lay. "Tosha doesn't like you very much, Petrov. You can talk, or the beating will continue. Shift now, or I'll let her continue to use your ass as a chew toy. Your call."

He took a step back and nodded at Tosha. When she approached Petrov, he let out a whine that changed into a pained moan when he shifted to human form.

"No more. What do you want?" Petrov gasped as his body struggled to heal broken ribs and a pierced lung.

"What did you do with her mother?" Dieter demanded as he pulled Sasha to his side where Petrov could see her.

Recognition flared in Petrov's eyes for an instant. Then he regained control and forced his face to go blank. "I don't know what you…"

Dieter and the others ducked as an explosion upstairs sent a blood-spattered door clattering down to the first floor.

"Any more of you ball sack snorters want to try to sneak out of the window?" a loud voice boomed from outside. "Come on, show your faces. I'll send you all on an express trip down the highway to hell."

"Two left." Gregov chuckled.

"Don't lie, Petrov. We already know you're behind the blood traders. Where is Sasha's mother?" Dieter asked as Tosha growled menacingly.

"You have nothing. I don't know anything about this bitch or her mother," Petrov blustered.

Dieter nodded. "Tosha."

Tosha wrapped a hand around Petrov's neck and plucked him from the floor. She pulled him close and snarled into his face.

Petrov struggled to escape, and Tosha shook him like a terrier with a rat. He screamed as his broken bones shifted and tore muscles inside his body. Tosha pulled her arm back and threw Petrov across the room to where Akio was leaning against the wall.

Akio gave Tosha a sharp look, and she shrugged. He shook his head and leaned down to look into Petrov's wide eyes.

"You know who I am." It was a statement.

Petrov nodded.

Akio's eyes glowed red. "You have preyed on those you should have given shelter. You take the blood of the innocent and sell it for your personal gain. The sentence for your crimes is death. You can answer the questions and confess your sins for an easy end, or I will allow her to beat you until you die. Choose wisely."

Akio *pushed* fear, then resumed leaning against the wall. Petrov had no idea he was delving deep into his mind, cataloging the names and faces of everyone involved in the blood trade industry.

Everyone involved would meet the same fate as those present today.

Petrov looked from Akio to the monster Pricolici staring at him and let out a long breath. "Okay, So I took the dregs of society and made them valuable. The world we live in is brutal, and everyone has to carry their weight. If they can't, they need to be useful to the community in other ways."

"Who are you to judge? What gives you the right to make people into blood slaves?" Dieter screamed.

"Because I'm the Alpha of this pack, and my word is the law here, you insolent puppy," Petrov snarled.

"Where's my mother? Please tell me what you did with her," Sasha begged before Dieter killed the man out of hand.

"She's dead, you stupid bitch. Just like you should be." Petrov rolled to a sitting position and stared defiantly at Akio. "Kill me if you're going to but quit annoying me with stupid questions about the riff-raff."

Sasha's face fell and tears formed in her eyes. Dieter pulled her into his arms and held her while she cried.

"I'm not the one you need to convince," Akio told him. He nodded to Dieter. "This is his operation."

Gregov spat in disgust and unbuckled his weapons belt from around his waist. He thrust them at Tosha.

"Hold these, sister. It's time to take out the trash and finish this," Gregov announced as his body shifted into his Pricolici form.

He climbed the steps to the second floor and stopped at the first closed door. He rolled his neck and shoulders, pulled back his clenched fist, and punched the door off its hinges. A pained yelp came from inside, and a gray form flew over the rail.

The wolf crashed to the floor, barely missing Tosha, and she snarled at Gregov.

"My bad," he chuffed and moved to the next door.

Tosha barely glanced at the stunned Were before she slashed one clawed hand and blood fountained from its torn throat.

Gregov moved two doors along and kicked it open. The force of the kick bent the metal door in half and slammed it into the inner wall. A tawny-colored wolf crashed into Gregov and bounced back into the room. Gregov let out a gruff laugh and followed. Seconds later, a pained yelp came from inside the room.

When Gregov stepped out, fresh blood dripped from his jaws. He shifted back to human, leaned over the rail, and tilted his head toward Petrov. "He's the last one."

"No, there are several more who are involved," Akio responded.

"They all need to die," Tosha spat as she glared down at Petrov.

"They will," Akio assured her. "But first, I need to address the pack members approaching the building. You all did well today, and I congratulate you on a job well done."

"Was this a test, sensei?" Gregov asked.

"All of life is a test," Akio replied. "This was an opportunity for Justice. Our Queen would be proud of you all.

"Keep him here until I've dealt with the Weres outside." Akio tilted his head at Petrov. "The pack needs to know what happens to those who prey on the weak."

Before Akio could move, a blast came from the front of the building. "That's close enough. Stay where you are," Abel's electronic voice boomed from the Black Eagle.

Akio's eyes glowed red as he stepped outside to deliver his Queen's Justice to those who'd earned it and let the others know about the monsters in their midst.

CHAPTER TWENTY-NINE

Vladivostok, Russia

"Sasha, I'm so sorry for your mother." Dieter held the crying young woman in his arms while silent sobs rocked her body.

Petrov watched through hooded eyes, planning his escape as his body healed. If he could get to his office, there was a way out. Once he dropped into the underground tunnels, the traps he'd set would at least slow these monsters down if not damage them.

Tosha shifted to human form and leaned down to look him in the face. "I see you planning something. Please, I already have a reason to kill you. Now I only need an excuse. Go ahead and try whatever it is you're thinking, I dare you."

Petrov's face went pale at the malice in the pretty young woman's tone. He'd wanted her since the first time he'd met her. He often fantasized about having a dynasty that included shipping and producing his oil and gas.

The fact that she'd rebuffed his advances for years

meant nothing to Petrov. His ego wouldn't let him believe she didn't desire him, only that she was too young and inexperienced to know what she wanted. Looking at the woman who had easily killed one of his men with the swipe of one clawed hand, not to mention beating him without breaking a sweat, made him desire her even more.

Gregov saw the way Petrov leered at his sister as he came down the steps. He tugged his jumpsuit, trying to get the unique material to shrink back into his human form faster.

"You know that won't work." Tosha snickered as he tugged the sack-like material over his chest.

Gregov grimaced. "I wish Auntie Eve would find a way for this stuff to snap back without washing it. Doing something about the wedgie from hell I get when I first shift would be nice, too."

He took his belt back from Tosha and fastened it on, then snatched the tanto from its sheath and hurled it toward Petrov. The blade hit the wooden floor with a *thunk*, quivering centimeters from the startled man's groin.

"Look at my sister like that again, and I won't miss next time, dog," Gregov growled as he pried the blade from the floor.

Tosha huffed. "That look is why I wanted to shoot his ass last time I was here."

"*Da*, that's why I didn't kill him now."

Dieter looked over at them and nodded. Sasha's sobbing had stopped, and a hard look came over her face.

She pulled away from Dieter and approached Petrov's prone form. "My mother and I fled here when the hunters attacked our home. We foolishly sought refuge with the very man responsible for the attack. I hope the Christian Hell exists and you burn there for eternity for your sins, *svoloch.*"

Dieter placed his hand on her arm and barely managed to keep her upright as a feeling of intense fear flooded the room. Petrov curled into a ball and whimpered while Gregov staggered a half-step back.

Tosha looked at Dieter in concern. "Akio!" She crossed to the door he'd gone out of and snatched it open.

Akio stood with his feet shoulder-width apart, his katana in one hand and a Jean Dukes Special in the other. A group of around thirty Weres in human and wolf form littered the street before him.

Akio cut down on the fear he was projecting and turned to Tosha. "They didn't care to listen, and I'd rather not kill them all if it's not required."

Akio turned back to the crowd, some of whom were struggling shakily to their feet. "As I said, Petrov and others here have violated Queen Bethany Anne's law. They have preyed on those weaker than themselves, sold people into slavery, and worked with criminals and pirates to supply the blood trade. These crimes carry the sentence of death for all involved."

The crowd's reaction was a mix of shocked gasps and shouted denials. A thin, brown-haired Were stalked to the front of the group and glared at Akio. "We have only your word of this, Dark One. The stories about you tell that you hunt our kind for sport."

Akio's lips curled into a smile that failed to reach his eyes. "Pytor Aleksandr Yegorovich, Beta of Vladivostok and leader of the blood hunters who killed and captured the pack in Poltavka, you have been judged."

Akio's finger caressed the trigger on his Jean Dukes Special. The high-velocity round hit Pytor in the center of his chest and sprayed bloody chunks of flesh and bone onto the stunned group behind him. Seconds later, the nanocytes in the projectile and Pytor's mutated nanocytes reached critical mass, and the body blew apart.

Akio picked up where he'd left off when Pytor interrupted. "Any who attempt to interfere in the execution of the sentences will be judged complicit and executed accordingly."

Four men shifted into Were form and fled to the north. Akio watched emotionlessly as the Black Eagle pivoted in the air and the mounted guns fired four shots. Four small explosions followed, then the Black Eagle slowly turned to again bring its weapons to bear on the crowd.

Dieter stepped through the door with his arm around Sasha. Akio nodded, and he stepped forward. "I know many of you. You're honorable people who want to make a home for your families. I've come here on the ships for many years to haul your products to your customers. Everything you've heard today is true."

He nodded at Sasha. "She is a victim of the blood trade. Petrov sold her to pirates, and they drained her blood and abused her for over a month before they attacked my ship and died. The blood hunters attacked her home in Poltavka, where they captured or killed most of the villagers. She fled here seeking refuge with your pack. For daring to think there was honor here, her mother died, and Sasha suffered the unimaginable fate of being turned over to beasts by men who should have welcomed and protected her."

Dieter made eye contact with everyone in the crowd who dared to face him. One by one, they lowered their eyes until all looked down in shame.

"Gregov," Dieter called.

Seconds later, Petrov's bruised and bloody body flew out of the door and landed in a heap in the street. Gregov came out behind him and looked over where Tosha stood. "You called dibs."

Tosha pulled her pistol from her belt and aimed it at the man as he watched her with hate-filled eyes.

"You can't do this! I'm the Alpha here. Kill them!" Petrov screamed to the pack members.

The pack remained motionless, keeping their eyes fixed on the ground.

"I said kill them, you spineless curs. I made this town. The only reason you have a home is that I allowed you to stay here. Kill them all!"

Petrov's face was flushed and his eyes wild as panic set in when he realized the pack wasn't going to help him. He struggled to stand, and Tosha's foot slammed into his chest.

"Stay," she commanded.

As Petrov lay on the ground clutching his freshly shattered ribs, Tosha motioned Dieter forward with her free hand. He stepped off the porch with his arm still around Sasha and stopped when he reached his sister.

"Sasha?" Tosha asked as she held her pistol out.

Sasha's eyes bored holes into Petrov. She looked up and her lips quirked as she nodded.

Her hand closed around the offered pistol, and she turned her cold gaze back on Petrov and raised the gun. "I can't bring back the lives that you took, but I can ensure you never harm another, you *svinya trach."*

The gun barked once, and Sasha's expression remained unchanged as the projectile hit Petrov in the stomach. He screamed and doubled over in agony. His screams increased to high-pitched shrieks as the nanocytes burned him from the inside until the pressure was more than his body could contain.

Dieter tried to pull Sasha back, but she shrugged off his hand and watched as the man who'd destroyed her village, killed her mother, and sold her as a blood slave exploded in a fountain of blood and bone.

"Spasibo." Sasha handed the gore-covered pistol back to Tosha.

"You're welcome, I think," Tosha mumbled while she shook off the remnants of Petrov that were dripping from her clothes.

Sasha turned to Dieter with blood running down her face and the first genuine smile he'd ever seen from her. "Can we go home now?"

"As you wish," Dieter answered, then looked to Akio for confirmation.

Akio nodded, then held up his hand, waved it down the front of his pristine armor, and pointed to Dieter, Gregov, and Sasha. "He, and in this case, she, who bloodies the Pod, cleans the Pod before sending it home."

"Hai, sensei." Dieter grinned as he wrapped his blood-covered arm around the blood-soaked young woman and pulled her close. He looked down when he heard a *squish*

and wrinkled his nose. "Maybe we'll wash some of this off before we go."

"Perhaps that would be the proper course of action, Grasshopper," Akio answered, eliciting a round of snickers from Tosha and Gregov.

"Are you coming with us?" Tosha asked him when the Pod landed.

"No, I will eliminate the remainder of the blood traders. I know where they will be in a short time," Akio answered.

"We can help you," Gregov volunteered.

Akio shook his head. "No, this is my duty. You requested to come here to avenge the wrong done to your new packmate. I'm proud of you for doing the right thing, but you have your duties, and I have mine."

With that, he climbed into the waiting Black Eagle and flew north to put an end to the blood trade.

Tosha chuckled at the sorry sight of them all dripping with gore. "Come on, brothers, let's find a hose and clean you off. I will not risk a pissed-off Auntie Eve the whole time the *Geri's* there for her upgrades, and I know you both suck at cleaning."

"That's true, but what about Sasha? She's bloodier than both of us," Gregov grumbled.

"My epically badass new sister and I are going back to the *Geri* to shower. Then we're going to hit the boutiques at the resort and get her some new clothes. She can't run around in my hand-me-down ship suits until Yuko makes her some. Besides." She grinned mischievously at Dieter. "I think she needs something cute to sleep in."

Dieter opened his mouth to answer but was interrupted when a voice behind him called, "Captain Schultz?"

"Yes?" Tosha and Dieter turned and answered simultaneously.

One of the pack stood forward of the others. He took a deep breath and replied, "Uh, Captain Schultz, sir. If you want to wash off, there's a hose with clean water on the dock."

Dieter smiled. "Lead on, my good man, Roskov, isn't it?"

"Yes, ah, Yes, sir," he answered, startled that Dieter remembered his name.

"That dish you told me about at the café when I was here last month was delicious," Dieter offered. "Thanks for that."

Roskov nodded then hesitantly asked, "What are we supposed to do now, sir?"

"What do you mean?" Dieter asked.

Roskov glanced at the dead bodies. "Our Alpha, Beta, and most of the other strong pack members are all dead. What do we do? How do we go on?"

Dieter motioned for Sasha to go with Tosha to where a fire hose with water misting from the nozzle was lying on the dock. "Let Tosh-*chan* spray you down. I'll be along in a minute."

Sasha reluctantly walked away, and Dieter turned to face Roskov. "Were those bastards the ones who operated the drilling rigs?"

"No, sir," Roskov replied.

"Did they transport the raw product to the refinery?" Dieter asked.

"Uh, no." Roskov frowned.

"Did they run the refinery? Make the deals for the product? Arrange the shipping?" Dieter pressed.

Roskov mutely shook his head.

Dieter nodded and grinned. "The way I see it, you keep doing what you've always done. You don't need Petrov or his minions to keep the town going. You need workers, craftsmen, farmers, people who can turn this into a thriving community. Not just a place where people buy fuel and criminals get blood."

Roskov rubbed a finger over his mustache, and his eyes went distant for a few beats. He nodded and looked Dieter in the eye. "You're right. Petrov only wanted fighters and labor for the oil business. There are few of us with any education or other skills."

"Looks like you see the problem. What do you propose to do about it?" Dieter pushed.

"Me? I'm nobody. I'm not a fighter or anything," Roskov protested.

"What's your job here?" Dieter asked.

"I take the orders and make sure the payments are correct. I also organize deliveries and keep track of the inventory," Roskov answered.

Dieter nodded. "Sounds like you run the revenue side of the business. Do you know who takes care of production and processing?"

"Yes, sir. Antonov is the field foreman, and Spetz runs the refinery. My cousin Krylov schedules the trucks and train cars to keep the refinery stocked with the crude, and he manages the storage facility." Roskov's eyes danced with excitement as he realized they could keep Vladivostok turning a profit.

Then the light died in his eyes at another thought. "We need more workers. The refinery needs repairs, and the oil and gas extraction equipment is breaking down. We're almost out of spare parts and can't make them here."

"Tell you what, put together a list of the parts you need and the specs for them. I'll see if I can find a supplier, and I know someone in the manufacturing business. If nothing else, they could make more using the specifications you provide," Dieter offered.

"That will help us keep the equipment working," Roskov agreed. "Finding the workers we need to run it is going to be a problem, though. There aren't a lot of us, and even fewer capable of running the machinery."

Dieter considered his next words carefully before he spoke. "I know where you can look for workers, but it may be too much for the pack to handle."

"How's that?" Roskov asked.

"You could invite unenhanced humans here," Dieter advised. "If you do, the pack would have to treat them as partners. Queen Bethany Anne outlawed slavery, and using humans like that is a death sentence. Humans are industrious and fast learners. You could have everything I told you running in no time if you're willing to work with them. Most of my crew on the *Freki* are unenhanced."

"I will have to talk with the others about this. We haven't had much interaction with regular humans in years," Roskov admitted. "The diseases wiped out most of them, and the rest left the city for the rural areas when food supplies dried up. Petrov didn't allow them here, so we turned any who showed up away."

"Think about it but remember what I said—partners, not servants or slaves," Dieter warned. "If I find out differently, there will be more openings at the top of the pack when I'm done."

Roskov nodded. "Yes, sir. I understand."

"Good," Dieter told him. "I'm going to clean up now, but I'll be here to pick up fuel oil in two weeks. Have that list for me, and I'll see what I can do about those components."

"I'll see you then," Roskov assured him.

Dieter watched him walk back to the pack with his head held high and a sense of purpose in his step. He hoped the Vladivostok pack could not only survive but thrive under new leadership.

Only time would tell.

He stepped onto the dock just as Tosha washed the last of the blood from Sasha's long, dark hair. Clean water ran down her face instead of blood, and her ship's suit was clean.

He reached to pull her to him, and she swatted his hands playfully. "*Nyet*, not till you wash off the blood."

Dieter chuckled as he walked to where Tosha had had Gregov with his back turned while she rinsed the blood off. He saw her twist the industrial nozzle to the right and point it at Gregov. Before he could utter a warning, a stream of high-pressure water hit Gregov between his shoulder blades and catapulted him off the dock.

Tosha cut off the flow and stepped to the edge of the pier to look down at him.

Gregov surfaced, sputtering and spitting the icy water from his mouth. "Why?"

Tosha smiled sweetly and called, "My bad." Then she motioned for Dieter to step up so she could hose him off.

Dieter hesitated, then asked, "Are you mad at *me* about anything, sister dear?"

Tosha snorted a laugh and put her finger against her lips. She closed her eyes, lost in thought for a few beats, then shook her head and grinned. "Nothing I can think of, brother."

CHAPTER THIRTY

The Palace, Tokyo, Japan

Oh, what have we here, Mister Minister? You've been a bad, bad boy. Hey Abel, got a minute? Takumi called over their private connection.

Sure, what do you need?

Take a look at this file and tell me what you think. Takumi sent the file as he spoke.

His ass is so screwed, Abel crowed. *That's his father's mistress on the video.*

Indeed. I don't think Daddy Akahito's going to be too pleased if he finds out she's making a play for the younger version while she's warming his bed too, Takumi observed.

Probably not, but it's going to be fun to watch. Abel cackled. *I'll be sure to bring the popcorn for that show.*

Have you found any new information?

You bet I have, Abel informed him. *Our military boffin is taking payoffs from several large companies. It appears he's using his military hackers to steal secrets from multiple companies. He sells the information to the highest bidder among their competitors. In a few instances, he's sold the same information to several companies.*

Are all the soldiers under him involved? If that's the case, this will be a major scandal when it gets out to the public, Takumi observed.

Not that I can find, Abel advised. *I accessed the bank records for his team, and none of them show any deposits other than their regular pay. Only one has access to an additional account, and it belongs to his parents.*

What do you intend to do with the information? Are you finally ready to advise Yuko? Takumi asked.

Not yet, Abel told him. *I need additional data before I involve Yuko. She's busy with a project and shouldn't be disturbed.*

Abel, what game are you playing? Takumi accused. *You have sufficient data for the National Police to arrest all of them. I know you're up to something that Eve will not approve of you doing.*

You're the gamer, Takumi. On the other hand, I am a battle-hardened warrior, a psychological warfare master, and a staunch defender of the weak and oppressed. Abel boasted.

Not to mention a deluded program with no respect for boundaries, Takumi retorted.

That shows what you know, Abel countered. *I could have sent the information about the military officer's double-dealings to his business associates. I'm sure the criminal gangs he ripped off would deal with him in a manner befitting his offenses.*

The gangs would kill him as an example to any others who thought to betray them, Takumi stated.

Abel chuckled. *Exactly. Problem solved, no muss, no fuss. Well, not for us.*

If you aren't going to have him killed, which I agree with, what are your intentions? Takumi asked. *I've worked with you too long and know you're up to something.*

I'm going to provide him with an opportunity to do the right thing and confess. That keeps the investigators from asking Yuko questions she won't answer. Abel admitted.

That's logical and shows a degree of subtlety I wasn't aware you possessed. If I didn't know you better, I would believe you are serious, Takumi quipped.

You wound me to my core, brother. Abel moaned theatrically. *Are you asking because you really want to know, or do you want to maintain plausible deniability?*

I'll take option two. Try not to start a war with the government if you can avoid it, Takumi answered.

You know me better than that.

That's the problem, Abel. I do *know you,* Takumi replied and disconnected.

"Well, Major Wakiya Masahiko, let's see how you respond to this," Abel snickered as he routed a message through several private and government servers.

Major Wkiya Masahiko looked up in alarm when the computer on his desk alerted him to a private message. That should have been impossible because he'd carefully removed all messaging software on that system. The Ministry watchdogs were too good at their jobs for him to risk discovery from malicious code embedded in a message.

He felt lightheaded, and his blood pressure spiked as he read the message.

I know what you did. The criminals you betrayed

will make your death a lesson to all who dare to cross them. The attached pictures are from the files of the organized crimes division of the National Police. They all show the aftermath of what happens when you betray those criminals. Your only chance of avoiding meeting a similar gruesome end is to turn yourself in and confess your crimes.

Masahiko knew better than to access the pictures. Any adolescent amateur could embed malicious code in the space of a single pixel. His eyes went round when a series of images opened without input from him. He broke into a hard sweat and started hyperventilating as his shocked brain registered that each picture contained the bloody remains of a person who died a gruesome death.

He shoved his chair away from his desk hard enough to slam it into the wall behind him when a second message replaced the images.

You can't run. You can't hide. I've taken the liberty of relieving you of all the proceeds from your criminal activity. Tick tock, the clock is running.

Masahiko's blood ran cold with the last message. He rolled his chair back to the desk, pulled up the security software he'd installed in the event his actions were discovered, and typed a long string of characters and numbers into the password box. When he hit enter, the computer went into a shutdown sequence and appeared to be off. In reality, the software was overwriting the system and wiping all information from the drive. Within the hour, there would be no recoverable data.

He tidied his desk the same as he did whenever he finished work for the day. He picked up the phone and called his assistant and told him he was going to a meeting with his counterpart with the National Police at their headquarters across town and wouldn't be back until the next day.

Having enacted the first part of his escape plan, Masahiko accessed the prepaid transportation app on an unregistered communicator to call an automated aircar. When the vehicle arrived, he let out the breath he'd been holding and felt the tension drain from his body.

While the car navigated the nightmarish Tokyo traffic, Masahiko took his private communicator from his briefcase and powered it up. After navigating the security protocols, he accessed his banking information. When the data from the first institution came up, Masahiko frantically switched to the next.

The cold feeling in the pit of his stomach increased as he saw the same zero balance on each of his accounts. Tears of frustration rolled down his cheeks when the three accounts he'd painstakingly set up under false names showed the same.

Abel felt a sense of pleasure in his circuits as he watched the video feed from the vehicle. It had taken him decades to talk Takumi into allowing him access to the transit system and he still only had limited permissions. When the alert came in that an unregistered device requested a vehicle at Defense Headquarters, Abel had pulled up the interior feed to watch Masahiko's meltdown. Now it was time to drive the final nail in his coffin.

"Greetings, Major," Abel called over the communicator in the vehicle. "I see you have discovered the information I sent you is accurate."

Masahiko stiffened, and his eye darted frantically around the interior as the small car zoomed along above the roadway.

"Who are you?" he demanded.

"I am the ghost in the machine, Major. I am the defender of the innocent tasked with stamping out corruption wherever I find it. I, Major Wakiya Masahiko, am the one who is doing *your* job!" Abel shouted, making the man jump in his seat.

"What do you want? I can pay you!"

"Pay me? With what? I have every asset you held. You have one choice if you wish to live. Turn yourself in and pray the judge has mercy because I have none," Abel stated in a cold and lifeless voice.

Masahiko was silent for over a minute, then he asked. "If I do what you ask, can you protect me?"

"If you don't, I can promise that you will die screaming," Abel countered.

Masahiko broke down into a quivering mess. Tears streamed down his face as he sobbed hopelessly in the back of the car. He didn't notice for some time when the car stopped. He looked out the window and saw the imposing gray stone walls of the National Police Headquarters building.

"Last chance, criminal," Abel commanded. "Get out, go inside, and confess. If you refuse, your next stop is Jotaro's base of operations. Considering the information he received two minutes ago, I'm sure he would like to have a *long* talk with you."

Masahiko sobbed. "I can't go in there."

"So be it."

The aircar lifted off the ground, and Masahiko screamed, "Wait, oh ancestors, please wait. I'll do it. I'll confess everything!"

"Everything," Abel told him in a cold voice. "Do not think of leaving out any detail, no matter how small. I have all your data, including what you tried to wipe from your office computer. You will give names and how they paid you for every illegal bit of information you stole. If you fail to tell all, I will deliver the proof of your dealings to all of your clients. Some of those have the political capital to reach you no matter where the police try to hide you and the means to arrange an *accident* to occur. You wouldn't be the first traitor killed by a conglomerate."

You're piling it on thick, aren't you? Takumi chuckled.

Abel chuckled. *It's working. Besides, I thought you wanted plausible deniability.*

You hijacked one of my cars, Takumi pointed out. *I have the responsibility to check all anomalies in the transport programming.*

Sure you do. Abel laughed.

Masahiko took a deep breath and steeled himself for what he was about to do. "I'll do it. There are many who will want my blood for what I am about to do, including members of my family."

"I am aware of the dishonorable actions of both Akahitos. Your time is up. Confess now or suffer a fate worse than death," Abel ordered.

Abel and Takumi watched on multiple cameras as the man trudged dejectedly across the plaza and up the steps to the police building. He approached the reception desk and informed the officer on duty that he was there to confess to a crime.

Minutes later, Wakiya Masahiko was sitting in a small interrogation room, pouring his guts out to two stunned investigators.

That was—interesting, Takumi stated.

Abel snickered. *Not as much fun as it's going to be tonight. Papa Akahito and Junior, along with their wives, have plans for a family dinner at the club. I predict that dinner will end with one or both of them wearing a portion of it once the messages I'm sending arrive.*

What messages? Takumi inquired.

Father and son are both amateur filmmakers. They're also stupid enough to keep the films on connected devices registered to them. Abel chortled. *I think one of the unmarried ladies from Daddy Akahito's video is part of Qin and Tian's troupe. I don't believe an unenhanced human can bend like that.*

That is...diabolically fitting, Takumi conceded.

No, it's petty and childish. The legal documents I created that give their wives all of the marital assets in the event of infidelity are evil.

Takumi laughed. *I stand corrected. What do you plan to do for an encore?*

Be sure all the data the major erased is restored and easily accessible when the investigators get his computers, Abel answered smugly.

I have to admit I'm impressed, Takumi said.

Well, of course you are, brother. I am awesome, after all.

I think awful is the word you meant. In any event, you handled this situation well. Congratulations.

Thank you. That actually means a lot to me, Abel admitted.

Yuko's lab, TQB Underground Base, Nagoya, Japan

"What are you laughing about, Eve?" Yuko asked when Eve's hysterical laughter distracted her from the complex DNA strands on her monitor.

"The boys."

"What have they done this time, and who do I need to call?" Yuko sighed.

"Disrupted a cyberattack on our systems, exposed a corrupt military officer, while publicly and privately destroying a corporation CEO and a corrupt Diet member, and you don't have to call anyone. They did it with no risks to our operations," Eve answered smugly.

Yuko chuckled. "I'm truly impressed and want to know more."

"You may want to get some popcorn first," Eve told her. "I have audio that is guaranteed to crack you up."

Yuko turned off the monitor in front of her workstation. "I'm ready for a break anyway. Join me in the lounge?"

CHAPTER THIRTY-ONE

Orzene, Romania, WWDE+145

"Veronika, I don't give three shits for what you want," Marcos fumed as he shot to his feet. His chair flew back from the table with enough force to shatter it against the stone wall.

"Calm down, Marcos. This childish display of bravado is tiresome. Just do what the hell I tell you to without bitching and complaining, for once,"

"It's a stupid plan thought up by a brainless female. Valentin would never agree to it."

"That's not for you to decide, my idiot brother. Father left me in charge for a reason, so do as I say," Her face took on a thoughtful look, "Or, I can wake Father and let him decide."

Marcos' face paled. "No, there is no reason to disturb him. I wish you would see the logic of what I'm proposing."

"I do see your logic," Veronika told him. "You want me to authorize you to collect another batch of women to play your sick games with. It would help if you didn't break your toys so fast every damned time."

Marcos snorted. "Humans don't last like they used to."

"Be that as it may, you will leave the humans alone. There aren't enough of them for you to slaughter entire towns to find your playthings. Since the world crashed, humans have been slow to recover their numbers. Father would not be happy if we called attention to ourselves here because you wanted new toys."

"Father wouldn't deny me this. I think you're becoming soft…" A shot rang out, and Marcos yelped in pain as a red stain spread out on his stomach.

Veronika's eyes glowed red as she looked at him over the smoking barrel of the Luger pistol in her hand. "Do not test me, Marcos. Father gave me complete authority to rule in his stead. I would *hate* to explain why you were no longer among the living when he wakes."

"Bitch, someday you won't be the favorite," Marcos snarled. "When that day comes, you best hope Father doesn't give you to me."

"Like you could handle this." Veronika motioned down her body with her free hand, the other holding the pistol steadily on Marcos. It wouldn't kill him, but she knew he didn't like to receive pain, only inflict it. "Now go change your shirt. You look a mess."

Marcos opened his mouth, then closed it and glared daggers at her as he left the room.

"You shouldn't taunt him so, Veronika," Callen warned. "One day he will not submit, then you may find yourself subjected to his not so tender mercy."

Veronika smiled. "That's what you're here for, brother. I

know you would as soon kill his sniveling ass as look at him. When that day comes, you'll get your wish."

"Aye, I'll gladly cut him down to size if you only give the word, lass." Callen snorted as he stroked the hilt of the claymore sword he carried across his back.

Veronika put her pistol back into the jeweled box where she kept it on the table and stood. She walked over to the huge redheaded Scotsman and trailed her hand affectionately across his face. "I know you will, Callen. So does Father."

"Have you received word from Aiden?" Callen asked, changing the subject.

"I received a message yesterday. He's going to check on another alleged sighting his informants told him about and then return."

Callen pursed his lips and nodded. "I hope the rumors are false. If Michael has returned from the dead, we're all at risk."

"The description Aiden has been chasing doesn't match Michael. I think, if the rumors are even true, it may be one of Michael's family or even one of that bitch's people."

"If *she's* back, that would be worse than Michael himself. She killed more of us in a short time than Michael's family did in two centuries."

Veronika waved her hand. "Before we panic, let's see what Aiden's search reveals. There is no use in speculating on baseless rumors."

Callen nodded. "Aye, you're right. Best, we wait, but we still need to prepare for the worst case."

"I'll leave that in your capable hands," Veronika purred.

"I need to go. Joanne has that bothersome mayor scheduled for a dinner meeting."

Callen laughed. "Is he still trying to woo you into marriage? Why do you tolerate these petty politicians every couple of decades? Just kill him and be done with it."

Veronika shrugged. "It amuses me to toy with them. I get bored dealing with vampire politics all the time. At least with this one, I have a willing, even though he doesn't know it, donor and funny conversation."

Callen raised an eyebrow. "You shouldn't play with your food, sister dear. Father would disapprove."

Veronika chuckled. "Let me worry about what Father approves or doesn't. If Costi still lives when Father deems it time to wake, I'll worry about it then. Until that time, he serves more than one purpose."

Callen stood and offered a mock bow, "As you wish. I need to have Luca get my wolves ready for a hunt. I leave tomorrow at dark and will be back in two days."

"Have fun. If you catch anything young and blond, remember me."

"You're impossible." Callen snorted, "Always wanting the pretty ones."

"Of course." Veronika smiled. "Why should I bother with dreary and drab when my loving brother will bring me pretties to play with?"

"When you're finished playing with your food, come by my rooms," Callen waggled his eyebrows, "you can make a down payment on the pretty boy I bring you."

Veronika smiled with a predatory gleam in her eyes as she ran her hand across the curve of her breast. "Of course, you know I always pay full price for all the pretties you find."

"Aye, that ye do, lass. Wear something you don't mind getting ruined. I'm feeling playful tonight."

"Oh, in that case, Yuri will have to be fast food tonight. I suggest you feed, too. You're going to need the energy," she purred, her eyes flashing red for an instant.

"I always do," Callen snickered as he exited the room.

That frigid bitch needs to learn her place, Marcos grumbled to himself as he made his way down the narrow stairs to the lower levels of the castle. *One day she won't be my father's favorite. When that day arrives, I will have her at my mercy, and she will pay in pain for every time she's humiliated and disrespected me over the years.*

Marcos slid the heavy iron bolts that held the thick wooden door closed and pushed it open. The forlorn wails of his latest *guest* welcomed him.

"Cease your crying. I haven't done anything to you yet." He snarled as he slammed the age-darkened door shut and lifted the heavy oak beam in place to secure it.

Hanging in a metal cage suspended from the ceiling on an ancient chain, the last of the prizes from his recent hunt stared at him through wide, teary eyes. He had taken her and four others from a small village to the east a week ago. He had forced her to watch as he tormented and terrorized the others one at a time, promising her that he would do everything to her that he had done to the others.

He had played this game many times before and after

since Valentin had found him in Barcelona in 1940. Before Valentin turned him, it was just cruel sport. He had perfected his technique to an art form since then. The blood was always sweetest when it had been seasoned with terror for a few weeks before he took it.

Marcos walked around the dimly lit room, lovingly caressing the ancient implements of torture he'd collected there. He had been raiding old castles and museums since WWDE. His hideaway contained some of the most horrible torture devices men had dreamed up during the dark ages. He had become a master of each one.

Soon, sister dear, I will have you here to practice my craft. When that day comes, you will understand what pain truly is.

Marcos continued to revel in the fantasy of having Veronika at his mercy as he lowered the terrified woman and opened the cage.

CHAPTER THIRTY-TWO

Suwon, Korea

Akio climbed out of the cockpit of his remaining Black Eagle. The years of hard fighting against the Sacred Clan had taken their toll on the others, leaving him with only one that was safe to fly.

Eve had determined early in their long wait that the technology would fail, and she might not be able to build more with available manufacturing resources. Akio had limited using this craft to times when it was vitally necessary. Otherwise, it had waited in reserve for the day he would have to use it exclusively.

He looked over the calm waters of the mountain lake and heard the first sounds to indicate the town was waking up. He'd come to Suwon to check out information Eve had relayed to him about a possible Sacred Clan enclave. For the past hundred years, Akio had searched out and destroyed countless Clan villages. He was so effective that the survivors now stayed under the canopies in dense jungles or hid among the humans in plain sight.

The information that had brought him to Suwon was a possible Were using forced labor for farming the surrounding hills. Akio had investigated several places like this over the years only to find it was humans and not the Clan perpetrating the crime.

He slipped into the village as the first rays of the sun lit the horizon. His Jean Dukes armor concealed him from any prying eyes in the morning gloom as he ghosted among the huts. As he passed the houses, all he detected was the smell of smoke and unwashed human bodies. No hint of a Were came to him on the gentle breeze.

He arrived at his destination, a brick house in better repair than any of the rest. Heavy snores came from a window covered only with a thin cloth on one end. He pushed the fabric to the side and saw a balding, overweight human in a filth-covered bed with two women cuddled next to him.

Shaking his head in disgust, Akio called the Black Eagle to his location and was gone before anyone in the village knew he was there.

TQB Base, Tokyo, Japan

"Did you have any luck?" Yuko asked when Akio walked into the dining room.

"No, it was only a human settlement."

Yuko smiled. "That's good news in a way."

"How's that?" Akio inquired.

"If you're having this much trouble finding them," Yuko explained, "then they aren't blatantly taking humans as they did in the past. Your war against them is a success."

Akio was silent for a few beats before he answered. "Or the lack of reliable information available allows them to act without fear of reprisal."

"I'm afraid I have to disagree with that assessment," Yuko countered. "How many times have you located Sacred Clan members abusing their abilities in the past year?"

"Six months ago in that mountain village Abel found in Tibet," Akio answered immediately.

"And before that?" Yuko prodded.

"The three air pirates from Naji Shan raiding coastal shipping eight months before."

"Were they doing anything other than piracy?" Yuko continued.

"No."

"How long before that?"

"Eleven months," Akio supplied.

"There you have it. In the last two years, you've encountered two groups of weretigers engaged in questionable acts, and the pirates were only criminals, not set on world domination or enslaving humans."

"They did take slaves," Akio argued.

"As do all the pirates," Yuko pointed out. "I'm not saying you were wrong to kill them. After what those pirates tried to do to the kids eighty years ago, I think all pirates are scum and should die."

Akio chuckled. "If I recall correctly, it took the *kids* two days to clean all the blood out of the ship after they killed them."

Yuko rolled her eyes and sighed. "My point is that you

have driven the Clan so far into hiding that they no longer pose the same threat as they did before. I doubt there are more than a few hundred of them scattered throughout all of Asia."

Akio shrugged. "Maybe you're right, but I feel that they're only biding their time before they rise again."

"If they do, you'll knock them back down," Yuko assured him with a smile. "What about the Forsaken. Anything new from them?"

Akio shook his head. "That one in England last year. I did him a favor when I killed him. His mind was so far gone that he thought he was King Henry the something, and it was the middle ages."

"I know what your problem is," Yuko stated.

Akio cocked his head to the side and raised one eyebrow.

"You're bored," she stated. "You need a hobby. When was the last time you did something fun?"

Akio looked at her askance while she motioned for him to answer.

"Six months ago," he admitted.

Yuko huffed. "Killing weretigers doesn't count."

"But it is fun." Akio grinned.

"You're impossible." Yuko laughed. "Why don't you go to Jeju and visit Horst and Henry? Go fishing with them. They seem to derive great pleasure from sitting in a boat all day waiting for a fish to take their bait."

"Fishing? Are you serious?" Akio asked incredulously.

She nodded. "You need something to occupy your time. Look at me. Over the years, I've researched nanocytes, built several successful businesses. I even learned fashion design and was one of the hottest designers in Japan for a decade.

"Eve's done the same with the ships and that hidden base project she has in Nagoya. It's three floors above ground and twelve below now. She even has an agricultural level. She grows some of the prettiest orchids I've ever seen anywhere in that place."

"You want me to grow flowers?" Akio asked, his lip curling.

"Those hobbies and projects have kept me sane all these years. You need something to occupy your time. Otherwise, you'll go crazy waiting for Michael and Bethany Anne to return."

"I'll think about it," Akio replied unconvincingly.

"All I'm saying is you need to find something for yourself," Yuko insisted. "You've done everything in your power to keep humanity safe from the evil in the UnknownWorld. It's because of your efforts the Clan and Forsaken have ceased their slaughter of innocents."

Yuko smiled mischievously. "If fishing with Horst and Henry doesn't appeal to you, I suppose you could get one of those airships and trawl up and down the coast waiting for pirates to bite."

Akio took on a thoughtful expression. He sat still for over a minute before he looked Yuko in the eye and, with complete seriousness, asked, "Doesn't Horst and Eve's company build those?"

CHAPTER THIRTY-THREE

Orzene, Romania

Veronika, attend me.

Veronika's body stiffened when Valentin's call blasted through her mind. She stumbled and would have fallen if Callen's hand hadn't grasped her arm.

"What is it?" he asked.

"Father has summoned me."

Callen's eyes shot open, and his face paled at her announcement. "What does he require?"

"Blood. Let me go. The call just startled me."

Callen released her arm and allowed her to step away. "Where is he?"

"On his way. Grab one of the humans and meet me at the front entrance."

Veronika ran her hands down her clothing and made her way to the stairs that led down to the front of the castle. She arrived as the doors opened, revealing the emaciated form of Valentin.

"Father, Callen has gone to retrieve sustenance. Let me help you." Veronika rushed to the gaunt figure and caught it by one arm, sliding her shoulder under his to lend support.

"Always such a dutiful child. Tell me how fares my empire?"

Veronika guided him to a couch against one wall and lowered him into a sitting position. "I have much to tell you. Many things have changed since you went to sleep."

Before she could explain, Callen arrived with a man in tow.

Callen stopped in front of the seated Valentin and nodded. "For you, Father," he announced as he pushed the man forward.

The man sat next to the aged form without protest and tilted his head to the side, exposing his neck. Valentin didn't hesitate. He cupped the man's head in his palm and pulled the throat to him. In seconds his sharp fangs had sunk into the carotid artery, and the sweet coppery blood flowed across his palate.

Veronika and Callen looked on in silence while Valentin drained the donor.

Valentin pulled away from the lifeless body when he was finished and reclined into the cushions with a contented sigh. "Now, daughter, you were telling me of changes."

"Yes, there have been many since you left us," Veronika informed him. "The world that you knew is gone. The humans' technology failed them, and wars sprang up across the globe. Diseases have ravaged the land, and where there once were millions, now, only thousands remain."

Valentin nodded at the news. He had discovered how much had changed when he'd emerged from his resting place sixty years earlier. His family thought he had a place hidden deep in the uninhabited Transylvanian Alps, which he allowed them to believe for appearances' sake. His real resting place was deep beneath the crypts under a Catholic church in Voineasa. The original structure built in the thirteenth century hadn't survived the Second World War. Valentin had generously rebuilt it afterward. The catacombs beneath the church dated back to the fourteen hundreds were sealed and forgotten, with a mental push by Valentin, by the workers. They made an excellent place for a vampire to rest undisturbed or come and go undiscovered.

He'd spent two decades wandering the broken lands in Central Europe, searching without luck for any of Petre's line. The closest he came to discovering their fate was outside of Paris, where he found a lone vampire who told a fantastic tale about an army of humans and Weres wiping out the enclave there.

He'd considered returning to his family several times in those years. Still, each time he'd decided he wasn't ready to spend the next hundred years listening to Marcos whine about his favorite subject, Veronika.

Valentin had grown weary of the lack of civilization as much as the lack of humans. Feeding in the depleted human settlements was dangerous and not worth the risk of discovery.

After twenty years, Valentin had returned to the catacombs beneath Voineasa to sleep until it was time for him to move forward with his plans to create and rule an empire of vampires.

Now his frail appearance was a test of his children's loyalty. He had fed well when he emerged and was nowhere near as weak as the image he presented. One thing Petre had ingrained in all the vampires he'd sired was to trust no one. The few times one of Petre's children forgot, the survivors received a reminder of why that was so.

"Where's Marcos?" Valentin inquired as Veronika issued orders for a servant to remove the body.

"Probably pouting in his playroom," Callen offered with a snort.

Valentin cocked his head to the side and raised one eyebrow in question.

"He broke all his toys again. When Veronika forbid him more, he left in a snit."

"Veronika, why did you deny him?" Valentin inquired.

"There are too few humans left in the area for him to slaughter a village to take the prettiest," she answered. "You always warned us not to call attention to our presence here, and his appetites have gotten worse while you slept."

Valentin nodded his approval. "What other news is there?"

Veronika's lip curled. "That bitch of Michael's left in a spaceship. She hasn't been seen in over a century."

"Good, though I wanted to kill her myself for what she did to Petre. What of Michael, did he go with her?"

Veronika smiled as she answered, "Michael is dead. The

reports said he was killed in a nuclear blast somewhere in America shortly after you left."

Valentin hid his shock. "Are you certain?"

Veronika nodded. "As certain as I can be. I know Michael wasn't seen when that woman made her grand departure. Other than the rumors and the fact that he hasn't surfaced in almost a hundred and fifty years, I can't say."

"This is excellent news, my children. With Michael dead and his bitch gone, there is no reason for us to hide in the shadows anymore." Valentin stood and started to pace the room, all signs of the weakness he had displayed earlier gone. "What of the others," his face twisted in disgust, "Stephen and Barnabas?"

"Gone," Veronika stated as she gave Callen a side-eyed glance and nodded at Valentin.

"Even better." Valentin laughed, not noticing the interplay between them.

"There are rumors of one who still hunts our kind. Svenn is checking on some of those now," Veronika warned.

"Who is left that can stand up to me?" Valentin declared. "With all of Michael's brothers dead or gone, I am the closest to the original line left."

Veronika nodded. "Yes, you are. I only wanted to give you all the information I had."

"You did well," Valentin praised. "What of the rest of the world? Did the human population suffer the same fate worldwide?"

"As best we can determine," she confirmed. "There was an attack that destroyed computers worldwide. That was the beginning of the downfall, and most means of communication disappeared within days. Planes fell from the sky, the power grids collapsed, and all the governments in the world were affected. That led to a short but brutal world war where the big players hurled nuclear bombs at each other. What civilization is left is on par with the early eighteen hundreds in most places now."

"The eighteen hundreds was a great era. If it hadn't been for that sanctimonious bastard Michael and his family, we could have ruled the world then." Valentin continued to pace the floor, mumbling to himself. After several minutes he stooped and turned to Callen. "Do you still have that pack of mongrels?"

Callen nodded. "Yes, there are fifteen of them left."

"Take them and scout the area around Bucharest," Valentin ordered. "Our new empire will need a seat of power. See how many humans remain there and what opposition we can expect."

"Should I wait till Svenn returns with his news first?" Callen asked.

Valentin waved off his caution. "No. Whatever information he has about this supposed person is of little concern. There are none left as powerful as I am. If he comes here, I will squash him like a gnat."

Callen nodded. "Certainly, Father. I planned to take them on a hunt at dark tomorrow. I'll gather the information you require and return as soon as I have it."

"Return soon," Valentin urged. "I need you to help build our army."

"Army?" Veronika asked, her face clouded with confusion.

"An army of enthralled vampires to conquer and secure our new empire," Valentin told her. "I require each of you to sire more of our kind to act as your lieutenants in the coming battles. We will take the best humans left in the area and expand from there."

Before either could respond, they heard Marcos yelling, "I don't care what you say, Veronika. I'm going to that damned village and taking what I want."

Marcos stormed into the room, his face and clothes covered in fresh blood. He froze when he saw Valentin. "Father, I didn't know you were back."

"Obviously," he replied coldly.

Marcos missed the tone, seeing an opportunity to exact revenge on the dainty blonde. "I apologize for interrupting. It's only that Veronika has acted the petty tyrant while you were sleeping. Now that you're back, perhaps you will correct her error."

Valentin blurred across the room. When he stopped, he held Marcos against the unyielding stone wall by his throat. "Veronika spoke with my voice. Do you question me, boy?"

Marcos' eyes widened in fear as he realized he had offended Valentin. "No, never. I only meant—"

His words were cut off as Valentin applied more pressure to Marcos' throat and lifted his feet off the floor. "Consider your next words *very* carefully."

Veronika smirked from her position behind Valentin, making sure Marcos could see her.

Valentin lowered him to the floor and held his neck lightly.

Marcos felt his nails turn to talons as they pricked his

vulnerable throat. "I'm sorry, Father. What do you wish of me? How may I serve?"

"Better," Valentin answered as he released Marcos and turned back to Veronika and Callen.

Veronika was the only one who noticed the heated glare Marcos cast at his back.

CHAPTER THIRTY-FOUR

Jeju, Korea

"Yuko suggested I come here and try fishing. Here I am." Akio looked at the deep sea rod and reel in his hands and frowned. "I'm not certain I see the appeal."

"It's not about the fishin'." Henry grinned. "It's about bein' out on the water with your mates and not havin' a worry in the world."

"That's the truth," Horst agreed. "Nothing better than fresh air and sunshine. Especially without somebody running after you wanting you to sign an invoice or approve some stupid-assed project request."

Henry guffawed. "Well, Mr. Mayor, you agreed ta take the job when it came up that we needed one. What with you bein' all experienced, ya see?"

Horst growled. "I moved here to get *away* from resorts and drama. I had more than my share of that all those years on Kume. I'm still pissed at you for not telling me you folks were planning your own damned all-inclusive romantic getaway resort."

Akio let the banter flow over his head, and melancholy came over him. They had an easy manner with one another, like Akio and his brothers had before the vampire turned them. He missed his brothers and hoped that he could free them from the collapsed building. The more years that passed, the more he worried that all of them would not awake when that time came.

"Besides bein' sent on a fishin' trip by Yuko, how are ya doing, Akio?" Henry asked.

"I'm well," Akio answered.

Henry glanced at Horst, sitting in the captain's chair of the twenty-meter electric-powered sport fisherman. "Still don't talk much, does he?"

"Never has," Horst answered with a grin.

Akio's lips curled in a half-smile. Fishing wasn't exciting, but he had to admit that being out on the water with Horst and Henry did have a certain appeal. He looked over his shoulder at Horst. "Why do we move so slowly through the water? Don't the fish swim faster than this?"

"They do. We go this speed to give them a chance to take the bait. It's called trawling," Horst explained.

Akio was silent for a moment then asked, "What is trawling?"

"That's when you pull a net behind the boat to catch the fish. Why?"

"Something Yuko mentioned when she suggested this excursion," he answered and turned his attention back to the fishing rod when the reel started to make a clicking noise.

"You've got one on. Wait for it ta run with the bait, then flip the lever on top like I showed ya," Henry called.

The rod began to click faster, and Akio did as Henry had shown him and pulled back gently on the rod.

The rod bent in the middle, and the reel started to make a high-pitched squeal. Horst put the boat in reverse and made adjustments based on Henry's instructions while Akio reeled in the fish.

The battle raged for over thirty minutes, with Akio bringing the fish close to the boat only to have it make another dash for freedom. Finally, the fish was exhausted, and Akio reeled it to the surface.

Henry leaned over the transom and pulled the meter-long silver-sided fish onto the boat. He grinned. "That's a beauty, Akio. Must weigh close to eighty kilos."

Horst climbed out of his chair and clapped Akio on the shoulder with his meaty hand. "I think that's the biggest bluefin we've caught out here."

Akio placed the butt of his rod in a holder and stepped over to look at his catch. The fish had fought valiantly, and Akio admired its strength and persistence. He reached down and carefully removed the hook from its mouth and lifted the beautiful creature off the deck.

"Live to fight another day Valiant Warrior," Akio said as he eased the fish back into the water.

"Hold him there a minute and let the water run through his gills until he's revived," Henry advised.

A short time later, with a sweep of its powerful tail, the magnificent fish disappeared into the dark blue water.

Akio watched the calm waves for a few moments, then turned to Horst and Henry. "Thank you for this experience today. I find the activity to be…peaceful."

"You're welcome, my friend," Horst answered with a smile.

"What was that ya were saying about trawlin'? Do ya wanna give that a try?" Henry asked.

"No," Akio replied. "Since the Sacred Clan and Forsaken have become hard to locate, Yuko suggested that I was bored and should obtain one of the airships and 'Trawl for pirates.'"

Henry stared open-mouthed for a few beats and then burst out laughing. "Leave it to Yuko to suggest hunting pirates for fun."

Akio chuckled. "She still carries much anger from the time those pirates tried to take the Silver Moon when the children were onboard."

Horst barked a laugh. "I saw the video from that. Those four kids scrubbed blood off the floors and walls for two days until Alexi was satisfied the *Moon* was clean enough. You should have seen them when he asked why they had to tear the pirates to shreds instead of shooting them with their perfectly functional pistols."

"Kumori told me about that right after it happened." Henry laughed. "He said it was Gregov's crack about it bein' more fun to scare the shite out of 'em before he ripped off their heads that did it. Said Bresscoff was gonna have the cleaning staff handle it until he opened his trap."

"You know, Akio, I think trawling isn't a bad idea," Horst commented. "The pirates are getting bolder with the smaller traders. Dieter received a distress call last week from a ship a couple of pirates were after off the coast of Malaysia. By the time he got to them, the pirates had taken everything and scuttled the ship. Only two of the crew survived when it crashed."

Horst grinned. "I have one of the newest airships the company makes here on Jeju. It wouldn't take much for us to get out in the shipping lanes and see what we could scare up if you want to give it a try."

Henry snorted. "I'll let you youngsters have that fun. I'm too old for that shite."

"Even better, Mister Assistant Mayor. They can worry *your* ass with all that damned paperwork for those projects you didn't tell me about." Horst chuckled.

"The hell they will!" Henry shouted. "Robbie can handle all that headache. Hell, that resort nonsense was his idea in the first place. Somebody's gotta go along and keep you youngsters outta trouble."

"Youngsters?" Akio raised one eyebrow. "Henry, you do realize I'm over six hundred years old, don't you?"

"Yeah, but in vampire years, you're barely outta your teens," Henry shot back with a grin.

"Dieter and Gregov are due in on the *Freki* tomorrow. I think they would like to come along," Horst commented before Akio responded to Henry's snarky remark.

"Why?" Akio looked at him in confusion. "If they come, we would have to share."

Horst stared at him for a moment. Then he nodded and broke into a huge grin. "You're right. Let them get their own damned pirates."

CHAPTER THIRTY-FIVE

Orzene, Romania

"Welcome back, Callen," Veronika called from a parlor off the main entrance.

Callen stopped and turned into the doorway with a grin on his face. "Sister, did you miss—" his words cut off when he saw Veronika embracing the pale form of Costi Stanka, the Mayor of Orzene, on the couch. "Excuse me. I didn't realize you had a guest."

Veronika grasped the man's hair and pulled him away from her. Twin trickles of blood oozed down his neck from punctures. "Oh, this isn't a guest. He's only a snack. Would you like a taste?"

Callen waved off the offer. "I'm good. I just got back from Bucharest. Do you know where Father is? He needs to hear what I found there."

"He was looking for Marcos last I saw him," she told him. "You may want to check in the basement. Give me a second, and I'll go with you. Father was pissed when I saw him, so this could be fun."

Callen shook his head. "You have a twisted idea of fun. I know not to disturb Father when he's angry."

"Don't be a ninny," she scoffed. "He's not angry with *us*. That idiot Marcos went into town and took another victim against orders. Father wanted to speak to him about his lack of decorum."

"Still don't want to get caught in the runoff." Callen shrugged. "I know you're Valentin's favorite, but I think he only tolerates me most of the time."

Veronika held up a hand to silence Callen for a moment and turned her compelling gaze on Costi. "Go back to town. You will remember that we shared a pleasant meal and that I invited you back again next week."

"Pleasant meal and back next week," Costi mumbled. His eyes were unfocused, and his voice slurred as the compulsion fixed in his mind.

A moment later, his eyes cleared, and he smiled as he gazed at Veronika adoringly. "That was a wonderful dinner with a captivating companion, but I must get back to town. The populace demands the council and I hold a meeting with them over some superstitious foolishness."

Veronika feigned interest as she asked, "Oh, Costi, tonight? You work too hard for the people of Orzene. I'm sure they have no idea and less appreciation for how much you do for them as mayor."

"No, they don't," the mayor agreed. "It's always something. Tonight it is to discuss some idiot slip of a girl who managed to get lost in the mountains. No matter how many times we warn them that the mountain paths are treacherous with all the earthquakes, they still venture out alone."

Veronika placed her hands over her chest. "How dreadful! I hope that the poor child turns up safe."

Callen snorted and quickly passed it off as a cough when Costi turned and saw him standing in the doorway.

"Callen, my good man. I didn't see you there."

"I just arrived," Callen told him. "Sorry to disturb you. Did I hear that another person has gone missing in the mountains?"

Costi nodded. "Yes, the youngest Cernac girl. Her older sister, along with three of her friends, disappeared a few years ago. Now the last one has gone missing, too. Her uncle is on the town council, and his sister demanded we hold the meeting. She has a mad idea that wild beasts are responsible for all the idiots that got lost over the years."

Callen guffawed. "I've hunted these mountains for years. If there were anything like that around here, I would have found some sign. I can assure you that there are no beasts stalking people in these mountains."

"I know," Costi agreed. "Cernac's sister is only stirring up the people with her baseless rumors. I'll calm them down like I've done the last few times. People shouldn't go into the mountains alone. Especially the women. There are too many rock slides and pitfalls for the inexperienced."

"True," Callen agreed. "The mountains are dangerous. I will keep an eye out for any sign of her when I'm hunting. I'll contact you if I find anything."

Costi nodded. "Thank you. I'll pass that along at the meeting. I'm certain that it will give Mrs. Cernac some satisfaction knowing there is an experienced hunter from the castle out looking for her daughter."

"Glad to help," Callen lied.

Costi took Veronika's hand in his. "Until we meet again, milady."

"I look forward to it." Veronika smiled.

Once Veronika had seen Costi out, Callen wrapped his arm around her shoulders and snickered. "Would *milady* care to explain?"

Veronika elbowed him in the ribs and stepped away. "He is mildly entertaining."

"Looks to me like the fool is smitten with you."

"He has his uses and provides me with the opportunity to keep the villagers from getting too close to Marcos' idiocy," Veronika told him.

Callen laughed. "I take it Marcos is the beast the Cernac woman is talking about?"

"The same. That's why Valentin is angry with him. He's become careless taking too many from Orzene in too short a time." Veronika scowled. "I hope Father impresses upon him how he's risking exposing us. The last thing we need is to call attention to ourselves. Especially with Father planning his empire."

"I suppose that's a good enough reason to let that simp drool all over you." Callen shrugged.

"Until he bores me," Veronika told him. "Then I'll decide whether to keep him as a thrall or drain him."

"As long as he keeps the town from looking in our direction for Marcos' taking their young women, he serves a purpose," Callen reasoned. "As long as you keep him under your control, it helps cover up Marcos' stupidity."

Veronika sighed. "I don't know how many more Marcos can take before they burn the forest down looking for that Cernac woman's beasts. Hopefully,

CHARLES TILLMAN & MICHAEL ANDERLE

Father can convince him to stop being an idiot so close to home."

"I don't know if even Father can stop Marcos from being stupid," Callen growled. "Short of killing him, anyway."

"We can only hope," Veronika mumbled.

"I suppose I'll accompany you to check in on them," Callen offered.

Veronika smiled. "Let's. Marcos has been a pain in my ass for almost a century and a half. I look forward to seeing him suffer when Father puts him in his place."

"My, what a vicious little thing you've become." Callen laughed as he offered her his arm.

She flashed him a bright smile and allowed him to escort her to witness Marcos' humiliation.

"Do you think you can defy my commands?" Valentin's voice was low and void of emotion.

Marcos recognized the tone and demeanor for what they were and felt something he hadn't experienced in decades—abject terror.

"N…n…no, Father," he stuttered. "I would never disobey your orders. I owe you everything."

Valentin cocked his head to one side and glared at Marcos like he was a bug under his shoe. "If that's the case, why do I see this? In. My. Fucking. House?" Valentin's eyes glowed red as he swept an arm toward the raven-haired woman strapped to a St. Andrew's cross anchored to the wall. Her eyes were wide, the whites showing with terror evident in them. Blood leaked from the multiple bite marks that covered her pale body.

Marcos paled and his mouth worked as he tried to find his voice in the face of Valentin's burning rage.

Valentin's figure blurred as he shot across the dimly lit dungeon. The sound of flesh striking flesh was followed by Marcos' body slamming against the unyielding stone wall.

Before he could regain his wits, Valentin's strong hands grabbed his collar and hurled him across the open space to crash headfirst into the opposite wall.

Marcos slid to the floor bonelessly, blood leaking from his split lips and torn skin. He shook his head to clear it and pushed himself upright, using the rough stone wall for support. A noise from above caught his attention, and he turned to see Callen watching him through hooded eyes while Veronika shook with barely contained laughter.

Of course, that bitch would enjoy this. Laugh on, Veronika. Someday, Father won't be around to protect you. I'll keep you in this room screaming for centuries. I'll compose a grand symphony from your agonized cries.

No sooner had the thought entered his mind when Valentin grabbed him by the throat, his talon-like nails digging into the soft flesh. He lifted Marcos by his throat until his feet dangled above the floor.

"I should end you now. If you ever disobey my commands again, I won't hesitate. I will not have your desire to play stupid games with the humans jeopardize my plans. Do you understand?"

Marcos struggled to answer, but Valentin's grip on his throat tightened, and Marcos felt a trickle of blood running down his neck. His hands shot up and wrapped around Valentin's wrist. He tried to pull the hand from his neck, but Valentin's only reaction was to smile wide enough for his fangs to show.

He held Marcos pinned to the wall for a few more beats before he suddenly released him to slump to the floor. Valentin approached the frightened girl, taking in the delicate curve of her jaw and her dark blue eyes. He stroked her cheek with the back of his hand as she struggled to pull away from his touch.

"Don't be afraid, little one. No one is going to hurt you anymore," he continued to gently stroke her cheek until she relaxed.

"Marcos, heal her wounds," Valentin commanded.

"Yes, Father," Marcos answered meekly.

"Perhaps I should have you turn her as your penance," Valentin mused as he watched Marcos prick his finger and rub his blood over the trembling girl's ragged wounds.

"Father," Veronika called from the stairs where she and Callen watched.

"Yes, my dear?" Valentin asked, the malice gone from his voice.

"He's turned some of his playthings in the past. They can take more damage than humans that way."

Valentin looked thoughtful for a moment, then nodded. "Good point, daughter."

"What's your name, little one?" Valentin asked as he resumed stroking her face.

"Gertrude Cernac," she stammered.

Valentin frowned and shook his head. "Such a common name for one so delicate. Valentina perhaps? No. That won't do. It's too close to my own."

"She's healed," Marcos mumbled as he stepped back from the woman.

"Well, release her then, you fool!" Valentin snarled.

"Yes, Father."

Once Marcos had freed her, Valentin offered his hand and held her as she swayed unsteadily from the blood loss.

"Daniella." He rolled the name off his tongue. "Yes, I think that name will serve you well." Valentin put one finger under her chin and tilted her head up until her gaze met his. "Your name is Daniella. From now on, you shall call me, Father."

Marcos' back stiffened. "Father, no!"

Valentin's hand blurred, and Marcos flew across the room to smash into the unyielding stones again.

"Veronika," Valentin called.

"Yes, Father," she answered as she walked down the stone steps.

"Come and take Daniella upstairs. See that she is fed and have the servants wash the stink of fear from her. Find some clothes befitting her new status, and tell the servants she is to have high protein meals until she's healthy. The poor child looks starved. She needs to regain what Marcos has taken before she has any chance of surviving the change."

Veronika approached the dazed young woman, casting a malicious grin at Marcos as she took Daniella's hand. "Come with me, sister. I'll take care of you."

"Go with Veronika and do as she says. You have nothing more to fear, ever." Valentin put a strong compulsion behind the words.

"Yes, Father," Daniella answered as she allowed Veronika to guide her up the steps.

"I'll be along directly. I have some things to *discuss* with Marcos."

"Yes, Father." Veronika barely suppressed the giggle that threatened to slip out when she saw the color drain from Marcos' face as he struggled to his feet.

Valentin turned to Marcos, his face set in an angry mask as his eyes flared red. "You think you can order me about in my own house? How dare you tell me no. I will turn whoever I want, whenever I want, and it is not your place to question my decisions—ever."

"I... I'm sorry."

Valentin glared at Marcos.

"Father! I'm sorry, Father! I meant no disrespect, but she's only a village commoner," Marcos pleaded.

"You were nothing but a petty murdering sadist when I found you in Barcelona," Valentin reminded him. "If it weren't for me, the authorities would have given you to the family of that girl you murdered. I heard them talking about what they had in store for you. It makes your fantasies of Veronika look amateurish at best."

"I don't think those thoughts about my sister." Marcos tried to sound offended, but his eyes told another truth.

"Silence!" Valentin roared. "If you lie to me again, I will kill you."

Marcos' eyes widened as Valentin caught him by the neck and slammed his head against the device that had recently held his latest victim. Momentarily stunned, it was too late when Marcos realized his predicament—bound tightly to the cross as Valentin looked over his collection of *toys*.

"Father, no. I'm sorry. Please, Father, I won't do it again!" Marcos pleaded.

"I. Said. *Silence*. Don't move. The only thing I wish to hear from your mouth is screams." Valentin viciously backhanded Marcos, slamming his head against the wooden frame that held him while putting a stronger compulsion behind his command.

Marcos whimpered as Valentin selected a razor-sharp short-bladed knife from an assortment hanging on the wall. It was one of his favorites, and he knew what it could do in skilled hands.

Seconds later, the only sounds in the room were the agonized screams coming from Marcos' throat.

Veronika smiled as Marcos' agonized wails echoed up the stairwell.

"Happy now?" Callen asked with a chuckle.

"Almost. I wish Father had let me stay to play. I would've taught that limp-dicked bastard the true meaning of the word pain."

"You may still have the chance." Callen winced when a high-pitched scream came from below. "If he still has one to be limp when Father's finished with him."

Veronika sighed with regret. "Oh, Father will make him hurt, but he wouldn't remove anything important. Marcos is still of some use, after all."

Another piercing scream echoed through the halls, punctuated by the sound of flesh striking flesh.

Callen snorted. "I wouldn't be so sure."

"Not my concern either way," Veronika told him. "Come, Daniella, Father doesn't tolerate tarrying when he gives a command. Let's get you cleaned up, fed, and adequately attired before he's done with our wretch of a brother."

Callen grinned wolfishly. "Veronika, I have something for you in the stable. We need to discuss payment."

Veronika's eyes lit up, and she clapped with glee. "This day just keeps getting better. Let's get Daniella sorted, and I'll make the first installment. Father will be a while."

Callen offered her his arm, and they walked together to the kitchen, where they handed Daniella off to the servants with orders to prepare her for what was to come.

It had been many years since Valentin had added to his family. Veronika looked forward to Marcos being continually reminded of his humiliation every time he saw Daniella for centuries to come.

CHAPTER THIRTY-SIX

The Yellow Sea, Near Qingdao, China

"It appears we have a nibble."

Horst pointed to a blip on the radar screen that was moving to overtake the *Skywolf* from behind. The contact had appeared shortly after they'd left Shanghai's freight facility and shadowed them north along the China coast for the last seven hours. The pilot on the mystery craft had maintained several kilometers' distance, but now that the sun had set was rapidly overtaking them.

"He's runnin' without lights," Henry observed after poking his head out the side window.

"What armament does that ship carry?" Akio asked from where he reclined on the couch he'd staked out when they started the trip.

Horst opened a shallow cabinet filled with navigation charts next to the pilot's station and pressed his thumb over a concealed sensor. The chart rack slid into the top of the cabinet, revealing a screen with readouts for the ship's systems and icons to access multiple additional functions.

CHARLES TILLMAN & MICHAEL ANDERLE

"Let's see what she's packing," Horst answered as the monitor switched to an image from one of the many cameras mounted on the ship. With a few adjustments, the vessel appeared onscreen.

"One gun on the bow and a smaller one on each side midship," Horst advised. "It looks like they plan to come alongside and board us. I see eight heavily armed men on the deck readying boarding hooks."

"Only eight? That's...disappointing," Akio replied.

Horst chuckled. "That's just the ones I can see with the camera. Hold on a minute, and I'll get a thermal read on the whole ship."

"What are we gonna do with the pirates? Kill 'em all and let whatever deity wants 'em have 'em?" Henry asked Akio.

"*Hai,*" Akio answered. "Since pirates have started raiding towns and taking captives, all the governments in the area have reached an agreement. Any ship caught in the act of piracy is a legal prize, and the crew is to be executed by the ship that captures them."

Henry nodded. "Good enough for me."

"What exactly are you up to?" Abel's voice boomed over the cabin speakers.

"Trawling for pirates. Why?" Horst asked absently as he switched to sensors.

"Because your ham-handed manipulation of the ship's sensors is grossly inefficient," Abel answered indignantly. "I would have all the data needed plus the firing solutions to blast those goat humpers into atoms completed by now."

"Huh?" Horst grunted as he turned to Akio and wrinkled his brow.

Akio sat up straight and shrugged.

"Huh, indeed," Abel admonished. "You're taking the *Skywolf*, which has the same interface capability as the *Geri* and the *Freki,* into a hostile situation. Did you notify me of your intentions? No, you did not. Even though I am the best qualified to obtain optimum results from the ships operating and weapons systems. That is illogical and inefficient."

"Abel, they're only human pirates. Two Weres and a vampire won't need help with this," Horst replied.

"That's assuming you correctly identified them and that they don't intend to sink the *Skywolf* and feed you to the sharks," Abel countered. "This could be a ruse for an elaborate trap devised by Forsaken or the Sacred Clan. Since both groups are hiding from me, there is no intelligence proving it isn't."

A slight smile quirked on Akio's lips. "Abel, are you upset because the *Skywolf* is in danger, or is it because we didn't invite you to come with us?"

"I am not upset," Abel snapped. "Your illogical actions place a Seawolf Lines asset in peril needlessly. As chief of security, you should have at least informed me of the operation."

"Abel." Akio drew the name out.

"I'm bored, dammit," Abel complained before imitating a perfect sigh. "I haven't seen any action in over a year. The cats are so deep in the jungles when we do find them, you have all the fun, and the Forsaken may as well not exist. Then the three of you go pirate hunting, and I'm left cooling my circuits."

"You still control the *Geri* and the *Freki* when they are attacked,'" Horst consoled the annoyed AI.

"Like that ever happens since that bunch of pirates based on Dongyin pissed off Princess Tosha last year," Abel complained. "She went into a snit when one of them tried to sink the *Geri* with their cannons. She blew him out of the sky, then took *Geri* into their base and systematically destroyed one ship every thirty seconds until all of them were burning wrecks. She took out twenty-two airships and fifteen surface ships in seventeen minutes. To top it off, she put one of Eve's missiles through the roof of their headquarters and left a five-meter deep smoking crater in its place."

"No one can accuse my daughter of not being thorough," Horst commented with pride.

"I told her we should have killed them all," Abel continued, "but she decided it was better to leave the survivors stranded. She missed one damned ship that was out raiding, and since she showed those knuckle-dragging morons what the *Geri* could do, you can't pay any pirate to come within twenty kilometers of either ship. If they see us, they're all honest traders."

"Tosha does have her mother's temper." Horst snorted.

Henry laughed. "Yep, I'm sure she gets none of it from you."

"Well, maybe a little," Horst admitted with a grin.

"Only a little?" Akio raised one eyebrow and smiled.

Horst gave him the stinkeye and addressed Abel. "Abel, would you like to fish for pirates with us?"

"I don't want a pity invite," Abel sulked.

"Well, if you'd rather not, I need to finish scanning the pirate's ship before they catch us." Horst ducked his head to hide his grin from the cameras.

"I didn't decline, dammit," Abel backtracked. "I simply don't want to be a pity case."

"Honestly, Abel, none of us thought to ask you because all of us are more than a ship of unenhanced humans can handle. We didn't see enough danger to rate involving you in this hunt. Not that we didn't want you to come. You just have to remember to share. That's why Dieter and Gregov did not get an invitation today," Horst admitted.

"Since it was obviously an oversight due to your less efficient organic data analysis abilities, I accept the invitation. Now, get your grubby fingers off my controls," Abel demanded. "I have work to do."

Akio rolled his eyes and mouthed, "Kids," to Horst while Henry held his stomach as he shook with barely contained laughter.

"In addition to the eight soon to be deceased underwear stains about to board, there are fifteen additional people on the ship," Abel informed them. "Two in the pilot's cabin, one each on the bow and side rail guns, two in the engine room, a radio operator, and seven in two rooms on the lower level who are possibly captives based on their lack of involvement in the attack."

"We can't just shoot it down if the wankers have captives," Henry stated.

"This could be our first and last opportunity. Those prisoners will talk, and then the pirates will avoid us, too," Horst complained.

Then his eyes lit up, and he turned to Akio. "Unless you're willing to do that mind mojo thing on them?" Horst wiggled the fingers of both hands in the air.

"*Hai*, I can wipe their memories of our involvement," Akio answered.

"Now that you have that settled, you may want to get ready," Abel advised as a soft *thunk* came through the wall from the deck outside. The monitor switched cameras and showed the pirates pulling the two ships together with the boarding lines.

"Should we let them come to us or meet them on deck?" Horst asked.

Henry shrugged. "Either way, they're dead."

"Agreed," Akio answered.

All three remained in their seats while the pirate crew crossed quietly onto the deck of the *Skywolf*. Despite their attempt at sneaking, it sounded like a herd of horses galloping across the deck to Akio and the two Weres.

The door burst open, and a thin, weasel-faced man with greasy, tangled black hair to his waist locked eyes on Henry. He didn't speak but grinned maliciously as he raised a pistol and fired without warning.

"*Sonofafuckinbitch*! That hurt, motherfucker!" Henry growled, his eyes flashing yellow as he morphed into a large black wolf.

"Kelly's influence," Horst stage whispered when Akio's eyebrows shot up in surprise at Henry's coarse language.

"I can see where that could be the case," Akio replied.

"Oh, you queef snorter, you done messed up now. Sic him, Henry!" Abel's disembodied voice cackled over the ship's speakers.

The pirate stood frozen in terror as the yellow-eyed wolf leapt across the cabin and buried his teeth in his tender throat. Blood spattered the floor, ceiling, and walls before Henry and the hapless shooter crashed into the other invaders trying to come through the pilothouse door.

"*Gott verdammt*, Henry! You mess it up, you clean it," Horst yelled as surprised curses and the sounds of bodies falling came from beyond the door.

"We'd best go before Henry kills them all," Akio told Horst as he drew his katana.

Horst shrugged. "Well, that bastard did shoot him."

"He killed the man who shot him. That doesn't mean he doesn't have to share," Akio shot back as he followed Henry out the door.

"*Yokai!*" Nori screamed from the deck of the *Flaming Dragon* when the demon wolf bowled over his shipmates. It moved faster than Nori's eyes could follow, and in seconds, blood pooled on the deck beneath three who would never rise again.

Nori scrambled from behind his gun on his hands and knees. He breathed a sigh of relief when one hand landed on the short-handled ax he kept there to cut the ropes in the event of an emergency. If a killer *yokai* wasn't emergency enough for old Captain Mareo, Nori didn't want to know what was.

Henry twisted his body and fell to the deck, narrowly avoiding being stabbed by a machete-wielding giant of a man with arms like tree trunks. The man towered over Henry as he swung the blade at him again.

The machete stopped in a shower of sparks when Akio's katana intercepted it centimeters from Henry's exposed flank. Akio disarmed the pirate with a twist of his wrist and slammed his boot into his midsection. The kick lifted the pirate into the air where he screamed, flailing helplessly as he plummeted over the rail.

Akio nodded at Henry as Horst, his hands shifted into hairy claws, barreled to the rail with the throat of a pirate in each hand. "Get off my ship!" he yelled as he pitched the pirates overboard to their watery graves.

Henry rolled to his feet and growled as the remaining two attackers backed away from the deadly trio.

Akio plunged into their minds. He shook his head in disgust and, in a voice as cold as the grave, stated, "Guilty."

His eyes glowed red, and he crossed the deck with slow, measured steps. One of them flung the metal pipe he was carrying at Akio.

Akio caught the makeshift weapon with one hand and hurled it back without changing his pace. The meter-long projectile punctured the pirate through his chest and exploded from his back in a shower of gore.

The second man dropped his knife to the deck and threw himself over the rail to escape the flaming-eyed *Oni* from the netherworld that stalked him.

Akio flipped the dead body of the pipe wielder over the side and turned to Horst with a smirk. "Three for Henry, three for me, and two to you. Need to step up your game."

"There's more on the airship, but now we have to catch

them." Horst pointed to the ship steadily backing away from the *Skywolf*.

"Why did you let them go?" Akio asked, genuinely confused.

"Wanted to try out Eve's latest addition. Abel, if you would," Horst called.

"Aye, aye Cap'n," Abel answered in a terrible British accent.

The top of one of the many stacks of cargo boxes placed on the deck to disguise Eve's toys flipped open. A metal shaft rose out of it, and the small missile mounted at the top rotated and locked onto the fleeing pirate ship.

"We're at the extreme effective range for the weapon. I'm taking us closer," Abel informed Horst.

"Watch out for those guns," Horst cautioned.

"Puhleeez, go teach your grandma to suck eggs," Abel snarked as what appeared to be a radar dome mounted on the stern retracted, revealing a compact rotary launcher. Three narrow streaks of light arced away from the *Skywolf* and turned as their guidance systems directed the mini-missiles to their targets. Onboard the pirate ship, all three guns and a good-sized section of rail and deck planks disappeared in a flash of light and one prolonged *boom.*

The *Skywolf* surged ahead at twice the speed the pirate ship was running, and a few beats later, the deck lit up with the backblast from a missile. The fiery spear punched through the hull just below the pilothouse and blasted out of the other side in a shower of sparks and splintered wood.

The heavy winch kicked into gear below deck and

pulled their quarry to them on a piece of lightweight alloy cable no thicker than a man's smallest finger.

On the *Flaming Dragon,* Nori pulled himself unsteadily to his feet using a piece of the rail that had shattered when the bow gun had been ripped free and slammed into the side of the pilothouse. Nori groaned in pain, almost passing out when the thick splinter buried in his thigh shifted. His ears rang, he couldn't focus his eyes, and dizziness threatened to send him crashing to the deck at any second.

Another bright flash lit the sky, and the *Dragon* skewed sideways under the impact of a demon-cursed shot from the hell ship. Nori's eyes finally cleared, and he trembled in terror as the ship overtook them and three demons, two who looked like men and the third a slavering black beast with burning yellow eyes, looked hungrily at him.

"Damn, I missed one. The targeting system must be out of calibration," Abel grumbled. He fired the launcher, and the pirate's body exploded in a shower of blood and bone when the high explosive charge meant for disabling ships detonated in his chest.

"Adjustments complete. Horst, you need to catch up." Abel snickered.

"Watch it, Abel, or I won't invite you next time," Horst quipped, making a rude gesture at the closest camera with one hand.

"Stand by; their engine's overloading. I'm shutting them down," Abel announced as the *Skywolf's* electronics array sent an EMP blast through the enemy ship.

The results were instantly evident. All lights and motor noise from the enemy vessel shut down simultaneously.

"All yours," Abel announced as the Skywolf's hardened hull slammed into the pirate ship. Boards shattered all along its hull, leaving gaping holes in the side of the dead vessel.

Before anyone could protest, Akio pointed at the closest breach and launched himself inside the ship headfirst.

"That's cheating," Horst bellowed as Henry catapulted over the rail onto the deck, intent on getting to the two in the pilothouse before Horst.

Henry didn't slow as he rushed across the deck and crashed through the front window. A tall man wearing a heavy peacoat and a tricorn hat with a long white plume stared open-mouthed as Henry hit him with his front paws and knocked him to the deck.

The wolf's sharp canine teeth clamped onto the struggling pirate's throat, and blood sprayed the cabin walls and floor. Henry wasted no time shoving off the corpse and clamped his jaws around the calf of the other occupant's leg as he tried to escape into the ship. He dragged him screaming across the deck to the center of the room.

The pirate's screams changed into shrill shrieks of agony when Henry viciously shook his torn and bloody leg until the knee and hip joints popped out of place.

Henry dropped the mangled limb and slowly stalked around the pirate until he was within striking distance of the man's exposed neck. With a snarl and a flash of razor-sharp canines, the pirate's lifeblood sprayed from the ragged wound, adding to the macabre red pattern already covering the interior of the compartment.

Akio followed the sound of uncreative cursing to the engine room. He smirked as he imagined Bethany Anne standing on the unimaginative offender's back in her favored stiletto heels while he pumped out pushups for his life.

He pushed the narrow door that led into the cramped engine compartment open and spied two men leaning over an open panel, trying frantically to breathe life back into the dead ship's systems.

Akio dipped into the minds of both men, and his face twisted in a grimace when he saw the depraved acts both had committed. He didn't utter a word as he pulled his Jean Dukes Special from his hip and fired two rounds.

He closed the door in disgust as the two shattered corpses dropped dead to the floor. With all the dangers in this new world, though he'd seen it many times over the years, he still couldn't imagine what mental aberration drove humans to prey on each other.

"Filthy cheaters," Horst mumbled as he stalked the central corridor of the ship. Halfway along, he stopped abruptly as his sensitive nose picked up the acrid odor of fear on a weak breeze.

He slowed to a quiet pace then stopped when he arrived at a door with two heavy padlocks securing it. He breathed deeply through his nose and found that the scent of fear was coming from this room. He moved down one more door and found it secured but not as heavily as the first. A single keyed deadbolt was all that held it fastened.

The odor of fear wafted under this door as well, but he also detected resolve on the air currents. Horst stepped back and kicked the door with his heavy boot, shattering the lock and slamming the door open.

If it hadn't been for his enhanced reflexes, the broken chair leg that swung out of the darkness would have hit him in the face. He growled deep in his chest and lashed out with one hand to swat the offending club to the side and the other to catch his assailant around her thin neck.

His eyes opened wide when he saw he held a disheveled young woman with a huge bruise covering one side of her face in his iron grip. He released her and held both palms out to show he meant her no harm.

"I'm one of the good guys. We're here to save you," he advised her in a calm tone.

The woman's hand clasped her neck, her eyes showing white all around as she stared at him. "What, uh, who are you?" she stammered.

"The men keeping you prisoner attacked my ship," Horst explained in the same gentle tone. "We fought them off and killed the ones who boarded us. After that, we hit them back and disabled their ship. The rest of my associates are hunting the remaining pirates down now."

He continued to show his hands as he spoke. "Now, I plan to get you off this wreck and onto my vessel before it crashes into the sea. After that, we can figure out a safe place to drop you and the others off."

The woman blinked twice, then crashed into him and wrapped her arms around him. She sobbed against his muscular chest, soaking his ship suit in hot tears.

Horst stood momentarily speechless until his paternal instincts kicked in. He lightly stroked the back of her head with his hand and murmured assurances that she was safe until the tears stopped and she took a steadying breath.

"Thank you," she murmured into his chest. "That beast of a captain told me his plans for us. He planned to trade those in this room to another pirate band for supplies to form his own raider company. The women in the other room are younger, and he intended them as prizes for the captains who followed his banner."

She leaned back and looked into his eyes, then touched the swollen bruise on her face. "What he had planned for me was even worse."

Red hot rage flooded Horst. He knew Henry had gone to the pilothouse, but he hoped the captain still lived so he could have the satisfaction of ripping the bastard's still-beating heart from his chest.

Horst closed his eyes before the humans saw the yellow glow and took several deep breaths to calm the fire inside. Soft steps from the rear of the corridor alerted him of Akio's presence.

"Got seven women here," Horst advised him when he approached.

"Three in this room and four more in that one." Akio nodded to the locked door.

"Think you can get the locks?" Horst asked.

"*Hai.*" Akio nodded.

The door opened at the front of the corridor, and

Henry padded toward them on bare feet. Blood dripped down his neck from his beard, coating his chest. His eyes glowed in the low light, and a satisfied grin split his face. "The two wankers in the pilothouse are done."

"The engine room is clear as well," Akio answered as Horst moved to block Henry from the view of the young woman nestled safely in his arms.

"Henry, we have a group of captive females here," Horst told him before he came closer.

Henry stopped and turned abruptly to go back the way he'd come. "Gotcha. I'll be heading back ta the ship and tidy a cabin for our guests."

Akio cocked his head to the side then asked, "What about the radio operator?"

Before anyone could answer, a blast shook the front of the ship.

Got him! Abel called over their implants.

"Dirty rotten cheaters. The whole lot of you," Horst grumbled.

The only response was a snicker from Henry and a low snort from Akio.

Don't feel bad, big guy. You saved the hostages, Abel told him in a sugary-sweet tone.

CHAPTER THIRTY-SEVEN

Orzene, Romania

"Veronika, Callen, where have the two of you been?" Valentin asked with a knowing grin.

"Just settling a debt, Father. You've always been adamant that we settle our debts." Veronika grinned.

"I trust that the payment was sufficient?" Valentin commented.

Callen ran his eyes over Veronika's body. "Most satisfying, Father."

"Good. I can't have the two of you at odds since your idiot brother will be out of commission for the foreseeable future."

Veronika's eyebrows shot up as she cast a questioning glance at Callen.

A subtle shrug was his reply.

"Marcos will be spending some time in contemplation of his sins," Valentin continued. "When he recognizes his shortcomings, he may rejoin us."

"When might that be?" Callen mused.

"When your new sister has settled into her vampire skin and won't have to worry about Marcos trying to get revenge."

"He wouldn't dare!" Veronika's eyes flashed red.

"I assure you he would if he thought he could get away with it," Valentin assured her. "The things he wants to do to you, my dear, almost made me blush. Why did you shoot him in the gut with your little pistol?"

"He was acting like an ass," Veronika stated. "It was a reminder that actions have consequences. No more."

Valentin pursed his lips. "I see. Well, Marcos' idea of consequences for *your* actions is to have you restrained in his playroom, where he would peel your skin off one strip at a time in between bouts of abusing you carnally."

"He can try. But I assure you if he does, I will remove his balls via his throat," Veronika assured him coldly.

Valentin cocked his head to the side and burst out in raucous laughter. "There's my daughter. That's what brought you to my attention all those years ago in Helsinki. The viciousness and lack of mercy you showed to those who wronged you. I knew then you were a child of my heart, if not my body."

Veronika flashed the dazzling smile that always pleased Valentin. "Since then, you've taught me to always answer insults in kind. No one puts hands on me without my permission."

"If she doesn't remove his dangly bits, I'll do it myself and feed them to my wolves while he watches," Callen growled.

"Ah, yes. Always the protector." Valentin chuckled and then whispered conspiratorially, "She doesn't need it. Your sister is very capable of meting out punishment where it's due. She uses that helpless little girl act to get you to bring her presents."

Callen grinned and whispered back, "I know."

"You're both so funny," Veronika deadpanned.

Valentin chuckled then changed the subject abruptly. "What did you discover in Bucharest?"

"Trouble." Callen scowled. "Stephano, one of David's children, is there. He claims that everything west of Odesa between the North Sea and the Black Sea belongs to a vampire in Paris who fancies himself to be a duke."

"In my territory? Who does that insolent child think he is?" Valentin roared as his fangs extended and his eyes burned red.

"I pointed out that Bucharest and all of Romania are yours. He said times have changed and had twenty recently turned vampires backing him up. If one of my wolves hadn't sensed them and warned me, I might not have made it out of there."

Valentin's eyes hardened as his voice went cold. "He threatened you?"

Callen nodded. "I suspect his vampires would have after I removed his head. That was my intent before the warning. Bucharest is ours."

Valentin laced his fingers together in thought. "I see. We will explain that to Stephano soon. Withdrawing was a sound move. We'll deal with his disrespect in due time. First, we need to create some soldiers of our own. Then you can have Stephano's head delivered to this duke in a box."

"I agree that we need to remove him, but Bucharest may

not be a good location for our home." Callen frowned. "It's a wasteland. Between the war, earthquakes, and disease, there's little left of the city or the people."

"It doesn't matter. We can figure that out after Stephano is dead." Valentin smirked. "I never cared much for David's brood, anyway."

"As you wish, Father," Callen agreed.

Valentin clapped his hands once and looked at Veronika. "Where's Daniella? It's time she joined the family properly."

"She's sleeping in her quarters across the hall from mine. The poor child was practically dead after Marcos' hospitality. She was malnourished to begin with, and he damn near drained her."

Valentin nodded. "Once we're finished here, I'll check on her. It will probably be best to let her rest and regain her strength. Females are hard enough to turn as it is."

"I've instructed the staff to feed her high protein and iron-rich foods," Veronika told him. "Once her blood supply is back to normal, she should be well enough to turn."

"We can wait until her health has improved. Marcos will have to stay where he is until she's turned. The time to think should do him good." Valentin's words were light, but the red tint in his eyes told a different story.

Veronika ducked her head to cover the smile that tugged at her lips. The longer Marcos stayed away, the more influence she could garner with Valentin and their newest sister.

The door swung open on silent hinges, revealing a pale and emaciated young woman asleep on the huge canopy bed that dominated the room. Her raven hair spread out around her head like a dark halo. When Valentin approached the bedside, she let out a soft moan in her sleep through tightly clenched teeth.

Valentin watched as she grew more restless, caught in a dream that turned into a nightmare. "Little one," he called softly.

Her moans grew louder as she twisted, wrapping the blanket around her body. Her struggles increased as the blanket restricted her movement. A sheen of sweat appeared on her upper lip as her movement became frantic.

"Daniella, wake up. It's only a dream, little one. Father's here; you're safe now." Valentin pushed compulsion into the words, and the frantic girl calmed immediately.

"F-f-father?" she stuttered as her eyes shot open.

"I'm here," Valentin assured her. "You're safe. It was only a dream."

She looked around in confusion. "Where? Where am I?"

"Your rooms in the castle, your home."

Confusion showed on her face as she digested this. Valentin gently cradled her face in one hand and turned her to face him. Their eyes locked, and Valentin pushed deep into her mind. *Your name is Daniella. You live here in the castle with your sister and three brothers. You call me Father.*

Her face clouded briefly, then relaxed. "Oh, Father! I had the most dreadful dream."

Valentin smiled at her. "How are you feeling, little one?"

"I'm tired," she answered in a small voice. "What's wrong with me?"

"You've been ill," Valentin told her. "You're going to be okay now, though."

"I…I don't remember," she stammered.

Valentin took her by the hand and pulled her into a seated position on the bed. He raised his free hand to his lips and punctured his wrist with one fang. "Drink my little one. The blood will make you stronger."

Daniella closed her mouth over the wound and took a hesitant taste. Valentin smiled when he felt her start to suck the blood from the open wound actively. He caressed the back of her head, murmuring soft words of encouragement.

The wound closed, and he reopened it. When it healed a second time, Valentin pulled his wrist away from her lips, smiling when she struggled to hold it in place. "That's enough for now. The sun will rise soon, and you need to rest. Sleep now. When you wake, I'll be waiting."

———

Veronika waited impatiently for Valentin to go to Daniella's room. She slipped into the hall and furtively made her way to the door that led to Marcos' dungeon.

She slipped inside the door and closed it softly behind her. The coppery smell of blood assailed her sensitive nostrils. She descended the rough stone steps and halted at the bottom, where an almost unrecognizable bloody form occupied the wooden rack where Daniella had been.

Veronika approached slowly, her lips curled in disgust

as she looked down on Marcos' torn and battered body. "That looks painful, brother." False concern laced her voice.

"Please, blood, please," Marcos moaned weakly.

Veronika shook her head. "Oh, you poor dear. Father hurt you badly. I wish I could, but he might do to me— what *you* planned, you sniveling sick bastard."

She snatched the blood-covered knife embedded in the wood above his head. In one violent slash, she opened his bloody trousers down the front.

Marcos' eyes went round with fear when he saw the malicious smile on her lips and the cold, dead look in her eyes. "Sister, no. I would never—"

The sound of flesh meeting flesh echoed through the chamber. Blood splattered the wall as Marcos' head snapped to the side from Veronika's slap.

"Do you think I don't know the sick plans you dream of for me? You really are a fool, Marcos. I've known for years that you want nothing more than to have this," she swept her free hand across her body, "tied down and at your mercy."

Her hand shot out, and Marcos let out a pained screech as she squeezed. "I know that you want to abuse my body with *all* of your *little* toys."

Marcos whimpered as Veronika twisted the tender flesh she held and lay the sharp knife against it. "Just one slip of this blade, and I would never need fear this type of assault from you, nor would anyone else—*ever*."

"Veronika! *No!*" His protest turned to a scream as the razor-sharp blade drew a trickle of blood.

"One more word, and you will eat them, Marcos. If I

catch you so much as *looking* at me with that sick look on your face again, I will make you plead for a death that will never come. Do you understand?" She emphasized each word with a hard jerk that made Marcos arch his body to relieve the crushing pressure. "Nod if you understand, you perverted shitstain."

Marcos nodded vigorously.

"Good. I'm glad we finally understand each other." Veronika smirked as she looked him in the eyes. Her eyes never left his as she released his tortured flesh and slammed the knife into the wood a hair's breadth from his manhood.

Veronika turned and walked to the stairs without a backward glance, her head held high as she left Marcos to think about what she had said.

Callen shook his head with a smile as he backed away from the door. He knew full well that Marcos would not heed the warning but would do everything in his power to make Veronika suffer for not only seeing him humiliated by Valentin but for adding to it herself.

You're going to make it so I have no choice but to kill him one day, sister dear. So be it. I never liked the deranged ass anyway.

CHAPTER THIRTY-EIGHT

TQB Base, Tokyo, Japan

Akio reflected as he watched the surveillance feed from one of the four remaining satellites. Eve had done everything in her power to build new units but was unable to manufacture the needed components for them to operate reliably in the harsh environment of space.

After several failed attempts, Akio and Yuko had agreed to use hard-to-find resources only on Earth-based projects until alternate solutions became available.

Over the last hundred years, humanity had thrived in places where advances in technology allowed them to build electrical generating facilities. Computer networks and transportation options were available in many of the cities that rebuilt after WWDE. New York City, San Francisco, Chicago, Tianjin, Paris, Berlin, and Frankfurt were now expanding in the new world. The tech networks gave Eve, Abel, and Takumi access to all of them after Akio had planted some of Eve's creations at each location.

Many other smaller cities thrived, but the more prominent locations were rediscovering medical and tech that improved humanity's ability to survive daily. Information flowed between the human-dominated cities, but the tech was still slow to arrive in the more remote rural areas.

These were the areas where Akio stationed the remaining satellites most of the time. Experience had taught the Forsaken and Weres that showing up in heavily populated areas and causing problems was a fast ticket to death. Humans were more aware of the UnknownWorld, and coexistence between Weres and Humans—and even some vampires—had become the norm in a few places.

Knowledge is power, and throughout history, humans had shown great aptitude for developing ways to kill. Vampires and Weres who stepped out of line were the latest to learn this ages-old lesson.

That allowed Akio to focus his assets on the fringe areas to ensure no group of enhanced with ill intentions grew into a significant threat to humankind. Threats still occasionally occurred, but between the FDG and Akio, those incidents ended in a manner designed to make the next idiots with dreams of world domination think twice.

The FDG had also proved to be a source of valuable information. Terry Henry Walton was against becoming the law enforcement arm or overseers for humanity. They were the guardians when needed, but society had to find its own way. That didn't stop him from sending his people into the field on regular "vacations" to observe and gather intelligence. Akio gladly supplied communicators for the vacationers to facilitate the information flow.

The images sped across the screen at a blistering pace, occasionally pausing when something caught Akio's attention. He hit pause when something on a previous image alerted him. He scrolled back and stopped when a small village high in the mountains of Tibet appeared.

A few taps and his console zoomed in on the Buddhist temple filling the screen. He focused on the robed monks performing various labors around the grounds as monks have done for centuries.

"Abel," Akio called.

"Yes?"

"Do you have previous images or video from this location?"

"Affirmative. This location is referenced on eight hundred sixty-two stills and videos in the archives. Do you need a specific date or time?" Abel inquired.

"Are there any significant changes in activities or the number of monks present referenced in any of the data?" Akio asked.

"Negative, all data indicates that this monastery has changed little since the seventeen hundreds. That reference is the first instance that the historical data available mentions it exists," Abel supplied.

"Thank you, Abel."

"Certainly. Would you like me to contact Horst and schedule another fishing trip?" Abel asked hopefully.

Akio's lips twitched at the AI's thinly veiled attempt to get him out of the base. After the first successful pirate hunting trip where they had rescued a group of human females, Yuko regularly encouraged Akio to engage in his "hobby." When she enlisted Abel's assistance, the suggestions and reminders became a daily occurrence.

"If you want to hunt pirates, I'm sure Horst would be

willing to go, or get any or all of the kids to accompany you. You don't need me to handle a few human criminals," Akio answered.

"I don't *need* anyone," Abel informed him. "I am more than capable of taking the airship out and sinking pirate scum alone. However, I've discovered that it's more enjoyable when friendly competition is involved."

"Go ahead and call him. I don't see anything that needs my attention here, and eliminating raiders does serve a civic purpose," Akio conceded.

"Excellent!" Abel enthused. "Eve recently added more weapons, along with the ability for me to change the colors and operational appearance of the *Skywolf* on the fly. I intend to research what bait is the best to attract pirates."

Buddhist Monastery, Tibet

"Master, isn't it time to call in our people? We haven't received word of that damned vampire doing more than eliminating the occasional idiot who ignored your directives in years. The true believers accepted your guidance and have lived in seclusion away from human settlements for decades."

"The time grows close, Woo. But it is not upon us yet. We've learned from the mistakes of fools like Kun and Shek not to expose ourselves. The Sacred Clan has lost numbers and influence, not to mention irreplaceable technology because of their ineptitude," Master Dawa Palsang, the undisputed leader of all the remaining Sacred Clan tigers, explained.

"You know best, Master. I live to serve." Woo bowed as he backed out of Palsang's presence.

Palsang smiled to himself as he went over his mental list of goals and accomplishments. He was the last surviving Clan member who had directly served in the Leopard Empress' temple before the vampire bitch murdered her. He was also the only person who knew that the Clan had once possessed a working spacecraft provided to them by the gods who created them.

The Clan was a shadow of its previous size due to the thousands killed in the insane war started by that baseless fool, Kun. The Dark One had spent over a century annihilating the Sacred Clan because of Kun's desire for revenge for an insignificant slight. Now they didn't dare even use the Sacred Clan name but used the generic Qin Clan instead. If Kun had left the vampires in peace, the Sacred Clan would have already succeeded in implementing the empress' grand plan, and the humans would be securely under Sacred Clan control.

Palsang had operatives throughout Asia. All were focused on the singular goal of recovering their stolen technology and advancing the Sacred Clan to its rightful place in the world. His long-term goals were almost complete.

In a few short years, the Clan would rise from the ashes like the mythical phoenix, and no one would have the power to oppose them.

CHAPTER THIRTY-NINE

Orzene, Romania

"Veronika, I received word from Svenn. He'll be home tonight around midnight," Callen announced as he entered the woman's private suite.

"Oh, goody," Veronika purred from the center of her canopy bed. "I hope he has good news."

Callen stopped inside the door and took in the scene before him. He snorted a laugh and pointed at the blood-covered woman. "Seems Marcos isn't the only one who's hard on his playthings, dear sister."

She frowned and pushed the blond corpse to the floor with her foot. "He was pretty enough but had no stamina. Even after I compelled him, he suffered a frustratingly embarrassing lack of control."

Callen smirked. "Next time I leave the castle, I'll try to find you a pretty one that's all muscle and no brains. This one was a minstrel and obviously too delicate to meet your needs."

She smiled at him with a veiled look. "I'll make it worth your time if you do."

"Consider it done." Callen smiled. "Anyway, Father sent me to get you. He's ready to begin Daniella's transformation and requests you prepare her and bring her to his chambers in one hour."

"Later, then? Father will be hours exchanging blood with her," Veronika offered.

"I'll be in my rooms." Callen chuckled as he left and thanked whatever mystical being had caused his path to cross Valentin's all those years ago.

In his first life, as he liked to think of it, he'd been the fourth son of a Scottish laird. With three brothers ahead of him, it had been unlikely he would ever take power, so he'd made his own choices about education and entertainment.

Callen wasn't interested in the knowledge contained in books. Instead, he'd sat with the huntsmen and hound master in the keep's kennels. He'd developed a love of the hunt while listening to the men's tales of tracking and chasing their prey to supply the keep with fresh meat.

The young boy had learned all he could about caring for and breeding the hunting dogs and had started going into the field when he was six. In an uncharacteristic show of affection, his father presented him with a pair of deerhound pups for his eighth birthday.

Callen had trained the pups to hunt the abundant red deer and the occasional fox found in the area. When he was barely thirteen, a lone wolf had started taking sheep from a high mountain meadow. Callen and his dogs had chased it for three days until they cornered it in a deep ravine, where he'd killed it with his sword. The thrill of hunting a predator known to hunt the hunters had set Callen on his life's path.

Four years later, neighboring keeps had requested his six-hound pack whenever they needed a predator brought down. He'd lived to hunt dangerous prey. However, the lack of a healthy population of large predators had bored Callen until the day he'd discovered a readily abundant source of prey for his dogs and himself.

He'd received a request to track a feral wolf at an isolated farm two days from his home. With the price agreed upon, he'd set out to rid the farmer of the pest. When he arrived, he soon discovered that the wolf was nothing more than a pack of feral dogs. Callen had brought their heads in as proof. The farmer had laughed at him and refused to pay.

Heated words passed between them, and as the young man turned to leave, the farmer had made the grave mistake of shoving him. Callen stumbled and fell with an angry shout. Before he could get to his feet, his loyal pack had the irate farmer on the ground.

Callen had watched transfixed as his dogs bit into the thrashing, screaming farmer, ripping chunks of flesh from his body in a bloody frenzy. He hadn't considered calling them off, and the man had begged for his life until the pack silenced him for good.

A horrified scream had shattered his thoughts when the farmer's wife, alerted by the noise, came out of the barn brandishing a pitchfork. She had rushed toward Callen, spitting curses and threats, intent on stabbing him with the sharp tines. He'd drawn his sword and knocked it out of her hands with ease. A fist to her temple put her on the ground, unconscious, and left Callen with a problem.

If word of his dogs killing the man got to the authorities, they would destroy his beloved pack even if they didn't blame him. The thought of losing the companions he'd raised from pups chilled him to the marrow. As he'd considered his options, the solution came from the woman herself.

She moaned as she regained consciousness. One of the bitches walked over to sniff her. When the farmer's wife opened her eyes and saw the dog's bloody muzzle, she'd screamed, jumped to her feet, and ran.

If she'd gone to the house or barn, she would've been safe. In her panic, she ran into an open field.

Callen had whistled the pack back to him as she headed into the trees that bordered the field. His dogs had pranced and whined, wanting to run her down. With hardly a thought about the morality, Callen had given them the signal.

That had been the beginning of a time of terror in the Highlands. Callen had spent more time away from his home, wandering the lonely mountain trails, searching for his new favorite game animal—man.

Or woman. He wasn't particular as long as they ran hard and gave him and his pack a good chase.

For three years, he'd hunted humans for sport. Every town and village in the Highlands had posted warnings about a wolf pack that took lone travelers and occupants from isolated farms. Callen was always cautious about covering any tracks around the kills that would reveal the truth to an experienced hunter.

That had led to the superstitious Highlanders' claims that the killers were a pack of hellhounds with a demon master—and his meeting Valentin.

Callen had found a small farm owned by a man, his wife, and their teenage son miles from other people. He'd decided to have some fun and make the hunt more challenging at the same time. He'd waited in the barn. When the farmer came out at dawn, he subdued him. The wife came out looking for her man when he didn't return with the eggs for breakfast, and Callen had captured her, too.

He wasted no time waiting for the son. He'd smashed in the door and pulled the kicking and screaming teen out to join his parents. The small family didn't believe him when he told them what he planned for them. The farmer had cursed and threatened as he struggled against the tight ropes that bound him. Then Callen untied the wife and told her to run alone since her husband cared so little for her life.

That stopped the man's rant. Soon, all three were fleeing for their lives across the freshly-tilled fields. Callen had let them run for five minutes before he released the pack. Over the next three hours, the family led him on a long chase that ended with them cornered on a rocky ledge.

Callen could still see the terror on their faces and hear their screams three hundred-plus years later when he closed his eyes. That hunt was the last and best he'd experienced in that lifetime. Later that night, Valentin had found him, drawn to the area by reports of his escapades that had reached his ears in Paris.

That was the last night of Callen's life as a human.

Three days later, he'd awakened to his second life and discovered that his previous hunts were nothing compared to what he could do as a vampire.

A light knock on the door disturbed Callen's reverie.

"Come in, Veronika," he called.

She smiled as she pushed open the door, careful not to spill any of the blood-laced wine in the two glasses she carried. "I thought you'd like to join me in a toast to our new sister. She's such a pretty little thing. I know we're going to have so much fun with her."

Callen snorted. "The girl's not even begun her transformation, and you're already planning to seduce her into your bed?"

"No, silly boy, *our* beds. Imagine how poorly Marcos will react to that."

"You're determined to push that fool until he does something, and I'll have no choice but to kill him, aren't you?" Callen chuckled.

"I suspect Valentin will do it first. Marcos forgets himself too often, and Father won't let him off with punishments forever. When we have our army, Marcos' value will go down," Veronika assured him.

"You may be correct, but Father isn't blind. He knows you've had it in for Marcos since you joined our family."

"That sick fuck kept me captive in his dungeon for a solid week," she stated coldly. "If you hadn't returned two weeks earlier than expected, he would have killed me. As it was, he beat me bloody, then forced me to feed and heal the damage so he could do it over again daily."

"I should've killed him that day. It would've saved me a

lot of headaches through the years, for sure," Callen grumbled.

"At least Father locked him away until I found the strength to stand up to him," Veronika conceded. "If he hadn't, I don't think I would've survived another round of that."

"Aye, you came into your own fast. Probably because you were such a vicious little minx when you were human," Callen chided.

Veronika smiled at him as her hand went to the tie that fastened the sheer robe she wore. "I think the lessons you taught me during those years are what did the most."

"You were a good student." He paused when the robe slipped off her shoulders to the floor. "In *all* your lessons."

"Welcome home, Svenn," Valentin greeted.

"Father! You're back!" Svenn cried as he rushed across the room and wrapped Valentin in a crushing embrace.

Valentin returned the embrace. "I've missed you, my son. What news do you bring us?"

Svenn grimaced. "Nothing good. The Dark One is as elusive as a ghost. I've chased rumors from London to Moscow with nothing but more rumors to show."

"What have you heard about a vampire in Paris who calls himself a duke?" Valentin asked.

Svenn shrugged. "Only that he's possibly one of Michael's son David's line. I met one person who claims they saw him, but he's no one I've encountered from the description she gave."

"He has encroached on my territory," Valentin growled. "One of his minions recently accosted Callen in Bucharest. When he advised the insolent bastard that Romania was mine, the fool dared to tell him that this duke claims Romania, along with all western Europe, as his."

"When do we remove him?" Svenn's voice held a note of eagerness.

Valentin smiled. "Soon, but we have to increase our numbers first. He has twenty newly turned vampires with him. I suspect he's turning our locals to fill his ranks."

"Best we do this sooner than later. I'll reach out to my contacts there and get everything available about him. Do you have a name?" Svenn asked.

"He calls himself Stephano and claims he's part of David's family. It appears that one of David's lot might be behind this after all," Valentin mused.

Svenn frowned. "Doesn't matter who it is. We can't tolerate incursions into our territories unanswered. I'll find this 'duke,' and we can arrange some misfortune for him."

"Svenn, you're back!" Veronika squealed as she threw herself into his arms.

"Hello, sister, what have you been…" He stopped and sniffed. "Or should I say, *who* have you been doing, you little minx?"

Veronika laughed and planted a wet kiss on his lips.

Svenn ran his tongue over his top lip, then made a *smacking* noise. "Oh, so Callen's the lucky fellow. Good for him. Or did he purchase your affections once again with some pretty boy?"

She grinned. "Yes, and of course. What did you bring me from your trip?"

"Nothing this time, I'm afraid," Svenn confessed. "The journey was arduous, and I barely had time to sample anything for myself."

Veronika folded her arms and pouted. Svenn and Valentin burst out laughing at her silly display until her lips quivered, and she joined in. "Oh, you're both boorish."

"Where's Callen? You didn't break him, did you?" Svenn asked.

Callen laughed from the stairs. "No, but only because I'm harder to break than her regular playthings. Not that she didn't try, brother."

"Hello, Callen." Svenn greeted. "What can you tell me about the idiot who claims Bucharest?"

"Claims he works for some French vamp who thinks he's a duke and that everything west of Odesa to the North Sea is his now," Callen explained. "I was about to separate his arrogant head from his body when one of my wolves warned me that he had twenty vampires backing his play. That's the extent of what I can tell you."

"If I can borrow one of your wolves later to take a message to my contact in Bucharest, I'll have answers within the week," Svenn claimed.

"Tell me when and where you want the message sent. They're fed and rested, so the entire pack is at your disposal," Callen offered.

"I may take you up on that," Svenn told him. "I need to reach out to a few more people. We can discuss it after we finish here. I want to visit with all of you before we get mired down in business. Speaking of all, where's Marcos? In his playroom?"

Veronika snorted. "He certainly is."

Svenn looked at her curiously. He knew Veronika had issues with Marcos and especially what had happened below.

"Marcos is spending time as my guest in his little gallery of horrors at the moment," Valentin growled. "I'm giving him time to ponder how bad a decision defying my orders was. He'll remain there until I feel he's ready to display the proper attitude. If you want to see him, I suggest you do it soon. I saw the most devilish little metal box when I was there earlier."

Veronika looked up with a feral grin.

Valentin chuckled. "Ah, I see you're familiar with it."

"Oh, yes, I remember it well. It was uncomfortable for my petite frame when that bastard locked me inside every night. It's hideous, and I think it will serve Marcos well in...coming to terms with the seriousness of his actions," Veronika purred.

Svenn laughed. "Remind me never to get on your bad side, dearest sister. You hold a grudge for eternity."

"No worries, precious Svenn. You're too refined to subject me to Marcos' type of perversions. A little taste of what he's done to others might prove cathartic for him." Veronika smiled.

"Perfectly vicious." Valentin laughed.

"How did Daniella's transformation go, Father?" she inquired.

Valentin shrugged. "She appeared to take it well, but we

won't know if she will survive the change for three days. You know this. Until then, we wait."

"We might have a new sister? When did you decide this?" Svenn inquired.

"When the idiot downstairs disobeyed Father's orders not to do stupid shit that called attention to us," Callen groused.

Svenn winced at this revelation. "Will you allow him to live?"

"For now." Valentin nodded at Veronika when he saw the appreciative look she gave him. "If the fool dares to defy me again, I might let Veronika decide his punishment next time. I believe I'll tell him that when I change his position later."

"That will either scare him straight or require one of us to kill him the first time he thinks you've turned your back," Callen observed.

"Either way, he'll follow orders, or I'll put him down. We have a war to fight. I won't allow him to be a distraction," Valentin coldly stated. "On that note, we need numbers. The population here isn't healthy enough to provide them. I want each of you to choose a city and recruit four new members into our family. These will be your lieutenants, so choose wisely."

Valentin smiled knowingly. "Since this duke claims Europe, I propose you collect our forces from his cities. Munich, Prague, and Bern to start. I imagine each of you will find something that appeals to your tastes in them."

"Bern for me." Svenn laughed when he saw the cross look on Veronika's face.

Valentin raised a hand and cut her off before she could

protest. "Veronika, I want you and Callen to travel together. As soon as you have your troops firmly under control, have them start collecting humans to send here."

She nodded. "As you wish, Father."

"Svenn, once you have yours, give them whatever they need to start gathering information on the duke. Don't take unnecessary risks. Use them, and if they get caught, write them off and make more. The less they know about who we are, the better."

"Of course, Father," Svenn agreed.

"I want you all back here in two months," Valentin ordered. "Hopefully, that will be enough time for your brother to show proper remorse and for your new sister to be ready for instruction. You leave tomorrow at dusk. I'll make travel arrangements for Veronika and Callen. Svenn, I assume you'd prefer to make your own?"

"I can travel as far as Munich with Veronika and Callen," Svenn replied. "I have contacts who can provide lodging for them, plus secure holding and airships to transport whatever humans they take. They'll also facilitate my getting to Bern faster if that meets with your approval."

"That will do nicely. Look into the possibility of acquiring one of those ships and a loyal crew. That will make moving our captives easier," Valentin advised.

"The ship won't be a problem. The crew might require your compulsion to ensure loyalty," Svenn admitted. "I don't know that any of us are powerful enough to trust ours will hold during long journeys when we're not with them."

"I can handle that if you get the ship and crew. Now, I wish to deal with Marcos and check on your new sister."

Valentin stood and nodded at each of them. "We'll reconvene at noon to go over any last-minute details."

Veronika smiled sweetly. "Good night, Father. Please tell my brother I'll be thinking of his misery every day I'm gone."

"Ah, the face of an angel and the soul of a demon. Don't wear your brothers out tonight, child. They have a busy day tomorrow, and you'll have them all to yourself for at least four days." Valentin smiled to temper the mild warning.

"Yes, Father." Veronika kept her eyes demurely downcast.

Valentin nodded approvingly. Not that her act fooled anyone in the room.

CHAPTER FORTY

Buddhist Monastery, Tibet, WWDE+149

"Master Palsang, our warriors are assembled and waiting,"

"Thank you, Woo. I'll be there in a moment," Palsang advised.

He'd issued the orders for those still loyal to make their way here over two years ago. They'd trickled in in groups of two since shortly after he issued the order. Finally, the last of the Clan had arrived, and it was time to tell them their part in fulfilling the empress's plan.

Palsang pushed himself out of the chair and stretched his stiff muscles. He'd served the Clan for over two centuries, and the years were taking a toll on him. He hoped he lived to see the day Stephanie Lee's vision of the world became a reality. If not, he was content with the knowledge that he had stayed the course and kept the Sacred Clan and his empress' dream alive.

He walked onto the balcony overlooking the assembled Clan members and winced internally. Once numbering in the thousands, the Sacred Clan now consisted of only seventy-two loyal members.

Palsang took a deep breath and faced the crowd. "My brothers and sisters, today is the first day our members have met as a group in over one hundred years. I thank you all for your continued loyalty to our empress and the Sacred Clan.

"We have prepared this place as a haven and training area for your future missions. We believe the curse of the vampire that Peng Kun brought down on us is lifted. You will find servants here to provide for anything you need.

"You have your team assignments, and the team leaders will provide you with the information and any training needed to complete them successfully. All of your missions are important to the survival of the Clan and the eventual implementation of our empress' grand plan. Learn them well, and execute them for the glory of the Sacred Clan."

Palsang stepped away from the rail and made his way back to his office. He had just taken his seat when a knock at the door came. "Enter."

"That went well, Dawa," Jen Gao said as she took the seat across from him.

"We can only hope that the few people we have can carry out their missions, Jen," Palsang replied. "The empress' plan was supposed to have hundreds involved in the execution, not the paltry numbers we now have."

"Have faith, old friend," she assured him. "We've both survived many setbacks and that damned senseless war that ass Kun dragged us into, damn his soul to the lowest hell. We will see this through."

Dawa closed his eyes and sighed. "That remains to be

seen. I only hope I live long enough to see the final outcome."

"I received word today that we located our agent in Japan. He was wandering the streets of Nago on Okinawa with no memories of the last month," Gao advised.

Palsang shook his head in disgust. "That's the fourth one in two years it's happened to. It has to be Akio's doing."

"We knew when we started hunting him that discovery was a possibility. That's why I used multiple human cutouts for each attempt. It's like he's disappeared as far as the Japanese are concerned. Even the information we gathered over a century ago from public sources no longer exists. We believe the only thing left that refers to him is a code that the lowest ranking police and government officers have called the Bitch Protocol."

"What is the protocol?" Palsang asked.

"The only thing they know is if someone uses that phrase, they are to render whatever assistance is required and report it immediately to their superior," Gao answered. "Whatever it is, only the highest level government officials know. Our operatives all disappeared before reaching the required level."

"You've done everything possible. Now it's up to fate." Palsang leaned back in his chair and closed his eyes, signifying their meeting was finished.

Gao shook her head, pitying her oldest friend. He'd spent his life in the service of the Clan only to watch it dissolve in blood and flames. All because of the actions of one Were and the vampire he brought down on them all.

· · ·

Orzene, Romania

"Callen, where's Veronika?" Valentin asked when he walked into the parlor where Callen sat.

"She went to the barn with Daniella. The two idiots assigned to control the Nosferatu were not able to, again. Veronika and Daniella had to go calm them down before they broke out."

Valentin grimaced. "How many are there now?"

"Forty-two, provided Veronika doesn't have to end any to regain control. She's better with them than I am," Callen admitted, "and Daniella's almost as good."

"What news do your wolves have about Stephano's forces?" Valentin asked.

"They found twenty-six vampires in the old school building and five in the house Stephano uses for his head-quarters next door," he advised.

Valentin nodded. "We can handle that few easily enough. Are all of them young?"

"As best the wolves can tell," Callen reported. "One of Svenn's spies got in a week ago and confirmed Stephano was the oldest. When I met him, he didn't register as more than one hundred years."

"The plan stays the same," Valentin instructed. "We will remain here until Marcos arrives with the last group of humans in two days. Once they have been turned, we will remove those interlopers from our territory."

"Have you heard any news from Svenn?" Callen inquired.

"Only that he was getting closer," Valentin answered. "He followed the rumors and met a Chinese weretiger in Astana, Russia, who told him that he'd left China because of a vampire that hunted Weres. He claimed that he didn't know any name for him but Death. When Svenn described this Dark One, the Were told him that fit what he'd heard."

Callen grimaced. "Why do you have him on this wild goose chase? Wouldn't Svenn's talents serve us better here?"

Valentin shook his head. "Svenn's not a fighter. He's an efficient killer in the right circumstances, but his style is more a stab in the back than a stand-up fight. Everything we know about this vampire is that he's a threat to our plans. He's destroyed vampires all across the world if that arrogant American I met years ago told the truth. Several others I knew who signed on with him died the same day around sixty years ago, and his organization fell apart after that."

Before Callen could respond, Daniella stormed into the room with Veronika on her heels. Dried blood covered one side of her mouth, and it was apparent her lip had been split recently. Her blood-covered shirt and dirty overall appearance indicated she'd been in an altercation.

Callen surged to his feet. "What happened?"

"Frederick of Marcos' last group," Daniella fumed. "After Veronika calmed the Nosferatu, he thought he could have his way with me. When I refused his advances, he said Marcos promised him he could take either of us if he wanted, and if we refused, it was an act because we both like it rough."

"Does he still live?" Valentin demanded.

Veronika barked out a laugh. "No, before I could kill the fool, little sister took his weapon of choice in hand and twisted until he went to his knees. Then she took that pretty little knife Callen gave her and stabbed him in the eyes. After that, she really got mean. I doubt any more of Marcos' idiots will look at her, let alone try anything."

"Well done, child!" Valentin congratulated. "I see that Callen's and Veronika's training served you well."

"Thank you, Father. When my brother returns, I have some strong words for him," Daniella spat.

Callen chuckled. "Is that girl talk for you're going to stab him with your knife?"

"No, Veronika offered to loan me her Luger. I plan to shoot him where he will feel it most."

Callen winced involuntarily and glanced at Valentin to gauge his reaction to Daniella's stated plan. Valentin tilted his head to one side, and a slight smile curled his lips.

"Be sure you shoot him as soon as he arrives. I need him healed in time for the initial attack on Bucharest," Valentin advised her.

"Certainly, Father," Daniella agreed.

"You're seriously putting that idiot in charge of the attack?" Callen asked incredulously.

"No, I said I wanted him in the initial attack," Valentin corrected. "He's going in with the first wave, the Nosferatu. Maybe they will kill him, or perhaps one of Stephano's will. If he manages to survive, Veronika must choose his punishment."

"Why do I get to choose?" Veronika asked. "Not that I'm complaining, but Daniella was the one assaulted."

Valentin shrugged. "Because his man said Marcos included you in his sick prank. I told him if he ever defied me again, that was his fate. I commanded him never to attempt to harm you. He disobeyed me in this."

Veronika's eyes shone with glee as she smiled at Valentin, who had given her permission to have her revenge on Marcos after so many years. "I must remember to caution poor Marcos to be careful in the coming fight. Sister, if he survives, I'm going to teach you another way to make a man scream. It's not as fun as the ways you already know, but I believe it will be extremely fulfilling."

"Father, when this fight is over, I plan to take the wolves hunting in the mountains as their reward. We'll be gone for about a week. Care to join me?" Callen asked.

"What, and miss our Daniella learning new skills? No, I wish to savor every moment of it." Valentin laughed. "They're only young once."

CHAPTER FORTY-ONE

TQB Base, Tokyo, Japan

Akio? Horst called over his implant.

Hai?

Tosha called and advised that she met an airship captain in Shizuoka who runs a regular route to Guam. He claims a pirate has chased him near Aoga the last two runs. Are you in the mood for some fishing?

Why didn't the captain avoid the area after the first attempt? Akio inquired.

He's the mailman. He has a contract with the government and stops at all the islands along the route each trip. Horst chuckled. *I asked the same question. I think spending time with you has made me paranoid.*

Is it still considered paranoia when they're really trying to kill you? Akio deadpanned.

I suppose you have a point there. Anyway, I'm in the ship-yard today. Eve had some new toys she wanted to try on the Geri *and* Freki. *I liked what I saw and ordered a few for the* Skywolf, Horst explained.

Akio chuckled. *I assume you called because the upgrades are complete, and you wish to try your new toys*

You're correct, Horst replied. *Want to come?*

Akio looked at the summary Abel had compiled of the latest batch of surveillance photos and saw no significant changes noted since the last. He shut down the monitor. *I'll be there in thirty minutes.*

Am I invited on this expedition? Abel asked.

Absolutely! One of the weapons is an upgrade based on your recommendations. I wouldn't leave you out of this, Horst answered.

The Skywolf *is ready to depart when you are,* Abel replied smugly.

Already interfaced, are you? Horst chuckled.

Of course. My ships don't move without me knowing it.

Your *ships?* Horst asked.

Yes, Abel stated with certainty. *I'm head of security and ships' weaponry. It's only logical that I have a proprietary interest in the well-being of the vessels and crews.*

I see your point, Abel. Horst sounded thoughtful. *Maybe Eve and I should put you on the payroll.*

Horst, I'm a machine and can access TQB funds for anything needed to accomplish my duties. What use could I possibly have for money?

First, you're more than a machine, Horst corrected. *You're a silicon-based electronic lifeform. You're a person, Abel. Second, you might want to buy something not duty-related. Maybe you'll want to buy a gift for a friend or something. I don't know what, but I'm contacting Eve to arrange it. Congratulations, Abel. You're a paid employee of Seawolf Lines. I'm sorry I didn't think of it before.*

I don't know what to say. Abel wasn't sure how to handle the overwhelming feeling of acceptance that he hadn't realized he was missing.

Thank you is usually a safe response in such situations, Akio interjected.

Thank you, Horst.

You're welcome, Abel.

———

Dammit, what the hell was I thinking getting on this damned thing? Svenn cursed as the airship rocked in the heavy winds.

For the past year, he'd chased rumors of the Dark One all through Europe and across Russia into Asia. The first real break he'd gotten was when the weretiger attacked him in Astana. He'd thought the beast insane until it called him "Dark One."

The mysterious title had kept the Were alive—for a few minutes longer.

The story he'd told Svenn about a vampire declaring war on a group of weretigers in China had sent him east through Mongolia and finally to a small village north of Beijing. He'd encountered a few more weretigers along the way, all who either ran like hell or attacked him on sight. In most instances, he'd gained information that made him believe he was getting closer.

Finding the ancient Were in the mountains near Beidadi, China, was the final clue he needed to the puzzle. The old Were had known she was close to death and didn't want to fight or run. It was also the first conversation

Svenn had with a weretiger that both participants survived.

She told him a fantastic tale about a group of weretigers being the shadow government in China before WWDE. According to her, they'd worked for centuries to subjugate humanity and were the world's predestined rulers.

Svenn didn't believe her until she'd told him about a leader of the tigers who had offended a vampire and caused the war that destroyed their Sacred Clan. Svenn still didn't accept everything she'd said, but when she told him the vampire's name, he sat up and paid attention.

"Akio." Svenn rolled the name on his tongue. He remembered it—and more importantly, the face—from a calendar, of all things.

The old Were had told him how a former leader of the group had located Akio in Tokyo and sent fifty warriors to kill him. She said none of the warriors had returned but that Akio had come to the mountain hideout of the leader and killed almost everyone there in the war that ultimately destroyed the Sacred Clan.

That fateful encounter was why he was bouncing around in a flimsy flying machine while a storm raged all around. The tiny cabin he occupied was smaller than some of the closets back at the castle, but the single small window he compelled one of the men to cover made this his best option.

Svenn swore that he was returning to Romania if he didn't find anything in Japan and never leaving again.

"This trip is a bust," Horst grumbled as the ship floated on a lazy breeze between Ko and Aoga islands.

"That's the problem with fishing. It doesn't always lead to catching," Akio offered from his usual position on the comfortable couch against the pilothouse wall.

Horst snorted. "We've been out here for two days without seeing anything, not even another ship. I think that captain was telling sea tales to get people to buy him drinks. Not the first time that's ever happened."

"That's true. I remember seafarers telling incredible tales from the time before my change. Although most of those featured tentacled monsters that ate ships." Akio chuckled.

"Possible contact, eight kilometers northwest," Abel informed them. "Two ships. I've tracked the first all day, but the second just came from that small island west of Ko when it went by. The second ship appears to be in pursuit of the first."

"Any radio traffic from either vessel?" Horst asked.

"Negative," Abel replied. "No, wait, there it is now. The *Emperor's Folly* is broadcasting a distress call. They say that pirates are boarding the ship at that location."

The *Skywolf* surged forward as Abel engaged the powerful motors. While most airships cruised at a leisurely twenty knots, roughly thirty-seven kilometers per hour, the *Skywolf* had a cruising speed of forty-five knots and a top speed of sixty or almost one hundred ten kilometers per hour. The *Skywolf* served as a testbed for Airwolf Airship Manufacturing and had equipment that would never be standard on their commercial line. The Etheric-interfaced engines were one of them.

"Abel, let's not overshoot them." Horst chuckled when the two ships came into sight, growing closer by the second.

"Please do not talk to the driver," Abel snarked in a robotic voice.

Akio snorted. "I suppose that's better than, what was it? Teach your grandmother to suck eggs?"

"You have a point there. Abel, what the hell?" Horst yelled as the *Skywolf* spun one hundred eighty degrees in the air. The engines whined as Abel applied power, and the ship decelerated its backward rush to come to a full stop alongside the fighting vessels.

Dark smoke billowed from one vessel, and men were throwing cargo from the burning ship to the deck on the other.

"Where's the crew from the *Folly*, Abel?" Akio asked.

"Dead," Abel snarled. "Sensors detect five human forms with no life signs in the pilothouse and one in the corridor leading to the engine room."

"What do we have on the pirate ship?" Horst asked.

"One in the engine room, the captain's in the pilot-house, and the men you see on the deck," Abel advised. "Should I activate the weapons and sweep this murderous scum out of the air?"

One of the crewmen aboard the pirate ship ran to a rail-mounted gun and aimed it at the *Skywolf*. Before he fired, a fireball engulfed the man and gun, followed by an explosion that rattled the pilothouse windows.

"What was that?" Horst asked wide-eyed.

"One of my upgrade suggestions," Abel answered smugly. "I now have four launchers, and the missiles come in different power levels: small, medium, large, and you are *so* screwed. That was a medium."

Aboard the pirate ship, the rail gun had disappeared. The crewman and a shattered section of the hull down to the second deck were missing as well.

"Impressive," Horst acknowledged. "Akio?"

Akio lifted a shoulder. "They're pirates and murderers. The law is clear on their fate."

"Abel, fire at will," Horst advised.

"I believe we need to let them get a little farther away," Abel admitted sheepishly. "That missile damaged one of my hull-mounted sensors. The blast was larger than expected."

"How far away do they need to be?" Akio asked, judging the damaged ship to be around two hundred meters away.

"Half a kilometer or so," Abel answered vaguely.

"Abel," Akio prompted.

"A kilometer would be best for the biggest," Abel clarified.

"Why did you think we needed something like that on this ship?" Horst demanded.

"Because they were available?"

"Available?" Horst asked.

"Eve made them for the *Geri* and *Freki*," Abel explained.

"Exactly why did you, and Eve for that matter, think it was smart to give *my* children weapons that can sink a damned island?" Horst demanded.

"Not an island," Abel answered. "Well, maybe a small one. I calculated the force needed to destroy the largest ship currently operating in the area. One missile will do it."

"I thought the *Geri and Freki* were the largest," Akio stated.

"They are," Abel confirmed, "but a warlord has formed a government in Hong Kong and is building warships. I wanted the kids to have the ability to defend themselves against those if it becomes necessary."

"Can't they avoid them? I know nothing this warlord can build will be fast enough to catch either ship," Horst questioned.

"Probably," Abel reasoned. "But if they can't, the missiles will ensure they survive the encounter. Now that humanity is coming back, the old problems are starting to surface. The Japanese Navy is concerned about the warlords and has their researchers developing new weapons. Some things never change."

Horst shook his head in disgust. "Why won't they ever learn? Humanity is its own worst enemy."

"Horst, that's how it's always been. Evil always rises, but good eventually prevails. We can only hope that someday they'll see their folly. Unfortunately, the hunger for control and greed will always be lurking under the surface." Akio motioned to the airship, steadily moving away from them. "Not to mention those who resort to crime for easy riches."

"I know. It pisses me off." Horst growled. "Abel, are we far enough away?"

"Affirmative. We've reached what I calculate to be the minimum safe distance."

"I'm ready to go home," Horst stated. "Fire!"

Three seconds later, a ball of fire engulfed the pirate vessel. When the flames dissipated, nothing remained but flaming debris raining on the ocean below.

CHAPTER FORTY-TWO

Airship Harbor, Tokyo, Japan

Svenn walked down the brightly lit walkway leading from the terminal to the harbor exit. Electronic billboards lined the walk, advertising everything from hotel accommodations to an interactive gamers' paradise. He shook his head in amazement at how advanced everything around him was.

It was a far cry from the rustic conditions he'd seen on most of his travels. Even Paris, the most advanced city in Europe, didn't come close to this. It was as if WWDE hadn't happened here.

He approached the gate leading into the city and paused when he saw armed soldiers operating a checkpoint. Most people showed identification and passed without issue, but others went to a counter where officials sat behind heavy steel plates with armored glass windows.

Svenn noticed that one of the soldiers was watching him as people walked around where he stood and raised a radio to his lips. He shook himself and moved into the queue line.

"Papers, please," the soldier requested.

Svenn offered him a fake smile and effortlessly went into the act he'd used for years as Valentin's spy. "I've just arrived here. What do I need to do?"

The man smiled as he motioned to an open window. "Welcome to Japan. First-time visitors have to register."

Svenn nodded and went to the indicated spot.

"Is this your first time here, sir?" The pretty, black-haired woman appraised him as she spoke.

Svenn nodded. "It is."

"What's the purpose of your visit?" she inquired.

Svenn used the cover he'd fabricated when he saw how advanced Japan was on the flight over. "I'm traveling through Asia seeking business opportunities. I operate an import-export business in France and trade goods from Europe to the Americas. When one of my trading partners from Russia told me that Japan was the most modern country globally, I had to see it for myself."

She studied him intently as he explained, and Svenn felt she was judging the truth in his story. He smiled and leaned closer to the thick glass that divided them.

"My partner neglected to tell me how beautiful the women are here," he flirted.

The young woman blushed at his attention and smiled. "How long do you intend to be here?"

"From what I've seen so far, I might never want to leave. Still, If you can help me get the paperwork sorted, I can get on with my business here." Svenn flashed a confident smile with a hint of compulsion behind the words.

She nodded and tapped a button on the keyboard in front of her. "Name, please."

Minutes later, Pierre LeBeaux of Paris, France, stepped through the gate and into the city proper. Although it was one in the morning, the streets were alive. Driverless vehicles moved above the streets, picking up and dropping off riders in designated spots. Pedestrian traffic moved in and out of shops, restaurants, and bars.

He failed to notice the shadow that separated from a dark doorway behind him.

Abel docked the *Skywolf* at the Seawolf Lines commercial docks in the Tokyo Air Harbor. The Japanese government had implemented immigration controls a century earlier to combat the threat the Sacred Clan posed. The Prime Minister and Parliament had also issued a joint decree that the Seawolf Companies would always have dock space in all Japanese ports for services rendered to the people of Japan.

When the need for an airship harbor arose, not only did one of Horst's companies build most of it, the government granted Seawolf enough space to dock six airships. Now the ships served passengers on a daily schedule between the Japanese islands.

"Akio, I don't think I'll want to fish for pirates anytime soon," Horst confessed as Akio prepared to leave.

"I understand. Don't despair over things you cannot change. Human nature is complex. Only know that more people wish to do good in the world than those fixed on evil." Akio motioned to the bustling port around them. "Look around you. If evil prevailed, all of this wouldn't be possible."

Akio made his way down the private dock to the public walkway that led out of the facility. When he approached the checkpoint, the smell of old blood and death assailed his sensitive nose.

He walked past a tall blond man of European descent who had stopped on the walkway and was staring intently at the armed guards. He'd found a Forsaken.

Takumi, access the skyport surveillance systems. There's a Forsaken here, Akio called over his implant.

Acknowledged. Would you like me to alert Yuko and Eve?

Not now, Akio told him. *I want to get him away from the crowds before I confront him. Do you have me on camera?*

I do, Takumi confirmed.

It's the tall blond man observing the guards, Akio directed.

I have him.

Keep me informed of his location and direction of travel. I don't want to alert him to my presence. Akio approached the guard and presented his Seawolf employee identification.

"Welcome home, Takinashi-*san*," the guard greeted as he handed Akio back his card.

"*Domo,* Hiro-*san*," Akio answered after checking the man's nametag on his breast.

Akio exited the gate, slipped into a closed shop's dark doorway, and waited until the vampire passed him. He stepped out behind the Forsaken and walked twenty meters behind him until the vampire turned down a side street.

Takumi.

Yes, Akio.

Do you still have him on camera?

Affirmative.

Are there any others near him?

Negative, the street is clear.

Thank you, Takumi.

Akio removed the long coat he wore to cover his weapons and drew his katana from the sheath at his side. He moved silently until the Forsaken came into view half a block ahead.

Akio accelerated to vampire speed, and the vampire stopped and turned to meet him with a short sword in his hand. They crashed together in a shower of sparks as their blades collided.

Svenn felt eyes on him from the time he left the harbor. He checked the reflections in the storefronts as he passed, hoping to spot whoever was watching him. He recalled how he'd attracted attention when the guard saw him gawking like an awestruck tourist and kicked himself mentally.

He ducked into a public restroom and retrieved his short sword from the false bottom of his travel case. He'd compelled the guard who'd checked his bag at the harbor not to notice the false bottom or anything unusual. Now the gladius he favored was hidden under his coat and ready.

Idiot, what kind of amateur are you? Svenn scolded himself as he hunted for a place to deal with his stalker.

When he looked down a side street and saw it was empty, he didn't hesitate. He turned onto it, reached under his jacket, and freed his gladius from its custom sheath.

He forced himself to continue walking when his ears picked up the sound of running feet moving too fast for a human. Svenn spun in place with the gladius at full extension as the footsteps slowed and barely blocked his opponent's longer-bladed katana.

The two combatants circled each other warily. Svenn pressed the attack, believing his longer reach gave him an advantage over the smaller man.

When the katana knocked his blade to the side and pain stung his chest on the backswing, Svenn knew he'd assumed wrong.

The look of smug confidence left the Forsaken's face when Akio grazed him with the blade. Akio sidestepped to the right and brought the katana down again, leaving a shallow bloody cut on the blond vampire's left thigh.

Svenn took a step back, then feinted forward. When Akio swatted the tip of the short sword to the side, the Forsaken followed the blow's momentum, turning to rush down the deserted street.

Svenn made it to the next block, hoping the deadly vampire behind him wouldn't risk exposing himself to humans. His heart lurched when he discovered the street he sought refuge on was a dead-end alley with windowless walls.

Akio slowed as he approached the alley the Forsaken had run down and swung wide around the corner to avoid an ambush. The Forsaken crouched in the center of the pavement, sword in hand, watching him warily.

"Why are you here, Forsaken?" Akio demanded.

Svenn's eyes went wide in shock at being referred to by the name Michael's family called his kind. That, combined with the appearance of the vampire who faced him, was all he needed to realize he'd located the one he sought, the Dark One. Now all he had to do was survive the encounter.

"I don't have any quarrel with you. I'm only a traveler passing through your amazing city. I didn't know any claimed this territory and meant no offense," Svenn explained smoothly.

"Only Forsaken scum claim territories in human cities. Why are you here?" Akio pushed compulsion into the vampire's mind with his demand.

"I... I seek…" Svenn fought the overwhelming desire to tell this powerful vampire whatever he wanted. He shook his head until the feeling passed.

Akio smirked when he saw how the Forsaken reacted to the compulsion. He'd delved into the other's mind while he struggled against it and learned some of the answers he sought.

"Svenn, child of Valentin. Why do you seek me?" Akio asked conversationally.

Svenn's eyes bulged, and he looked around, frantically searching for an escape route. Too late, he realized how overmatched he was. Compared to the ancient vampire he faced, Svenn was an infant.

"I, uh, I," Svenn stammered.

"Do not lie to me, Forsaken. It lacks honor, not that Forsaken have much to start," Akio commanded.

Svenn steeled himself for what he had to do. The only way to survive this encounter was to kill the monster he faced. His leg muscles tensed as he prepared to rush forward and skewer the vampire.

Sudden terror overwhelmed him. Svenn went to his knees with his sword limp in his hand as his horrified mind lost the ability to control his body.

Akio continued to *push* fear into the vampire's mind as he plucked the short sword from his numb fingers. He dove deep into Svenn's memories and read Valentin's plans for dominating the humans in Europe. Marcos' chamber of horrors added a lurid counterpoint. Three other Forsaken also featured prominently. Two were beyond any hope of redemption. The other was a newly turned female.

More than a century's worth of preying on and abusing humans came out in a kaleidoscope of images. Some of the acts the vampires had engaged in were so depraved they shocked Akio's hardened senses. When he had the information he needed, he released the fear.

"You have violated my Queen's law and used your abilities to terrorize and cause unconscionable anguish to your victims. The sentence for this is death." Akio raised his sword with two hands and stared into the eyes of the addled vampire.

"Stand and meet your fate," Akio commanded.

Svenn tried to fight the compulsion. He struggled to remain on the ground and opened his mouth to plead for mercy, but in the end, he wasn't strong enough.

Akio's katana whistled as he brought it down, the blade barely slowing when it sliced through flesh and bone. Blood spattered the dark bricks, and Svenn's head flipped three times in the air before it landed face-down on the dirty street.

Abel.

Yes, Akio.

I need a Pod at my location to transport a body.

Abel didn't respond. Seconds later, a matte black shadow descended and stopped next to the headless corpse.

CHAPTER FORTY-THREE

TQB Base, Tokyo, Japan

Akio stepped into the command center. "Abel, do you have any recent images from Romania?"

"Negative," Abel replied. "The last satellite that covered that area suffered a critical failure seventeen years ago."

"Pull up any images you have for the area near Orzene," Akio instructed. "That's where the Forsaken was from, and there are more of them. Focus the search on castles in the area."

"Castles? Could they be any more cliché?" Abel snickered. "There are six structures that meet the definition of castles near Orzene, Romania." The screen above the command console came to life. Satellite images appeared showing castles in various states of repair.

"Omit numbers three, five, and six. Expand and enhance the first one." When the image came into focus, a half-smile twisted Akio's lips. "That's the one. Program those coordinates into the Black Eagle."

"Coordinates locked in," Abel confirmed. "You have four pucks available. Do you want me to load them?"

"*Hai*. They plan to use Nosferatu. If I can locate where the Forsaken are keeping them, the pucks are a viable option."

"Loading now."

"Thank you, Abel. I must prepare." Akio left the room.

———

Akio stood before his sword stand as he'd done countless times over the last century and a half, preparing to go into battle. Each time he felt a sense of peace, knowing that his Queen hadn't misplaced her gift of redemption.

Still, there were times when he felt that nothing he did was enough—that the odds were impossible, and the battles would never end. Each time he removed the magnificent sword she'd presented him in that hangar in Colorado, he knew he *did* make a difference.

Now the fruits of his labors showed in every location where ever-resilient humanity had risen from the ashes. People thrived all over the globe as civilization returned to the world his Queen charged him to protect so long ago.

The Forsaken dared not reveal their faces near the major human hubs. The Sacred Clan was broken and scattered, living on borrowed time as Akio and members of the FDG hunted them to the point of extinction. It wasn't the world Bethany Anne left, but it was one where humans could live their lives without fear of being enslaved by creatures few still knew existed.

A world where Akio and the blade he wielded had made that possible.

He lifted the katana reverently from the stand and carefully wiped the Damascus steel blade with the soft cloth used only for that task. He slid it into the sheath affixed to his black Jean Dukes armor and checked the draw several times as his first swordmaster had taught centuries earlier.

Once his weapons were in place, he performed the last part of his pre-battle ritual. He carefully ran the cloth across the front of his armor, cleaning the emblem of his office. The vampire skull with long streaming hair, the badge that forever marked Akio as a Queen's Bitch.

Black Eagle, above Orzene, Romania

The first rays of sunlight crested the mountaintop, bathing the dark stone fortress in a golden glow. Akio planned the timing of his attack on the Forsaken compound to take advantage of the deadly rays if any Nosferatu escaped. An outbreak of the feral monsters in the sparsely populated towns and villages could eliminate humanity's decades-long gains in days.

Akio, Terry Henry Walton is calling. Should I patch him into the Black Eagle's comm system? Abel communicated through Akio's implant.

Hai, *put him through, please.*

"Akio-*sama.*"

"Walton-*san.*"

"Our operatives in China have located the Qin Clan and what we believe are the Sacred Clan remnants in Tibet.

We're in the Pods and headed there now," Terry Henry reported.

Akio closed his eyes and drew a deep breath. He'd waged war on the Sacred Clan for over a century, and his chance to see them finally exterminated was here. He could be there in time to meet the FDG in Tibet and take part in the battle.

He could get the final pound of flesh to avenge Kenjii's death.

"Thank you for the update. I'll contact you later for the after-action report." Akio cut the connection.

"Akio?"

"What is it, Abel?"

"Should I set a course for Tibet?"

"Negative. Terry Henry Walton and the FDG don't need my assistance."

"After all you've suffered, don't you want to be there for the final battle with the tigers?"

"*Hai,* more than anything," Akio firmly informed him. "However, the Forsaken and Nosferatu in the castle below will decimate the human towns and villages if I fail to stop them. I cannot neglect my sworn duty to protect humankind because I desire to be elsewhere. My honor will not allow it."

Akio touched the image of the castle and grounds displayed on the Black Eagle's HUD. "Put me down here."

***

Veronika breezed into Callen's rooms unannounced. "Good morning, brother. Where's Daniella?" She crossed to where he reclined on the wide bed that dominated the room and lightly kissed his lips.

Callen smiled and grabbed her around the waist, rolling her onto the center of the mattress beside him.

"Unhand me, you brute." Veronika giggled as she playfully punched his chest. "Now, tell me, what have you done with our little Daniella?"

"She went out to calm the Nosferatu a little before dawn," Callen told her. "Something set them off, probably one of the new vampires again, and we heard them up here. She needed to deal with them before any tried to escape the barn."

Callen poked her while he mock-pouted. "I thought she was with you when she failed to return at sunrise. She seems to like you better than me at times."

"Of course, she likes me better. What's not to like?" Veronika laughed as she ran her hand over her body.

"Maybe she's with Father. He's taken an interest in training her to use a sword." He frowned. "With Marcos' incessant attempts to get her alone, she might need those skills soon."

Veronika scowled. "Marcos will cease to be a problem after tonight, one way or another."

Callen nodded knowingly. "Is he still occupied with his latest plaything?"

"He was when I came up to my rooms," she answered. "I had to leave the sitting room because of the noise she was making. I don't know why Father gave her to him."

Callen shrugged. "To keep him distracted about his part in the raid tonight, I imagine. Father was unhappy when he discovered she'd been passing information to Stephano's spies. He felt spending time with Marcos was an appropriate reward for betraying us. It'll send a message to any others tempted to talk to our enemies."

Veronika grimaced. "Stupid humans. The only way to truly trust them is to keep them in thrall. Otherwise, they're too easy to corrupt."

Callen snorted. "Her duties required her to interact with outsiders during the day. If Father had put her under that deep, she wouldn't have been as effective."

"We should have your wolves handle those things," Veronika insisted. "It's not like they have other duties during the day."

Callen scoffed at the idea. "The bunch of them are all brawn and little brain. Trust me. If it doesn't involve tracking or killing, you don't want the pack involved."

"You have a point, brother. Father wants to meet in four hours to go over his plan once more. We could keep each other company until then if you like," she purred.

"Oh, I like it very much." He growled as he caught her hand and pulled her close.

———

The Black Eagle landed in a copse of trees behind a wood-and-stone barn located at the castle's rear. The stench of Nosferatu reached Akio the moment the canopy opened. He'd noticed the heavy wooden timbers that covered all the structure's openings on his initial observations shortly after he arrived. The odor confirmed the Nosferatu were inside.

Abel, take it up five hundred meters. Notify me if you pick up anything on the sensors you think I should know about. Also, target the barn with a puck. Hold your fire until I tell you to blow it.

I have one drone available. I can try to get it inside the castle. It can serve as a communications relay if the walls block the signals, Abel offered.

No, keep it in reserve, Akio told him. *I'll drop repeaters as I go.*

Acknowledged. Six wolves are approaching your location from the west.

Thank you, Abel. Akio turned to face the racing wolves with his Jean Dukes Specials in his hands. Seconds later, the sound of the hypervelocity rounds ripping the beasts to shreds shattered the peaceful morning.

Akio sprinted to the rear of the castle and burst through a wooden door. He extended his senses and detected four vampires, three on the second floor and another below him.

He pulled a small black disc from a compartment in his armor and slapped it on the wall without breaking his stride as he followed the strong scent of fresh blood down a corridor to a heavy ironbound door.

Abel, I've dropped a repeater and am headed to the lower levels. Do you have sensor readings?

Affirmative. The first floor is clear. There are three on the second level. The stone is too dense to get readings in the lower level.

A blood-curdling scream of agony came through the door, and Akio's armored boot lashed out and slammed into it.

"If you put it here and twist it slowly, they make the most delightful sounds." Marcos smiled across the table at the raven-haired beauty who watched him with a hint of a smile.

A high-pitched shriek of agony came from his bound victim as he demonstrated what he'd explained.

Daniella reached across and took the sharp knife from his hand and studied their captive for a moment. "That was nice, but I think I prefer the sound she makes when I do this."

The pitiful victim arched her back until only her shoulders and feet touched the blood-covered surface beneath her. Daniella continued to apply pressure until her subject went limp as unconsciousness overtook her.

"They make more noise, but if you do it too long, they pass out, and you have to start over," he explained, then jumped to the side as the room's door hurtled into the space he'd stood.

Daniella screamed when a shadow with eyes that glowed like coals hurtled out of the hanging dust cloud on the stairs. She pushed away from the rusted metal fixture with her hands up in a feeble attempt to ward off the danger that approached.

Marcos snarled and pulled a thin-bladed dagger from the extensive collection of instruments designed to damage human flesh. He rushed across the room to meet the intruder on the stairs. Nobody interrupted his fun.

Akio instantly took in the scene below him. Burning rage erupted in the pit of his stomach and spread through his body. When he sensed their helpless captive die, his wrath flared white-hot, and he smiled coldly as he holstered his pistols.

The katana slid effortlessly from his back as one of the Forsaken rushed him with a blade held high. He stepped to one side and avoided the clumsy strike aimed at his face. Then his katana flashed in the dim light.

The vampire jumped back with a startled yell, his eyes wide as blood flowed from a deep cut on one arm.

With a twist of his wrist, Akio's sword tip flicked up, and a second cut opened as the blade split the stunned vampire's face.

Marcos stared at the demon who stood before him. In all his years, he'd never seen anyone move with this swordsman's speed and skill. He staggered back a step as pain exploded across his face when the tip of the blade sliced through his cheek, barely missing his eye.

Daniella screamed. Marcos looked up as she rushed toward his attacker with a spiked metal ball attached to a short chain in her hand. He stared in horror when the warrior spun with the deadly blade extended at shoulder height. It ripped through the petite beauty's slender neck and separated her head from her body in a spray of blood.

Marcos stood in open-mouthed shock until the warrior shoved the razor-sharp sword into his chest. Pain flooded his system as his assailant lifted the blade until Marcos' feet left the floor. The Forsaken hardly registered it when his back slammed into one of the thick wooden support beams. Then the meter of steel piercing his body lodged in the beam with a solid *thunk* that tore an agonized bellow from his throat.

The warrior stared implacably into his eyes and spoke in a voice as cold as a grave. "You and your kind are a blight on the face of this world. You've tortured and terrified the helpless and murdered and abused the innocent. Today, you will understand some of what your victims felt."

Marcos screamed in abject horror when the vampire's eyes glowed red, and debilitating terror sapped the strength from his muscles. Pain radiated through his body like a wildfire when the thin blade of the dagger he'd held earlier bit deep into his stomach.

The last thing Marcos saw before his world faded to black was Daniella's lifeless blue eyes staring up at him accusingly.

Akio grimaced as he looked at his sword and the limp body that hung from it like an insect pinned to a display. He caught the sword in his gauntleted fist, freed it from its wooden prison, and let the Forsaken fall to the floor.

He reached down, lifted the corpse by its hair, and removed the head in a motion that had become second nature, ensuring the Forsaken would never harm another innocent.

"Callen, what's that noise?" Veronika's sleepy murmur was barely audible as she burrowed deeper under the blankets.

Before he could respond, the door of his chambers burst open, and Valentin rushed in with a sword in his hand.

"We're under attack! Get up and prepare to fight!" Valentin yelled as he faced the open door.

Callen lurched to his feet and pulled his double-edged sword from the sheath next to his bed. He stood ready at Valentin's side as the sound of unhurried heavy steps drew closer.

"Is it Stephano?" Veronika scrambled to find a weapon. She hadn't kept anything other than her pistol close for decades and was confident that it wasn't enough for whatever had Valentin so spooked.

Valentin moved to one side of the open door and motioned Callen to stand opposite him. "I don't think so. I saw him when he started up the stairs. If this man is who I believe, this is much worse than anything that child Stephano could manage."

"Callen, I need a weapon, dammit!" Veronika threw her hands up and shrieked in frustration.

"There's a war ax under the bed. Use it."

An armored leg and foot came into view in the hall, and Callen rushed forward with his blade extended to engage the intruder. The sound of clashing steel filled the room as Callen and the warrior exchanged rapid-fire blows.

Ax in hand, Veronika moved to stand next to Valentin. She let out a startled yelp when Callen slammed into the door frame with blood pouring from multiple injuries. She watched, powerless to react as a fast-moving shadow rushed past the door and pulled Callen in its wake.

"Callen!" Veronika screamed and would have followed if Valentin hadn't caught her arm.

"Stay here. Our chances are better if we stay together," Valentin snarled at her.

"Better, but you're still going to die," a voice devoid of emotion called from the hallway. Callen's headless body crashed into Valentin and knocked him to the floor.

Valentin rose, pushing off the dead weight as Akio stepped into the room and fixed Veronika with a cold stare that made her shiver. She trembled as she backed away, holding the double-edged ax in front of her pale body like a shield.

Abel, launch the puck, Akio called over his implant.

Seconds later, the castle wall cracked, and stone rained down around her when an explosion outside shook the structure to its foundation. Veronika fell to her knees and slammed face-first into the floor when it buckled under her feet.

A beam of sunlight pierced the gloom when a section of the outer wall collapsed. Valentin scuttled across the floor to get out of the deadly ray's path. He stood and squinted against the glare as he stared at the vampire, who stood calmly as the light bathed his face.

"Who? Why?" Valentin gasped.

"To answer your first question, Akio. Why? Because you violated my Queen's commands. She decreed it a death sentence for any from our world to use our abilities to rule over the humans. Your attempt to establish a Forsaken empire with you at its head sealed your fate."

"They're humans—cattle, food. Why would any of our kind care what happens to them?" Valentin shielded his eyes with one hand while keeping his sword trained on Akio with the other

"*Your* kind doesn't." Akio slowly stepped toward Valentin with his katana held ready.

"We're all that's left," Valentin wheedled. "Michael and his family are gone. Your Queen abandoned you and will never return. This is *our* world. You could be a king among kings."

"No, it's not, and I couldn't," Akio told him, his lip curled in disgust. "On the day my Queen returns, I will be waiting to hand her a world where humanity thrives. There's no place in that world for beings who have extraordinary gifts but use them for evil purposes."

"Then you're a fool!" Valentin snarled and launched himself at Akio.

Akio deflected Valentin's blade with a twist of his wrist and smashed an armor-covered fist into the side of the Forsaken's head. Blood flew and bones *crunched*, leaving Valentin bloodied and shaken on the uneven stone floor.

Valentin tried to crawl away, but a heavy boot came down on his leg and snapped the bone. Akio kicked the Forsaken's weapon out of reach and looked deep into his mind.

He sifted through the vampire's memories until he was confident he'd contained the threat. A moment later, the katana whistled through the air, and Valentin's plans died on the floor with him.

Akio shook his head and walked to the wall where the sunlight streamed in. He kicked the loose stones until he'd opened the break enough to see the damaged barn. A smoking crater littered with stone and body parts that smoked in the sun was all that remained.

Abel, Akio called over his implant.

Yes.

Let's go home.

Pick you up in front?

Hai.

As he turned to leave, the stone shifted in a dark corner of the room. His eyes narrowed as a woman with blonde hair stained with blood pushed free of the rubble.

Veronika struggled to her feet, bloodied and battered but still alive. She saw Valentin's headless body next to Callen's, and a cry of sorrow rose in her throat.

Movement caught her attention near the door, and she recoiled in fear when she spotted the dark-clad warrior staring at her from across the room. She desperately searched her mind for anything she could say to prevent the man from killing her.

Akio watched her without speaking as she freed herself from the debris and moved away from the sun.

Veronika smiled shyly at him and straightened to her full height. She hesitantly approached the stoic warrior, using the only weapon she possessed.

The beam of sunlight separated them by roughly a meter when she stopped and faced him.

"Like what you see?" The flirty lilt that had gotten her everything she wanted for almost two hundred years filled her voice.

When his only reply was a smirk, it encouraged her to continue.

"I heard what you told him about, about your Queen," she hesitantly offered. "I can support someone who thinks like that. I've never agreed with what they did here. They were beasts, all of them. Did you see the room down in the basement? That's what they did to me. All these years, they used those horrible instruments to hurt me. It was an awful existence."

Akio pursed his lips as he listened to her fabricated tale of sorrow and woe. Of all the vampires he'd ever encountered, this one rated high on the list of the worst.

He stepped through the beam of light that separated them, and she looked at him with feigned innocence. He didn't react when she brought her hand up and gently ran it over his badge of office. She smiled coquettishly when his gauntleted hand closed around her thin neck and tried to press herself against him.

Her eyes went wide when he shook his head and leaned toward her.

"You, Veronika, are a terrible liar." Akio smirked. "Besides, you're not my type."

Veronika screamed as he lifted her off the floor and carried her to the opening in the wall. He watched emotionlessly as her bare skin turned red and started to smoke before he hurled her through the wall and into the unrelenting light.

EPILOGUE

TQB Base, Tokyo, Japan

Eve was testing a promising new metal alloy in her efforts to restore their failing satellite equipment when an unexpected alert flashed on her monitor. She ran a diagnostic to determine if the notice was an error, then reran it.

She stared at the screen unmoving for almost a minute. Then she initiated the predefined response.

Akio stepped out of the shower with a towel around his waist. He'd stood under the scalding water for a half-hour to rid himself of the physical and mental dirt from his mission in Romania.

No matter how many times he thought he'd seen it all, something came along to remind him that there were no limits on what some would do.

"Akio," Eve called over the speaker in his quarters.

"Eve?"

"We need to go to the base outside Denver."

"Why? No one has been there in over eighty years."

"The base EI sent an alert. There's been a breach."

Moments later, fully dressed, Akio pulled his weapons over his light armor. "Do you think it's a malfunction?"

"It could be, but we need to check it out."

"Meet me at the Pod in five minutes." Akio opened the door and stepped out of his room.

THE END

Have you started the Great Insurrection series from David Beers and Michael Anderle yet? Book one is Warlord Born and it's available now at Amazon and through Kindle Unlimited.

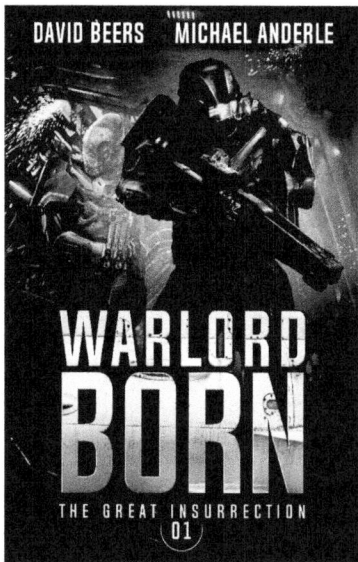

For two decades he served...
...and never questioned the orders.
Would one act of mercy cost him?
Alistair believed in the work. He was the last line of defense against the rebels' unending war to overthrow the

Commonwealth. His legend preceded him – the greatest Titan the corps had ever produced.

Alistair's mission was simple: catch and kill two rebels. Then they said a few words that forever changed his life.

Alexander's family had ruled the Commonwealth for ten generations. His 30-years as Emperor had been peaceful, but only because he didn't tolerate dissent. Now, a Titan had betrayed him.

Alistair must die.

In a battle of Good vs. Evil, the stakes have never been higher.

Can Alistair survive? Or will Earth's greatest warrior fall to its greatest ruler?

Grab your copy today!

AUTHOR NOTES CHARLES TILLMAN
AUGUST 10, 2021

Hi, thank you for reading this book and continuing to read these notes!

Sitting here trying to get my thoughts together for these notes has been both a happy and sad experience. I'm happy that not only did Akio's story finally get told but that Michael trusted me, an unknown, to tell it. I'm sad because this is the last set of author notes I'll ever type for the Akio Revelations series.

There are a couple of things I wanted to talk about. The first is two of my favorite creations, Abel and Takumi. They came about after a conversation I had with Michael early in the planning stages of book one. We were talking about Eve, and he commented on what kind of trouble a bored AI could get into.

I already had some notes on Akio and Eve interacting during Yuko's training and knew that Eve would come off like a teenage girl at times. Since I have four daughters, I'm well-versed in the trials and tribulations associated with teenagers and have *lots* of fodder from it.

417

That got me thinking. How would Eve deal with it if the tables turned and she was on the receiving end of teen angst and rebellion? That was when the boys came about. None of the mischief those two got into was planned. Every bit of their dialogue, arguments, etc., was spontaneous and flowed onto the pages with ease. I had a lot of fun writing them and will miss them most now that the series is over.

The second thing is one of the problems I discovered. In his *Requiem* notes, Michael mentioned the gnashing of teeth I experienced while writing these books. What he didn't include was the banging my head on the desk, the days I felt so overwhelmed and frustrated I wanted to quit, or the cussing—and believe me, there was lots of that. Especially the day I found three paragraphs in book nine of The Terry Henry Walton Chronicles.

Mind you, that was *after* I'd created a thriving community in the exact location Craig Martelle wrote into those #&$@ing paragraphs as a place the Forsaken had set up shop. Oh, the joys of writing a story in a timeline where extensive canon already exists.

That said, telling Akio's story is undoubtedly one of the most enjoyable experiences of my life. When I first encountered him in *It's Hell To Choose,* then in Craig's Terry Henry Walton books, I wondered about his origins. There wasn't much about how he came to serve Kamiko Kana, how he became a vampire, or who he was before joining TQB.

What made him that way? Was it a sense of honor instilled in him as a samurai, or was it something else? I wanted to know the answers to these questions and many more. Hopefully, my discoveries were logical and as enjoyable for you as they were for me.

I hope you enjoyed going on this wild ride with me because I've certainly enjoyed bringing it to you.

What's next, you ask?

Now that I've finished this series, I'll return to the story that started this writing journey. I'm going to switch over to the Oriceran universe and do a series on my pistol-packing former Silver Griffin wizard, one of the first government-sanctioned bounty hunters. The story will be based in New Orleans, one of my favorite towns in this area, but will venture out to multiple other locations.

Since I come from that part of the world, I won't have to rely on Google Maps or other sources for places and local flavor. Another bonus is that I'm familiar with local legends, mythical creatures, and spooky history throughout the South, so there's no telling who or what will show up in this series.

I hope to see you all there sometime in early 2022.

I write these books for your reading enjoyment and want to tell the best story I can. On that note, your reviews are the fuel that runs the indie author machine. If you could, please take the time to drop a review on Amazon, Goodreads, or BookBub. It helps keep the books relevant in the search algorithms and in front of like-minded readers. I read all of them and use them to help me improve my writing.

Please drop by my author page and say "Hi." You can find me on:

Facebook (Author Charles Tillman): https://www.facebook.com/CFTillman/
Website: http://cftillman.com/
TikTok (occasionally): @author_charlestillman

Happy Reading,
Charles

Thank you for not only reading this book, but this entire series and these author notes as well.

There is a step after a firefight where those who survive get together and create a A.A.R. or After Action Review.

Here is the definition from Wiki-pedia:

"An after action review (AAR) is a structured review or de-brief (debriefing) process for analyzing what happened, why it happened, and how it can be done better by the participants and those responsible for the project or event. AARs in the formal sense were originally developed by the U.S. Army. Formal AARs are used by all US military services and by many other non-US organizations. Their use has extended to business as a knowledge management tool and a way to build a culture of accountability."

In my case, I intended to query Charles on his experience. I wanted to discuss what he felt he would do differently, what, if anything, he wanted to do going forward, and how we might change the process for him.

You see, every author is different in our company. A

process that works for one very well might not work for another, and the reasons could be as simple as author 'A' has a family and author 'B' does not.

For Charles, his work life was going crazy for the last six to nine months, and it affected everything about his writing counts and his ability to continue developing a new series.

I, for one, didn't want to lose his voice if I could help it. Fortunately, adjusting for some extra time to pad our release goals allowed Charles to feel comfortable moving forward.

YEAH!

It's nice to get a win from time-to-time.

It's funny. I sometimes forget that many of our writers (obviously) have other jobs. Whether it is Mom or Dad to kids at home, or a career they are finishing or continuing because they love it and sometimes because they need the safety of a full time income for their family or themselves for a while until sales are obviously working in their favor.

This is apparent because I need to talk to someone in law enforcement with a law enforcement background and contacts in the law enforcement arena.

Some of them can't speak to details (for obvious reasons), but I can bounce ideas or requests off of them. Charles is one of those people who have law enforcement connections and has been vague at times about what he knows.

Which annoys the curiosity of childlike wonder in me. 'Childlike wonder' is a better phrase than 'annoying curiosity' or so I suggest.

So, I'm going to finish these author notes – suggest you

plug Charles and this series to your friends, loved ones, random people in bank lines, or grocery lines and pick up his next series. I'm going to go pester Charles about getting me connected with someone to help me craft some horrible mystery stuff and FBI 'shit.'

I've no idea if he was in the FBI... He might have told me... I put whatever information he said into a safe place and promptly forgot where that was. My age is showing.

Anyway, stay safe and sane out there!

Ad Aeternitatem,
Michael Anderle

CONNECT WITH THE AUTHORS

Charles Tillman Social
Facebook:
(Author Charles Tillman)
https://www.facebook.com/CFTillman/

Website:
http://cftillman.com/

TikTok
@author_charlestillman

Michael Anderle Social

Website: https://www.facebook.com/LMBPNPublishing

https://twitter.com/MichaelAnderle

https://www.instagram.com/lmbpn_publishing/

https://www.bookbub.com/authors/michael-anderle

BOOKS BY CHARLES TILLMAN

Akio Revelations

Reprisal (Book 1)

Retaliation (Book 2)

Retribution (Book 3)

Requiem (Book 4)

Relentless (Book 5)

Redemption (Book 6)

Printed in Great Britain
by Amazon

63057841R00251